D1246503

ROAR

VOLUME 2

Edited by Buck C. Turner

Bad Dog Books

2010

ROAR Volume 2
First publication 2010

Edited by Buck C. Turner
baddogbooks@gmail.com

Cover by ConfusedOO
www.furaffinity.net/user/confusedoo

Published by Bad Dog Books
www . baddogbooks . com

TABLE OF CONTENTS

Preface

Welcome to the second volume of ROAR. It has been a long time coming, the result of much effort from the authors and editorial staff. It was just about a year since I stepped in, grabbing the reins from Alex Vance and Ben Goodridge, and what a ride it has been.

I was particularly keen on picking up the standard for ROAR, as it is one of only a very few publications that are both general audience and general in theme. There are a number of wonderful anthologies that have been and are being published centered around a specific setting, theme, or genre; what I wanted to see as a reader was a book that would bring a wider variety of stories to its audience.

I have been happy to see the success of a number of recent books, and the upswing in popularity of furry fiction in general. Many of the highest profile works in the past few years have been decidedly erotic, and while I have nothing against that (indeed, I have enjoyed them quite a bit) I wanted to see an equivalent success for stories enjoyable by furs of all ages.

It was one year ago at Further Confusion that I was able to lay the groundwork to make this a reality. I am fortunate enough to know many of the movers and shakers in the furry publishing game, and count several among my friends. It was Fuzzwolf, proprietor of Fur Planet publishing, that connected me with Alex Vance when I expressed an interest in getting a new general audience anthology onto furry bookshelves.

Had I known just how much work goes into an anthology, I might not have entered into the enterprise so lightly. Rest assured that my participation had no bearing on my desire to read the works of my favorite authors before they are released to the general public.

Perhaps the most heady and exciting part of this process was back at the very beginning, combing through the submissions that had accumulated prior to joining the project.

After the initial flush of excitement at reading the unreleased submissions came the task of selecting authors and stories, building the thematic connections to make this a book that hung together as a collection. I think the volume manages this well, for while each story may be very different in tone and subject, they all have a game to play. The games and their stakes vary widely, but the moves remain familiar.

Something else you may notice about this volume compared to most other anthologies is the brevity of the Table of Contents. This collection has a number of stories which explore the gap between short story and novel. These stories tend to get much less love from the publication world. They aren't long enough to warrant a book to themselves, but at the same time they take page counts that could be used to showcase three to four writers in a short story collection.

As editor, I found myself in a position where I could accept stories that are quite compelling, but would be rejected at other publications for space constraints. At the outset it wasn't my intention that so many of the stories would be this length, but as I went through my submission pile and built the anthology around the primary theme, it naturally grew into a showcase for these longer pieces.

The production of this volume has been quite the learning experience—to say nothing of the juggling practice it gave me. As I write this, the heavy lifting in creating the finished product is almost entirely behind me, and it is nearly out of my hands entirely, onto the hands of the printer, distributors, and ultimately you, the readers. I can only hope that you find as much satisfaction from the stories herein as I found in bringing them all together.

Buck C. Turner, Editor

A group of college friends reunite for a vacation from the tedium of their new professional lives—but a visit from the Trickster ensures this trip will be more exciting than planned.

Trickster

Shepherd J. Wolf

"D o you think it's safe?" Allison finally asked.

It was hard to tell in the near-total darkness, even in such close quarters, but Mikey suddenly realized that all four pairs of eyes were on him, including his brother's. *Especially* his brother's. Setting his jaw, the wolf steeled himself and pivoted on the cold vinyl tile.

Remaining seated, he squirmed around and pressed one pointy ear against the thin wood. Like all motel bathroom doors, it was intended for privacy only, and manufactured as cheaply as possible. Based on how the building had been shuddering, it was a miracle the door had held at all.

He concentrated for a moment, listening. His keen lupine ears picked up a number of howling wails in the distance, but nothing of the air-raid variety. "I don't hear tornado sirens anymore. There's nothing but car alarms." He frowned. "I'm pretty sure one of them is mine."

He eased himself to his feet, pounding his shoulder on the doorknob in the process. "*Ow!*" he barked. The little room was lit with nothing more than their cell phones—his and Allison's were basic phones on competing networks, Gabe and Sarah had matching Blackberries, and of course Louie had nothing at all.

TRICKSTER

Standing up, he grumbled under his breath. "Gabe, care to assist me?" To his right, he saw the ferret get effortlessly to his feet. Gabe was slim and quiet, and all too happy to defer to Mikey's request, just like back at school. In the near-darkness, the only part of Gabe that was visible was the white part of his face, tinted bluish-green by their cell phones. It was a weird effect.

"Are we sure it's safe out there?" the ferret asked, his deep voice resonating in the tiny bathroom.

"No," Mikey answered. He tried the knob.

Nothing happened.

He turned it again, pushing hard. The wood creaked softly, as if bothered by his insistence, but did not budge. The door felt like it was nailed shut.

He frowned. "It's jammed. The building must not be in great shape."

"I think it follows that we should leave right now, then," Sarah advised. It was an obvious statement, but the mouse had a lot of credibility right now. It had been her suggestion to take cover in the bathroom.

"I'm working on it," Mikey muttered, checking the door for hinges. They weren't on this side; the door opened outward. "Hey, Louie, can I get an assist?" He turned and looked down.

From the floor, his brother stared back at him. His eyes grew so wide they were nearly luminescent in the darkness. He didn't respond.

"I need you to push the door open, okay, buddy? It's jammed and I need some serious strength here."

He could see Louie working it out, looking the door up and down, and then he nodded. "Okay…if you say 's'alright…" Louie was braced against the bathtub, and he simply extended his massive legs and pushed against the door.

The wood creaked shrilly, and when Mikey twisted the knob, it burst free from the door frame and banged against the room's back wall.

3

He looked back to where Louie was cowering unhappily from the noise. Allison was next to him, with a comforting hand on his massive forearm, but Mikey didn't know how much good that was going to do.

"Okay, people, here I go." Waving his Nokia in front of him, he slowly padded out into the room.

He frowned. The room was now a movie set—that was the only way to explain it.

Strange white light from the emergency LED lighting cast bizarre, stark shadows all around the room. Everything was wet—water trickled down the walls, the carpet squished under his sneakers, and moisture dripped from a new low point in the ceiling, which sagged dangerously over the two beds.

The entire picture window was conspicuously missing from its frame, letting in a mixture of gray light and soft rain. The shards of the window were scattered around the room like confetti, mingling with marble-sized chunks of hail. The front door lay against the foot of the beds, in a heap of plastic fragments and large jagged segments of particle board, which had probably once been the bureau and TV.

Their luggage, clothes, and the curtains had landed in haphazard, soggy piles all over the floor. The air smelled like wet cloth and foliage. A car alarm screamed outside, just out of sight. Thunder rumbled in the distance.

Mikey took a few hesitant steps, Gabe trailing a few inches behind him. "I think we're okay," he said softly. "Sarah, what's your take?" he said, guessing the mouse was just a few steps behind them.

Sure enough, Sarah appeared in the doorway. She was short and straightforward, the sort of girl who perpetually wore a ponytail. "I think we're through the worst of it. These systems really only have one big punch." She took off her glasses, which had steamed up in the humid room, and wiped them on her camisole.

Gabe frowned. "I thought tornado season didn't start until *next* week." He crossed his arms. "I want a refund."

4

Sarah smiled. "It doesn't. These were straightline winds. If it was a tornado we wouldn't be standing here right now." She started picking her way toward the door.

"Um…great. Good to know, sweetie. Thanks," Gabe said. He turned to Mikey. "Scientific detachment," he explained.

"Yeah, I guess," Mikey replied, frowning. "Allison, Louie, it's okay out here. C'mon—"

He stopped at the sight of Allison backing out of the room, leading Louie by his massive front paws. She was a red-haired doe in size 0 jeans, looking frail and delicate, dwarfed by Louie's huge lupine frame, but he allowed himself to be led unhappily out of the bathroom.

Most of the time, Louie's oversized, fierce-looking muzzle and generally feral-looking features were enough to stop strangers in their tracks, but at the moment he just looked like a frightened puppy. Mikey swallowed the lump in his throat.

"There, there," Allison said comfortingly, carefully stepping backward over the threshold. "The storm is over, Sarah said so." She sounded soothing, even over the wail of the car alarm. "Careful of the glass."

Louie glanced around nervously, his ears flattened against his skull. "You sure?" he asked softly, his deep voice rumbling like the thunder in the distance. He ducked as they went under the doorframe.

"Mmm-hmm!" Allison said brightly. "Won't it be nice to get out of this nasty, smelly room?" she asked. Mikey listened—he knew she was a teacher, and a very relevant sort of teacher at that, but he'd never really seen her in action, even after four years of college. The four of them, Gabe, Sarah, Allison and Mikey, had all been in different programs.

"Doesn't it smell yucky?" Allison asked, a hint of amusement in her voice. Mikey smiled.

Louie's nose wrinkled. "Yeah," he admitted softly. They passed the first bed. "Floor's squishy," he noted, unhappily.

As they passed, Mikey reached up and put a comforting arm on his brother's shoulder. "You're doing good, big guy," he said. "Wait'll we tell Mom about *this*."

Louie actually smiled at that, and Mikey felt himself grin. Breathing a sigh of relief, he started to relax, for the first time since the tornado sirens had begun wailing.

And then he caught sight of his brother in the dresser mirror, across the dark, shadowed room. Mirror-Louie towered over his reflection, and—it must have been a trick of the light—in the shadows he looked *angry*, deadly, like a beast rearing for attack.

The effect that was so startling that Mikey gasped, and mirror-Louie turned to glare at him, showing nothing so much as his teeth. Mikey's fur stood on end.

He snapped his head to look at his brother, who had whirled to look at the dresser mirror, and then at him. Wide-eyed and baffled, Louie stared at him. "What's wrong?" he asked, and ever-so-subtly, began shaking.

Allison shot him as angry a look as a doe could produce. Mikey frowned. "Nothing, big guy...uh, just realized it's probably *my* car making all that racket. Go on ahead." He patted his brother on the back.

Glancing at the mirror again, Mikey saw nothing but himself—gray fur and hard lines. Deep in the back of his head, some sadistic part of his brain wondered if that was how other people—just at first, of course—saw his very special brother.

Frowning, he shoved the thought back down, like swallowed vomit. This was just nerves. And wasn't that to be expected? This was Louie's first trip out of the state, his first road trip in his entire life, and in barely five hours they'd nearly been killed by a freak storm.

People saw things, in mirrors in dark rooms, under far less stress than this.

Then they were outside, in the hazy sunlight, where there weren't any shadows at all.

The car alarm did turn out to be Mikey's, of course, and it took him several tries to get it to stop screaming. The vehicle was a black Scion xB, and now it sat with its front wheels on the sidewalk, nose nearly against the motel wall. The rear window was a gaping hole, rimmed with jagged black bits of safety glass, and the inside of the car appeared to be filled with landscaping remnants. The windows were splotchy and opaque, fogged from the inside by the rain and melting hail inside.

The parking lot was otherwise empty, littered with bits of foliage, everything from leaf-stripped twigs the size of pencils to a 20-foot section of branch blocking the entrance to the parking lot. The pavement looked more green and brown than black.

Strewn around the blacktop like confetti were small, jagged chips of bright orange plastic. It took Mikey a moment to realize that they were remnants of the huge orange "Super 8" sign for the motel at which they were staying. He and Gabe had run directly underneath it when the sirens had fired. They'd made it into the room barely thirty seconds before the windows had blown in.

All up and down the line of rooms, windows and doors had been blown out of their respective frames. A few of the rooms, including the one next door, were also missing parts of the wall. Not a pane of glass was left in the entire strip.

Gabe rubbed his black muzzle fur. "*I* wanted to go to Vegas," he pointed out.

Despite himself, Mikey smiled. "Vegas was too far to drive."

Gabe scoffed. "Yeah? Well, the Wisconsin Dells was the only travel destination inside tornado alley."

Sarah frowned, wringing out her sweatshirt. "I *said* it wasn't a tornado." Her nose twitched in annoyance.

Louie was nervously watching the skies. Again, Allison put a comforting hand on his arm. The clouds were the color of ocean water and roiled ominously.

"Are you sure something *worse* isn't coming?" Louie whispered.

From across the parking lot came the sound of running.

They looked up. Sprinting across the lot from the direction of the office was an older coyote in a plaid shirt, eyes wide and panicked. He looked vaguely familiar.

Mikey straightened up, heart pounding. "Who's that?" he asked, alarmed. Louie picked up on his tone and shrank back against the car.

Allison stepped forward. "He's the owner of the motel," she said quickly to the group. "We checked in with him yesterday. There's practically nobody else at the hotel this early in the season; I talked to him for like twenty minutes."

The barrel-chested coyote thundered toward them, pumping his arms, his baseball cap sailing off his head. "Are you kids alright?" he boomed, skidding to a stop. "All the windows in the office just blew in! Oh my Lord, this one hit us bad."

"We're fine," Allison said, brown eyes a little wide. "Are *you* alright?"

The coyote staggered toward them, panting desperately, pink tongue lolling out. He was carrying a few extra pounds—Mikey began wondering if he was going to blow a heart valve in front of them. He frowned.

The coyote made his way to their room, peered in through the missing window, and let out a slow breath. "Sweet Jesus," he said, "You coulda been *killed*." He turned back to them, eyes wide.

Not knowing what else to do, Mikey shrugged. "Yeah, guess we picked the wrong room, huh?" He smiled lopsidedly.

The coyote frowned. "*I* picked that room." He leaned against the wall.

Allison cleared her throat. "Sir, it's fine. I'm sure your insurance will cover everything."

The coyote pulled a red bandanna from his pocket and began wringing it between his hands. "Oh, I know it will, honey, but this is always a shock. This has happened before, believe it or not... we're right on the edge of the lake and the winds just come roaring right in." He twisted the bandanna into a little knot, and then unraveled it, turning to the rooms. "Not as bad as all *this*, usually, but..." He trailed off. "These rooms all needed new windows anyway," he said, smiling weakly.

Then even that paltry amusement dropped off his face. "Oh, but your vacation is *ruined*, that's just awful." He turned to Allison. "And here you were sayin' you haven't even seen each other in years..."

They all turned to look at Allison. She colored under her tawny fur.

He cleared his throat. "This is just terrible." The grizzled old canine thought for a moment, frowning intently. "But I think...I think I just might have an idea."

Mike and Gabe exchanged glances.

"Oh boy, the Missus would kill me for saying this, but we've got a cabin a ways further up north, on a lake... sort of a retirement home. S'real nice—got a big TV and a big pantry." He stared at them expectantly. "If you're still in a vacation sort of mood, I suppose I could lend it to'ya for the week..."

Mikey narrowed his eyes. "You're offering us your...personal cabin?"

"For the *week*?" Gabe added.

The coyote nodded. "We don't use it much," he said, as if that explained his offer. "'Specially going into tourist season."

Sarah blinked in surprise. "You're very trusting."

The grizzled coyote smiled. "I've got your credit card numbers."

Mikey smiled. "That's true. Well...how big is it? Decent size?"

The innkeeper nodded. "Four bedrooms. Built a long time ago, but barely finished renovating it last year. S'got a boathouse... you can use the canoe." He glanced into their room one more time, frowned, and looked back to the group. "Whatcha think? I can refund your money but it'll take a week or so to go through..." he said, wringing the bandanna again.

Mikey was staring at the storm-assaulted remains of his car. "You know what? The Dells have sort of lost a bit of their charm in the last hour or so. I don't really feel like finding another hotel… anyone else leaning toward yes?"

Allison smiled faintly. "Actually, that sounds kind of nice. A cabin by the lake…we can go swimming!"

Louie's eyes brightened. "Swimming!"

Gabe's brow furrowed. "Um…I'm not really the spontaneous type, but if you guys think it'll be fun…I'm up for it."

Sarah frowned. "Well, I'm sure there's undamaged hotels here in the strip. We could always come back and find one if it doesn't, ah, work out."

Mikey turned to the innkeeper. "I guess we're taking you up on your offer," he said.

Behind them, Louie cheered.

The innkeeper turned to glance at the large wolf's outburst, but to Mikey's mild surprise, he didn't stare, as most folks would. In fact, Mikey thought he saw the hint of a smile.

Later, it was a moment he would come back to.

"Dude, are you *sure* we didn't pass it?"

It was 7:30 p.m. They were far along Route 10, the Scion's lights the only artificial illumination for miles.

Mikey sighed. "Yes, Gabe, for the *fourth* time, I'm sure. Mr. GPS is up here with me, remember?" He pointed at the tiny screen of the knockoff-Garmin stuck to the windshield. The little electronic arrow pointed confidently forward. "I'll let you know if it starts displaying a Michigan zip code, huh?"

"Or Canada," Gabe muttered.

Mikey chuckled. "Right." The zip code was displayed in the top right corner of the GPS map, and it had stayed the same— 55407—for about an hour. Back home in Chicago, it had been changing every 20 minutes or so…they must really be out in the sticks now.

10

Next to him, Louie yawned toothily, staring vacantly out into the darkness. He slumped in his seat, looking drowsy, but couldn't slump too far before his knees hit the dashboard. Even the vast expanses of the Scion's interior were a little cramped for Louie—at 6'6", Mikey had purchased the car solely because his brother fit into it. He had bought Louie a bright green Packers hat at a gas station, and the top of it was barely four inches from the headliner. Mikey had bought him a giant Diet Coke, too—his favorite—and his brother cradled the empty cup between his legs. Mikey smiled.

In the backseat, Sarah and Allison sat on opposite ends, looking bored. Gabe pouted between them. He was blocking the view out the back, but since the entire rear window was covered in opaque plastic sheeting, that didn't really matter.

"So, how's teaching at the new school?" Mikey asked him.

In the rearview, he saw Gabe's brow furrow. "Pretty much the same. High school kids are still stupid." He smiled wryly. "I'm still trying to teach them history, sociology, and the life skills to come in out of the rain."

Sarah sighed. "If you succeed, we could use you at my job. The new department head doesn't know the difference between an outflow boundary and an ascending bifurcated cold front."

There was silence for a moment.

Sarah colored. "Never mind. Allison, did you ever get that classroom aide?"

Allison smiled. "Yes, and it is *great* just to finally have one. I could use two more, though—I've got two kids in wheelchairs this year."

"So move to Illinois!" Mikey said. "Special Ed actually has a budget for things like classroom aides."

Louie straightened up. "My teacher Miss Laura has two aides! One of them is named Brandy and she lets me help lift David into his chair sometimes." He frowned. "Not allowed to push it, though. Brandy says it's a…lie…lie…" He trailed off, thinking feverishly.

"Li-aaaaaa…." Mikey prompted.

"Lie-bility!" Louie pronounced triumphantly. He grinned.

"*Turn right, 20 meters,*" the GPS announced. Mikey glanced up at it.

"Finally!" Gabe announced from the backseat. "Boy, I hope this place is up to par, or else it's going to be a looonnng drive back."

Mikey frowned. They came to a tiny road, labeled on a hand-carved wooden plank nailed to a birch tree. SHELTER ROAD, it read.

"This is it," Mikey announced. "And if the innkeeper was right, this should be right around the point where we—"

"*Signal lost,*" the GPS announced. The artificial voice had an urgency to it that Mikey had never heard before. "*Signal lost. Signal lost.*" Mikey reached up and held down the power button.

The rearview lit up as Gabe's Blackberry illuminated. "Yep, no service on this thing either. This must be one of them *enforced* relaxation vacations."

Sarah sighed. "I didn't know a GPS could even lose a signal. This takes 'rural' to a whole new level."

Mikey kept an eye on the car's odometer. "Well, according to the Kindly Old Innkeeper, it's supposed to be nine miles further, exactly." Next to the odometer, he spotted something wooden on the dashboard, about the size of a pack of cigarettes. "What is *that?*" he asked.

Louie reached for it with one giant hand. "A toy," he said proudly. "Found it. In the room."

Mikey blinked. "Where?" He glanced at it. "Can I see it?" He held out his paw.

The bigger wolf slipped the little figurine into Mikey's fingers. Mikey glanced at it, quickly looking back to the dark road. It was made of wood, carved like a coyote and worn smooth with age. It looked distinctly Native American, decorated with dusty red war paint.

Sarah was looking over his shoulder from the backseat. "Doesn't exactly look like gift shop fare," she pointed out.

"No…it doesn't," Mikey added. Raising his head and watching the dark road, he lifted the little coyote in his brother's direction. Louie held out his giant hands eagerly. "This was in the room?"

Louie nodded. "Uh-huh. I heard the stuff in hotels is free like…" He paused to think of an example. "Soap. And…shower cap." His eyes suddenly widened. "Was this not free?" he asked. "Did I steal it?" he asked, alarmed.

Mikey shook his head dismissively. "No, no, it's fine! Where'd you pick it up, though?" He glanced at the odometer. It had racked up six more miles.

Louie traced one thick claw over the figure's blunt muzzle and ears. "Table. Between the beds."

Mikey frowned. "When we checked in?"

Louie turned the figure over and over. "Nope, when we were leaving."

Gabe asked what Mikey was thinking, "*After* the storm?"

Louie twisted his great mass around, looking worried. "Lots of questions," he said softly. His ears began to tilt backward.

Mikey put a hand on his arm. "No, Louie, it's fine. It's just that there was a lot of wind in the room; it's weird it was still on the table. But tornadoes do weird things." He smiled. "Maybe it even flew in from outside. Just for you."

Louie stared at him for a moment, processing, and then looked down at the figure in his hands. "Wow," he breathed softly.

"Hey, *heads up!*" Gabe called from the backseat.

Mikey snapped his head upward, and slammed on the brakes. The tires shrieked for a moment and the antilock brakes grumbled under his feet. The car screamed to a halt, and sat rumbling softly in the road.

"What?!" Allison cried. Louie covered his muzzle in shock.

"Sorry, sorry," Mikey muttered. "I wasn't paying attention."

"To what?" Sarah asked.

Mikey gestured with his head. "We're here."

The car sat idling in front of a sign post. The number 11 had been nailed to a tree.

The cabin seemed more like the innkeeper and the Missus intended to open a bed'n'breakfast than retire in peace. It was huge, immaculate, and charmingly decorated with what seemed like twenty years' worth of estate-sale finds. The place was full of end tables and thick wooden shelves, covered in old books, framed pictures and all manner of knickknacks, from crystal vases to cheesy-looking vacation souvenirs. The log bones of the structure had been preserved, in the perfect mix of historic and comfortable.

"Look at this! I bet these are the original plank floors!" Allison was saying in the kitchen, as Mikey and Gabe set the last of the luggage in the living room. Louie was right behind them, carrying the heavy cooler full of their groceries, a faint, dopey smile on his face.

Setting the cooler down, Louie looked longingly down at it and licked his teeth; somewhere inside were six frozen pizzas. He whined plaintively. "Food?" he asked.

"Alright, dinner's comin'," Mikey announced, grinning. "Allison, care to join me?" He grabbed one end of the cooler and began dragging it into the kitchen. "Gabe, Sarah, you want to have a look around? Maybe start assigning rooms?"

"Seen one cabin, seen 'em all," Gabe mumbled. "I seen the '*Friday the 13*th' movies, I can pretty much paint a picture for you." He picked up a duffel and wandered out of the room, smirking.

Mikey rolled his eyes. "Louie, you want a soda?"

Louie's eyes lit up. "Soooda!" he said, grinning.

Mikey tossed him a Diet Coke from the cooler. "Go hang out in the living room, okay? Do what Gabe and Sarah tell you." He smiled. "Give your little coyote a tour of the living room."

Clutching his Diet Coke, Louie thumped off, his tail wagging ecstatically.

14

Twenty minutes later, Mike and Allison had three pizzas coming out of the oven.

"Do you think there's a pizza cutter in here somewhere?" Mikey asked. He began pulling drawers open, frowning in concentration. "There's *got* to be."

Allison suddenly crossed her arms.

Mikey felt her gaze. He looked up. "Um…what's up?" he asked, ears tilted back.

Allison smiled. "Nothing. Here in this kitchen is just the most relaxed I've seen you since…uh, college?"

He sighed, digging through the top drawer. "Yeah. It's Louie's first trip. I've been a little on-edge."

Allison opened a drawer on her side of the kitchen. "You're a *lot* on-edge. Is it because you're nervous about Louie, or about the fine people of the state of Wisconsin?"

Mikey glanced up, frowning. "Wow, I'm transparent. Look… it's not like he doesn't have feelings. He can tell when people are staring. Let's just say it's not so bad to be way out here in the woods." He slammed his drawer and began working on the next one down. He held up a whisk in each hand. "Do you *believe* how many whisks these people have? How many could you possibly need at one time?"

The doe suddenly appeared at his side with a pizza cutter. He blinked. "Oh."

While Mikey cut the pizzas, Allison leaned against the counter. "Did I ever tell you about our class trip to Denny's?"

Mikey cocked his head. "No. With your special kids?"

She smiled. "Mmm-hmm. Our field trips are a little simpler…ordering food, how to act in public places, basic functioning…it's good for them. We went to a Denny's this spring." She rolled up the sleeves on her sweatshirt. "Seven kids, two wheelchairs, two parent volunteers…it was quite a troupe. We took up the whole middle section of the restaurant."

Mikey stopped what he was doing. He felt the blood drain

from his face. "Did somebody start shit with you?"

Allison stared at him. "No, just the opposite. When I went up to pay, the girl grinned at me and said the bill had been taken care of. 'Taken care of,' that's exactly the wording she used."

He set the cutter down on the stove. He didn't get it. "Did the restaurant...?"

Smiling, Allison shook her head. "No. It was one of the other customers. Some random businessman or soccer mom walked up, paid our three-hundred-dollar tab, and left without a word." She sighed happily, remembering.

Mikey stared at her, his brow furrowed. He didn't know what to make of the story.

"I think," she said gently, "I think the average person isn't nearly as hateful as you've come to believe. I think people are basically tolerant and understanding, and your brother's going to be just fine."

Mikey stared at her for a moment, and then looked away. It took him a moment to speak. "I just...can't stand to see him get hurt, you know? I want him to be happy."

Allison nodded. She thought for a moment, and then put a hand on Mikey's shoulder. "I know. And he will be. But you should be, too."

He frowned.

She looked intently at him. "And I am hungry. So you should serve the goddamn pizzas."

He laughed.

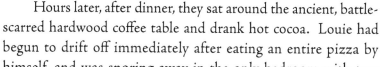

Hours later, after dinner, they sat around the ancient, battle-scarred hardwood coffee table and drank hot cocoa. Louie had begun to drift off immediately after eating an entire pizza by himself, and was snoring away in the only bedroom with two beds in it. Mikey was proud of him for going to sleep by himself

16

in a strange place, though Louie had insisted on taking the little coyote totem for company.

"This place is *great*," Gabe announced. "We should almost die in freak weather disasters more often." The ferret and the mouse were curled up under a gigantic hand-sewn quilt, a habit they'd taken up on cold college nights and never quite broken. "I can't wait to get into the boathouse tomorrow. I bet the lake is small enough that we're the only ones on it."

Mikey smiled tiredly. He had changed into a sweatshirt that was so huge on him it could only have been Louie's. "I know. This is so much better than that crappy motel would have been. I love you all, but I was really not looking forward to the thought of sharing one room with everybody. And Louie snores like a truck downshifting, so this is going to work much better. There's only one thing missing."

"What's that?" Allison asked.

Mikey leaned forward and picked up his mug. "I need a blanket...with some kind of *sleeves* on it."

They laughed.

He leaned forward and set his mug on the coffee table, next to a large, old fabric-bound book.

Unnoticed by the rest of them, Sarah happened to glance at the book's cover. She leaned forward and picked up the tome, cracking it open with a leathery creak.

"So, how's everybody's life going?" Gabe asked, out of nowhere. "Are you where you thought you'd be?"

Mikey frowned. "Jesus, Gabe. We graduated, like, three years ago. That's not a lot of time to reach self-actualization, huh?"

Gabe sighed. "I know. I'm just...bored. Life got ungodly routine a lot faster than I expected."

Allison curled her legs up under her. "Not enough adventure in your life?"

Gabe shrugged. "Well...I dunno. I *like* my life, that's for sure....Sarah and I have a nice place and good jobs...but nothing *happens* anymore. I'm only on my third year and it's already like I'm watching reruns. Not exactly life in interesting times, if you catch my meaning."

Allison furrowed her brow. "Interesting times?" she repeated.

Gabe paused. "It's an old Chinese saying, 'May you live in interesting times.'"

Mikey frowned. "That's not a saying," he said flatly. "That's a *curse*."

Allison cocked her head. "It's a what?"

Suddenly, Sarah inhaled sharply. They all turned to look at her.

"I *knew* it," she said, definitively. "You guys—take a look at this." She turned the book around and set it on the coffee table, squirming out from under the blanket.

They started at the large, grainy, black and white picture.

"Whoa," Mikey said. "That's *Louie's*."

The carving pictured in the grainy photograph was an exact match for Louie's newfound toy. The accompanying caption was a small wall of text, all but unreadable in the scant lighting, but the entry's heading was clearly visible.

It read THE TRICKSTER.

"Weird," Gabe pronounced. "What the hell is it?"

"I was sure I'd seen that totem before," Sarah muttered. "My department hosted an exposition on native mythology last quarter. The Trickster is one of the major players in Native American folklore."

Mikey nodded. "The Creator. I remember stories from when I was a pup."

Sarah nodded. "Yeah. The originator of all things." She paused for a moment. "Um, you wouldn't happen to remember the significance of the war paint, would you?"

Gabe narrowed his dark eyes. "I don't like the way you said that. That's your 'bad news' voice."

Sarah opened her mouth, closed it, and then started again. "Well…this is a subset of the Trickster myth. There were a number of pieces at the show addressing this aspect. Louie's little, um, 'toy' is a *Dark Trickster* totem, characteristic of the somewhat more… grim…aspects of his trickery."

Allison leaned forward. She looked a little sick. "How grim? Like, *Saw IV* grim?"

Sarah swallowed. "…yeah. Like, 'wouldn't it be funny if I tricked you into eating your own children' grim."

"Jesus, what culture produced *that*?" Gabe asked.

"The Sioux," Mikey and Sarah said, together.

They all looked at Mikey.

Mikey felt his ears tilt backward. "Um…yeah. I never got around to mentioning this during college, but…Louie and I are part Sioux. Not a lot, but…enough to be familiar."

Gabe stared at him in utter disbelief. "And you never thought to mention this?"

"It's not a big deal! I didn't want to seem like I was milking it." He frowned. "If you say it too loudly somebody runs up and gives you a scholarship."

Allison leaned back in her chair. "I'd guessed it, at any rate. I mean…you'd have to be, for Louie to…well, be the way he is."

Mikey dipped his head. "…yeah."

There was a quiet pause.

Allison pursed her lips thoughtfully. "There still aren't any recorded occurrences of Gregar Disorder outside of the Sioux bloodlines, huh?"

He didn't look up. "Nope," he said.

All four of them were silent for a moment. When Louie came lumbering down the hallway, they all heard him coming from the moment he left the bedroom.

He appeared in the hall in just his running shorts, rubbing his eyes, looking massive and fluffy and disheveled. He was still wearing his bright green Packers hat.

Mildly concerned, Mikey straightened up. "What's the matter, big guy?" he said. "Can't sleep?"

19

Louie yawned, eyes half-closed. "No," he said, brow furrowing. "All I can hear is talking." They exchanged embarrassed glances.

"Sorry, buddy," Mikey said. "We'll move it to the kitchen."

Louie frowned and opened his eyes, looking baffled at them from under his cap. "Not from *you*," he said. He turned to the enormous picture window. The forest was so black that the window appeared as a colossal mirror, even with the dim lighting in the living room. "It's the man out *there*." Louie frowned severely, his brow furrowing.

There was a thump as the book slid from Sarah's hands and hit the floor.

"Louie, what did you say?" Allison said, in a voice that was barely a whisper.

The big wolf picked up on their fear and shrank back. "There's someone out there," he said, mirroring her soft tone. "He wants me to come outside." He frowned. "I don't like him."

There was another moment of silence, and then Mikey stood up. He set his mug down on the coffee table. It landed half on the book and then tipped over, gushing thick liquid cocoa all over the antique wood. Mikey didn't notice.

"Kitchen," he said simply.

They went.

Mikey entered first. The kitchen light was already on. He flipped open his phone, checking it for a signal. There was nothing, of course. This was the sort of situation where no phone ever worked, if his two semesters as a film major had taught him anything.

The others were right behind him. "Louie, I need you to tell us exactly what you heard."

Wide-eyed and alarmed, Louie's head dipped, like he was afraid he was in trouble. "Just w-whispering," he whispered himself. "A stranger." He swallowed. "He say, 'Come outside, I got something to show you.'" He mimicked a deep, gruff voice for the quote, and it made Mikey's fur stand on end.

The smaller wolf turned to the group. He lowered his voice nearly to a whisper. "Okay. Louie doesn't lie, so there's somebody out here. Can we agree that this is too far out into nowhere for a simple robbery?"

Gabe swallowed, tried to lower his impossibly-deep voice. "Maybe they're interested in your stereo. Say they saw the car at a gas station, it stuck out, they decided it must have a pretty decent stereo in it, want it for themselves. It's an easy target with half the windows missing."

Mikey stared impassively at him. "And they need Louie to come out and get it for them? No, whoever this is, they came here to fuck with us." He turned away, opened the kitchen drawer from which Allison had previously retrieved a pizza cutter, and came out with a 12-inch long butcher knife. Everyone's eyes widened. "And they're targeting Louie, which makes me think they don't like a feral in their town." He handed the first knife to Sarah, reached in for another. "So we're getting the fuck out of here."

He found another knife, handed it to Gabe. "Allison, you're in charge of Louie." He snatched his car keys off the counter with a sharp staccato jangle, and turned to his brother. "Louie, remember what Mom said, about never biting or growling at anybody?" He looked into his brother's eyes.

"Yeeeaahhhh," Louie said slowly, brow furrowed like an old man's.

"I want you to forget it. If you see anybody who's not one of us, I want you to bite and scratch and kick and do whatever you can to hurt that person until one of us tells you to stop."

Louie stared back, horrified. His jaw hung open and his ears tilted back.

Mikey grabbed his brother's cheek ruff. "Do you understand me, Louie? This is a bad situation. We're in real trouble here."

Terrified, Louie nodded. He was so scared that tears were beginning to form in the corners of his eyes, but Mikey didn't have time to address that right now. He leaned in, kissed his brother on the nose, and went to the back door.

"Okay, I'm going to unlock the car first. Everybody run like hell, slash at anything that moves, and get in the same seats we were all in for the ride up. Any questions?"

Nobody said a word.

"Okay, here we go," Mikey said. He put a hand on the knob and quietly flipped the deadbolt open with his thumbclaw. Steeling himself, he set his thumb on the upper button of the Scion's key fob, eyes locked on the brake lights, which would flare when the vehicle was unlocked. Tensing to run, he jabbed the UNLOCK button.

Outside—predictably—nothing happened.

They stared for a moment. Allison gasped, but the others weren't nearly so surprised.

"I could have told you *that* was going to happen," Gabe said unhappily. "You wrote your film thesis on scary movies, for fuck's sake. Does the car *ever* work?!"

"Oh crap, I'm having a really hard time chalking that up to coincidence," Allison said, her ears tilting backward.

Growling softly under his breath, flipping the lock back shut, Mikey turned back into the room. "Okay. New plan. We spend the night in here, this kitchen, together. Armed to the teeth, maybe make a nice Molotov Cocktail for good measure, and we don't leave this room for *anything*."

There was silence for a moment, and then laughter. It was coming from Louie. He was laughing, slowly and deliberately.

It was unlike any laugh Mikey had ever heard before. It made his fur stand on end. Allison stepped away from the bigger wolf.

Grinning from ear to ear, Louie crossed his massive arms. "I don't think that's going to work out very well for you."

Mikey swallowed. "Louie, what's wrong with you?" he asked, his voice shaking. "This is serious."

Louie raised an eyebrow defiantly. It was a gesture so unlike him that Mikey couldn't speak. He couldn't even move.

His mannerisms, even his posture, were not those of a developmentally-delayed individual. It was like someone else was inside Louie's head, speaking through his mouth.

"...Louie?" he whispered, hesitantly.

The Louie-thing just grinned back at him. Mikey suddenly hit the kitchen counter, and he realized he'd been backing up slowly. His ears folded back against his head.

The bigger wolf let out a slow breath, looked at each of them one by one. "Come, now. I've left you enough clues. Surely *one* of you has figured it out."

There was a moment of silence.

Sarah cleared her throat. "I have," she said.

The hulking wolf smiled toothily. "Have you, now." He played with the claws on one finger. "And have you figured out what comes next, mouse?"

Sarah frowned. "A game."

The wolf's face lit up. It was a terrible smile. "Brilliant! You *have* been paying attention!"

"So what's in this for you?"

The big wolf shrugged his massive shoulders. "Entertainment. I grow bored." His teeth showed again. "But no longer. This is exciting. I'm especially curious in what I will get from this one." He pointed one of Louie's thick fingers at Mikey.

Mikey's ears popped up and his eyes grew angry.

"And what if we don't want to play?" Sarah challenged him.

The larger wolf slowly turned to look at her. "You will," he said deliberately. "The prize is too good to pass up."

23

Sarah bit her lip. "You leave him *alone*. He's as innocent as anyone ever was."

The big wolf scoffed. "No mortal is innocent. Now…choose your path. Choose your path carefully." He raised one oversized hand, and snapped Louie's thick fingers.

And with that, the lights went out.

It took them ten minutes to find the flashlight they'd come in with, and by the time they did, Mikey was nearly hysterical with anxiety. When they discovered that Louie was not among them, it took another ten minutes to convince Mikey not to go charging out into the night. Gabe actually had to physically restrain him; they lay on the kitchen floor now, panting.

"It's not going to help," Sarah insisted again. "We have to play the game. Don't you get it? The prize is *Louie*."

"Are you out of your mind?!" Mikey spat. "This is not the fucking *X-Files*! He's…he's had some kind of a breakdown or something, and run off, and *we have to find him!*"

Gabe put an arm on the wolf's shoulder. "And we *will*. But you cannot honestly tell me you think that was actually your brother talking to us."

Mikey didn't have a response to that. He looked frantically around the room, a low, plaintive whine building in the back of his throat.

They sat on the kitchen floor, the room lit only by the flashlight. It was eerily reminiscent of the motel bathroom, with the exception of the missing participant.

"Okay, so *now* what?" Mikey suddenly demanded, startling them all. "I'll play along for a minute. Let's assume that the Trickster god is not only real, but has decided to spend an evening fucking with us, and possessed my brother. We don't get Louie back until we win the game, right?"

They all looked at one another.

"So what the fuck is the game?" he demanded.

In the dim yellow glow of the flashlight, they all stared at one another.

Sarah swallowed. "I've been thinking about that. I think it might be a clue game."

Allison frowned skeptically. "Clue game? As in, Colonel Mustard in the Observatory, Clue?"

Sarah shook her head. "No, like, a logic puzzle. Figure it out, that sort of thing." She looked at each one of them. "Think about it: he left us all sorts of hints...the little figurine, the book explaining it...I think he's left us a series of clues, and if we figure them out, we win the game." She paused. "It stands to reason that...maybe the last one even leads us to Louie."

"So where's the first clue?" Allison asked.

Sarah sighed. "That's what I *haven't* figured out."

Gabe blinked at her. "So, is this like, something that's left for us, or something we have to find...?"

The small gray mouse leaned back against one of the cabinets. "I don't know. For all I know it could have been something he said to us."

Mikey stared for a moment. "Choose your path," he said.

"What?"

The small wolf cleared his throat. "'Choose your path.' Louie—uh, whoever—said it right before the lights cut out." He swallowed. "It didn't make sense with the rest of what he was saying—What the fuck is the other path? Leaving my brother? He knows damn well we only have *one* path." He scowled, the top of his muzzle wrinkling in a silent snarl.

"Do you think that's—" Allison began, but Gabe cut her off.

"Oh, God, of *course*," he said. He leapt to his feet. "The Garmin."

The others scrambled after him. He was holding the sheer white curtains open in the kitchen window. "Look," he said, and pointed at Mikey's car, huddled silently in the driveway.

They all gathered around and stared. "What the fuck are we looking at?" Mikey asked. "It's dead. We already tried that."

"Look *harder*," Gabe insisted.

They did. Now that their eyes were adjusted to the darkness, they saw it; the interior of the car was lit with a bizarre green glow.

It was the screen of the GPS.

"I saw it when we were getting ready to run," Gabe said. "The GPS is on, even though Mikey turned it off. *That's* the first clue."

Sarah let out a breath. "Choose your path…of course. The navigation system."

Mikey turned and strode away from the window. There was a jingle as he snatched his car keys off the kitchen floor and headed for the back door.

"Where are you going?!" Allison demanded. "How do you know it's safe out there?"

He turned, and Gabe just happened to catch his eyes with the light. They flared bright yellow. "Do you honestly think we're safe in *here*?" he demanded, and turned back to the door.

Allison didn't have a response for that.

Reflexively, he tried to unlock the car with the fob, but of course that didn't work. Reaching the vehicle, he jabbed the key at the keyhole, scratching the paint in the process.

Fumbling the door open, Mikey dropped into the driver's seat. He didn't even bother with the power lock button, instead lunging across the passenger cabin to yank on the other door's handle and straightened himself up. Not knowing what else to do with the keys, he stuck them in the ignition, as Sarah dropped into the seat next to him, and Gabe and Allison leaned in across them.

They looked at the little screen.

It was a map. A vague, incomprehensible little map.

"So…?" Gabe said, slowly.

Allison leaned forward. She peered closer to the screen, leaning over Mikey's chest. "I was kind of expecting a riddle or something. What is that, just a map?"

It was. The GPS was in turn-by-turn mode. Directly ahead of the little pixilated navi car was a street labeled Big Mine Road. Other roads snaked out from the main drag, but none close enough to list any street names. No buildings, either; though Big Mine Road appeared to be fairly wide, it was apparently in the middle of a series of empty lots. In the top right corner was a string of question marks, five of them. In the lower left corner were the words SIGNAL LOST - CHECK CONNECTION.

"I think a better question is, *where* is that?" Sarah muttered. "I was thinking we'd have to drive to the location, but this doesn't exactly look local, does it?"

Mikey frowned. "I've never even heard of 'Big Mine Road,' and I've been coming here since I was six. When's the last time you saw a mine in Wisconsin?"

Gabe grunted. "It's in turn-by-turn mode...can we go back a screen? That should be an overhead map." He reached for the device.

"*Don't!*" Mikey exploded, grabbing Gabe's wrist and startling them all. "It doesn't have a signal. It's not like a web browser; it refreshes every time. If you back up it'll just dump the current screen."

"What is *this?*" Sarah asked. She pointed to the ????? in the upper corner.

Mikey took a breath and then let it out. "I...don't know. I've never seen that before. It's *supposed* to be the zip code, but if it loaded the map it should have loaded the zip code. I guess it can't find one." He paused. "But that's absurd—What American city doesn't have a zip code?"

"Maybe it's not American," Gabe offered. "Maybe it's a European city, or even South American. They have a lot of mines."

"Canada, too," Sarah added.

"No, not this one," Allison said quietly. "This one's in Pennsylvania."

They all turned to stare at her.

"Allison?" Gabe asked through his pointy little teeth. "Something you'd care to share?"

She stared back at them, frowning unhappily, and then let out a slow breath. "Big Mine Road sounded vaguely familiar, but I didn't remember until you mentioned zip codes. It's Centralia. Centralia, Pennsylvania."

"I've heard of that," Sarah said softly. "But...the zip code...?"

Allison crossed her arms. She took a step back. The others followed, Gabe and Sarah taking a few steps to listen over the car's small hood. "The zip code is gone because the Postal Service revoked it. Once enough of the townspeople had fled there was really no point in keeping it."

"Sorry, *fled?*" Mikey demanded. He stared at her. "What happened there?"

Allison blinked at him. "Surely you've heard of this place. Little mining town with a fire burning in the coal veins under it? The fire's been going for over forty years; it was started accidentally in the 60's, and it's not even close to running out of fuel. The city is filled with smoke and poisonous gasses, and now there's only half a dozen people still stupid or suicidal enough to live there. You've seen *Silent Hill*, right?"

He nodded slowly.

She pointed at the GPS. "You're looking at the inspiration."

Gabe frowned at her, his black eyes narrowed. "How do you know all this?"

She looked embarrassed. "We did a unit on it. For Halloween."

Gabe stared. "You taught a bunch of mentally impaired kids about a poison-swathed ghost town," he said flatly.

She shrugged. "The town's empty. I wanted something vaguely scary but not actually threatening. I left out the gory details."

Mikey cleared his throat. "*HEY*, guys, there's a more pressing question—such as what the fuck does this have to do with my brother?"

The rest of them were silent.

"Okay, so…" said Gabe. "Fire? Mining? Are we supposed to dig something up?" He turned to Allison. "How did the fire start?"

She looked up, thinking. "Uh, it was something stupid. I think they were burning out the town dump or something, and the pit was connected to one of the mine shafts."

Sarah frowned. "The mine seems pretty significant. They were mining coal, right?"

Allison nodded.

Mikey growled softly. "Yeah, but there are coal mines all over the country. Why *this* mine? Why not a list of mining towns?"

Gabe blinked at him. "So you think it's the fire."

Mike frowned. "Yeah. I think it's the fire. A 30-year-fire burning underneath a town is pretty fucking distinctive."

Sarah thought for a moment, and then turned and looked over her shoulder. She was looking at the house. "Hey…how old do you think this cabin is?"

Gabe shrugged. "I don't know, a hundred years?"

Mikey narrowed his eyes. "Why do you ask?"

She paused before answering. "Old enough to have a coal stove?"

They all thought about that for a moment.

"Yeah, I think it is," Mikey said thoughtfully.

"Coal fire," Gabe said.

Sarah nodded. "Yeah. There's one in my parents' cabin up north," she noted. "I saw a stove in the living room. I assumed it was decorative, but if the cabin is old enough it's probably real. I guess there must be another stove in the basement."

Allison stared at her, startled. "The basement? Why the basement?"

29

Sarah took a deep breath. "Well, it's Centralia, right? Where's the coal fire?"

Mikey figured it out first. "...under the ground."

They were all quiet for a moment.

"Well, let's go," Mikey said. He popped open one of the car's rear doors, leaned into the cargo bay, and hefted a hunter green duffel bag out of the back. He rummaged through it and produced a pair of bright yellow flashlights. "Louie isn't going to save himself."

The night sky had been dark and cloudy, but not *completely* without light—the stars had been out in patches, and even a half-moon produced enough light to see one another. Back in the house, it was as black as pitch.

Apparently, the lights were not coming back on.

The door to the basement was in the first place they looked, the kitchen. It looked like it was part of the original structure, composed of thick, uneven panels of oak, nailed and bolted together. The knob was dented and misshapen, like a rotting piece of fruit.

"Wow, this is probably the last place on the entire earth I want to go right now," Gabe said. He swallowed.

"Move it," Mikey snapped. He pushed Gabe out of the way. "I have a feeling the clock is ticking here."

Gabe looked at him sideways. "What?"

Mikey paused with his hand on the knob. He turned. "The Trickster is basically the biggest asshole in all of mythology. I'm worried if we don't find Louie in time, we're going to find him in pieces."

Gabe looked horrified. He lowered his flashlight in shock, and with the light now pointing at the floor, his eyemask blacked out entirely. It was like looking into a skull.

Mikey shook it off. "You guys ready?"

"No," said Sarah and Allison.

"Me neither," he said quietly, and twisted the knob. It made a loud CLACK! noise that made them all jump.

"Oh my God, I can't take this scary movie shit." Gabe muttered.

Mikey pulled the door open and shined the flashlight down the stairs. The basement had obviously *not* been on the remodel list—the wooden stairs were so worn they were shiny in the center, uneven and occasionally sagging. The floor beyond them was nothing more than dirtpack. A musty smell washed over them, like rotting wood, so powerful that they wondered how they had missed it before now.

"Louie?" Mikey whispered.

There was no response.

He swallowed, steeled himself, and started thumping down the steps. There was no railing. "All I can think of is the fucking *Blair Witch Project*," he said.

"Thanks for that," Gabe muttered behind him.

He reached the bottom of the steps, planted two feet in the hard-pack dirt, and shined his Maglite around. The three-foot circle of light played over the features of the room, making it impossible to get an accurate idea of the size of the room.

The walls were crumbling uneven plaster, streaked with water trails and covered with soft mold. There were stacks of discolored cardboard file boxes, small piles of leftover tile and brickwork, the old kitchen appliances, and what was obviously a coal stove on the far side of the room.

He held the beam on the stove, like it was a spotlight. The stove was about the size of an oil barrel, with a long, cylindrical post coming out of it.

The fuel door was slightly ajar.

Mikey felt himself drawn toward it. He walked forward, his boots scuffling through the light dirt floor. As he neared the stove, he detected another detail; the stove was covered in a thick layer of dust, except for a light patch near the door. It was a handprint.

A very big handprint.

His mouth suddenly tasted metallic. He padded slowly toward the stove, stopped in front of it, and raised one hand.

Allison appeared at his side. "I'm sure it's just the next clue," she said with authority, and reached for the door, yanking it open.

"*Wait!*" Mikey said, but it was just nerves, and when he saw what was inside the stove he forgot he even said it.

In the center of the round barrel, on top of eighty years' worth of coal ashes, was a bright green Packers baseball cap.

Mikey could feel the corners of his mouth tugging back, and tears welling in his eyes, and he fought them both. He reached for the cap.

Suddenly, something black and formless dropped onto his hand. With a panicked yelp, he yanked his arm back, but not fast enough. He felt something hit his fur and stick to it. Flailing his arm around like mad, he howled in panic. His flashlight flew from his fingers and dropped to the floor.

Gabe grabbed him by the back of the arms, held the smaller wolf tightly. "It's okay, it's okay! It's just coal dust!"

"Mother*fucking* God fucking dammit!" spat Mikey, stumbling, heart pounding. "Really? *Really?!*" he yelled into the darkness. "You're resorting to cheap scares? Is this supposed to be *I Know What You Fucking Did Last Summer?!*"

The ferret's eyes went wide. "Um, should you really be antagonizing this guy?"

Mikey broke loose and shook his fingers through his arm fur, trying unsuccessfully to dislodge the thick black dust. It stuck to his fur like Velcro. "Son of a bitch," he whispered. His hands were shaking and his heart was pounding.

Sarah was now standing in front of the stove. She reached into the barrel—without incident, Mikey noted—and picked up the hat, examining it.

He caught Louie's scent for half a moment, and then it was lost in the mildew and dirt. His breath caught in his throat.

Sarah brushed off the cap with the back of her hand, picking up her own share of ash. "Well, this is our next clue...though I can't imagine what we're meant to infer from this kind of—"

While the hat was upside down, something small and shiny slid out of the inside brim, where it had been tucked inside the fabric. It dropped to the floor and landed directly in front of Mikey's dropped flashlight, glinting in the bright LED glow and throwing weird reflections in all directions.

The slight mouse set the hat on top of the stove, and bent over to pick up the small metal object from between her feet. It was a small silver key, round at the top, and well-worn. She turned it over, looking for a name or a manufacturer. On the back was only a series of deep scratches.

She sighed. "The name's been filed off. I didn't *think* it would be that easy."

Allison crossed her thin arms. "Well, I can't imagine the lock is in the basement, so I think we're safe to go back upstairs."

"Wait," Mikey said. He reached for the stove and retrieved Louie's baseball cap. He looked down at it, willing his eyes to stay dry. "Okay," he said softly, for fear his voice would break.

Gabe led the way back up the stairs.

"What time is it?" Allison asked again.

Mikey was rubbing his eyes. He turned and blinked at her for a moment, and then lit up his watch. "Uh, two a.m."

The doe frowned, and looked at her flashlight. "You'd better turn off your light. They aren't going to hold out all night. And we should start looking for extra batteries."

"Yuh-huh," he said. He clicked off his Maglite and resumed rubbing his eyes.

There was thumping from the stairs. Another swinging light revealed Gabe and Sarah wearily descending the stairs from the upper levels. Sarah's flashlight looked dangerously dim.

Mikey perked up, swiveled his ears in their direction. "So...?" he asked, hopefully.

Gabe sighed. "Two file cabinets, a luggage lock that wasn't even the right size, three closets that weren't even locked, and one door. I was betting on the file cabinets."

Allison sagged in her chair. "Same here. The only thing we even found that *had* a lock was a gun rack—and it certainly didn't match." She frowned at the small key. "Two hours of searching and we've got nothing. Maybe it was in the basement...?"

She set the key on the coffee table. In their searching of the kitchen cabinets, they had found some emergency candles, which were now lit across the table's surface. The key glinted at them in the flickering light.

Mikey growled, low and dangerous. "I don't know what kind of a goddamn clue this is supposed to be."

"Okay, let's go over this again," said Sarah. She sat on the couch next to Mikey, winding her fingers together. "Are we approaching this correctly?"

Gabe grunted, his whiskers twitching. "It seems pretty clear to me. You get a key, you find the lock."

"Maybe it's a metaphorical key," Allison said. "Like a key to someone's heart, or the key to a mystery?"

Sarah shook her head. "I don't think so. Would a metaphorical key be cut?" She peered at the small bit of metal. "Plus, it's worn—very worn. It obviously fits a lock somewhere."

Mikey threw his hands up, and snarled. "So what the fuck does it open? We've checked every lock in the goddamn house!"

"So maybe it's not inside the house," Allison said quietly.

They exchanged looks.

Mikey swallowed. "Like a shed, or something?" He thought for a moment. "This place supposed to have a boathouse, isn't it?"

34

Gabe suddenly gasped. "Oh shit," he said. "Let me see that key." He held out one black hand.

Allison picked up the little key and dropped it into Gabe's palm. The ferret peered at it, turning it over and over. He frowned severely. "Oh, Christ," he whispered. "I can't believe I didn't see it before."

They all stared expectantly.

He swallowed visibly, looking sick, and turned to Mikey. "So…I know what this will open. But we aren't going to find it in the house." He frowned. "And you aren't going to like it."

It took them only a few minutes to find the garage. It was built into the back of the cabin, little more than an enclosure under the second-floor deck. Its walls were corrugated metal, leaning haphazardly and universally rusted almost to crimson. It had one huge door, made of gray, weathered wood, like it started life on the side of a barn. The entire structure looked on the verge of collapse - there wasn't a true right angle in the entire mess.

It was cold outside, now. The wind was blowing like it was going to storm again, and the air smelled like moisture. Mikey hoped they found Louie soon – Louie was terrified of thunder, doubly so when he was alone.

He hoped that thunder was the biggest of Louie's worries right now.

When they pulled the garage door open, the hinges squealed like an injured animal.

In the darkness their flashlights illuminated an unstable-looking workbench with rusty tools scattered across it like bad fruit around an apple tree. The floor was covered in leaves and foliage debris, six inches deep in places. Filling the rest of the structure was a massive gray sedan, blocky and anonymous. The car was covered in greasy-looking dust, and every inch of glass was so dirty as to look fogged over.

At a glance, they could tell it was undriveable. It was crouched like a hunchbacked old man. Its tires were all but flat and its springs were no doubt in comparable condition.

Mikey shined his light on the rear of the vehicle. Above a three-part, cracked, perfectly square tail light was the word "ᴄᴇʟᴇʙʀɪᴛ𝗒," in a cheerful, dated-looking font.

They stared at the abandoned sedan.

"Son of a bitch," Mikey said. "It's a *car* key."

"Yep," Gabe said. "Vintage eighties General Motors key. My Corsica had a set just like it. Chevy used the same key blocks for about two decades. I completely forgot they were so small, though. I didn't make the connection." He crossed his arms, looking embarrassed. "Sorry, man."

"I don't get it," Allison said. "Are we supposed to *drive* somewhere?"

"We're not going anywhere without my brother," Mikey said flatly.

Gabe played his light over the rest of the car. The paint was so dirty the light didn't even reflect. "We're not going anywhere, *period*. There's no way in hell you're starting the car with that key. We're not even getting inside the cabin, unless someone wants to break a window."

Sarah shined the light on his chest. "Then what's the key for?"

Gabe frowned at her. "The car. Don't you remember my old Corsica? I didn't recognize the key right away because *I'm used to seeing them in pairs.*"

Allison held her hand up. "Is someone going to explain this? I come from a Ford family."

Gabe turned to her. "What we've got here is half a set. Older GM's came with two keys. One is for the ignition and the doors, that's the square one. The other one, the *round* one, the one we have, is for—"

Mikey interrupted him, in a voice like gravel. "The trunk."

36

Gabe swallowed, and then nodded. "I told you that you weren't gonna like it."

Mikey sighed softly. "Alright, let's get this over with." He held a paw out for the key.

Gabe steeled his eyes. "No way, man. In fact, why don't you find something else to do?"

Mikey stared at Gabe for a moment. "Just open it," he whispered.

"Alright," Gabe said. He swallowed. "The trunk's too small for Louie, anyway."

Mikey winced.

With deft black fingers, Gabe jabbed the key home in the Celebrity's trunk lock. He tried to twist it, and for one sickening moment, it looked like it wasn't going to turn and they had the wrong idea after all. Then—worse, somehow—the trunk emitted a distinctive clunk.

He had to reach under the lid with both hands to open it. Sarah shined her light inside.

For the most part, the trunk was empty. Mikey let out a relieved breath.

The trunk light was long-dead, and Sarah had to seek out individual objects. The space was full of some vintage back-of-car detritus; oil cans from long-bankrupt manufacturers, weathered old screwdrivers, an aluminum flashlight, road maps yellowed with age.

One object stuck out.

Mikey frowned. "What the hell is *that*?" he demanded, pointing.

It was tucked in the back of the vast expanse, perched on top of the spare tire; a large black metal box, about the size of an old VCR. It looked like a mutant piece of stereo equipment, with a vaguely professional, expensive feel to it. It had five stubby antennae poking out of it, in addition to a handful of dials and switches. There was one light on it, a little red dome, and it was lit. A thick cord ran out the back, and disappeared into the bowels of the car. It appeared to run upward, toward the car's battery.

Mikey lit his Maglite and aimed it at the mysterious piece of equipment. There were words on the side. "It says 'CPB 3000P.'" He sighed. "No help there."

"What on earth uses five antennae?" Gabe muttered. "Must be broadcasting a hell of a signal."

"Or blocking one," Sarah said quietly.

They processed that for a moment.

"Oh, no fucking way," Mikey snapped. "CPB – Cell Phone Blocker? Are those even *real*?"

They stared at the innocuous little device.

Sarah leaned over the rear bumper, even her sleight weight making the car sink and creak. "There's a frequency range on the dial here. Does anybody know what range cell phones operate in?"

Gabe grunted. "Or satellite navigation systems?"

"I've got a better idea," Allison said, and appeared over the device with an ancient pair of bolt cutters. The cord resisted the cleaving blade, but only for a moment.

The machine gave an angry little squeal, and then the red light went out. The others stared at her, astonished.

"*Allison!*" Mikey snapped at the doe. "Jesus, what the *fuck?!*"

"I hope we were supposed to do that," Gabe said, through his teeth.

Suddenly, a synthetic, tinny chirp made them all jump. Sarah squeaked in alarm—it had come from her pocket.

A moment later, as if answering, Gabe's Blackberry chimed a response. Half a second later, Mikey's pocket began blasting a snippet of Incubus.

"Messages," he said simply.

Allison sighed. "My purse is still in the kitchen. Let's go inside and get our next clue."

They gathered around the kitchen table. No one moved to sit down.

Mikey sighed. "I'll go first." He retrieved his Nokia from his side pocket. "It's a text message," he muttered, clicking through the menus. "Number not available, big surprise." He stared at the phone for a moment. "'*You must end your great quest as this one began. As they began this greatest of disasters, so you shall end yours.*'" He looked up at his friends, scowling. "Could use some context on that one. Anybody?"

Allison went next, flipping open her Motorola RAZR. She paled. "Oh Jesus, it's a picture message." She swallowed hard. "I'm almost afraid to look at it." Squinting at her phone like she was watching a horror film, she brought up the image, then opened her eyes and stared blankly. "What on earth...?"

The doe held out her phone to show the others. It was a blurry photo, which appeared to be taken from inside a large bed, with the interior of a simple, well-lit bedroom in the background. The bedclothes were clear, but the air around the bed was hazy and opaque.

"Is that smoke?" Mikey asked, frowning at the tiny screen.

"I think it's *cloth*," Sarah said. She blinked. "Like...mosquito netting?"

They stared at it. "Yeah, I think you're right," Allison said to her. "It's mosquito netting." She played with her phone. "What's on yours?"

Sarah scrolled through the inbox on her Blackberry. "Mine appears to be a video file. We each have a different sort of medium - interesting." She selected LOAD, and the Blackberry displayed the words LOADING 47.MOV for a moment.

"It's *interesting*, huh?" Mikey said flatly. Sarah colored.

Gabe was about to say something when the video began playing. It had a loud, tinny sound, and when the plink of metal rang out over the small speakers it startled them all. The camera was out of focus and vibrating so they could barely see what they were looking at, but it appeared to be small, shiny rings – metal, maybe? – striking a flat surface in front of the camera. Another small ring *Ping!*ed off whatever the camera was lying on, and this time its sound was clearly identifiable as some kind of metal. The video ran for nearly minute of the much of the same. After 45 seconds, Sarah set the phone on the table just before the last *Plink!*

Mikey sighed. "Gabe's message had better be a hell of a fucking clue."

Gabe was already bringing it up. "Mine's a sound file," he muttered. "Hold on, I'll put it on speaker…" He clicked a series of buttons, and suddenly his phone was speaking loudly and with authority—In German.

"*Wenn es dem internationalen Finanzjudentum in und außerhalb Europas gelingen sollte, die Völker noch einmal in einen Weltkrieg…*"

Mikey was so surprised his jaw dropped open. "What the fuck is that?"

They listened for a moment.

"*… zu stürzen, dann wird das Ergebnis nicht der Sieg des Judentums sein…*" It was obviously a speech – the speaker was loud, authoritative, full of passion. The recording was incredibly old, half-composed of white noise. It sounded like it had been recorded off the radio, on worse-than-ancient equipment.

"Does this sound familiar to anybody else?" Sarah asked with dread. Gabe nodded, ashen-faced.

"*…sondern die Vernichtung der jüdischen Rasse in Europa!*" The speaker finished with a flourish, and the cheer of a crowd swelled up like an ocean wave.

The recording ended.

"So, uh, anybody else recognize that?" Gabe asked quietly. He looked sick.

Mike and Allison shook their heads.

"It's *Hitler*," Sarah said. "Hitler denouncing the Jews. My German is a little rusty, but the content isn't a difficult guess."

Mikey felt a chill run down his back. "What…" he began, and then he couldn't finish. The fur on his arms was standing up.

"Jesus Christ, this is fucked up," Allison said, and that pretty much covered it for Mikey.

Gabe clicked his phone off and swallowed. "Well, actually, that clears a lot of things up."

Sarah blinked at him. "How do you figure?"

He shrugged. "Well, it's Hitler, right? This is him putting the wheels into motion for World War II."

"The greatest of disasters," Mikey alluded, looking at his phone. "World War I was called the Great War, wasn't it? I guess that would make part II the 'greatest.'"

"The video and photo cinch it. The Iron Curtain—it's metal rings and a curtain around a bed."

Sarah frowned. "Are you sure? He called it a 'disaster,' not a war."

Allison thought it through. "Actually, that sounds about right…WWII was the deadliest conflict in human history. And I can't imagine what else the curtain and the iron could mean."

Mikey thought for a moment. "So how did that disaster begin?"

Gabe blinked. "Germany invaded Poland."

Mikey stared at him. "Are you serious? We're supposed to invade…*Poland*?"

Gabe shrugged, his whiskers twitching. "It's obviously not *literal*. Maybe it's a cultural thing. Or a reference to a specific event."

"Look, *think*," Sarah said, "Because if we can solve this, we find Louie," she said.

Mikey's eyes narrowed. His ears tilted forward, crazily. "How do you figure?"

She shrugged . "It's the third clue. There's *always* three clues in stories like this. Think about it—have you ever heard of a quartet in all of mythology?"

He thought about it, and then nodded slowly. "No, I haven't. God, I hope you're right."

Allison was looking around the room. "It could refer to something in the house. There are knickknacks all over the place." She pushed open the door to the living room. "This place is like a freaking museum."

The rest of them followed. They entered the candlelit room and ran their flashlights over the bookshelves, littered with figurines and photographs and books and vases and an entire swap meet's worth of crap. Before it had looked charming. Now it looked daunting and oppressive.

"Any ideas what we're looking for?" Allison asked, eyes searching.

Gabe inhaled deeply, his dark eyes wide, and swallowed. "Um...something distinctly cultural? German steins, Russian nesting dolls...anything related to one of the Axis or Allied countries. It could be a ceramic Polish sausage for all we know."

"Great, if I see the fucking Weinermobile I'll let you know," Mikey muttered, and set off for the bookshelves.

Gabe coughed. "Uh, why don't you girls give us a minute?" he said. "Check out the kitchen. Mikey could probably use a minute."

Sarah and Allison exchanged glances.

"Sure thing," Allison said.

Sarah nodded. "We'll check the kitchen."

From Mikey's direction came the sound of glass breaking as he dropped something off a shelf. He growled, low and threatening.

The girls slipped back through the kitchen door.

Their phones were still on the kitchen table. Allison briefly considered dialing 911, and then sighed. She wouldn't even know how to direct the police to their cabin, let alone explain to them what was happening. She began looking around the kitchen, starting with a trio of dark green wine bottles on the back of the stove, thinking they might be German wine.

The label showed an outline of the state of California. She sighed.

"You know what's been bothering me?" Sarah asked, out of nowhere. "Each of us received a question in an area of expertise— except Mikey." She frowned. "Why? "

Allison looked up from the bottle, blinking. "What do you mean, an area of expertise?"

Sarah picked up a small ceramic vase from the counter, running her fingers over it. "Well, for instance, the coal mine question: it was obviously intended for you, because there's no way the rest of us would have known the answer to that. And Gabe was the only one who has owned the right car to identify the key. But Mikey never got a question. Meanwhile, Gabe *teaches* history, so he's the obvious authority on World War II. Why did he get *two* questions?"

Allison frowned. "I don't really see what you mean...you didn't get a question, either."

Sarah blinked at her. "Yes I did. I'm the only one who's studied mythology."

Allison set the wine bottle back on the counter. "Yes, but that wasn't a clue," she said gently. "The Trickster stuff was... supplemental. You knew the background information, but any of us could have picked up that book...and Mikey is part Sioux, he knew it off the top of his head."

Sarah set the vase back down, eyes widening. "You're right."

"So in order to validate your one-question-per-person theory, and assuming this is our third and final question...this would have to be *your* question, too."

Sarah frowned, her mind a flurry of thought. "*My* question." She blinked. "But why Mikey and me together?"

Allison shrugged. "I don't know. Maybe because of your history?"

Sarah crossed her arms, coloring behind her glasses. "Surely you aren't referring to our *two dates* when you say 'history.' There obviously wasn't any ill will or he wouldn't have introduced me to Gabe."

Allison stared at her. "Yes. And Mikey and I started hanging out so we could double with you and Gabe. So if you and Mikey hadn't gone on those two dates, none of us would be friends."

Sarah frowned, thinking for a moment. "I still don't see the connection. Where's my portion of the clue, then? What does my clue have that the others didn't?"

Allison shrugged. "I don't know. How do you send a secret message to a nerd?"

Sarah stared at her down her nose. "...that was uncalled for."

"No, seriously," Allison said, playing with her hair. "Like, a scientific formula. Or a math inside joke. Fractals or something. Fibonacci sequence. Fujita Scale."

Sarah thought for a moment, her nose twitching. She whirled for her Blackberry.

Allison narrowed her eyes. "You've got something."

Sarah snatched the device off the table. "The image you received, did it have a filename?" she said quickly.

Allison stared at her. "No. It was just 'image.jpg.' What was yours?"

Sarah flipped frantically through the Blackberry menus. "It was called 47.*mov*. I thought it was randomly generated, just the forty-seventh file to be created, but that must've been part of the clue..." She loaded the message files. "Oh my God, it's in there *twice*! The file is 47 seconds long." She looked up excitedly.

Allison nodded breathlessly. "So...what's it mean?"

They both watched the video, listening to the little pings of metal striking something hard.

At the very last moment, as the file clock reached 00:00:47, the camera pivoted to reveal a splotchy shape in the background.

It was shaped vaguely like an upside-down arch, several shades of blue in the center, with a hint of pink on one side and orange on the other. It was far too blurry to make out in the distance. The shape was only visible for half a second, and then the media player started it at the beginning.

Allison gasped. "How on earth did we miss that bef—"

Sarah sucked in a breath, her whiskers twitching madly. "*That's it!*"

"What is it?!"

Sarah held up the phone and chattered excitedly. "Look, the video's blurry, so you can't tell what the metal is, right? Even if it was clearly visible, you'd have no idea – most metals look the same, right? So how do you identify it?"

Allison frowned. "You...you can't! You'd basically have to be *told* what it was."

"Exactly! So how do you do that with a two-digit number? Using something shaped vaguely like that *colored upside-down arch*, which also happens to be a staple of nerd décor?"

Allison thought for a moment, and then covered her muzzle with her hands. "Oh my God. It's the Periodic Table of the Elements."

Sarah leaned forward and grabbed her shoulders excitedly. "It *is*! He *did* tell us what metal it was! He told us by including that metal's atomic number!"

Allison leaned back. She stared into space, thinking feverishly. "Oh geez, there's even a Periodic Table hanging right in my classroom. I stare at it on the back wall, every day. But, uh, iron isn't 47. It's...um...uh..."

"Twenty-six!" Sarah supplied cheerfully.

Allison's brown eyes widened. "So we were wrong about the Iron Curtain." She swallowed. "This changes the entire clue. But what the hell is 47?"

Sarah thought for a minute, lifting her head and staring into space. "Well, 47 would be second-tier, which means it's a transition

45

element, so that still puts it within the realm of...um..." She looked down. "What are you doing?"

Allison had picked up Sarah's Blackberry and was stabbing buttons on it. "I'm going to freaking Wikipedia and looking at a picture of the Periodic Table."

Sarah opened her mouth, and then closed it. "I guess that works, too."

A moment later, Allison had her answer. "I got it! I found it! Atomic element number 47 is...is *silver.*"

They thought for a moment.

"This changes my clue, too, doesn't it?" Allison muttered. "This couldn't possibly refer to an Iron Curtain if the metal rings weren't iron. So what else could mosquito netting mean?"

"I don't know." Sarah wrung her fingers together. "It's not even really a curtain at all. It's more like a barrier."

Allison pursed her lips. "But there are lots of barriers he could have picked. Why *this* one, which is barely strong enough to keep out insects?"

Sarah's eyes widened behind her glasses. "Maybe it's because it's not a very effective barrier...and it's not really a barrier at all, since people can get right through it, it's more like a, a, a *screen!*" She sucked in a breath. "*That's it!* Silver, screen! It's a movie question!"

They stared at each other for a moment.

"Mikey was a film major," Allison said.

Sarah's hands flew up over her mouth.

They raced into the living room.

"Are you *sure?*" Gabe asked, for the fifth time.

Sarah nodded. "We each got one question. It makes sense." She swallowed, still breathing hard, and adjusted her glasses. "Mythology is very big on symmetry," she explained.

"It makes about as much sense as any of this shit," Mikey said, rubbing hard at his eyes. He was sitting on the couch, with his brother's hat in his lap. His eyes were narrowed to slits and his teeth were bared—he looked like he was starting to lose it.

"So if Hitler is the only element from World War II, what's the connection?" Gabe asked.

"Timeframe, I would guess," Allison said. "A movie that came out during World War II."

Gabe scowled. "That wasn't exactly cinema's golden age," he snapped. "Largely due to the aforementioned genocidal dictator and his attempts to take over the world!"

"We're not looking for a classic film here," Sarah said. "The clue even says the movie was a *disaster*."

"So that's what we're looking for," Allison said. "A movie that came out at the beginning of World War II, failed terribly, and holds some clue in its opening that we can use to find Louie."

"Sounds about right," Sarah said thoughtfully.

They all looked expectantly at Mikey.

The wolf closed his eyes.

Gabe sat down next to him. "Mikey, c'mon," he said quietly. "I know you're barely keeping it together here, but your brother's counting on you."

Mikey furrowed his brow, squeezing his eyes shut. "Gabe, I was a film major for *two semesters*. Sophomore year. The last class I took was half a decade ago—"

"Think," Gabe instructed forcefully. "What did you study in your classic film classes?"

Mikey swallowed, rubbing at his eyes with the back of his hands, face twisted in agony. "The same shit every new film student studies. *Casablanca. The Maltese Falcon. Vertigo.* "

"The answer has to be something you know," Sarah put in, leaning deftly over the coffee table. "The rest of the clues were easy, once we got down the right track. What's a film that *every* film student would know?"

Mikey suddenly straightened up. "*Citizen Kane*," he gasped.

The mouse frowned. "That can't be right," she said. "This is supposed to be a *failed* movie. Citizen Kane is supposed to be the greatest movie of all time."

Mikey stared at her, yellow eyes wide and panicky. "That's what most people think, yeah. But what *every film student* would know is that the film originally tanked. It was the *greatest disaster!*"

Allison perched on the edge of the coffee table. "It flopped? *Citizen Kane?* Like, Rosebud-Citizen Kane? Are we talking about the same movie here?"

Mikey swallowed. "It was all in the timing. It was a dark, depressing movie coming out right at the beginning of World War II. It didn't get popular until it made the rounds in Europe, almost until the fifties."

Sarah cocked her head. "The greatest film of all time was a failure." She frowned thoughtfully. "Well, that certainly fits the bill."

"Alright," Allison said. "Let's apply it to the clue."

Gabe produced Mikey's cell phone. "'*As they began this greatest of disasters, so you shall end yours.*' I only know that Rosebud was the sled." He looked up. "So how does it begin? What does Mr. Kane start his movie with?"

Mikey stared at him, ears flat against his head. "He dies," he said.

They all stared at him.

Mikey looked around, corners of his mouth pulled down and back. "That's what 'Rosebud' is from. He whispers the word, and then he keels over in his chair. That's it. He dies."

Gabe flopped back on the couch, stunned. "...seriously?"

Mikey nodded dejectedly. "Yeah. Seriously. The whole rest of the movie is the rest of the moron cast scrambling around trying to solve the mystery. But if they'd paid a little more attention they'd have known, all they had to do was look at the goddamn—"

His eyes widened.

"...snow-globe." The last word was a whisper.

Allison moved into his frame of vision. "What are you talking about?"

Mikey's eyes widened, too much. "It's the beginning of the movie, I'd completely forgotten…he's holding a snow-globe with a little cabin in it. It's supposed to represent his childhood home, where he went sledding, where his life was simple. He drops it when he dies." They all looked at one another.

Mikey got to his feet, took a few steps forward, and stopped in front of the bookshelves, where a snow globe sat silently at eye level, perched a few feet from where they had been sitting.

Inside it was a little cabin.

"This has to be it," Mikey whispered, staring at the snow-globe like it might be electrified. "It looks just like the one in the movie."

Gabe cleared his throat. "So, are we supposed to—"

Mikey reached up and tipped the snow globe off the shelf. It landed between his feet and exploded onto the hardwood floor, bits of glass rocketing out in all directions and glittery water splattering everywhere.

Gabe closed his eyes. "I wish you guys would stop doing that."

The wolf dropped to his knees and began pawing through the pieces. "There's got to be a note in here, or something…" A piece of glass cut the side of his paw. He ignored it, leaving bloody little splotches on the light-colored wood.

"Hey, look at this," Gabe said, leaning down a few feet away. The little plastic cabin was sitting scattered among glass shards and wet glitter. He carefully picked it up between two slim fingers.

They all peered at the tiny house.

"This is weird," Gabe continued. "It's not a cabin at all. The bottom part was just hidden in the base, under the snow."

He turned it in his fingers. Sure enough, the plastic log cabin had the angular stern of a small boat stuck on to the bottom of it. "It's a *houseboat*."

Mikey stood up and stared at it. "Houseboat," he said. "Houseboat. House...boat."

They both got it at once. *"Boathouse!"* they shouted.

Mikey was on his feet in a moment, snatching his flashlight off the coffee table. *"Come on, hurry!"* he cried, bolting for the door, though his friends were already right behind him.

The forest was still dark, with no hint of the upcoming lightening slated for the next hour, but after several hours in the darkened house, they had no problem negotiating the narrow forest path, even at the frenetic pace Mikey set. He raced into the night as his ancestors must have, his breath streaming out behind him in the cold night air like the vapor trail behind a jet. The thumping of footsteps behind him told him his friends were a heartbeat behind.

They reached the boathouse in a matter of minutes. The lake spread out before them, an expanse of silver set in the black of the forest. The boathouse itself was simply a corrugated metal shed, twenty feet tall, set a dozen paces off the beach.

Mikey hit the door first. He glanced momentarily back at the others, twisted the handle, and swung the wide doors open.

The interior of the boathouse was all but black, but it was light enough. To step inside, as they did, was to know its contents.

A figure dangled from the center of the shed. It was silent and unmoving, completely stiff, still except for a gentle sway in the breeze from the open door. It was a large figure. Too large to be anyone else.

Mikey crumpled to his knees. He made an inhuman howling, shrieking noise and clamped his paws over his muzzle. Gabe grabbed him from behind and tried to turn him around, but Mikey fought him, thrashing like a thing possessed, all flailing limbs and fur.

"Louieeeeeeeeeeeee!" he shrieked, and then what came out wasn't words at all.

"Don't look, dammit!" Gabe snarled, struggling desperately to pull his thrashing friend out of the shed, but Mikey fought him like the devil.

In the end, it was Allison who finally picked up Mikey's flashlight and, with shaking hands, lifted it to the hanged figure.

"It's not him," she said softly.

Shaking, Sarah turned. "What?"

"It's not him," she said again. "It's not *him!*" she said again, and this time she was screaming it. "It's not *anybody!*" It's a pair of stuffed coveralls and old rags! It's a trick! *It's just another trick!*"

Mikey was shrieking incoherently now, clutching at his face. Gabe backhanded him, hard.

Mikey's muzzle snapped to the side. He turned back and stared up at his friend, shocked, tears running down his face.

"It's *not him,*" Gabe hissed at him, his voice shaking.

Mikey writhed, lifting himself onto one elbow, wiping the tears from his face with his forearm. "Wh-whu-whut?"

Gabe rolled off him, grunting. "It isn't your brother." He picked up his own flashlight from the dirt and directed it at the dummy hanging from the ceiling. Its face was nothing more than a bundle of cloth, such an obvious fake that it didn't even look lupine anymore.

"But..." Mikey swallowed shakily. "But where is he?" He sat up, eyes wide and terrified. "*Where is he?! Louuuuiiiieeee!*" he screamed. "*LOOOUUUIIIIEEE!*"

Mikey's shout echoed off the walls, and died in the corners. The boathouse fell silent.

And then, they heard whimpering.

Mikey scrambled to his feet. "Louie, are you in here?!" His ears pivoted for half a second of feverish concentration, and then he lunged toward a far corner of the small building. There was a stack of wooden crates, and he tore through them.

Behind them, he found the prize.

It was Louie, safe and sound, though clearly unhappy. He was on his stomach, his ankles and wrists tied in the small of his back, secured with the same rope supporting the dummy. He was still wearing only his gym shorts, and his muzzle was tied shut with a large red bandanna. He craned his neck to look at them, whining plaintively, staring at them with wide, frightened eyes.

Mikey collapsed onto him, shivering, and wrapped his arms around him. "I got you, buddy, I'm here, you're okay, you're okay." He lunged at the thick rope knots but could barely grip them; he was shaking so badly he could hardly stay upright.

Allison put a hand on his forearm. "It's okay, Mikey, we got this one."

Next to her, Gabe lifted two paws full of sharp ferret claws, and leapt upon the ropes. "All over it, man, I'll chew through them if I have to. Why don't you work on that bandanna?"

Nodding dumbly, biting his lip, Mikey crawled to his brother's head and tugged on the red bandana until it came free. "You're okay, Louie," he said, and then the tears started. "You're okay."

Louie whined and nuzzled his palms. He looked absolutely miserable.

"I wanna go home," he said.

Hugging his brother's big shaggy head, Mikey nodded. "Yeah, buddy. Me, too."

The walk back to the cabin took considerably longer—they took their time, with the big wolf limping, and the small wolf huddled up against him as they walked. By the time they made it halfway, the sky was starting to lighten.

They heard the shrill cry of the Scion before they were even around the last bend. It was the car's interior alarm keening into the morning, advising all within earshot that the vehicle's keys had been left in its ignition, its doors were ajar, and it was not particularly happy about either condition.

They reached it after a few moments, finding it sad and abandoned, its front doors still hanging open. Still wiping tears from his eyes, looking dumbfounded, Mikey climbed behind the wheel and tried the key. The engine cranked on the first try, the roar of its small engine thundering like a tractor in the near-silent dawn. It idled roughly for a moment and then set to rumbling contentedly.

Mikey turned to his friends. "I guess we won," he said.

The cabin's front door was still hanging open, as they had left it. Though the morning sky was yellow-light enough for them to travel without the flashlights, the inside of the house was still filled with shadows.

As soon as they entered the front door, they saw it—a bottle of Diet Coke set conspicuously on the narrow table behind the couch, its cap removed and neatly placed on its side next to the bottle, facing the doorway. It was right inside the front door and set up between two lit candles, unquestionably placed to be noticed. To be any more prominent would have required a spotlight.

Allison shivered, glancing nervously around.

Gabe frowned. "*Please*, somebody tell me that was there when we left."

Sarah stared at it. "Nope. That was Louie's, from dinner. Look, it's half empty."

Louie glared suspiciously at it. "I was saving that. I don't want it any more." The front of his lips pulled up in revulsion.

Mikey squeezed his brother's massive paw and wandered over to the bottle. He picked up the cap, stared at it a moment. And then, for the first time since Louie had disappeared, he smiled.

Everyone was staring at him. "Well?" Gabe said. "That better not be another clue."

Mikey grinned. "Nope," he said. "Just a message." He held up the bottle top.

They all peered into the little white plastic cap.

SORRY, it said, in little pixilated letters. **THANKS FOR PLAYING**.

Mikey was grinning, waiting for them to get the joke. Nobody laughed. Nobody even smiled.

Mike sighed. "Well, *I* think it's funny." He dropped the cap back on the table and shrugged.

They slowly filed into the cabin.

Louie took a few steps toward the soda and stared at it, with a mixture of longing and suspicion.

"You thirsty, sweetie?" Allison asked. She touched Louie's forearm.

Edging past the bottle, Louie nodded.

"I'll be right back," she said. She disappeared into the kitchen and reappeared a moment later, holding a new bottle.

"It's a little warm, but it's the last one," the doe said, twisting the cap off for him and glancing inside it. "Besides, it's-" Falling silent, she stopped in her tracks.

Sarah appeared at her side. "Please tell me you just won another Coke," she said. "Because otherwise the Trickster just needs to shut up."

Allison showed her the cap.

Sarah's eyes went comically wide. "Is this what I think it is?!" She snatched up the cap for a closer look. "'*Winner: 25K. Congrats!*' It's a winner! It's a *grand prize* winner!" She looked up in disbelief. "This cap is worth twenty-five thousand dollars!"

"No fucking way," Gabe said, and then clamped his paws over his muzzle. "Are you *serious?*"

Mikey just stared, showing a hint of a smile. "Dinner's on Allison."

She blinked at him, and then stepped back, eyes wide. She held out the winning cap like it was a poisonous snake. "Oh no! This was *Louie's* soda." They all turned to look at the big wolf.

Louie's eyes grew wide. "Don't want it!" he announced, alarmed.

Gabe stared at the two of them like he thought they were crazy. "Uh, if *nobody* wants it, I think I could take it off your hands…"

Mikey thought for a moment, and then nodded to himself. "We split it," he said. "We'll split it five ways. Everybody played the game. This is everybody's prize." They were all quiet for a moment.

"Okay," Allison said.

"Works for me," Gabe chimed in.

"Seems fair!" Sarah added.

Louie just smiled.

"But I get the best prize of all," Mikey said, leaning over the couch to pick up his brother's Packers hat. Reaching to his full extension, lifting himself onto the tips of his toes, he planted the cap on his brother's head.

Grinning foolishly, tail swishing behind him, Louie nodded.

There was a moment of silence.

"Soooo…now what?" Gabe asked.

Mikey thought for a moment. He turned and regarded the group. "Now? Now we pack the car up, drive far enough to find a chain hotel, sleep for about nine hours…and then get back in the car and drive."

"To where?" Allison asked, incredulously.

Mikey grinned. "To Vegas."

Gabe grinned. "*Now* we're talking."

How do you make it through the day and still get home on time? It's hard enough for a normal person, much less a superhero wrapping up a big case—on date night at that.

KNOW WHEN TO HOLD 'EM

D.J. Fahl

The cool afternoon air whipped over Star Coyote's large ears. The wind was scented with a hint of pollen now that it was spring. He soared through the sky in his blue and yellow costume, which hugged his trim body. The sun was going to set soon. Star Coyote glanced at his wrist and remembered he had taken his watch off to put his costume on. After he broke his last watch in a fight he decided to save his money and just stash it with his clothes.

He was still new at being a super hero. He looked at the ground below and saw people pointing up at him, some were even waving. They probably assumed he was out on patrol. Instead he was headed to a time sensitive mission. He couldn't arrive too early, as that would risk the DA's ability to get at the information. Too late and the data might be gone, or worse he would be late for his date.

He blushed a bit as the wind ruffled his fur. It was hard to believe he had started dating someone; it had been completely unplanned. Originally when he decided to put on the costume he figured he had to forget about long term relationships. It would be too much work to mesh with a crime fighter's lifestyle. Yet, thanks to a spilled slushie, he had ended up juggling a blossoming romance and a costumed identity. Star smiled, Jay was certainly worth the work. He couldn't help but think about that collie's firm body and soft thick fur. He had to make sure he was on time for this date. He didn't want to ruin his chances.

He had to admit that flying over his city was fun. He had only put the mask and costume on a few months ago. Going from Ted Rodriguez to a superhero was a transition he had considered for a long time. It was a decision he didn't make until well after he achieved his powers and learned how to control them. Well, perhaps control was too strong a word. He still slipped up sometimes, floating when really excited and accidentally smashing coffee mugs, but he was getting better with his tricky powers now. The name Star Coyote was given to him by the Portland Gazette. Honestly he would have chosen something else, like Sidereal or Gravity Guy, but he hadn't gotten to the papers in time and the name had stuck. He didn't mind it too much, and people seemed to like it if the booming sales of street corner knock off t-shirts were any indication.

Flight was easily the most enjoyable power he had. He loved making himself light and soaring over the street. Propelling himself above the populace with forces he didn't even understand himself, Star Coyote swooped down and waved at the people below as he flew over the city. He had to be careful about flying too fast. He might break windows, and he didn't think it would look good for a super hero to rain shards of glass onto watching denizens. This was simply a relaxed patrol over the city.

Portland in general was pretty happy to have a hero; there had been local calls to try getting one for years. Having a hero ensured a lot of super criminals steered away from the city. Ideally, if any came they could be countered without risking police or civilian lives. Oregon and Washington had been trying to attract a superhero for a while with more lax laws involving superbeing activity and other benefits. The irony was that Ted had lived in Oregon most of his life and already had a job in the city of Portland. The welcoming atmosphere hadn't swayed him, it just made his life easier than working in Atlanta or Salt Lake City. Star still couldn't believe he had been given a PR agent by the Mayor's office. That was a very nice perk. There was also the fact that the police department was extremely helpful coordinating with him, especially Officer Belinda Ramirez.

Officer Ramirez recently asked him for some help. Belinda had become the go to girl for interacting with the police department, and she was easily his best ally on the force so far. He was only too happy to return the favour for the help he received. The coyote's thoughts were interrupted when he heard a scream. Some guy was grabbing a pedestrian's wallet; a woman had seen it and was calling for help.

Star Coyote floated downwards as the guy pulled a gun. Oh joy, Star grimaced to himself, this would make things tricky for his schedule. He wasn't bullet proof, not that he wanted anyone to know that. The gun wielder was a lapin, brown fur, big ears, and very twitchy. Star Coyote landed behind him. The attempted mugging victim suddenly went from panicked to flabbergasted, which caused the rabbit to whirl around. Star was ready for him and grabbed the gun in his paw, smirking as he said, "Sorry sir, I need to see your permit for this."

Before he could respond Star had already focused, making his relative gravity heavier than the rabbit's and he easily tore the gun from his paw. Keeping the gun away from the rabbit he motioned at the mugger saying, "Now why not be smart? Drop the wallet and wait here for the cops, hmm?"

The rabbit turned and bolted. With an exaggerated sigh Star Coyote lifted off into the air. He lessened gravity around himself and tucked the gun safely in his utility belt as he gave chase after the mugger. Star Coyote had figured out long ago that his powers revolved around altering his personal gravity field and the fields of those he touched. No one really knew the mechanism behind his amazing feats; it was safer for him that everyone just assumed he was super strong and able to fly. The rabbit didn't make it far. Star Coyote simply flew into the air, and then swooped down, barrelling into him. Pushing the rabbit to the ground Star Coyote quickly clasped the brown furry paws in police cuffs. He did enjoy getting those from the cops; they were quite helpful. He was also getting better at using them after some practice.

The bunny swore and struggled under the confidently grinning coyote, "Oh don't feel bad, you were just in the wrong place at the wrong time and committing a crime. Why not avoid that next time by not mugging someone?"

Getting up, Star Coyote grinned as a police car approached. Dropping the gun out of reach of the rabbit he jauntily saluted the cops as they got out of their car. With the police on the scene, he immediately flew into the air. He would normally stay and make a report, but he was going to be late if he delayed much longer. He was trying very hard to be on time.

His cell phone rang and the coyote smiled as he fiddled it out of his belt pocket. He didn't like to talk on the phone while flying, but he still answered, "Hello?"

"Ted?" Star Coyote's heart fluttered and a man's voice on the other end of the phone asked, "Are you on the freeway? I'm hearing a lot of wind."

"Hello Jay!" The coyote said happily. He grinned despite himself just hearing the collie talking to him. He wagged his tail, slowing down a bit, "Oh, um, just running some errands for tonight."

"So the boss let you go early?" asked Jay. Ted detected a hint of excitement in his voice.

"Yeah," Ted licked his nose and lied. He disliked keeping the truth from Jay but it had to be done, "I've still got to get these errands finished off."

"Alright," he heard the collie say over the phone, "but try not to be late. We have a big night tonight."

61

Star Coyote laughed, "You know me too well."

"I hope so," said the voice on the other end and Star could just imagine the collie putting a paw on his hip and smiling, "I just want to prove the gang wrong about you being a flake."

"Have they been saying that?" Star Coyote asked in surprise. He could see the surly otter Brandon making such a comment, but Mattie and Gary seemed like nice friends of Jay's. They were hardly the type to call him a flake.

"They've just noted that you tend to be late," Jay reassured him. "It's starting to become a running gag with them."

"I'll try very hard to get there," said Star Coyote truthfully. "I've just got a huge errand to deal with."

Jay paused for a long moment and then said, "I don't really care, we always manage to have fun no matter how late you are."

"A little patronizing there Jay," said Ted even though his tail wagged faster. That pause was worrying; he knew that Jay didn't like him being late. He had arrived late to three of their past five dates.

"I'm just saying I enjoy your company Mr. Rodriguez, so hurry on over here so we can have a fun night," Jay said easily and Ted grinned.

"Of course," he said simply, and then seeing his destination ahead he added, "have to go now, I'll be there soon."

"Bye," Jay said as the flying coyote turned off his phone. Now he really had to make sure he got there on time. He moved a little quicker towards the tower, the business office of Phillip Larson.

Councilman Larson was a very well liked ferret in Portland. He was an elected official known for some popular legislation, as well as a successful business man. Everyone knew he had his eyes on the mayor's office, if not the Governor's mansion. He was also, according to the cops in vice, the dirtiest man in the city. He was behind a string of prostitution rings, illegal gambling on the riverfront, money laundering, and a host of other illegal activities. He was also impossible to get thanks to an impressive network of informants, dirty cops, and a top notch legal defence team on retainer. The cops and Assistant District Attorney Swain were having an impossible time shutting his operation down.

That was where Star Coyote came into the picture. There was a quirk in the legal structure, thanks to all those lax superhero laws, that ADA Swain wanted to try. Star Coyote could arrest Larson if he deemed it necessary for the common good. It was a quirky bit of language that gave enough probable cause for the DA's office to cut through Larson's defences and dodges to spearhead an investigation that could finally bring him down. It was a loophole that was too powerful, and would need to be closed eventually, but for now it was the only avenue of attack.

Star Coyote was angry at the councilman; he had voted for the guy after all. It felt more then a little galling to find out about his ties to a host of illegal ventures. He had found out most of the information from the councilman himself. Belinda Ramirez couldn't show him the records; just point him to the starting line. He had gotten the rest of the way staking out the councilman for the last month, watching his movements and eavesdropping where he could. Today he would finally arrest the creep. This would be enough to get a warrant from a Judge. Although Star couldn't testify in court on the evidence he had personally collected, it was inadmissible, he could spur the investigation. It would become very public and be much harder to for the ferret's cronies to deflect.

He was sure he was right; he had to be. If he wasn't he was about to ruin the reputation of the councilman and his own as a superhero. He grimaced at the entire situation and the gnawing reminder that he was on a strict schedule. It set his teeth on edge. Tonight was a big opportunity. Larson's partners were running a huge gambling event which meant he would, hopefully, not have all his records as hidden away. Time was short to arrest the guy, jump start the investigation, and get it all wrapped up before Larson could obscure everything.

He landed on the roof of Larson's business headquarters. The man was well off but he didn't own the building, he only rented a few of the top floors. He also hadn't thought to put more security on the roof door. Star Coyote concentrated a moment at the door, making his paw very, very heavy and pulled down on the handle ripping the lock off and swinging the door open. He floated down the stairwell, something he always wanted to do at work. He suppressed a giggle and tried to look stern. Arresting a councilman was serious business, but the action did make him think of awful vampire movies.

He got onto Larson's floor and confidently strode down the hallway. It was dark and the lights were off. It was late, but he was still surprised that no one was on the floor. Larson usually had people in his office at this time of day. Not even the stern secretary who guarded Larson's door was at her post. The thick carpet absorbed the sound of his footfalls as he walked. The lack of life in Councilman Larson's office was unsettling. Quickening his pace he barged into Larson's office.

The doors swung open and he entered the room; richly appointed, spacious, and grand. Larson obviously had a taste for impressive digs. Maybe it stemmed from the fact that he was such a short man. The windows opening over the city gave an impression of a lord looking over his domain. The carved ebony desk seemed to suck in light. The fact that the councilman was gagged and hog tied on his desk underlined that Star Coyote had just walked into something unexpected.

"Oh-kay," Star Coyote mumbled as he arched an eyebrow, his ears flicking. This was unexpected. When the door slammed closed behind him he knew he was not alone.

"Well look at what we have here, sister," said a vixen in a very revealing leather outfit. A cap perched between her ears, black mask on her face. She had deep russet fur with bright white highlights. Her whiskers were trimmed, and she had a smooth jaunty waggle of her hips as a fluffy tail trailed behind her easily.

Star Coyote also noticed a bull whip and a utility belt perched on her hips.

"A dashing hero come to save the day?" asked another voice with a rhetorical flourish. Star Coyote glanced at the other side of the room as another vixen in a similar outfit revealed herself from behind Larson's desk. Her fur was a lighter tone, and she had a similar gait. The two weren't twins despite how similar they looked. Even from here Star Coyote could smell that. The second vixen added, "What a unique surprise."

"But whatever is he doing here? In the offices of such an esteemed businessman and politician?" mused the first vixen aloud as they moved closer to the coyote. Their bodies moved in mirror of each other as they slowly circled Star. They were trying to box him in. Star may not been on the job long, but he had learned group tactics well enough to spot that. The masks on their faces suggested they were either superbeings with a lean towards criminal activates or they were posers. It was always hard to tell. Nowadays some people did wear masks as a fashion statement. There was an entire underground antiauthority culture that enjoyed using supervillain gear and styles. Not to mention a more, well, kinky aspect. He looked between the two of them, waiting for their next move.

"I agree sister dear, what could Twinkle Doggy be thinking?" asked the second one as she slid back to the desk and sat down near the councilman. The ferret wiggled on the desk as a paw patted his ears. The name calling was a rather transparent gambit, an attempt to manoeuver themselves into a better position. Their implied threat to the councilman was an obvious play for his attention as well. Larson had shifted from the center of their little game to a helpless bystander.

"Well I think Mr. Shiny Pup might be here to stop us," said the first vixen with a wide grin, "isn't that adorable sister? He thinks he can play with the big girls."

"Well I'd like to know who you are," Star Coyote cut in. Their coy smiles were just as off putting as their attitude. They acted like they had this entire situation perfectly in paw. It was as if they had expected him from the beginning and this was their endgame for the evening. Star Coyote retorted, asking the obvious question, "I mean am I fighting the Leather Lasses or something?"

Both vixens chuckled. The first one, who was getting very close and fondling the handle to her whip, spoke up, "Oh how droll. He's trying to be amusing. Well, Shiny Pup I happen to be Cinnamon."

"And I'm Spice," the one near Councilman Larson said with a girlish giggle.

"Isn't Cinnamon just a type of Spice?" Star Coyote asked putting his paws on his hips and looking at the two of them. The use of code names; another check in the column marking them supercriminals.

Both vixens laughed at that. It was sincere, unlike the other times which had a tint of condescending amusement. This time they seemed to find the comment genuinely funny. They glanced at each other and with a smile Cinnamon commented, "Well I suppose that is true. However, I don't think a grown coyote in tight blue spandex has much room to criticize our names."

"It's better then Sugar and Spice," said Spice with a charmed smile at Star, "After all, we weren't made with sugar. We vixens have a little more flare."

Star smirked at the two of them. They were trying to figure him out just like he was with them. They had to be. Their banter was an attempt to ferret out information on the opposing side. Turnabout was only fair play, "A high opinion of yourselves there. So may I ask what you think you two are doing with the councilman?"

"You don't know?" asked Spice with mock disappointment, "I had thought he called you in for help when we tied him up. You know, with one of those deus ex machina superhero devices so many government people carry around."

"Well no," Star looked at the two of them flicking his ears as he laid some of his cards on the table, "I didn't know you were here. I was coming to arrest him for graft."

Larson's eyes widened and he growled, wiggling on his desk, papers falling to the floor as he strained in his bonds. Spice playfully bopped his muzzle and he stopped struggling, looking up at her as he whimpered. The vixen on the desk looked at Star Coyote with a smile, "Why, that's why we're here as well."

Star Coyote arched his eye brow and flicked his ears. This was making less and less sense. Who ever heard of superheroes wearing skimpy leather costumes and tying a guy up like that? He looked at Cinnamon who was sauntering closer, "Oh?"

"Well, my sister exaggerates," said Cinnamon with a coy twist of her lips, "You see, we know all about his illegal deals."

"The drug money," Spice said with a girlish giggle.

Cinnamon grinned and flicking her tail and added, "The gangs he controls in the city."

"The illegal gambling parlors and money laundering," said Spice waving her tail in the bound ferret's face. The tail teasing his nose made him sneeze helplessly.

"The illegal arms shipments to Quebecois rebels in Canada and other fringe groups across the North American continent," said Cinnamon with an ear twitch.

"And of course the prostitution rings and escort services," said Spice with smug delight, "This dear boy controls most of the illegal sex business in the city."

"If not the state," said Cinnamon and Star detected a hint of hardness in that comment. Cinnamon seemed like the older one. Her paw gripped the handle of her whip tightly now, "Among his other illegal acts. You know he loves to sample his goods. Well, the women at least."

"Plays very rough with them too," said Spice offhandedly, "Well, when this one ordered a foxy for the night how could we resist the opportunity?"

"He thought he was getting a two for one deal," said Cinnamon with a flinty smile as she looked past Star Coyote at the ferret, "Getting him all tied up after that was far too easy."

"Indeed, I was almost looking for a challenge," said Spice. She glanced down at the politician, "almost."

"Perhaps we have one here Spice," said Cinnamon with a grin looking at Star Coyote, "Tell me Star-zy, will you help my sister and I have a good time hmm?"

Star Coyote looked between the two of them, his tail raised confidently as he decided his next move. Obviously these two enjoyed talking. Buying time made sense as he tried to figure out if they had any weird powers he should be concerned about. He floated off the floor almost imperceptibly. His super flying speed didn't work when he was firmly on the ground and he might need the extra edge. He looked at the two of them, "So we're not at cross purposes then. The police have been looking to get him for a while. So has the District Attorney. Why don't we work together and take him in?"

The two vixens laughed at that—it was a cold angry laugh. The tenor of their body language changed completely. Spice was the first to say her peace, "Dear silly coyote, why do you think the police will hold him? He's bought off so many of them."

"The system is dirty Twinkle Doggy," said Cinnamon, barely containing the bitterness in her words, "Honestly, you are far too trusting if you think they'll be able to keep him locked up for long."

Star flexed his fingers, getting ready for the fight. He knew now it had to come. These two were obviously not going to make this easy. The coyote just knew he was going to be late for his date with Jay. They didn't trust the system; they didn't want to work within the rules. He'd have to fight them. He hoped he could win, but he didn't know with these two, "So what are you planning?"

Cinnamon held up a data storage device for a computer with the utter confidence of someone who had just revealed their ace-in-the-hole, "This, my dear."

"And just what is on that?" asked Star Coyote as he watched the two, hoping they'd offer something he could use to his tactical advantage.

Spice slid off the desk and sauntered forward towards them, "Why, it is a copy of Larson's records. The complete books: his secret business deals, underground accountant's contact information, numbers to accounts in assorted banks and dummy corporations, Swiss accounts, names, dates, even a record of his assorted jewels from a brief stint in the black market gem stone business. The good councilman keeps immaculate records in a safe place."

"And now we have them," said Cinnamon with a wide grin, "just imagine the fun we'll have in Sao Paulo or Macau."

"So that's it?" asked Star looking between them with some irritation now, "You're robbing him? Taking his money after tying him up— With that information you could bring him down hard. Get the law on him and expose him to the public. Instead you'll just go spend it in some far off city and leave him to continue with his crimes?"

"Well listen to him," said Cinnamon with a smirk and a snap of her fingers, "getting all self righteous about what we're doing."

"Such a silly idealist," said Spice, "do you really think anyone could hold the councilman? Or stop him from achieving his goals? Be realistic coyote. We're just stealing from a rich criminal who will never be held accountable. His funds would just disappear and reappear somewhere else and who would that benefit?"

"Exactly," said Cinnamon with a smirk, "We're just going to take a nice chunk of change from this fellow. Have a little fun with it."

"And he can't go to the cops about it because," Spice grinned and twitched her tail, "he'd have to say where he got all that money from and admit two little fox girls overpowered him."

"You do realize I have to stop you," said Star Coyote simply looking between them sternly as he floated above the plush carpeted floor, "The councilman is rotten but I can't let you take evidence or steal from him. Two wrongs don't make a right."

"And make sure to brush your teeth and be in bed by ten, right doggy?" said Cinnamon as her whip unfurled. Star heard Spice's do the same thing as they slid towards him, circling him in earnest now.

"We do outnumber you," Spice said, "And the Rigger was really helpful in creating some fun inventions for us."

"Rigger?" The coyote grimaced. One of the older super criminals on record, he had taken on all of the world's most powerful heroes and was even victorious at times. He made weird inventions, like flash bombs made out of tuna cans and Christmas lights. Star had taken him on once before and it wasn't fun, especially when he hit him with that Frisbee containing a spring loaded device that had wrapped his arms in steel cables. The otter was known for training other super criminals if he liked them. If he had given these two pointers this fight really would not work out well.

"Oh yes," said Cinnamon. With that the battle had begun, and the whip cracked out toward the coyote. Star dodged the whip tip jut barely. Unfortunately he had underestimated Spice, who had leaped into the air. With an acrobatic twirl through the air her own whip cracked outwards. The tough leather wrapped around Star's paw as she landed and spun around pulling the now very lightweight coyote

Cinnamon was running towards him as he was slammed into the ground. The whip unfurled from his paws. Star Coyote braced himself as best he could from the prone position on the ground. Cinnamon leapt into the air with a frightening grace and speed. She pirouetted and slammed her boots against the glass of the large window looking out of the city. Surprisingly, the glass held as she rocketed away while throwing little knives at Star Coyote.

Star Coyote winced as the knives sliced through the air. They didn't touch him beyond a few scratches. The knives were thrown with care not to hurt him. They had, however, pinned his left arm and right leg to the ground through his costume. The sheer precision required to do that was incredible. He closed his eyes and made himself heavier and pulled his arm up, ripping the knives out and tearing his costume. He sighed inwardly; it was going to take days to repair those rips on his sewing machine. He kept that to himself, instead he said, "Cute moves."

Cinnamon and Spice looked at each other grinning. Obviously they were charmed. Spice said, "Oh someone wants a challenge then."

Before they could continue Star Coyote was up in the air and flying directly at them. They hadn't expected him to move so quickly and they were close enough together for his charge to hit both of them. He grabbed Cinnamon with his arm and pushed Spice down to the ground. Twirling up into the vaulted ceiling of the office he gripped Cinnamon and spun around. He planned to make her dizzy, but she squirmed out of his grip. She was slippery, and far too nimble to be normal. Out of his hold, she kicked him in the chest. He growled from the pain. She fell toward the ground head first, but she twisted with impeccable grace and landed daintily. Spice even gave her an amused clap as Cinnamon did a little bow.

Star swung around in the air and floated above them. He quickly interposed himself between the two of them, moving at a speed beyond most people's comprehension. The sudden change in air pressure caused by his rapid swoop was powerful enough to rattle the windows as he lashed out at both of the vixens.

Normally that little move worked on gang bangers and thugs. The streets toughs would be surprised and reel back from him. The vixens easily dodged his blows as they spun around, their whips cracking. They were trying the same feint again, but this time Star Coyote was ready. He grabbed both whips, wincing as he felt them cut through his gloves, giving him a rope burn on the pads of his paws.

Ignoring the pain he channelled his weightlessness down the whips. He had practiced this before; as long as they held the whips he could affect them. He smirked as they found themselves lifted into the air becoming weightless. They struggled awkwardly, having lost their purchase on solid ground. With that loss their unusual agility was nearly neutralized. They couldn't have practiced in a low gravity environment. Their surprise at the situation only caused them to grip the whips tighter. Star Coyote grinned confidently, "Now who's out of their league?"

He pulled at the whips, sending them careening around the room unable to control their motion. The two vixens were not phased as they were flung about the room. Instead of letting go, they skilfully rebounded from the walls and pushed towards the coyote. That was a surprise. Star let go of the whips and ducked down to the ground as they flew at him. Their return to gravity wasn't sudden, it never was, and they seemed to adjust as they fell down. They landed near a window while Star found himself back by the door. The councilman was still watching from on his desk, scared out of his wits and unable to escape from his bindings.

Spice went into a runner's starting crouch. Her body compressed like an elegant furry spring. She jumped at Star. The coyote swung out of the way of her fist as she leaped at him. He barely saw Cinnamon coming from behind in a coordinated attack. The two were a team and the coyote could see they trained hard together.

He was expecting their moves this time as he breezily dodged their blows. They weren't holding back; they focused on removing him as a threat. The earlier delicate moves and flourishes were replaced with elegant simplicity.

He swung around and a fist connected with Spice's side. She spun away, moving with the momentum of the blow. He felt a kick jostle him from Cinnamon. It knocked him forward but he was ready for it. He swung his leg back in a move he learned at the YMCA judo class. The hook of his leg caught her, but she flipped into the air before he could trip her to the ground.

The two went into defensive postures and circled him as Star Coyote floated into the air. The time for showing off abilities was at an end. Sheer brute force was needed. Sadly, when he floated he had less momentum; his punches and grabs wouldn't be as effective. He still had an edge, however. They hadn't expected him to be competent. The fact they underestimated him played to his advantage.

Cinnamon lashed out with a throwing star. It wasn't meant to kill, simply wound. Star Coyote dodged it; he was too quick while floating in the air. He swung around and neatly twisted out of a flying punch Spice tried to land. She was a prodigious jumper. Star had to admit the two had a lot of skill.

The lighter coloured bubbly vixen said nothing as she flew past him. She flipped in the air and landed beside her sister by the window. They glared at him for a moment and then both muzzles broke into wide grins.

"Well someone has some talent," said Cinnamon with a flaunted swish of her tail, "We seem to have underestimated him, didn't we Spice?"

"Oh yes," said Spice with a smile, "he might actually be a challenge."

"And I have to give him credit for not copping too much of a feel when he grabbed me," said Cinnamon.

"So why not just come quietly? The police won't throw the book at you," said Star with an easy smile.

Cinnamon motioned at the ferret, "Like that one wouldn't try. Sorry coyote boy, but we don't plan to stay in any old cell."

"We're getting Egyptian cotton sheets and fine caviar tonight," said Spice.

"On that note perhaps it is time for us to leave," said Cinnamon

"Couldn't agree with you more sister," said Spice, and with that the vixen threw what looked like a label-less soup can at the window. It had suspicious yellow and purple lights at the top which blinked as it approached the window. A powerful blast resounded in the room, making Star's ears ring. The glass shattered and seemed to dematerialize. One of Rigger's glass disintegration bombs, that confirmed their training. They had added some sort of smoke bomb, obscuring them from view. Star coughed as he looked around. The smoke was quickly swept away by the wind as the pressure in the room changed. They hadn't anticipated that; they had clearly expected to escape using the smoke for cover. The two vixens stood at the edge of the high rise building; backs to the city, facing the coyote.

"Ciao," said Cinnamon with a salute and in perfect synchronization the two fell backwards out of the open window.

Star Coyote gasped and flew after them as quickly as he could, but as he soared out into the air he watched the two twirl and use their whips to grab purchase on the city's buildings as they swung away in opposite directions. He would need to choose one to follow and he got the distinct feeling he wouldn't be able to catch up with either of them easily. They probably had some way to remove their costumes quickly and blend into the city. Foxes were common in Portland; these two wouldn't stick out. He grimaced as he floated, watching them escape. He heard sirens below as police cars pulled up, and he saw news vans as well. Looking back in the office he saw Larson still tied up on the desk. He had to take Larson in. Sighing, he flew back into the office and walked over to the desk. Whoever wrote that top ten song about superheroes not having responsibilities needed a serious talking to.

"Are you okay sir?" he asked as he undid the gag and started to work on the bindings that hog tied the councilman.

"No thanks to you," the ferret groused as he was freed, "Why the hell didn't you go after those sluts?"

"Well, I was concerned with your safety sir," Star Coyote said easily. He helped the ferret stand up off of his desk, but his hands were still bound behind him. Star coyote grabbed them with a paw and continued, "Besides, you're higher priority. You are under

74

arrest by the authority given to me by the city of Portland's citizen arrest laws."

He lifted him into the air and out the window. The ferret gasped and began to squirm as Star Coyote easily flew out of the window. "I wouldn't move around so much," Star said calmly, "I might lose my grip—and if I let go, who knows if I can catch you?"

The ferret looked up at him and his eyes bulged but he stopped moving around. The coyote knew he'd be able to catch him even if he did fall, but why not put a little fear into him. It was a small consolation after those vixens got away. Stratagem or Force Vixen never got duped by women in low cut leather halter tops. The hero floated easily to the ground, Councilman Philip Larson clutched tightly in one paw. Cameras flashed as he landed on the ground, police lights flashing as Star looked around. The ferret wrestled out of his paws and tried to resurrect some measure of dignity, but his paws were still tied behind him. He hobbled forward towards some paramedics while shouting, "I am going to sue that spandex off of you! You self righteous vigilante!"

The angry councilman found an ambulance easily as Star shook his head. He was somewhat shielded from legal retribution, a law the Larson himself had helped the city council to pass last year.

A grey and tan coyote woman approached him. Belinda Ramirez's uniform was not perfect; it had a crease there, a wrinkle here, caused by her ceaseless late nights. Star grinned at her as she sidled up beside him. Assistant district attorney John Swain joined them quickly, ducking the TV lights and flashing cameras as Larson raised a loud din.

"What's his problem?" asked Belinda as she looked at him.

"Well, being hog tied by super criminal vixens will make anyone irritable," said Star Coyote simply.

ADA Swain gave Star Coyote an odd look at that. The pine marten, in contrast to Belinda, was impeccably dressed. Star was never sure how the marten always appeared so put together and completely unflappable. He sighed after a few moments and asked Star the obvious question, "Super criminal vixens?"

"Uh, yeah," Star Coyote rolled his eyes blushing slightly as he held out his left arm, showing the torn costume, "We might have a new threat in town. They called themselves Cinnamon and Spice."

"Need to have that checked?" asked Belinda inclining her head towards the paramedics, "I'm pretty sure they'd be glad to take an injured hero before any loud mouths."

Star shook his head chuckling, "I'm not getting involved with that. He's under my citizen's arrest like we needed, but if I were you I'd read him his rights when he is done pontificating."

"I have the warrants ready to be signed," said Swain with a confident smile, "I am concerned about these super criminals, though. I don't like the idea of them setting up in our city."

"I guess they were the pair of foxes in the gauche and skimpy leather who swung over our heads earlier?" asked Belinda with an ear twitch.

"Yep," said Star with a chuckle and before he could stop himself he decided to add, "Someone needs to tell them that low cut leather push up bras went out with the 80's."

Belinda laughed but Swain just gave him an odd look. He shook his head, "I notice they escaped."

"Sorry," Star Coyote said, a little more chagrined, "I had to decide between them or Larson. He might have destroyed evidence and escaped before I got back from chasing them down."

"Those two might have contaminated evidence," said Swain with a note of worry," at the very least his defence lawyers will claim that."

"Yeah that might be a problem," Star coyote nodded his head, "especially since they targeted him specifically for his criminal dealings."

"Well you do have to respect that," said Belinda with a slight smile, "We've been after him for years and they get to tie him up first."

"Assuming they haven't been after him a while themselves," said Star Coyote with a nod.

"That may be but Larson will tell the defence lawyers that those supercriminals planted this evidence on him. I'm sure they can spin some conspiracy theory about discrediting the councilman or something else," said Swain irritably now, "And if Star Coyote takes the bench he'll corroborate it. Damn, they can make a good case of evidence contamination. Why didn't you catch them? At least then I could have them locked away and use that to pacify the jury. Nothing deflates a super criminal contamination argument harder than having the super locked up. Are you sure you're working with us?"

"Take it easy John," said Belinda coming to the fellow coyote's defence. "This plan was pretty hare-brained as it was. We'll work with what we have. I've got the crime scene boys here and they're good guys. Clean as a whistle. We've got the cards we were dealt so let's play them. Who could predict a supercriminal duo showing up?"

"Super criminal and superhero conspiracies get eaten up by the jury, especially if you don't have the criminals behind bars. People love to assume they did all the law breaking," said ADA Swain, his whiskers twitching in irritation, "Superheroes might be popular, but pundits and irresponsible politicians have played up their crazy persecution theories and lots of people have internalized it."

"Well, you're good Swain. You'll figure something out," said Belinda.

"They may have gotten away, but they can still help with the case," said Star with a wide grin as he turned to make sure Larson couldn't see him as he raised up a data storage device, "I got this off of Cinnamon."

"I assume that was one of the vixens," said Swain looking at it, "What is on it?"

"Not much," said Star with a wide panting grin, "just every last one of Larson's illegal dealings in digital format—Or so the vixens claimed at least."

As Star dropped it into Belinda's paws she grinned very widely with a sly coyote chuckle passing her black lips, "Oh my. That is perfect."

"I grabbed it while tussling with them. I don't even think they realized what I was doing in the fight, grabbing them like that. They probably thought I was just copping a feel," said Star with a smile, "It should help a lot."

"The courts will find it inadmissible," said ADA Swain with a shake of his head, "Which is a shame I bet it has some damning evidence on it."

"I'm positive it does," said Star Coyote.

"They won't take it though. Superhero evidence gathering is tricky at best. With what Larson's attorneys will bring to bear I doubt it will stand up in court."

"Well, who says I grabbed it while arresting him," asked Star Coyote, "I just happened to grab it off a pair of supercriminals while they were committing a crime. Rather high profile supercriminals I might add, who the press will publish salacious photos of."

Belinda's smile widened as she said, "So we'll have to check every record on here to find a connection to them so we can prosecute."

Swain's face broke out into a very toothy smile, "And with these files open to us, we'll be able to uncover and subpoena all of Larson's hidden dealings. They can be declared evidence found in the investigation of another crime."

Star Coyote gave a happy wag of his tail, "Yep. We might not be able to use the files directly but they're a smoking gun to everything else Larson has done."

"Definitely," said Swain with a chuckle, "I'll go make sure the paper work has all the dots and crosses in the right spots. Belinda, get that to evidence personally. Star Coyote, do you want to say a few words to the press with me?"

Star Coyote glanced at a bank clock that was flashing the time and winced, "Um, I can't. I'm sort of late for something."

ADA Swain shrugged, "Well, alright then. I'll make sure to mention you, but I think you're missing out on a golden press opportunity. What could be more important than sealing the deal with this case?"

"Talk to my agent," said Star leaping into the air and zooming away.

He was sure he heard Belinda ask the Assistant District Attorney, "Honestly where does he zoom off to all the time? Does he have a hot date or something?"

Star Coyote smiled at that as he flew home. The slight aches and pains of battle were forgotten after the successful mission. He landed on a roof near his apartment and quickly changed into his civilian clothes. Putting his costume into a duffle bag, he glanced around and then floated down into an alleyway. Landing on the ground he quickly walked out and joined the crowd of fellow Portlanders. He grinned to himself, happily ignoring the twinge from his paw as he almost skipped home. He didn't want to run for fear of drawing unnecessary attention. After all, why would Ted Rodriguez be running down the street? He was just an everyday citizen.

Getting home Ted took off his ratty civilian clothes and tossed on a denim jacket, some jeans and a nice looking casual shirt. He quickly brushed his fur, making sure he looked somewhat presentable. Ted smiled happily and wagged with glee. He looked nice. He took a moment to clean out the wounds on his hands and bandage them. He wasn't sure how he could explain that to anyone right now. Ted glanced at his clock. He was already late, and he couldn't fly like this so he just ran out the door and down the stairs. It was quicker than the elevator thanks to a judicious use of his power.

Ted was out the door and jogging down the street in moments. It took him a good fifteen minuets, but part of that was him stopping off at a florist for some lavender and baby's breath. He was soon at the door of Jay's apartment complex and ringing the bell to apartment 352B. The buzzer rang and he was up the stairs as quick as he could go. All this superhero work had put him in great shape, so he was barely panting when he reached the door and knocked.

The door opened and a collie, his own black and white fur brushed to a nice luster, smiled at him. He was wearing a simple light blue button up shirt and clean unwrinkled chinos. Everything about him spoke of an unaffected professional; his body firm, but still fluffy. His brown eyes brightened up as he looked up at the coyote. He grinned, stepping aside so Ted could enter the apartment and wagged his tail happily saying, "Glad to see you made it. Only twenty minutes late this time."

Ted chuckled and his tail went down slightly in contrition as he said, "Sorry abut that, maybe some flowers will help?"

Jay smiled, taking them and fetching something to put them in as he said, "So what happened? Not traffic this time I hope."

Ted blushed trying to think up a realistic excuse, really it was a wonder Jay put up with his tardiness. The coyote had been trying to manage his time better, "Well you know, just general stuff. I lost track of time."

"I need to buy you a better clock," Jay said, putting the flowers on a table in a pewter pitcher. The collie slid closer to the coyote and smiled, "but first something I wanted to give you."

The kiss was short but tender. Their lips brushed together and Ted found his arms creeping around the collie, holding him gingerly as they kissed. Finally their kiss broke. Jay looked down at Ted's paws and saw the bandages, "What happened?"

"Oh just a little mishap," said Ted with a slight roll of his eyes as he licked his nose slightly hoping the dog wouldn't press the issue.

"What sort of mishap?" asked Jay his eyes narrowing slightly looking at the bandaged paws.

Ted squirmed under his gaze and searching for an excuse he said, "Um, kitchen accident— I was trying to cook something."

Jay chuckled and shook his head. He seemed to believe that one, "You really should let me do the cooking. You have more accidents in your kitchen that everyone else I know put together. What was it a few weeks ago? Picking up a hot pan without an oven mitt?"

It had actually been a hot piece of roof he moved during a fire in an office park as he tried to save someone, but the pan worked for a cover story. He really wasn't sure he should tell Jay he was a superhero. How could he deal with that kind of information? Jay might not react well to dating a super powered freak who dressed up in a costume to fight crime. Better for now to keep it under his mask and keep the excuses to the mundane. Ted nodded and said, "Sorry, I guess you're just stuck with an accident prone coyote."

"Good. Though I do like your cooking I don't want you to die by pie," the collie said with a broad smile and then Jay added, "Try and be better about being on time. Brandon, Mattie, and Gary already left for the docks."

"The docks?" asked Ted quizzically turning his head.

"Well you had been talking so much about gambling lately I thought a night at that casino might be fun," said Jay with a grin, "It's funny, I never thought of you as a gambler type."

Ted blushed. He had been talking about it a lot. He had researched it for Larson's arrest today, but he never could resist talking about his latest reading material to everyone around him. He just said, "Well I haven't done it that often, I was just interested. I'm not really into it."

Jay wagged at him and gave him a smile, "I was hoping you'd say that. I was thinking we'd just enjoy a boat cruise around the river instead. You know, take in the city lights. I know a dinner boat that leaves pretty soon."

"Sounds fun to me," said Ted, a happy grin on his muzzle as he pressed against the warm body of the collie. He wasn't sure if they were boyfriends yet, but they had been getting closer and he enjoyed that as he looked into the collie's eyes.

Jay's phone rang just before he could give him another kiss. Jay broke the embrace and picked up his cell phone. For a few moments he was talking to someone on the other end. After a bit of garbled agitation from the receiver he closed the cell phone and looked at Ted, "Well good thing I made reservations on that dinner boat. Apparently that gambling ship just got impounded as evidence by the police. Gary said something about illegal money and profiteering or something. Apparently it will be on the news tonight and we should watch for him in the crowd."

The coyote guessed Belinda worked fast. He looked at Jay with some slight worry, "Everyone okay?"

"Yeah," Jay grinned, "thanks to your slow shuffle they weren't on the boat, so they're all fine and going over to that new coffee place I told you about."

Ted thought for a moment trying to remember the name of the place. Drawing a blank he asked, "What was the name again?"

"Somewhere over the Java," said Jay with a wag of his tail pleasantly as he added, "It's a nice spot. I think you should see about taking me there."

"If I play my cards right do I get a reward?" asked Ted with sly grin as he and Jay got ready to leave. The thought of that kiss lingering on both their minds as they looked at each other.

"Only if you don't overplay your hand," said Jay with a smile as they stepped out of the apartment. The two took the stairs down and out onto the street.

"Good thing I know when to hold them and when to fold them," said the coyote, wrapping an arm around Jay and drawing him close. Jay didn't resist the touch and instead seemed to smile leaning against him.

"I think I better stop with these puns. They're distracting me from a more important game," said Jay with a happy smile as the sun began to sink and twilight graced the city. The Collie's arm reached around the small of Ted's back as they walked. TVs and newspapers were already emblazoned with pictures of Star

Coyote arresting Larson and ADA Swain. Neither canine really noticed, as they were busy with more personal things and happily talking about their plans for the night.

Toras has been limping along in the same avatar for too long. He's in need of an upgrade. The only problem is how to get it, and at what cost?

THE HAIRCUT

H. A. Kirsch

"You look like someone took a leak on you."

Toras wasn't expecting that kind of greeting. He turned around, the virtual view from his augmented reality visor swinging around a split-second behind, showing a rough approximation of his college friend Jason standing in a very unnatural position by the door to the hallway. "What? It's just the lighting."

"No, you're all yellow and your uh, fur sticks out all funny, like you've been playing fire hydrant." Jason's failing in life was his mouth; he always opened it before thinking. The vulgar comment made him snerk, which made the simulation programming think he was coughing, which made his avatar cover his mouth in round-about politeness.

Toras flipped to vanity view. Despite the crass language, Jason was right about the outward appearance of Toras' avatar. "It's supposed to be gold, but they couldn't figure out how to make something shiny and furry at the same time back then, I guess."

Jason was 'visiting' from his new home in Seattle. He had the classic New England attitude, which didn't bother Boston-homed Toras, but the sudden output about the wolf avatar stung. "So, let's do this thing. I hate this stuff enough as it is, all this weird

crummy graphics and stuff, but I have a test tomorrow and the ol'
organic chemistry just isn't clicking."

"Maybe you shouldn't have decided to get a Masters in
material science engineering, then," Toras grinned. The wolf
grinned and shook its head a second or two afterwards, as Toras'
visor tried to pick up on the gesture. It often failed, one of the
reasons Toras had originally rejected the prototype during testing.
Most users figured out how to game it to do what they wanted,
creating elaborate movement routines out of idiosyncratic slight
movements and facial expressions. Toras was part of the team
testing the usability and user interface for the AR visors; he failed
them because the quirks made it so difficult to convincingly
inhabit an avatar, only to later discover that hardcore users liked
the challenge.

His latest assignment dealt with a new interface, electro-
haptics. Through a series of contacts that would press through hair
to the scalp, the electro-haptics could produce skin stimulation that
a human brain interprets as physical sensations anywhere on the
body. The technology was so limited and temperamental that he
couldn't see it really working out, but the struggle of taking limited
knowledge and framing it for even more limited users gave him
enough of a mental challenge to stick with it. With the exception
of his testing group, the haptics system was off limits, which added
a little bit of spice. He never verbalized it, but there was another
reason why he was sticking with the haptics project despite several
setbacks and continual frustration from users; it promised to open
the door to simulations far more intense than just pictures and
sound. It was good work, at least it would be until the project
inevitably got canceled or sold out to someone else.

"Whatever. Hey, so, is this your apartment on here or
something?" Jason walked his avatar around, peering at the stock
college-dorm art and surreal renders that Toras had stuck up.
The movement was smoother than someone walking in real life,
yet patterned like someone who could only give directions. Jason

was probably using his computer to walk through the simulation like it was a video game.

"Yeah, don't you recognize it? You freakin' lived here." Meanwhile, Toras was inspecting himself further. He made his avatar hold out an arm, comparing the ill-designed dark yellow and cartoony spiky fur reality with his mental notion of what it should look like. Then, his real self started digging in a drawer, pulling out the character picture that was the source for all things wolfy and Toras-y. The contrast of virtual pixels with watercolor-on-paper was alarming, but it was generally the same. Gold fur, utility kilt and belt, logger boots made to fit the toe-walk of wolf feet, an industrial-tinged wristwatch.

"I guess you're right, this body's kind of garish. You kind of don't notice after all the pierced Gothic princesses with angel wings and low-rise jeans." While he dug in his drawer, his virtual character rummaged in a virtual box that appeared out of nowhere. Toras stopped his visor from trying to scan and display the picture.

"Why are you a wolf, anyway? Are you one of those crazy people who walks around as a lion with angel wings and a tee-shirt that says, 'Yiff!'?"

Toras's avatar rolled its eyes, the real Toras poking a few buttons on his cell-phone-turned controller to accomplish the feat and force his avatar not to read his facial expression. In reality, he blushed hard and turned away from Jason to dodge the ignorant question. "Why do you look like yourself? That's boring. You can look like anything, but you just scanned yourself in."

"I didn't scan it, I played with that thing that lets you just uh, adjust everything. I'm boring enough that no one'd need to scan me. I'm not here to play games, I'm here to talk to people. The Internet's a tool, remember? Didn't you used to tell me that?"

Yeah, and the Internet's full of tools too, Toras thought. It made him grin.

"So anyway," Jason's avatar said, making a beeline for the couch. The animation was jerky as the fake Jason sat down, like older life sim games. He obviously hadn't invested much in new actions. "Orgo time. Come on, hit me with a molecule."

Toras fooled with his cell phone and the wolf avatar flung something out of a kilt pouch, the object expanding into a very large organic molecule. Jason sat forward. "What's that?"

"A caffeine molecule. Seemed appropriate for study time."

When Jason didn't laugh, Toras just grunted and opened up his notebook. Why are you a wolf? The question came back to him whenever he wasn't watching Jason simulate redox reactions. Despite Jason's claims of tech-stupidity, he got the hang of the molecules and was soon trying to do show-off tricks with them.

Toras welcomed the diversion, since it kept him from thinking about all the years that had passed since he decided he wanted to be a wolf.

The real Toras walked right past The Cave, the well-named Alter Realm hangout for anthropomorphic fans that he sometimes patronized. Alter Realm was a nickname born out by its genre: Augmented Reality. It was really three separate incarnations. The first was The Endless Age, an also-ran in the world of massive multi-player online role-playing games. Although the original publisher folded, the developers bought back the code, and the game could still be accessed on a few servers now run by MIT. The Endless Age spawned El Dorado, a strictly social virtual avatar system like Second Life that ran on the same game engine and network and allowed users to keep their same game character while talking with friends. El Dorado as a separate entity was now defunct, replaced by the all encompassing Alter Realm.

When a shoe shop burned out several years prior, the city parks committee jumped on the chance and put in a 'Mixed Use Pedestrian Facility', code words for a small corridor of benches and trees between two roads. Alter Realm users jumped on it and made it into one of their hangouts, primarily a group of furry-fans, saving it from homeless people and vandalism. The alley jogged, which meant that part of the park area wasn't very well-used since people were leery of hiding away out of sight. It was this area that anyone viewing through AR hardware saw a ceiling with stalactites and bats where clouds and birds hung in real life.

Normally, Toras would have stopped in, but here were too many real passers-by, too many tourist groups who wouldn't understand why someone was standing and talking to no-one, even in the age of the cell phone. The Cave was a kind of experiment that sounded good until people tried it, and then became popular only for a select niche. Augmented spaces were only useful to people who had equipment to view them, anything from a cell phone with a camera/GPS/compass up to the visors that Toras' research group were long-term testing, but only those with visors could walk around in real-space with their avatars. That meant anyone who wanted to buy the expensive units could make themselves into whatever they want and trot around the city streets, although the hardcore users were primarily college students who received a subsidy in exchange for being part of the equipment test.

Since Alter Realm included virtual representations of people, users could 'light-travel' their avatars in from anywhere in the simulation and other users would see them. The outside world just saw a wall, a tree, a bench. Toras hung out by the entrance, pretending to check something on his phone while the visor loaded up the room and overlaid it onto the real alley parkway. It was as close as he could get to see inside without having to trot his avatar through the small crowd.

The small crowd was entirely virtual, and entirely anthropomorphic that day. The lurking Toras found everyone gawking at one RedOrion, a fox who had recently put himself in debt over a full series of character commissions including a new avatar. His had realistic fur, although it didn't move with him. Compared with that, Toras's faux-gold wolf would look like a kindergarten-doodle. Disconnected from the group of admirers, the preening and fawning over the well-furred RedOrion had Toras morose. He was stung by the distaste of watching so much vanity, and because it reminded him of how he once felt years ago as a teenager.

It didn't help that RedOrion's vulpine appearance was truly 'good'. Jason wasn't the only one to complain about the state of Toras' wolf avatar. It had been cutting edge when he got it two years earlier, before the big Alter Realm upgrade, but now many of the other anthros had ones with physics engines and fur shaders. In comparison, Toras looked like a pixelated cartoon from the early days of 3D video games. When he'd first received the skin, he was surprised and elated to see how well it worked out in the days of runaway in-game inflation and fun-crushing lag. Now, it just separated him from those with their fingers on the pulse of Alter Realm, even though that was supposed to be his job. He could easily fix it by ditching the character and recreating it, but that just wasn't the same. It was like having a real early serial number on a collectible, a classic car, a pair of boots that had been repaired fifty times. It was a part of who he was, and his personality didn't want to give it up despite how threadbare the golden wolf was growing.

When he'd explained the conflict to anyone, they usually just laughed. Toras walked away from the scene just in case one of the other anthros came up to him and made a comment like Jason had earlier. He shut off his self-reflection, so he didn't have to see the dingy yellow 'fur' on his arms or see his old-school self in anything reflective that he passed.

Alter Realm was, among other things, a chance to turn fantasy into reality, or at least overwrite some of reality with the fantastic. It was the first socially-usable example of that 1980's computer science pipe-dream called Virtual Reality. Gone were the immense visors and huge projection screens, blocky polygonal avatars and supercomputers. Now, it lived in the land of cell-phones and relatively unobtrusive laser visors. Augmented reality had been tried numerous times before, overlaying all kinds of graphics and information onto the real world, but Alter Realm took it to the next level. It let people overwrite themselves with their avatars.

Turning a corner, Toras came face to face with a ten-foot-tall virtual gryphon and jumped to a halt. "None shall pass!" the creature said. The voice was modulated rather cheaply to sound like it matched the body, an expansive baritone. The effect was like listening to James Earl Jones through one of those voice-distorters like used in the movies. Aside from the startle, Toras stayed unfazed by the gryphon, although at least one person walking by gave him a funny look.

"Cliff, what's up?" Toras said, slinking his wolf up against the wall so the steady pedestrian traffic wouldn't collide with it. The real Cliff was several feet away from the virtual gryphon, demarcated with a general human form that vibrated slightly as it moved, human features covered over with solid color. The bifurcation was intended to keep users from trying to physically interact with virtual avatars that weren't really there—waving hands in space was embarrassing at best and could clock a pedestrian in the face at worst.

"Man, you still have that thing?" Cliff pointed a claw at Toras' pelt as the three forms moved over towards the wall of a building, out of the way of foot traffic.

"Oh come on, everyone's giving me the same crap lately! First time I see you VR in a couple of months and this is what I get? Look at you, you're cell shaded!"

Cliff proudly spread his wings, which knocked a barely-clad avatar girl off the sidewalk. The real girl, now visible, yelled something in Italian and flipped both off, avatar miming the action which Cliff ignored. "I got style. You look like a dog used-"

"No, don't say it, don't say it!" Toras stuck his real fingers in his ears, attracting a few more looks from passers-by. The city denizens had slowly grown used to people walking around with AR headsets on, but a finger in the ear was silly no matter what. "So what do I do? I'm too busy to work up all the money to buy some new Skin Physics. I'm not going to wreck my character and start over. I'm not going to try hacking around in The Endless Age to steal money and trade it to some kid in South Korea for better fur." The Endless Age, though a shadow of its former self in population, could still be farmed for items and currency for customizations that could be carried over into Altered Realm.

"You need to get rid of them morals, T-wolf," Cliff said, turning and starting to lumber down the sidewalk. Toras followed. "The hell's your weirdo problem? You're like that dude in sweatpants who always fixes up the rust spots on his old-ass car each spring, even though they come back over the winter. Remember that dude? Like at my old apart... Whatever. If there ain't a way to kill some guy who's plugged into all this, then you can just do whatever you want. You don't even need to pay money, you just walk around for free and someone hands you dough!"

"Whatever," Toras laughed. "I think you mean, you pay a subscription fee, and someone hands you a stipend, in hopes that you buy name brands and wear labels. It's just like out here. RedOrion's just a walking signboard for the guy who does all those fancy avatars for furs."

Cliff used one of his gryphon wings to brush Toras's sociology aside. "You know, I heard there's some alley over by the fish pier, it's got a Cartographer there. You know, for The Endless Age. Like that's real old-school. He does nautical stuff, but I heard he has like some map to some crazy guy who does Skin Physics. It's a crazy quest, for some kind of plus-one-billion beast shaman whatever points... It's taken out a couple friends. That little fox guy, wasshis name, Beeny?"

"I think it's with an I, like Biini?" Toras tried to air-spell it, but the constant pedestrian traffic made the letters distort into a profanity as soon as his finger traced them out. "He got taken out?"

"Yeah, deleted, wiped out... I guess he cared a lot, man, he gave up all this tech shit and went back to trade school, I think he's an electrician or some shit now."

Taken out was slang for erasure. Not just death, but deletion. It was as if the game suddenly decided you never existed, and subsequently removed you from friends lists, purged you from the database, name-recycled. Anyone in Alter Realm could take themselves out, although they had to pay to expedite the process to cut down on churn and lend some realistic gravity to the 'death'. An Endless Age quest taking someone out was rare, though, maybe even technically against the rules. "That's insane. He got taken out trying to get new fur?"

"I guess," Cliff's virtual gryphon shrugged. "I blew all my money on this rig. It's like wasting money on porno, you know? I'm happy with what I have. If you're not happy, do what it takes."

Toras processed the combination of wisdom and stupidity. "So you said this dude's in the fish pier?"

"Yeah, somewhere in there. Hold your nose, man, 'cuz you gotta go in person. You can't just light-travel an' go see him. You gotta walk with yo' feets."

"I think I'm gonna check it out, I'm kinda hungry anyway," Toras said, and spun. "Later!" The gryphon wing-waved, narrowly missing a virtual street lamp.

By the time Toras reached the fish pier, he was hungry enough for a pit stop at the No Name. It actually had no name, but by virtue of humanity needing labels, received the amazingly creative moniker over time. He turned off the AR headset and set it on the other side of his table, near the window so no one could swipe it. It was a prototype, separated from commercial distribution by just a model number and the temperamental haptic simulation circuits, but still expensive and probably worth too much on eBay.

After a good lunch of fish chowder and scallops, he paid up and dumped himself outside into the pier alley. On went the visor, the projector lasers tracing virtual reality into Toras's eyes on top of the real thing. Toras sniffed and frowned; he wished that he could switch on the haptics and somehow drown out the foul smell, but with his luck, he'd get a neck cramp from the creepy-crawly stimulations.

The augments for most places in town were just informational—names of businesses, menus, sales, geographical tidbits for tourists, graffiti. Money was always the deciding factor, so advertising and placement made up the core of the system. Hard-core users were a small portion of the user base, as niche as 'real goths', furry fans, and medieval reenactors. Hard-cores tried to make the system into the virtual reality of books and movies, while the bread-and-butter was just new ways to help people part with their money. Luckily for Toras' employment, hard-cores were often just coming out of their teenage years and waving around Daddy's credit card, and there was an endless stream of people looking to brand anything and everything.

The fish pier was exactly the same way, except for a simulated oak door in the middle of a concrete wall. Toras walked up and got out his phone to control his wolf, walking his avatar through the door while he stood around outside. That was the big failing of the mash-up between The Endless Age and Alter Realm—virtual places sounded cool on paper, but not so cool to the people left standing around in the cold while their virtual selves had a beer. Augmented social reality could be as alienating as old-fashioned text chat, turning human interaction into a lazy ass sitting in front of a screen. The only difference was that it sat your ass next to some stranger who thought you were crazy. As such, Toras tried to act like he was texting friends or waiting for someone, a task made difficult by the pervasive fish pier stench.

Inside the game, he was as far from Boston as possible. The room was a cartographer's shop, full of ships in bottles and map scrolls. Milling about behind the desk was the caretaker, a Hoppins Dragon whose name appeared as Aragh.

"What can I do for you, young traveller?" the dragon said. Toras scrolled through the responses with his phone, greeting and trying to extract information—Aragh was an NPC. Since the dragon sold mostly nautical maps, there was nothing for them to talk about. Toras didn't have a ship in The Endless Age, so a nautical map was pointless. He examined the entire room, finding no teases, hints or hidden doors. On a lark, he charmed the dragon: no luck. Toras gave up and walked his avatar back to the door. Bingo. Instead of the door creak as it opened, he heard, "Wait, one more thing..."

"I have a problem with rats," Aragh said. "It's all the fish from the merchants here. The rats love to hide in the cellar and scare away customers when I take them down to my map library. You don't happen to know any way to get rid of rats?"

Of course, Aragh's problem with rats was as real as he was. Toras paged through his inventory. Nothing seemed promising, except for his scrolls—almost all of them were activated as hints. Toras settled on one, "Control Small Animal", and offered it to Aragh.

"Ahh, you are a shaman beast master! I'm sure you have no use for such a middling spell. This will be perfect. Say, I happen to have heard of a reclusive hermit out in the Forest of Stone. He might be able to help you improve your lupine nature. Interested?" Aragh's response jerked as he mentioned the hermit—the action was clearly spliced in and hastily constructed, like it had been added as an afterthought.

Toras stared at it the dragon's glitchy motion, then Toras picked "Yes" out of the dialog selector and found himself with a secondary map and marker for the Forest of Stone. The dragon warned him that the area was very inhospitable and packed with wild animals, then sent him on his way.

Back home, Toras sent his avatar off to The Cave while he milled around, cleaning his apartment. Every now and then, he took a break, sitting on the couch and full-screening the action into his visor. The discussion apparently revolved around cartoon goof ball antics, which were only interesting with great concentration, and his own avatar. Many of the other anthros had cell-shaded graphics or artistic and unrealistic avatars, so whether or not they were poor quality wasn't an issue. Toras had the old-style realistic avatar, and the overlarge pixels were glaring in comparison, not to mention the poor color. He wanted to blame RedOrion for putting the bar up a notch, but the fox in question seemed too happy playing 'pounce the dark corner' to spend much time bragging. The fox appeared to have purchased the avatar just to look good—this was confirmed when he said as much, then let the entire room pet his new tail.

What a waste, Toras thought. His jealousy at the fox's avatar flared up, but withered just as quickly. Still, he couldn't stop obsessing over his own ancient avatar. He gave up with the virtual people-watching at The Cave and left, teleporting to Ash Gate to enter The Endless Age.

As soon as he did, a friend named SkwirlMastr popped up in the global chat window. Skwirl had been at The Cave, keeping an eye on the conversation. "Hey toras it was just you know friendly stuff. Where'd you go?" The words came up wrong, then auto-corrected on Toras' end. Skwirl was probably typing on a keyboard; he was a terrible typist, something he excused by putting all of his manual dexterity into artwork.

"If everyone wants me to look better, then I'll look better," Toras said. The subtitles popped into place second after he spoke.

"Oh come on ur not like that-"

"No, I'm not like that. I'm going to do it right. Look, this is important to me." Toras said it aloud, letting the voice recognition chew on the words. It gave him time to think about what he said, which made him flush. "I got this dingy wolf avatar for a reason, Skwirl. It was supposed to be me, but it's not me any more. It's like when you're a kid and scribble a picture of what you want to be when you grow up, then find it in your attic as an adult. It's just... a scribble. I guess the time just came around to notice." Toras felt enough gravity from the statement that he leaned back on his real couch.

"Hahaha I know what you mean, like this-" Skwirl's cartoony-cute avatar disappeared and was replaced with a vaguely squirrel-like object. It looked like it was drawn by a three year old. "I am da skwirl mastur!" was written on it. Toras couldn't tell if it was a joke, or an actual artifact of the hyper-kinetic artist's childhood.

"Anyway, I'm feeling profoundly affected, so I'm going to go on a quest Cliff told me about. I think it's gonna take about a week."

"A week!"

A week. Toras thought about taking time off work to pretend he was doing... something... in a pretend world for pretend results, all because he wanted to make believe he was something. He shook the idea. "I'm bound," Toras said, pushing his thoughts away to answer Skwirl's question.

"Ooooooh," Skwirl said, and his avatar produced cartoon eyelashes that it batted seductively.

"Not like that," Toras laughed. "I started off playing The Endless Age, back before El Dorado split off. When they started the whole thing back up again, I just... What'd they call it? I transplanted. So I can use everything in Alter Realm, and also go back to the game stuff. Just not at the same time. You can only be in one place at a time, right?" As soon as he said it, Toras realized how strange it was to say that about something so virtual and limitless.

"Aww. I'll miss you. Big nuts to you!"

Toras laughed, his avatar no doubt chuckling on Skwirl's end. "Thanks. Well, I'm out."

SkwirlMastr's chat window winked out, only to be replaced immediately with Jason's. "Okay, so you're going to be gone for a week, like you can't be reached with this chat stuff? You gotta be kidding me. I thought you wore that thing when you slept!"

Toras sighed. "Who told you?"

"One of your freaky little friends got my screen name from that Cliff guy you work with. Some squirrel thing." Jason smirked. "You love to do things the hard way."

"I do them the right way," Toras countered, and then grimaced as he tried to force his brain to assemble a good explanation. Jason and Cliff had gone to business school crossover classes for a while and must've kept in touch. Toras somehow hadn't paid attention and wished he had. Jason started to talk, but Toras cut him off.

"Alter Realm lets you do anything you want, but all anyone does is buy crappy fake versions of things they'll never be with money they didn't even earn. It's like the wrong kind of socialism." Toras's words started coming faster, his face heated up, as he accidentally summoned feelings he hadn't used since high school. He abruptly dropped that line of thought.

"Hey, you went to college, aren't you all for that kind of socio-whatever mumbo crap?"

"Oh come on, that's so tired," Toras rolled his eyes. "I want to do something more than sit around wait for virtual money to accumulate so I can buy... new fur. I want to earn it. Besides, it's going to be an adventure. It's like those teeshirts, you know, "Because It's There"."

Jason's chat window exploded with eye-rolling smileys.

Toras ignored the outburst. "I don't think this is even a regular game quest. There's something fishy about it," Toras said, sputtering at the end. Fishy. Fish. Fish pier. Another eye roll. "Maybe it'll be a wild goose chase, but so what? I might as well try. Pretend I'm joining, I don't know, a new-age movement for a week. Having a midlife crisis. Pretend... I'm going to France."

"Merde. Vous n'est... ungh, I totally forgot all my French. Jean, you're not even forty. You just turned... Fine, later dude," Jason said, and his avatar gave a dismissive wave as he turned away and vanished. Toras pulled up the main navigation screen and chose the Game Transplant option.

A big warning came up indicating that no Alter Realm communication would continue if he accepted the transplant shift. He accepted, and entered the world of The Endless Age. The blend of overlays, ads, buildings and concrete outside The Cave re-drew into the familiar seamless anachronism of a fantasy RPG.

The Stone Forest was not a typical forest. Legend had it that an entire lush forest and range of foothills had been turned to stone as the life was sucked out by some necromancer thousands of years earlier. The original forest was literally petrified as it stood, leaving trees with spindly rock branches, animals frozen in time, plants crunching to dust underfoot. The passage of years had worn things down, and new growth had started, along with a new ecosystem that served to make the petrified wildlife into shrine to the past.

In reality, some guy in a Star Wars tee shirt doodled it on a napkin after too much Mountain Dew and then gave it to the graphic designers. At the time it was a joke, and the designer who took hold of that napkin snatched a cell-phone photo of the stereotypical geek. The photo was later immortalized as a cave painting in the game world, and if you gestured over it the right way, the actual photo appeared, reminding everyone of the modern human touch in a world of anachronisms.

Toras paged through the quest details: several challenges meant to exercise the astuteness of the player, culminating in a meeting with one of the Masters who will grant a single wish. It's like the Wizard of Oz, Toras thought. Probably some short bald guy living in his mom's basement. Toras wondered if it was even an actual game thing, or one of the early hacks that broke the fourth wall in the days before the social El Dorado interface.

First, the player had to navigate through the hills that made up the Daunting Circle, impassable foothills that funnelled the player through a valley and an ancient ruin. After the ruin, he would have to traverse a field of Frost, which Toras swore was

100

a copy-paste duplication from a PC game he'd played in high school. The quest details were written as an in-game document on old parchment, and after the Frost, the text had been corrupted somehow, as if ink had spilled on it. After the garbled text came the final step: Your Reward, it read.

Toras wondered what the the prize was. The quest didn't mention anything about lupine nature, but that NPC dragon had. Toras remembered the jerky cut-in of that piece of diction. He broke out of the regular game and went into his testing log. He didn't have access to the actual online role playing game the same way he did on Alter Realm, but he still had a log of everything he did and everything people said to him. There it was—a specific reference to his piss-poor wolf avatar.

The quest was pathetic, he thought. Maybe even a red herring. The garbled text and strange behavior of that virtual dragon meant Toras had a more tangible reason to embark on it: curiosity. Someone was paying attention to him, and that made the reward more real. He wasn't going to be getting some paltry game reward—terrain challenges were pointless in a multi-player game anyway. There was a man behind a curtain somewhere, and that was Toras' ultimate goal.

The daunting circle looked like nothing in particular, certainly not impassable, as a valley ran straight through the hills. As soon as he headed towards the cut-through, Toras found his avatar quickly over encumbered and unable to do anything but sit cross-legged, panting like an untrimmed husky in July. After spending a few game hours milling around and going through every spell he had, dropping every item he carried, Toras gave up. Items and clothing strewn all around, his character still had the red "over encumbered" text hovering over its head.

He fumed to himself at whoever set up the quest. The Endless Age had once been a regularly updated MMORPG, but changed into a fan-driven system when it was resurrected as part of Alter Realm. At the top of its downward slide, achievement whores created quests to boost their numbers as quickly as possible, while real creativity languished. As it became a relic, TEA ended up a collection of non-player characters haunting a sprawling world, with the occasional bout of storytelling or unique challenge. A quest that made a character drop all his or her items was a simple obstacle from the world of 'real' RPGs, but one that was more often a trick to steal player items in The Endless Age. He cast a spell to lock his character and all the items strewn around on the virtual ground, the one special power he had as a tester, and logged off to clean his real apartment.

The next day, he came back online and had his eureka moment. The Daunting Circle was obviously some sort of gravitational effect, but the area was full of NPC wildlife. Previous challenges in other games he'd played never had animals in a gravity bog, presumably because everything was built off the same physics system and they would all simply stand still. NPC squirrels and birds cavorted around the valley with no problems, so maybe...

After waiting long enough, a rat wandered out of a nearby bush and came up to sniff Toras. He attacked and ate it, then watched as his weight meter dropped down by a fair chunk. After three more rats, he was able to move around. It was a good hour's work, as the rats didn't wander by very often and ran away if he tried to chase them. Three more rats, and he could pick his items back up. However, all of the magic supplements his character had were disabled or drained from his items. Even a Restoration Stone did nothing. Cute, he thought, rat meat that drained weight *and* magic.

An NPC wolf wandered up, nosing and nipping at the left-over rat carcasses. Toras tried to approach the animal but it just growled and attacked him, prompting a few swipes back with a weapon. Just before the wolf was critically injured, it quickly ran back and sat on its haunches, health bar creeping back up. Toras had been playing TEA since it had been in beta, back when he was in high school, and that behavior just wasn't something

NPC animals did. Animals were cannon fodder, walking bags of experience points. Their entire point was to die while adding to the scenery. Never had one escaped before dying, only to sit out of melee weapon range and recuperate.

Intrigued, Toras made his way further up through the foothills, then down into another valley, with the wolf following a ways behind. If Toras stopped for too long, the wolf jumped him, only to retreat at the last minute. Near the middle of the valley, the land spread out into a wide half circle dish-shaped area, almost like a spiral mashed in at one side. A stream wound its way around, disappearing through a hole in a great wall. It had to be the ruins from the quest description, although it really looked just like an enormous wall.

Toras led his virtual self up to the wall and its tunnel. A gate instantly crashed down and he barely managed to leap back before being hurt. Each time he tried, the gate crashed down, thwarting any attempt to pass through. Toras wandered around the strange wall and found no other entrance. On a lark, he dropped one of his items. It was sucked towards the wall, disappearing in an impressive graphical poof. The wild wolf stood by, head moving back and forth between Toras and the hole, watching the procession of disappearing item as Toras tossed them into the darkness. After a few minutes of it, Toras stuck his arm out and the visor picked it up. He waggled a gem around and then hurled it at the wall. "Here boy! Go Fetch!" The wolf just sniffed and sat, watching with staring eyes as the gem vanished in a puff of particle effects.

Toras shrugged and kept at it, until the only thing left was his avatar's external appearance. In reality, Toras growled at the stupidity of another item drop, this one whisking his collection of trinkets and weapons off to some unknown place. His visor read his frown and made the animated Toras growl. The following wolf tucked its ears back and returned it. Toras stared at it, then shrugged it off.

He tried the gate again, and this time it didn't crash down, allowing his avatar and the wild wolf to head through the passageway. The passage was somehow translucent despite being made of rock, showing Toras his progress through stone and dirt, finally expelling him on the other side of the foothills. Fully inside the Circle of Daunting, he could see for virtual miles. Cold white mist blanketed everything, trees and rocks peeking out here and there before the foothills rose again in the distance.

The breathtaking view lasted only until he started to walk. He was hit by a frost warning, visor buzzing its internal vibrator. The effect was profound enough that Toras could swear the cold crept over his skin, but it had to just be the immersion and the hours of sitting alone at home getting to him. His prototype haptics gear was always disabled. He quickly cast Dispel Environment, which only worked for a few seconds at a time. He had to cast it on the wolf as well, who wouldn't follow without it. He tried leaving the wolf behind, but as the animal was hurt, so was he. He went back to the perimeter and tried to leave the wolf, but then he wasn't even allowed to walk forward into the frost—the game just stopped him as if there was an invisible wall.

The travel was very irritating, a continual pause every fifteen seconds to re-cast the spell, his magic level hovering almost at zero. The timing necessary to avoid taking damage was precise and mind numbing, casting the spell and running forward, waiting for enough magic to come back to cast again. The frost seemed endless, and Toras spent the better part of an entire day wandering through it. Every half an hour or so, he took a break to stretch, wander around the apartment, look out the window, use the bathroom.

When he paused for lunch, he took a longer break and rode the subway down to Boston Commons sans visor. Everything he saw was actually there: real trees, real people, real dogs on real leashes, real sidewalks. Every time he looked at himself, he saw his real body, not the overlaid one of Toras. The compulsion to eat finally won out over the compulsion to get fresh air, leading him to the vendor stalls. There, standing at a cotton candy cart like a five year old, was the real life Cliff.

"Hey man, where you been at?" Cliff said, biting off a big fluffy chunk of candy. He looked like a cross between a pimp and a street thug, dog-fur coat mismatched with a POW-MIA hat and urban digital camo. He was actually a fellow researcher at the Advanced Visualization Laboratory, geeky insides coming out in the incongruous outfit.

Toras dug out a credit pass and bought an elephant ear from the street cart, then tipped with hard cash. "Didn't Skwirl tell you?"

"Man, you really been jacked in, huh? Skwirl's at Mass General! He got broke up in a wreck down in The Big Dig."

Toras mumbled through a mouthful of dough. "No way! When did this happen?"

"A couple days ago, some narcoleptic semi driver caught some Z's at the wheel, jackknifed his truck across the whole damn road. Skwirl slid right under the thing, almost got killed. Truck squashed down on the hatch of his back, man! He's all bashed up, but he ain't dead. Gonna be okay, he said." Cliff fought with his sugary puff through the entire statement, as if it was an obstacle between him and Toras. "Man, that damn Dig is like some kinda open sore on this city's ass. They started that crap when I was still in high school."

Toras looked around at the fall colors in the park, the pedestrians, the surrounding buildings. Everything was still real, including the real visors on a significant number of heads, including the people looking around the park with their cellphones held up like viewing glasses. "Boy, now I feel dumb telling you what I've been doing."

Cliff laughed hard. "You out there tryin' to buy yo'self a fancy fur coat? You oughta go my route, you shave your own dogs!" Cliff showed off the coat by pulling one lapel out and turning to the side, like someone demonstrating an expensive mink coat.

"I don't think I have to buy it. At least, I won't have anything to buy it with. I'm bound, remember? I had to drop all my stuff to go through a hole. It took all my Alter Realm money, too."

Binding could be a perk from his testing job, as a good subset of his developer rights to log and deconstruct Alter Realms carried over into the game world. It also gave an uncharacteristic weight to the virtual world, in that he could actually be damaged as an avatar through actions in The Endless Age.

"Man, you do everything the hard way." Cliff started eating the waffle cone out from underneath his cotton candy. Toras watched and felt a creeping sensation come up his spine. He wasn't watching the virtual Gryphon that was Cliff, but the real thing. The real Cliff was watching him right back, and certainly saw the frumpy cargo pants and hiking coat that made up Toras' fall attire. Not to mention the pale skin and unruly hair, and the fact that Toras was human... He took a deep breath and let it out with a huff.

"I wouldn't have a real job if I didn't stick with things, Cliff. I'd be trapped in school."

"Ha. You still are, man. You're trapped, you just get paid for it now." That was the truth—Toras was technically still a student, although a doctoral student doing his dissertation as part of a tech internship with the Alter Realm people. "Well, back to th'grind, you take care. Don't rot yo' eyeballs out with that thing. I seen some big ol' nerd-guys, they walk 'round like they zombies." Cliff pointed at Toras's forehead.

Toras didn't even remember putting the visor on when he left the apartment. He certainly didn't have it logged in. Realizing it was attached to his head made his stomach lurch. "Oh, I'm not even using it. I guess it's just habit. Seeya."

The two parted, Cliff swaggering off, Toras going to sit on a hill under a tree. Now when he looked out at the crowds of students and businesspeople and bums and tourists and hawkers and whatever else, all he saw were the people wearing their Alter Realm gear like a badge of honor.

They were different. They saw the world differently. He saw it differently, even with his own eyes. He got up, antsy again,

106

and headed for a sausage cart. On the way there, he poked at his cell-phone, sending Skwirl a few text messages, doing his best to create a bouquet of virtual flowers with ASCII art and expressing his condolences for the accident.

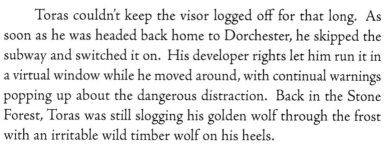

Toras couldn't keep the visor logged off for that long. As soon as he was headed back home to Dorchester, he skipped the subway and switched it on. His developer rights let him run it in a virtual window while he moved around, with continual warnings popping up about the dangerous distraction. Back in the Stone Forest, Toras was still slogging his golden wolf through the frost with an irritable wild timber wolf on his heels.

The frost let up after another couple of hours wandering and was replaced with something much worse. Walking through craggy, grass-grown fields of boulders, Toras's avatar energy would drain until he had to sit down, then lie down. The first few times he managed to cast Rejuvenation, but his magic didn't renew either. His avatar lay down and ended up staring at the sky.

"This is so stupid," the real Toras said to no one, as he wandered around his apartment fixing a real sandwich. His words bubbled up in his overlay, melting away after a few moments, unseen by all but the NPC wolf. He sat down at the kitchen counter, watching his useless wolf in vanity mode as it watched clouds move past over a red, then purple, then black sky. The clouds cleared, leaving stars gently shimmering. Toras could hear noises from the virtual world, the squeak of an animal, the squeal of the animal being attacked, the crunch of bone and flesh, the sound of paws in the grass approaching. The wolf's head appeared, holding a very odd red bird. Toras selected it and his energy restored, although it quickly started dropping again.

Toras ran his character as fast as he could in the only direction that held promise. The character ran out of energy just at the edge of the plain, falling down with an empty energy meter.

The wolf disappeared again, then came back. It whined and simply sat within view, muzzle appearing and disappearing as it looked around, anxious. Toras grumbled and started trying to talk to the wolf. He found it would apparently listen to him, and he told it to find another bird. It disappeared and came back with another whine, sans bird.

There was nothing left to do. No more magic, no more energy, no belongings, only a strange wolf. A wolf who could possibly retrieve some strange bird that restored energy, but either there were no more birds or the wolf was being stubborn. Normally NPC animals didn't have much AI, so it was odd that the wolf could understand human language. The Endless Age may have been a breakthrough, but this animal seemed too forward-thinking to be just another cog in the simulation.

Then Toras noticed something. While he couldn't cast spells without magic power, he could still cast abilities. Seeing in the dark was pointless, but his Beast Master powers were part of his Lupine Shaman abilities and never disappeared. Toras cursed himself for missing the obvious use earlier with the camp rats he had to eat, then set out to try it. Using the Beast Master power on the wolf made the creature irritable, and barely had an effect. As usual, it let him see as the wolf saw, but there was a catch. Without energy, he couldn't control his character at all, so all he did was see himself lying motionless through the wild wolf's eyes. Voice commands to the wolf didn't work, since without energy his avatar wouldn't 'talk' even if the real Toras could unleash a litany of profanity a mile long.

There was one last option: Toras had been a pretty adept user of Dream Walk and Possess, which allowed a user to control people or visit their dreams. Theoretically, Beast Master abilities worked the same way, but Toras had years earlier discovered that it tended to simply kill him when he walked into an animal's dreams, either intentionally or through a bug. He went to save the game progress and found that the load utilities had been disabled.

"Hey, what kind of mess is this?" Toras groused. There was now no recourse; death meant death. That meant a gigantic waste of time, not to mention the virtual failure of Toras Loup-d'Or. Toras tried to mentally avoid the reason why that was so important to him, and focused the intensity on his trials with the AR equipment. "Come on, bring up the stupid console…" He muttered, fooling with his cell phone to control the visor. The control app wouldn't connect. He walked over to his computer and loaded the world there, only it wouldn't transfer from the AR visor.

"Hey, god people, are you awake? I bet you're listening to me. I have tester access, so you better be listening. Or—or else. Nice quest, you've left me stuck somewhere watching a wolf jump at fireflies. You enjoying all my AR credits? Having fun watching this wolf stare at me? I bet you are that wolf. I bet this is some kind of scam."

The tech failures were either insane coincidences, or proof that someone really had put Toras up to the entire thing. A quick trip to the Endless Age wiki came up inconclusive: the quest Toras was on had never been completed, but it looked like a real quest, slowly honed over the past couple of years. Anyone who went on it either had their character reset or erased, just like Cliff had said a few days earlier when Toras ran into the virtual gryphon on the street.

All the pieces of the puzzle pointed to a red herring, a ruse, a dead end, nothing worthwhile. Toras turned red in reality, embarrassed that he hadn't bothered to RTFM. He knew about the wiki, but had just… avoided its authority. He sighed to himself and pondered giving up. He could create a new character, build it up all the way, get exactly what he wanted the first time around. Or, he could just hang out in Alter Realm like the more mundane members of virtual society, whiling away the days until he could simply click and buy. Or, he could just give up entirely and do something tangible with his life, maybe a skilled trade…

He posed the question to his mental demons and they came back with a resounding 'No'. Alter Realm was the future of tangibility, and finally he drew up the words to his core thought: he wanted to be a wolf. He had to be a wolf. He had to be his wolf, the design he'd had in his mind for years, that had been rendered onto paper numerous times. He tried to mill around his place without logging back in, but it was just one thought after another. Wolf, wolf, wolf, wolf, wolf, wolf. He kept seeing the picture Skwirl had drawn years earlier, the crummy rendition of said picture as an avatar, RedOrion's beautiful new fox fur... Everything that left Toras feeling out of place as a teenager, every desire to see his own arms sprout tawny fur, came back. He had to fulfil the quest.

Success was the only option, despite the written proof to the contrary. Of course, the written proof was communally editable, and thus inherently untrustworthy. He logged back in, and saw that his energy had crept up just enough to say something. "Hey wolf, go to sleep. Come on, put your head on me or something so I can click on you." Only the first five words registered. On a lark, Toras had managed to say something that exactly used up his energy store. His visor threw the remaining words out after ascertaining that not only was he unable to 'say' them, but that the speech recognition didn't know what to make of them.

After a pause and a yawn, the wild wolf appeared to go to sleep, its Talk icon turning to floating Z's. Toras equipped his Beast Master ability and clicked. Everything shimmered and vibrated, a creeping tickle crawling around the back of his scalp. Toras had just a split second to realize what was happening: Haptics. He had just registered the presence of those electrode contacts on his neck, forehead, and temples, when the simple presence turned into a monstrous itch. Toras reached up to the visor and went to flick it off, but there was no visor to flick off.

He opened his mouth and nothing came out. His character was sitting up, although it was still lying down. Toras was now a physical entity and a dream shape. The wild wolf was standing there, glowing an unhealthy shade of red. It kept creeping closer, and Toras stood up, then tried backing off. Nothing seemed to actually put distance between wolf and wolf-man.

The wolf lunged and bit down on Toras at the throat. He didn't feel pain, just a scratchy clutching grasp. He lifted his— real? virtual? hand to his throat, and the gold fur came away slathered in blood. It wasn't just red blood, but shimmering with some kind of gold-colored specks. The world started to throb and pulse, gold-speckled blood spilling everywhere from the wound.

When it hit the ground, the ground quivered and cracked, soon turning into a writhing mass of black and gold. The writhing mass started to push forward, forming a rivulet, then a narrow stream. Instead of flowing down and away, it started flowing up forward, spilling to the side, creating some kind of path, then steps, then a growing hill. Deep inside his head, Toras knew he was in a game, but it didn't feel fake. It felt like the buzzing vibration of a lucid dream or sleep paralysis. Toras had always wondered if immersive VR would really lead to brain-hacking the way it always did in science fiction, or if it would wither in lieu of something different. He no longer had to wonder.

Everything happening with his visor now was completely illegitimate and raw, like using a sledgehammer to crack an egg. Toras had nearly fallen off a cliff as a child; as he clung onto a small outcropping bush, his body had prickled with the pangs of shock. That sensation came back again, only with a back-of-the-mind focus on the crawling sensations around his neck as the root of his discomfort. Everything he saw now was forced upon him as someone somewhere subverted technology, as technology subverted his flesh, as flesh subverted his mind, all with the almost mocking ever-present Endless Age HUD printed on top.

Toras stared on, powerless to do anything, color draining out of the world, health meter dropping until it reached the danger level, the world flickering and draining to a dull red. Normally, it would be cause for anger, the symbol of death and rebirth, re-equip and restart. Now, Toras wondered if he was dying along with his avatar. The ground tilted up and everything disappeared.

The haptics shut off with a spine-twisting snap, and Toras found himself staring at his couch. Overlaid on the couch was a sideways view of the wolf, pacing back and forth and whining, nosing up so close that its nose chopped off at the front and showed a strange inside-out view of the wolf's avatar skin and skeletal physics. Toras himself sat up, and his character did the same, going the extra step to stand up fully. Magic was still completely depleted, but his energy slowly crept back up along with his health.

He was in the same clearing as before, but this time, there was a twisting path leading up to some sort of weird cave directly in front of him. It hadn't been there before. He started up forward, the wolf walking only as far as the beginning of the path. It sat down and refused to go further. The real Toras took a stop at the bathroom and discovered that he had 6 AM stubble and hollow dark eyes beneath the AR visor. A peek at his cell phone indicated that it was the next morning.

The thought that the haptics somehow knocked him out for hours made him feel woozy, a feeling that only cleared up a slight bit after several glassfuls of water. Light-headed, he scarfed down an entire bag of potato chips, leaving his stomach aching. Groggy, he tried to pretend he hadn't just been mind-wrangled by a computer simulation, his avatar acting out his very real obsessive pacing around the room as he hadn't even bothered to remove the visor.

After his stomach had settled and the warmth of food spread out, he sat back down and started his avatar up the winding path. At the top of the virtual hill, someone walked out of the cave opening. He looked very human, and very modern. Glasses, trimmed beard, graying hair, a Boston band T-shirt with the signature branded UFO, khakis and hiking boots. The person looked vaguely familiar.

"Hi there!" The man's voice filled Toras' ears, along with the mild static and background noise of an actual voice link. Toras' avatar stopped.

"Hi? Who are you?"

"The barber!" the person said. Toras mouthed it to himself. "Wait, here, lemme complete the effect..." The man waved his hand in a spiral and a barber pole grew out of the ground. Next to it, it said, "Eric the Barber: Open for Business".

Toras cautiously walked his avatar into the cave opening, following the man. "No, I mean it, who are you?"

"Says right here," the man tapped the pole. "Eric the Barber!"

"A barber— but, why..." Toras's eyes widened as he got the joke. "Oh, I get it. I need a haircut. Ha ha."

"It's an inside joke. Long story. Sorry about the little episode back there. The last person to go on this little quest didn't have haptics. He died—Not for real! But he was spared having his brain turned inside out for real... That stuff's damn tricky to program. Are you okay?" Eric had a decided southern accent.

Toras nodded. "I think so. I was out for a day or so, though. How the hell did you do that?" He wasn't really okay—he was cold and confused and his mouth tasted sour as the potato chips fought back. A belch just made his avatar look like it was yawning.

"You were just asleep. It induces your brain into a sleep cycle, knocks you out like a baby. I've done it myself. It's awesome if you run into some insomnia. Anyway, here's my barber shop!" Eric swung his hands around, morphing the boring torch-lit stone room into a middle-America old-school barber shop. Hair on the floor, a regular chair, one of those toy race car kiddie chairs, a pile of magazines. Toras looked at them: 'Visualization Systems', 'The Edge', 'American Journal of Neuropsychology'. A light bulb clicked in Toras' actual head. The familiar voice and first name drew connections in his head.

"You're not Eric the Barber. I bet you're Eric Montreaux."

Eric's avatar blushed a little. "Well, okay, but don't tell anyone."

'You're God', came to Toras's mind, but he didn't let it reach his mouth. Too tacky. Eric Montreaux was one of two founders of Alter Realm and the lead designer for The Endless Age. He was famous for not ever using the new world himself, not even playing it once in testing, because it would never live up to his expectations. Obviously that was either no longer true, or just a myth.

"Anyway, you're here for a haircut, huh? Get that mess of fur tidied up?" Eric cleaved the scissors in the air. His avatar moved so fluidly that it was hard to imagine it was the subject of careful choreography.

Toras nodded again, then smiled, then remembered to actually answer the question. "Sure. Yeah. Someone told me that if I went on this quest, I could 'improve my lupine nature'. I assume that means I get to upgrade my avatar, which really means realistically wolfy—"

"Well, sit down!" Eric said, and motioned. The world blurred in the visor as Toras was forcibly stuck into the 'chair'. "Here goes!"

"Wait, don't I get to pick? I don't want to be a frog or something!" Toras complained, voice rising back through time to a childish brat whine fueled by mental fatigue and shock denial at what the experimental haptics had just done to him.

Eric's avatar brandished some absurdly over-grown shears. "Well, you don't get to pick, nope. But I know just what you need..." With the first cut, the visual cut out. In its place, Toras saw a familiar picture: the picture of Toras Loup-d'Or, done by Skwirl.

"How do you know about that?" Toras continued to whine. He recalled being a teenager, doodling poorly-drawn werewolves in his notebook, slowly amassing a collection of lupine artifacts, wishing he could see his arms covered in tawny gold fur.

"You know, it's a funny thing..." Eric's disembodied voice said, as the wolf picture dissolved and flickered around into flecks, swirling into a physical form of shimmering colored spots. Every so often, a snip-snip sound effect trickled into his ears. "When I got the whole Alter Realm project started, furry fans were some of the first people to really try and make use of it all the way. They really pushed for scripting and reactive movement, face tracking, reflections—haptics. I've actually been good friends with a few since the late 90's. It wasn't too hard to find a few people who knew something about you."

"You mean you were stalking me?" Toras watched the colored spots fly around like a flock of birds, sometimes forming into vague shapes and disappearing like figures in the clouds.

"Don't think of it that way. Think of it as keeping an eye on you."

"I don't like that," Toras said, watching the 3D image dissolve to nothing again. The room reappeared. "That's pretty big-brother."

"Well, I don't expect you to. But I expect that you're going to love this. Did I take enough off the back?" Eric's avatar held up a hand-mirror. In it, Toras saw the same thing he did the last time he was near a virtual mirror, the virtual body that he'd finally grown tired of.

"Hey, it looks the same," he said.

"Maybe you need to let it grow in a bit," Eric's avatar grinned.

"This is so stupid!" Toras yelled, and dragged his avatar out of the chair.

"I'm not joking. Go sleep on it a little."

Toras panicked. "No! Don't do that weird shit again!" He didn't care if he sounded childlike in the outburst—it was self-preservation. His avatar flailed as his visor failed to interpret his panicked arm-wave in reality. "What the hell is going on around here? This pointless quest shit? Hacking my visor to—to— What, did you flash the firmware or something? The haptics were shut off! What if I was in public?"

Eric changed the subject. "Toras... that's just your last name backwards, isn't it?"

"What's my name have to do with anything?"

"Jean Sarot's a grad student at MIT, right? Playing with really awesome toys? And how happy is he? I give him something totally awesome, something few people get to experience, all that haptics stuff, and he panics. Just like everyone else, they all panic." Eric dissolved the barber shop and replaced it with a virtual home, just like Toras' apartment. "That's why we don't use that stuff yet. That's why we have guys like you working on it, hammering it out, plugging people into it to see how they twitch around. It's all a big test, and it's really damn important. This whole Alter Realm thing is still just the beginning of redefining identity and self. Even moreso when these haptics get worked out."

Toras stared, dumbfounded. "Yeah, I know."

"You know. You know and you're honest," Eric said. Toras stared as Eric's avatar gestured, almost pixel-perfect as an enthusiastic professor. "You're honest about your vanity, about wanting to look the way you want, maybe a little ashamed. You're vain because you're human, not because you need attention. Am I right?" Toras nodded enough for his lupine self to deliver a firm nod of approval. "I can empathize. I've made my body here the way I wish it was. I bet you have a million friends who wish they were wolves or bats or anteaters or whatever. What would happen if they got what they wanted? Would they be happy?"

"I don't know... wait. The way you wish it was?"

"Be careful what you wish for. You feel something inside, right? Underneath the vain need for your appearance? I feel something inside, too. I feel how I used to feel," Eric said, and the virtual environment flickered away. It was replaced by a low-quality real video feed of a man sitting at a computer, head tilted to the side. It was Eric; the face was the same, but his body was twisted, contorted in an electric wheelchair, left hand the only one capable of more than trivial movements. His face seemed half-lifeless, literally blank across the right side. "I'll never feel that way again, not unless they pony up those stem cells everyone's been talking about. On the best of days, I can be anything I want in here. On the worst of days, it does a damn good job of taking my mind off the fact I'm probably gonna die of pneumonia by the time I'm sixty."

Toras flinched. "I..." His realization stopped the words from coming out. Being a wolf was a very personal use for Alter Realm, but it wasn't the only one at all.

"Look, Toras. Jean. Whatever you really want to be called. You think that The Endless Age is a game? It's a graveyard. It's an idea that didn't work so well, and the only reason it's around is that people, well, they just love visiting graveyards. El Dorado, and now Alter Realm, that's better. That's pushing people's buttons. El Dorado was a place where you can have whatever you want, but you lost it all when you left. Right? Well, now that it's reborn in Alter Realm, no one has to leave." The real Eric's voice was harder to understand, slurred and halting. As he talked, the real image faded into the virtual, physically whole Eric. His voice evened out, virtualized, and Toras tried to imagine how much horsepower it was taking some system somewhere to throw inflection into a near flawlessly synthesized voice.

Eric kept on. "That whole quest, well, I just made it up. I felt like playing The Wizard, but I made it kill people so that I wouldn't actually have to grant everyone a wish or something. I made it because I liked the idea of having someone get something special, I guess. I wanted to give someone something to show what we're capable of, and I wanted it to be someone special. So, I figured anyone who had the haptics stuff in their headset was special enough, different enough. Someone with that stuff wouldn't die. Call it a total shot in the dark. Well, it turns out you're—"

Toras butted in. "That's bullshit. I'm not special. What are the chances someone like me would randomly blunder into that quest? You set it all up. You hacked something into that dragon, that cartographer or whatever, about me. If you wanted to give me something, you could have just talked to me. Why couldn't you just—"

"Toras, Jean, whatever, I did it because I could. You want to work at things because you feel shorted otherwise. Right? You want to be what you want because you're human. Right?

117

Besides, would you have even taken this if you hadn't felt you earned it somehow?" Eric was right, but that didn't make it any less unpleasant that he knew all that about Toras.

Confused, Toras nodded and then quivered as he reconsidered the motion only after it happened. "Earned what? A near death experience with haptics? I still look the same, and you keep dodging the question of, 'why me?'"

Eric didn't waver. "I said you should go sleep on it," he said, his face hardening slightly. "Sleep on it," he said with finality.

Toras sighed and bid Eric farewell. As soon as he made his final wave, his avatar instantly transported back to the starting point of the 'quest'. He worked over what had happened in his mind, and despite Eric's assurance to the contrary, the former lead programmer for The Endless Age seemed an awful lot like the bald little man pulling strings behind the curtain. Click your heels and go home. Go to sleep. Toras clicked his headset off instead.

The next time Toras logged on, his wolf was right where he'd left it, hidden as he'd long since turned off auto-sleep to make testing and research easier. He transplanted back into Alter Realm and wandered around his bedroom, both in real life and in the virtual simulation. His room was the same, his wolf avatar was the same, and the little quest was very likely to be some kind of pointless exercise to live out someone else's fantasy of playing wizard or fairy god-mother or choose-your-own-modern-equivalent. The use of the haptics was another puzzle, and maybe a dangerous precedent, as was Eric's refusal to answer Toras' questions.

On a complete lark, he called the person who had so often been the yang to Toras' yin: Jason. As soon as the line connected, he blurted, "Jason, this is crazy."

"Yeah? Telephones are pretty crazy. You can talk, and it comes out someone's ear instantly thousands of miles away! Next you'll tell me that you can write words and someone else can read them instantly somewhere else too!" Jason was eating something, probably potato chips.

Toras sighed and punched the sleep command in the game simulation without a second thought, then took his visor off and went old-fashioned with his phone up against his ear. "I just got to thinking how crazy this AR stuff really is, how it just takes away my friend on the street and replaces him with a freaking squirrel. And this damn Endless Age, it's just a roleplaying game mausoleum. I just spent a week of vacation on a quest because people were nagging me about my avatar, and what's the final outcome? I meet one of the programmers, but he doesn't do anything but go on about the future of AR and never answered my questions about what he was really up to."

"Huh. Hey, speaking of squirrels, I heard that guy you know was totally banged up in a wreck," Jason said, mid-chew.

"Yeah, he's doing okay." Toras' voice caught. I just heard from Cliff about it. Broke a lot of stuff but he's going to be alright, unless he gets one of those superbug things from the hospital.

"You know, I wasn't even thinking about that. Maybe I was. Maybe I was thinking about Skwirl and how I was... nevermind," Toras said. His face burned, the only relief coming from the fact that Jason couldn't see him. Toras omitted the fact that he hadn't even bothered to find out more about Skwirl since Cliff had told him.

"That's awful. Well, that he got banged up. Anyway, hey, a bunch of people and food showed up. So, I'm gonna have to cut off this crazy new fangled telephone thing and go get fatter. Later."

Toras barely had time to bid Jason farewell before the line went dead. He put the phone down and looked at his visor. He contemplated ditching it and his research tester position and his dissertation on virtual reality testing theory and all the old New England baggage that came from the area. For that matter, he wasn't a wolf and would never be a wolf, unless genetics advanced

119

far enough to fix everything and wave its magic wand over him. At that point, he could be whatever he wanted, Eric could have his body back, and everyone would live happily ever after.

Then, he remembered: Sleep on it. Sleep. Everything in Alter Realm/The Endless Age reloads after waking up from sleep, like starting up the environment from a cold save. That's why he never used auto-sleep; it got in the way of his testing efforts in case he had to take a real-life break for a moment or two. Either by twitch reflex he had put his avatar to sleep, or maybe he'd been acting on Eric's suggestion. He put the visor back on and logged in.

Buzzing swarmed over his head, focused around the scalp line just above his ears, as the haptic system turned on again. Just like before, Toras realized what was happening too late to stop it, his body numbed and stunned. His virtual self glowed and re-wove itself, sparkles crawling over the body in tune with the strange creeping sensations that the haptics used to indicate touch. Disoriented and half-panicked, the real Toras cowered onto his sofa, while a banner hung over his virtual head. It read: "Gratuitous Magical Transformation".

When the crawling sparkles died off, Toras was still a golden wolf, but everything was upgraded. His color was now an appropriately golden yellow, complete with a sheen to it when light hit a certain way. The body underneath was far from perfect, something more akin to Toras's actual self in its mesomorphic adequacy than the more typical over-built and perfect-toned musculature that users picked. The visual effect was on par with RedOrion's stunner of a fox avatar, a virtual adaptation of SkwirlMastr's expensive watercolor painting of Toras Loup-d'Or.

Along with the skin changes, Toras' avatar was now haptics-enabled, no doubt thanks to the forced circumvention of software locks in his visor. As he held his arms up in the game, the visor rendered over his hands with gold fur and black clawnails, but it also sent a strange new skitter over his skin.

When he reflexively touched over one arm, the skitter became like a monstrous tickle, sending shivers over every inch of his body. One hand felt fur, the other felt a hand stroking fur. The sensation came with a strange duality, some of the tickling from the electrical contacts at his neck confusing his brain as it tried to fool him into feeling. The tickling sensation made him want to giggle, and the emotional realization made him want to outright laugh. As he tried to stifle the reflex, another new feeling cropped up, like the sides of his head were rising up in twin points to the sky. Then another, this time extending from his backside in a borderline prurient way, producing a rhythmic sense of sweep. His smile grew even wider when he realized that he was wagging his tail.

Despite the glitches, it worked. It worked on such a deep level that he didn't want to believe it was real. He'd been through enough haptics tests of his own to know better. Pieces of the early haptics trials fell through his mind: simulating something brushing the skin as part of phobia exposure therapy, mapping radar coordinates to the skin for touch-reflex information in military combat, adding tactile sensation to virtual object manipulation. Toras had done it already, had touched the frontier of simulation science, but it had been imperfect, with enough failure that the general public would not have access to even the basics for at least another year. Never had it been assembled like this.

What he felt from his new avatar was beyond that frontier. Alter Realm gave him, and anyone else who was logged in, the power to overwrite his body with what he wanted, with what they wanted. Now, it gave him the power to overwrite his body with how it should feel, to himself and anyone else who was equipped with the technology. The new sensation of animal self felt like the missing piece of a puzzle, and as the image formed to completion, every moment of teenage angst and vanity over his in-world appearance died.

He didn't throw the visor in the trash and move to California. Jean Sarot finally knew what it was like to be Toras, what it had to be like for the paralyzed Eric Montreaux to get a new body, and what it was going to be like for everyone someday.

The new fur, the new body, the haircut Eric the Barber gave him—it was what he had been searching for. Now, all he had to do was find out why Eric had given it to him.

Kody is still reeling from his last breakup. What will it take for him to open his eyes and move on?

Total Opposites

Graveyard Greg

Kody was staring moodily into his bowl of cornflakes when he heard his roommate's footsteps rattle down the stairs. "Morning," the lean muscled otter said, yawning briefly before scratching his hip. He was naked as usual, his tail swaying rhythmically as he rummaged through the fridge for breakfast. He finally settled on a slice of cantaloupe and apple juice. "Kody, you know I love you like a brother, but you really should learn to not leave your underwear in the hallway where dainty otter paws might step on them, and would it kill you to put the dishes in the—" He paused as he finally saw the look on Kody's face. "You're thinking about him again, aren't you?" He sat down and studied his friend's face, brushing a lock of pink-dyed hair from his forehead as he did so. "Din't even try to deny it. So what's wrong?"

"I was too big for him," Kody replied, eyes staring blankly at his cornflakes.

"Okay. So?"

"I just read that in his blog."

"Ouch! Well, it's not a lie, but he's still a fucker for using that excuse. How long has it been since he lead you on and then dumped you?"

"He didn't lead me on, Dion."

"Hon, you went out for three months. I'd call that leading you on, most definitely."

Kody looked directly at the otter, causing his roommate to back away instinctively. "He didn't lead me on. I'm seven feet tall and weigh almost four hundred pounds. When we stayed at his place, we had to move the mattress on the floor if we didn't want to break his bed."

"Okay, so we have a difference of opinion. He still dumped you, and that means we have to make sure you go out tonight to forget Jimmy once and for all."

"Jeremy."

The otter grinned, his pearly teeth flashing in the morning sunlight. "See? We're going to have to work harder to make you forget his name."

"Not funny. I liked him. I might've even been in love with him."

The otter rolled his eyes and sucked on the cantaloupe. "Please! You only knew him for three months. I've dated people for a lot longer and never fell in love once."

Kody couldn't think of a suitable comeback. He wasn't witty like his roommate, nor did he consider himself an exceptionally fast thinker. "Well," he rumbled, "you move too fast anyway."

The otter laughed. "Live fast, die hard, and wear a condom." He sipped some of his apple juice delicately, then guided the conversation back to more important matters. "We need to go to the Discotheque tonight. The music will be loud, the bass will be thumping. It's perfect for a single bear on the hunt for some ass."

"I'm not on the hunt, Dion."

"Not yet, you're not. Once you get to the club your predatory nature will take over, and I'll bet you'll tell me not to come home tonight."

"I'm not going out with you tonight, Dion."

"Ohhh yes you are."

"Tonight is game night with my friends. I'm not cancelling just because you think I need to date someone."

The otter leaned back in his chair looking smug. "You are such a geek, I swear. When are you gonna start playing D&D again?"

"I'm not. Everyone wants to play Fourth Edition, and I think it sucks."

"Sure you do," smirked Dion, rising from his chair. He kissed the bear's cheek as he passed. "But we both know you'll play it eventually."

Kody was not going to admit Dion was right, so he quickly changed the subject. "You still going out?"

The otter shrugged as he walked back up the stairs, thick tail swishing behind him. "Yeah, but I might stop by Steve's place, just to see what you guys are playing. Some of your friends are kind of hot, and there might just be a bit of a geek inside me locked away."

Kody shook his head, wondering how in the world someone half his height could have such a monstrous ego.

Kody entered Steve's house, and this time managed to not bump his head as he ducked under the door. "Hey Steve," he said to the lanky greyhound.

Steve grinned and wagged his tail happily. "Kody! I didn't think you were going to make it tonight."

Kody rolled his eyes. "Let me guess. You already heard about Jeremy's parting shot."

Steve nodded. "He posted all the sordid details on his journal."

Kody shook his head slowly, a wry smile on his face. The greyhound was grinning like a lunatic. *Here comes the punchline,* he thought.

"You should have told us how much you like role playing in bed, Kody. I hear they have therapy for that!"

Kody faked a punch towards Steve, who jumped back giggling. "You're a dork, Steve."

"Can't hear you, Kody. You're too tall."

"Ha, ha. Very funny. So where is everybody?"

"Ronnie's going to be late: he's bringing some new guy with him. Just moved to the area. Chris is in the bathroom, and Jordan's gone to get some snack food."

Kody sat down on the sofa and stretched his legs. A few joints popped and he sighed in relief. "A new guy?"

Steve plopped down beside the bear. "Yeah, I don't know much about him, but Ronnie vouches for him, and you know he wouldn't do that unless he really trusts a guy."

"I dunno, he vouched for you, and the verdict's still out on that."

Steve jabbed at Kody's stomach, his knuckles barely brushing the bear. "Jerk."

"You love me anyway." He ruffled Steve's headfur with a grin.

A tall iguana emerged from the bathroom. "Hey Kody!"

"Chris!" Kody got up from the sofa to engulf his friend in a hug. "How was Vegas?"

While the iguana was tall, he was still shorter than Kody. "Going home is always nice, but I swear if I have to help my brother fix one more car I'll kill him."

Kody chuckled as he sat back down. "Hello, Mister Negative Attitude. You're never going to have fun if you don't think positive."

"I'm positive I'm going to kill my brother if I have to help him fix one more car when I'm in Vegas. There. Is that any better?"

Before Kody could answer, a kangaroo came in through the front door. "Oh, God," he said, feigning shock, "who let the bear in the house?" He set down the two bags he was carrying and folded his arms. Kody was pleased that the label on the snack chips read 'Moritos', his favorite.

"Don't you know how to knock, Rooboy?" Kody retorted as the kangaroo bounded over and jumped into the bear's lap to give him a brief hug.

"Haven't you learned my name yet? We've only been friends for years!"

"Fine, Jordan, but I still think Rooboy would be a great name for you."

"No it wouldn't—you know I hate that name."

"That's why he calls you that, Jordan," Steve said, with mock seriousness. "Kody's pure evil. Don't you read Jeremy's blog?"

"I am going to kill you, Steve." The bear snarled menacingly, then stuck out his tongue. "Whatever game we play, you're my target."

Steve stuck his tongue back at Kody. "Your loss, big guy," he shrugged, "we're playing a cooperative game tonight."

"That Settlers game?"

"Yup!"

It had been a while since Kody had last played Settlers. "And you're not going to trade with me at all now, are you?"

"Nope!"

A knock on the door interrupted the banter. Steve answered it. A stocky young bull terrier came in and hugged Steve the moment the door opened. "Sorry I'm late. Len got off work late, and needed to shower." He then saw Kody, and grinned. "Oh, good. Kody made it."

Kody arched an eyebrow as Ronnie went over to hug him. He remained on the sofa to hug the bull terrier, as Ronnie was barely over five feet tall. "Yeah, of course I made it. Why?"

"Oh...no reason."

Kody felt his pelt bristle at the suspicious remark. "You really drive me crazy sometimes," he said coldly as he straightened himself back up.

Ronnie gave a sad little look. "Only sometimes? I'll have to try harder." The terrier winked at Steve and grinned. "Leonard's bringing a cooler of sodas. I told him a couple of two liters would be fine, but he has this obsession with canned drinks." Another knock came to the door. "And that's gotta be him."

A tall giraffe stood outside, so tall Kody couldn't see his head from his seat on the couch. The lintel only came up to his shoulders. He wore a blue midriff shirt, the exposed white fur insufficient to hide the development of a nice six-pack of abs. He had a nice chest, reasonably developed, but what Kody found attractive were the long bangs of blond hair and blue eyes of the stranger that came into view once he ducked under the door frame. In his arms he carried a large container. "I hope you guys don't mind me bringing a cooler?"

"I already mentioned your thing for canned drinks, Len." Steve took one of the cooler's handles to help carry it in. "Guys, this is Leonard. Len, these are the guys."

"Pleasure to meet you all." He glanced around with a smile, but Kody thought his gaze seemed to linger on him a little longer than the others. "Please, call me Len. I don't have a clue why Stevie constantly calls me by my full name."

Steve's ears twitched at the nickname. "Because maybe you keep on calling me Stevie?"

"Well, you started it by refusing to call me Len."

"Hm, you win this round. Let's get the sodas in the kitchen."

It only took Len and Steve a moment to drain the melted ice from the cooler, while Jordan, Chris and Ronnie introduced themselves. Kody felt he should stand up to introduce himself properly. Secretly, he really wanted to see how he measured up against the giraffe.

Len smiled at the bear, saying "I don't think I've met many people almost as tall as me." Kody came up to his shoulders, which did make him feel strangely short compared to his spotty admirer. He stuck out his hand. "Like Steve said, I'm Leonard, but my friends call me Len," Kody stood there in silence, his eyes locked onto the giraffe's blue ones. "So, what's your name?"

"Huh?" The room cracked up, breaking the spell. Kody glared at his friends. Len grinned and pulled the bear's hand over to shake it.

"Your name?" he repeated teasingly. "You know, that thing you were given when you were born? The verbal tag people use to identify you?"

"Oh—Oh! My name's Kody."

Len's smile widened triumphantly. "And we have progress! It's a pleasure, Kody. Though it remains to be seen exactly how much of a pleasure it's going to be." He winked down at the bear, who was still slack-jawed. "You look thirsty. Can I offer you a drink?"

"I...I dunno," Kody stammered.

Len chuckled briefly, and nudged Kody on the shoulder lightly as he leaned forward to whisper in his ear. "Well? Do you want one or not?"

Kody blinked twice, snapping himself out of his daze. "Oh. Uhm. Sure, I'd love to have a drink."

Len smiled as he opened up the lid on the cooler. "I've got your choice of Sprite, Pepsi, Orange Fanta, and Pibb Extra."

"I like Pibb Extra," Kody replied.

"Oooh, I think I'm going to like you. I have a love affair with Pibb and the PhD equivalent." He handed Kody a can, then looked over the bear's shoulder at Steve. "So, what're we playing?"

"Settlers of Catan."

"I haven't played that game in ages," Len said happily as he slid his arm around Kody's and led him to the table. Ronnie was laying out the game board and pieces. "I call the red piece."

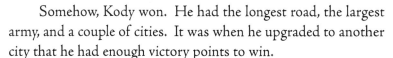

Somehow, Kody won. He had the longest road, the largest army, and a couple of cities. It was when he upgraded to another city that he had enough victory points to win.

"Damn," Len said, "I thought I was going to win next turn." He gave the bear a warm smile. "Good game."

Kody found Len's smile to be infectious, or perhaps it was the fact the giraffe was gracious in defeat. "Thanks."

"If you two lovebirds are done flattering each other," Ronnie interjected as gathered up the pieces, "why don't you two go to the store and get us more snacks?"

"Why us?" Kody started, but Len took him by the wrist.

"With victory comes the dreadful task of being the buyer of snacks," Len announced. "Don't worry, Kody, we'll buy snacks we like."

Kody let himself be led out towards the driveway, and Len grinned at him sheepishly. "I rode with Ronnie," he said, "so I promise to drive next time we're saddled with getting snacks."

"It's a deal, but..."

"But?"

"Why do I have a feeling we're being set up?" Kody asked as he walked over to his black truck, a "Super Duty" model large enough for his long legs and bulky frame.

"Because you are, to be honest. I admit, I asked Ronnie if he knew anyone who was single, and..."

Kody unlocked the doors. "And they knew I was single."

"Is that a problem?" Len asked as he climbed in.

Kody felt the blood rush to his cheeks. Len's eyes never left his. Everyone else he'd ever dated could never make eye contact with him, instead choosing to focus on his chest or his muscles. He understood women's "my eyes are up here" line all too well. While he wasn't a bodybuilder by anyone's standard, he was built solidly, like a wall. This giraffe, though...he was a bodybuilder. His physique was well developed through what must have been several years of dedication. He wasn't pumped to a steroid-induced size, but the sight was somewhat intimidating to the bear, and all the giraffe did was look into his eyes. "I...I guess not."

"You're a bear of few words, aren't you?" Len looked away for a moment as Kody pulled out of the driveway and drove down the street. "Am I being too forward?"

"No! It's just that...well, I haven't been single for that long." The words were difficult to force out, and he felt once he admitted it, that would be that, and the handsome giraffe wouldn't be interested anymore.

Instead, Len placed his hand over Kody's thigh. "You're not on the rebound, are you?"

"I don't think I am, but my ex just posted some really hateful things online."

"Some exes will do that. Lord only knows why they would. I'm not making you uncomfortable with all these personal questions, am I?"

Kody shook his head a bit too emphatically, and then regretted it, feeling desperate. "No, but I don't want to give you the wrong idea. I don't know if I'm really in the game right now."

"I'm always in the game until I win. Or I tackle the first cute guy I see." Len followed up that statement with a wink. "I'm just teasing. What do you do for a living?"

"I'm a stockperson at the Val-U-Mart."

Len nodded, his eyes trailing down to the bear's thick arms. "I can believe it, looking at you. I bet you're very strong, even for someone your size."

Kody felt himself nodding automatically, wishing he could look at the giraffe instead of the road. "You're probably a lot stronger than me, though."

Len grinned, and folded his hands on his lap. "Maybe, but I don't like to brag. Guess what I do for a living?"

Kody blurted out the first thing that came to mind. "Professional model?"

The giraffe's laugh was soft, which felt out of place for one as huge as he was. "Lord, no. Just because I'm built like an underwear model doesn't mean I want to be one!" He flashed Kody a pearly smile. "No, I work in construction. I lug around all kinds of heavy stuff when I'm not doing paperwork. Gives me a good workout, it does. The lifting, I mean."

Kody nodded automatically again, his eyes looking down at the giraffe's mightily well-developed arm and the hand that was

TOTAL OPPOSITES

previously on his leg. He didn't say anything—he was afraid he couldn't speak without stuttering.

"Kody? Are you sure I'm not being too forward?" Len asked with a tilt of his head.

Kody took a moment to work out his response. He wanted to make certain Len would believe him. "No, I was lost in thought. I'm just not used to someone taking an interest in me anymore."

"It must've been a bad breakup for you to end up thinking like that."

Kody kept his focus on the road, looking for the neon lights of the grocery store. Len was a bit too observant, or maybe Ronnie had informed the giraffe of the details. "I...kind of, yeah."

"I'll stop being nosy, then. I don't want to scare you off."

Kody parked the truck, got out and followed the giraffe into the store, but he found himself staring at that broad back, wondering what his spotty admirer saw in him, and why he was unable to reciprocate. Maybe he simply wanted to be left alone, but no one else seemed to want that for him. Could it be his friends knew him better than he knew himself? Most likely.

"What kind of chips do you think the guys would like?" Len asked, checking the labels of a couple of super-sized bags. "I'm partial to cheddar cheese flavored chips, myself."

"We usually buy sour cream, fiesta ranch mix, and corn chips."

"That's a good idea. How about you get the mix stuff, and I'll buy a couple bags of these?

"Sounds like a plan."

Len trawled through the selection as Kody headed to the dairy aisle for the sour cream, then crossed the store for the fiesta mix near the produce section. This gave him too much time to think about how handsome or good-natured Len was, and why he wouldn't be a good match for the giraffe. Len was too good to be true, while Kody felt anything but.

"You found the stuff you need?" asked Len, looking over the aisle. He waved two bags of white corn tortilla chips, Kody's

133

favourite. It was a lucky guess on Len's part, perhaps, but one that further ingratiated him to the bear.

"Yeah, I did. You ready?"

"Yup. You think these chips will do?"

"Yeah." Kody smiled up at Len. It was easy to feel good around someone as cheerful as the giraffe, and Kody decided to go with the flow.

On the drive back to Steve's house the giraffe was quiet compared to how much he talked up until now. Kody didn't feel that it was an awkward kind of silence, but it certainly was odd how Len didn't say anything. When Kody pulled up in the driveway, Len grinned at him.

"I've been doing some thinking, Kody."

"Oh?" Kody put the truck in park and turned off the engine.

Len nodded, then unbuckled his seat belt so he could turn to face the bear. "I think I have to give you this." He handed Kody a business card that looked too small between big fingers with well-manicured fingernails. The bear took it, conscious of his own rough, blunt claw tips, noticing a phone number was scrawled on it in blue ink. "That's my phone number. I normally don't give it out to people I just met, but you strike me as the shy type."

Kody felt the blood rush to his cheeks. Len was certainly right about that!

The giraffe grinned once again. It was almost a default setting. "You're too cute for your own good." He gently cupped Kody's face with his large hands and looked right into the bear's eyes for several seconds before nodding to himself, as if coming to some sort of conclusion. "I get home tomorrow around three. You can call me after four, alright?"

Kody nodded as best he could, the sides of his head still cradled between the giraffe's hands. "I can't make any promises, Len. I'm not sure if I want to date right now." He felt it was good to be honest with Len; as attracted as he was to the giraffe, he was a bit unsure of his own readiness to get back into the dating game.

Len released Kody's head, folding his arms across his chest. He studied Kody's expression a bit more before saying, "Fair enough...but that just brings me to my last point."

"And what's that?"

"That I think we're bound to be friends, and friends should know how to get in touch with one another. So now that you have my number, if you don't call me, I'll be forced to call you." Kody didn't ask how Len would be able to call him, because something about the giraffe told him he could easily get his phone number. "It's been nice to meet you for the first time, Kody. We'll have to find out if our second meet will be just as nice." The giraffe gave Kody's cheek one last pat, then stepped out of the truck and into the house.

They played Settlers of Catan again, but this time Len defeated Kody and the others soundly. Of course, this time Kody was terribly distracted by the immense weight of a small business card in his back pocket.

Kody was sure a phone call to Len the very next day would make him appear desperate, so he told himself he would ring the day after. He didn't, though. A voice in his head stopped him—an irritating little voice that convinced him that he wasn't good enough, regardless of the situation.

More days passed. He wanted to call, but hesitated every time. The old fears and doubts invaded his every thought. It also started to affect his mood at home, something Dion noticed after the second day.

"You haven't called him, have you?" Dion asked while the two were having lunch on the fifth day.

"Called who?" Kody replied, knowing full well who Dion was talking about.

"That guy who makes you look short. The one you met at Steve's? Why haven't you called him?"

Kody grunted and looked away stubbornly. "I don't want to talk about it."

"You never do, but if that's what you want, then fine." Dion went back to his lunch without another word. This was odd behaviour for the otter, as he usually kept after Kody until he 'fessed up; one of the many reasons why he loved him so much. Though he'd never admit it to Dion, he sometimes wondered why they never got together. Then he recalled how small the otter was compared to him. It was almost like an instant replay of his conversation with Jeremy.

The shrill electronic ring of the phone broke the bear out of his self pity, and he reached over to pick up the receiver. "Hello?"

A familiar deep voice replied, "You know, the usual waiting time to call someone you just met is three days. You're lucky you're cute. I don't usually call folks, even if I did threaten to call you. I have a rep to uphold."

Kody's mind went blank on him, the shock of the giraffe calling him too much to process for a moment. "Len? How did you get my..." His voice trailed off as he realized the culprit. "Who was it? Ronnie? Or did Steve give it to you?"

"Ronnie. Cute guy, but he's my best friend, and also a bit small for my tastes. Plus he's an alpha, and have you ever seen two of those dating? It's constant head butting, let me tell you. Still, he told me you might be shy about calling me, and gave me your number just in case. I hope you're okay with me being impatient."

"Yeah, I am. I would've called you eventually, because Dion would've bullied me into it," Kody said, sticking his tongue out at his roomie.

"Who's Dion?"

"My roommate."

"I like him already. He seems like a good pal to you. So are you going to ask me out, or do I have to be forward and see if you're free this weekend to hang out and practice the basics of being social?"

Kody took the bait. "Are you free this weekend?"

"Miraculously enough, I am. It's almost as if I was expecting a handsome critter of the ursine persuasion to ask me out." Kody could feel the smile Len must have had on his muzzle, and it made the bear grin in spite of himself.

"Dinner and a movie sound good?"

"That's very traditional, though I was going to suggest dinner at my place if you're okay with that—Unless you'd rather meet on a neutral field?"

Kody hesitated. The minute he sees how messy I am—wait, it's his place, not mine. Is that worse? He finally said "Sure. I'd love to do that."

"Then it's a date. I get off work on Friday at the usual time. Do you remember when that is?"

Kody did, and after saying his goodbyes he called Ronnie. "Thanks," he said when Ronnie answered.

The bull terrier chuckled on the other end. "I had to do it. You're so much happier when you're with someone. If you could only see the look you had on your face when you were talking to that big hulk. It was priceless."

Kody wondered if the current puzzled look on his features would be as priceless. "Huh. I'm surprised you didn't take pictures with your cell phone camera."

"I guess you'll have to find out if I did or not once I update my blog."

Kody thought better of challenging that. Instead he chose to end the conversation and get ready for work. It would be a long week until Friday, but he had something to look forward to that would get him through until then.

Naturally, by the time Friday rolled around he had to fight the urge to cancel the date. "I don't have anything to wear," he complained to Dion.

"You've got plenty of stuff to wear, you just have to wade through the pile of clothes that hides the floor," Dion replied, stepping over a small mountain of shirts as he carefully made his way to Kody's closet. "There is a floor here, right? It didn't get replaced by all the laundry, did it?"

"Thanks for trying to make me laugh, but this is serious. He's going to think I'm a slob."

"I was being serious, and by the way it's time for your reality check, Kody. You are a slob, you're just lucky I'm usually too busy being awesome to care."

"I never thought I'd be grateful for your ego. Now can you tell me what you're doing in my closet?"

Dion started sliding the clothes that were on the hangers from one side of the closet to the other. "I thought it would be obvious. I'm trying to find an outfit that actually looks good." He then smiled as he glanced over his shoulder towards the bear. "Of course, this may need a miracle or two, since all you ever wear are t-shirts and jeans."

Kody fell back against the bed, rubbing his face dejectedly. "I'm doomed. I'm going to screw this up. I just know it."

"Whine, whine. Ah, here we are!" Kody looked up to see Dion pulling out a purple buttondown shirt. It looked slightly wrinkled, but it was clean at least. "You'll have to iron this," Dion said, tossing the shirt to the bear.

"But I'm terrible at ironing."

"Oh, Christ, do I have to do everything to make sure you get some tail? Fine, I'll iron it later."

"I'm not going out with him to get laid, Dion," the bear started to protest, but knew it wouldn't do any good. With Dion, it was all about sex, and who to have sex with after that.

"Okay... I think these shorts will do. It's warm enough weather; I don't think Ben will think any less of you."

"His name's Len."

"It doesn't matter, because you'll be calling him 'Sir' soon enough."

Kody flumped on the bed again, rubbing his face with both hands this time. "It's hopeless."

Kody nervously brushed the wrinkles out of his shirt again, knowing full well they wouldn't go away. He pressed Len's doorbell. It's not too late to run like a scared cub, the little voice said, but it was. The fear of being a quitter outweighed the fear of embarrassing himself in front of the giraffe. Not by much maybe, but it was enough to keep him standing in place until Len answered the door.

Kody rang the doorbell again, starting to feel apprehensive. Why hasn't he answered yet? He brushed out the wrinkles yet again. Then the door opened and Len smiled down at Kody. He was dressed in a black turtleneck shirt, blue slacks, and there was the faint hint of cologne from him. The sight of Len threatened to turn the bear's legs into jelly. He stood upright through sheer fear of being embarrassed if he fainted.

"Kody! Sorry, I was putting the finishing touches on the pasta. I hope you have an appetite tonight, because I think I made too much." The giraffe then moved behind the door, making a sweeping gesture towards the interior of his house. "Come on in, would you like a drink?"

"Yes, please. Just water if you have it," Kody said, marveling at how the doorframe was tall enough for his ursine bulk, yet Len still towered above it. He took in the living room: there was a standard entertainment center with a nice wide-screen television, a set of bookshelves filled with hardback books and DVDs, and a large sofa facing the television. It was dust-free, and not a single thing was out of place. Even the pictures were perfectly straight.

"I'll be right back, then. Make yourself comfortable!" Len said as he headed into the kitchen. A pleasant aroma of cooking filled Kody's nostrils but did nothing to calm the butterflies in his stomach. He glanced at the hallway and the door leading to the outside world. It would be silly to leave now.

As soon as he sees what a messy person I am, he's going to be disgusted and never want to see me again, Kody thought miserably.

"Here's your water, Kody," Len said, holding a glass of water in front of the bear, who flinched in surprise.

"Oh! Thanks." To cover up his reaction, he quickly gestured at a picture of Len and a shorter female giraffe. "Who's that in the picture with you?"

Len looked at the picture in question, a small smile forming on his muzzle. "That's my sister Lynette. She lives here with me, and you might get to meet her. She's my best friend to boot."

"Really? Wow, that's nice. I'd drive my older sister crazy if I lived with her."

Len chuckled at that. "Oh, I can't see how that could happen." Before Kody could think up of a reason, a persistent beep came from the kitchen. "Dinner's ready! Come on and sit in the dining room, and I'll get the food. You like spaghetti?" Len asked as he ushered Kody into the next room, which already had plates and utensils for two on the table.

"I love spaghetti."

"Well good, because I make a very nice sauce, and pretty decent garlic bread. Now go on, sit. I'll be right back with dinner."

A few moments after Kody sat down Len brought in a large steaming pot, and then repeated this for the sauce and garlic bread. He served Kody first before getting some for himself, and then sat down to eat his meal.

Len was right about the sauce; the basil tomatoes it was made from gave it a zest that rivaled most restaurants and it had enough ground beef to satisfy any carnivore. The garlic bread was understated, as it practically melted in Kody's mouth with the buttery taste. Kody was enjoying the bread so much, as a matter of fact, that he didn't notice Len's gaze on him until he went for thirds on the spaghetti.

"Kody? You have some crumbs on your shirt," Len said, covering his mouth from what the bear first thought to be embarrassment, but after he heard the first quiet snicker, Kody realized the giraffe was trying hard not to laugh. "In fact," Len said, taking a napkin to catch the crumbs that he brushed off of the bear's shirt, "I'd say I could make half a loaf with all of them." He folded the napkin twice, setting it down next to his plate.

Kody glanced over that door, wondering how fast he would need to move to be through it before Len noticed his after-image fading. "I'm—I'm sorry. I didn't mean to make such a mess."

Len made a dismissive gesture. "Oh, don't worry about it. It's rather flattering, you know."

Kody canted his head slightly. "It is? How's that?"

"You must really love my cooking if you're not paying attention. That's a very nice compliment. Thank you."

Kody blinked, not expecting that reaction. In fact, Len almost seemed happy to clean up the crumbs from Kody's shirt. No, it's my imagination, he thought. "I do love your cooking. I'm stuffed, though; can't eat another bite!"

"Then let me put the leftovers on the oven to keep them warm for my sister. Why don't you sit down on the sofa and I'll bring in dessert?"

"Alright, but let me wash my plate."

"You're my guest, I won't let you. Now go," Len said, gently maneuvering Kody to the living room. "I'll just let the dishes soak in the sink. I hope you like strawberry shortcake."

Kody sat down on the sofa, the butterflies slightly mollified by the food in his belly. He was replaying the scene dealing with the crumbs in his head when suddenly the front door opened, and Kody saw a female giraffe duck through it. The resemblance to Lynette in the picture was perfect. "Oh, hi!" she said. "You must be Kody. My brother said he was having company over."

"Hi, you must be Lynette," Kody said as he stood up to shake her hand, and he couldn't help but notice how he was eye level to her neck. She was dressed in a basketball uniform, and after shaking Kody's hand she discarded her jacket onto the sofa, then

141

removed her shoes, tossing them casually on the floor where they bounced in separate directions.

"It's really nice to meet you, Kody," Lynette said before calling out to her brother. "Hey Len! I'm home! Where are you?"

Len emerged from the kitchen, holding two plates, each loaded with a large slice of cake. "You're home early. Would you like some spaghetti?" he asked, placing the desserts on the coffee table. He then casually picked up his sister's shoes and jacket, placing the former next to the door and hanging up the latter on the coat rack.

"I'd love some," Lynette answered, and Len went back into the kitchen to get her a plate. "It's so endearing," she said, sitting on the armrest of the sofa. "I think he actually enjoys picking up after me."

That statement made things click in Kody's brain: the immaculate apartment, the crumbs, the shoes—Len genuinely enjoyed cleaning. No wonder Ronnie set them up. "Do you think so?"

"Oh, I'm almost certain. I try not to be too messy, but I can't help it. I'm lazy at home. Len never complains, and he's the honest type. If something bothers him, he'll let you know all about it."

"Are you telling Kody all of my flaws already, sis? You move fast," Len chuckled, handing her a plate of spaghetti and a can of soda. "So, Kody, are you having a nice time?"

Kody smiled, genuinely feeling it. "I sure am, Len. I'll have to cook for you next time, though."

"I'd like that."

Kody did, admittedly, try to keep his shirt crumb-free, but he devoured the cake with relish and failed completely. Len happily cleaned him up with a wide grin.

As their evening drew to a close, Len walked Kody to his truck. "Tonight was fun," Kody said, and before Len could reply the bear took him by the hands and kissed him. Len stiffened from surprise, but quickly relaxed as he returned the kiss. It ended all too soon for Kody, but he knew there would be more opportunities to come.

To be a successful runner, you must constantly navigate the knife's edge. The lure of a big paycheck may prove deadly for Roland's crew as someone pulls the blade from beneath their feet.

DOUBLE BLIND

Teiran

The alleyway was quiet, even though there were close to fifty people waiting in line hoping to get into the Powerline club. The crowd of people in the queue was all dressed in trendy and expensive clothes, flashy gear that included leather and piercings, and they weren't talking much. The three of them were getting close to the front of the line now, and so Roland sub-vocalized, "We ready everybody?" The words were barely more than thoughts, but because of the otter's extensive cybernetic enhancements, they were transferred wirelessly to his crew. There was a slight hiss of static only Roland could hear as the radio transceiver built into the otter's ears connected with the rest of the team.

"Check," rumbled the deep voice of Boris, and even though the bull had sub vocalized the word, the big man was standing so close to Roland that the otter's unnaturally augmented hearing picked it up anyway.

A burst of powerful dance music crossed the line as Gina said "Check Baby," in a sultry whisper that would be lost in the noise of the club's interior.

"Check one, two," Richard quipped, and Roland twitched his thick tail in annoyance. The fool horse said the words in a normal voice, and the words echoed in the quiet alleyway. A couple other people waiting in line glanced at him oddly, but most ignored him before returning to their own personal worlds. Ever since the highly sophisticated internal computer commlinks that Roland, Boris, and Richard sported became so cheap and easy to install that you could get one in a mall like it was an ear piercing, people had gotten used to folks who talked to thin air and seeing things no one else could see. Funny how even brain surgery seems normal when everyone is doing it. Nobody even thought of Richard's chrome cybernetic arms as weird anymore.

"We're good Boss, everyone has good signal." Brian said quietly. "I'm bringing the tactical network feeds online now." Roland's vision of the world flickered for a moment, the way an old time video screen would flicker when changing channels.

Across the otter's vision, four windows opened in the air and after a moment of buffering, they began streaming the live feeds of everyone in his crew. Boris and Richard's video windows were déjà vu inducing picture in pictures of the alleyway from slightly different angles because they were both standing behind him. Brian's stream showed the inside of the van as the German Shepherd monitored several computer screens at once, his fingers dancing over keyboards and controls that existed only in the Shepherd's mind. Gina's window showed the interior of the club, and in the last hour the ferret had been able to find a very good spot to do surveillance from. You could see most of the dance floor and club interior from where she was positioned, and she was within twenty feet of their target.

Finally, the last person in line ahead of him was let into the club, leaving the three men in front of the stolid grizzly bear bouncer. He waited patiently as the three of them sent him their identity information wirelessly. All of it was fake of course, the complex code and passwords forged by Brian to provide them with clean identities for the night's work. As the bear was examining their information, Richard leaned forward and in a practiced way slapped Boris on the back. "Here to celebrate my boy's birthday, big man," the horse said happily. The bear bouncer took in Boris' grimace; Richard's smiling face, and Roland's slight nod of greeting. With that nod, the otter sent a signal to the big bear's commlink, a point to point wire transfer that was the modern equivalent of slipping the bear a pair of 20's without real money having to change hands.

   With that, the three of them were in.

   Roland made his way through the crowded club, politely pushing his way through the dancing crowd like an icebreaker. Behind the slim otter, Boris lumbered through the gap the otter was making, the big bull careful not to step on the smaller otter in front of him or any other other patrons. Behind them, Richard was glancing around the bar casually, as if he were just checking out the patrons of the Powerline. In fact, the horse was scanning the bar with his cyber eyes, recording every face he could see and sending everything to Brian out in the van. The German Shepherd was running facial recognition as fast as he could, using the high resolution camera's in the eyes of the three men making their way across the floor to see if anyone the team knew was here. They wanted to leave no traces tonight, and anyone who could identify them later would be a problem.

   Brian had already done his best with the surveillance that Gina had done, but the resolution from her glasses was never as good what was could be transmitted by a pair of cyber eyes. The ferret had never altered her body like the rest of them had, but she was the only one of them good looking enough to get into the club on her own merits so they made do with what they had.

   While Roland had made himself faster and stronger than any otter had the right to be, Gina had very good reasons for not going under the knife. She was one of the few people in the world gifted with magical power, and that required her to avoid the body modifications that Richard enjoyed so much. The body was your connection to magic, and Gina was not about to risk what made her special. Practically all of the horse was chrome by now, and even though Roland had never gone as far as getting cyber limbs like the horse's arms there was still enough wiring in the otter's body to furnish a house.

They pushed and jostled their way through the club, until they came to the back stairs and made their way up to the second floor. There, the three men bellied up to the bar and got a round of drinks. Richard put on a show of ordering something complicated for all of them to celebrate Boris' "birthday". It was a good cover, and it made the stolid bull scowl and blush slightly, which Richard loved to do. Roland lingered by the two of them, as Richard talked loudly about the game or some other nonsense as Boris sipped his drink and pretended to listen. That was the routine the two had developed over the years in situations like this. Boris watched as Richard made them look like real club patrons instead of criminals scoping out the place.

Roland meanwhile scanned the crowd for a bit, and then made a show of catching Gina's eye from across the room. The ferret glanced back at him and after a minute or two of eye contact she smiled demurely, making it look like she was interested in him. The otter grinned and made his way to Gina, as Richard started talking about him scoring with the lady in red. Boris just rolled his eyes, a dizzying motion in the picture in picture in Roland's head.

The otter sidled up to Gina at the railing of the second floor, whispering about how pretty she looked. They exchanged a few lines, pretending to get to know each other. This was another act, but unlike the one Richard was putting on behind them, it was a reprise of an actual conversation. Eventually the otter glanced at the back of the bar, where a small hallway led past the restrooms, to a locked door that protected their target. "Think we can do this without being noticed?" Roland said calmly, and Gina smiled at the way the otter touched her side.

"I'd always notice you, Roland," she said quietly, "but the idiots here? The yakuza should be ashamed of this security. You wouldn't even need a rhino to just barge into their secure room," the ferret grinned, her whiskers flaring out as she leaned in close. "Now kiss me, because this is going to be a milk run."

Roland grinned as Brian's muttered comment about tempting fate reached his ears via the radio, but he didn't care. He leaned in and kissed Gina softly all the same. It was a long slow moment of peace, just the two of them, before the run started in earnest. Then the otter stood up, guiding Gina away from the railing and towards the shadowy corridor, and anyone who saw them knew that they weren't ducking back into the shadows just to use the facilities.

Their act was so convincing that the bartender didn't even give them a glance as they slipped into the hallway. Roland grinned as he pushed Gina up against the wall at the end of the corridor, their bodies hiding the door's electronic lock and the little security reader that would open the door for the right badge. Roland pushed a small device against the reader and resumed his not quite an act making out with Gina. In the little window that was Brian's tactical video feed, he saw the dog eagerly begin cracking the system. It took less then a minute for the German Shepherd to crack the lock's code, and with a buzz the door unlocked beside them. Gina giggled, and the ferret worked her magic as the kiss broke.

Roland felt a pressure descend around him as the sound and lights of the club dimmed to a muted rumble as the ferret weaved an illusion around them both. It felt like his ears needed to pop, but he ignored the sensation and he opened the door. To anyone looking at the door from the other side, it appeared as if nothing had changed at all. To anyone looking down the hallway from the outside, it would look as though Gina and Roland were still making out calmly in front of the closed door, when the truth was they were now both creeping silently into the darkness beyond.

148

The hallway beyond the door was dark, and they crept down it slowly. Gina kept her paws up, weaving them through the air, altering the illusion around them as they moved. The darkness affected her more than it did Roland, whose cybernetic eyes switched smoothly to night vision. Roland slipped his paws into the back of his coat and pulled out a pistol and flicked the safety off. The gun's targeting system connected with his commlink, and when the two had synced a red target reticule appeared in his vision, tracing the spot where the gun was pointed. The otter mentally activated one of his favorite cyberwear devices and 'pinged' the room beyond the door, a wave of sonar going right through the door and walls, outlining the room beyond in silvery gray lines for the otter.

The room had only one occupant, a canine sitting in front of a computer terminal. Roland took the last few steps to the door alone, looked back at Gina, who gave him a nod. The otter's ears went dead as Gina's spell intensified, silencing him completely. "It's go time folks." Roland mentally sent the message to the rest of the team, and with that he activated all his cybernetic enhancements.

The wolf inside the control booth never stood a chance. Roland grabbed the doorknob, hit the door with his shoulder, and broke the door open in one smooth, soundless motion. The man began to turn, just catching a blur of motion as the door opened out of the corner of his eyes, and the last thing he saw was the end of Roland's gun as the otter pulled the trigger.

The gunshot made no sound, but it overloaded Gina's spell and the sounds of the club rushed back into the world in a wave. The beat of the club's music provided enough cover from then on as Roland sat down at the terminal and Gina slipped in behind him, closing the door behind her. The otter pulled a small black box out of his jacket, set it on the keyboard, and plugged the little wireless transmitter into one of the console's ports. The otter's fingers danced across the keys as he established a wireless link into the otherwise secure system, giving Brian full access to the

149

machine in front of him. "Brian, we've got five minutes max before somebody notices this guy's gone offline. Make it quick."

"Will do boss," the dog said happily, and the computer in front of him began to flicker and dance as Brian controlled it remotely. It only took him a minute to find what they wanted, and in three Roland and Gina were gone, slipping back out onto the club floor, their clothes rumpled and their faces red just like a couple that had had an extended make out session would look. The team was out of the building entirely before the body was found.

"The reservation is under Mr. Johnson."

Roland smiled slightly at the look the doe gave him. The woman was dressed in a beautiful kimono, her facial fur powdered to appear ghostly white, but it did not mask the way the color drained from her face. She had sneered at him when the short otter in his long, dusty coat had walked right past everyone else up to the podium in the lobby of the Gilded Pearl, Seattle's premier sushi restaurant. The five of them were not dressed for such a formal establishment. They hadn't had time to change after the club, and so they were decked out in leather and flash, but she should have known better than to be rude to them here. This wasn't just Seattle's best sushi bar, it was also a thriving meeting place for people who did what they did.

When powerful people or megacorps couldn't achieve their goals via legal means, they went to the shadows to get things done. Men and women like Roland and his crew were fairly common in the shadows of Seattle. They were known by many names. Fixers, guns for hire, terrorists, corporate headhunters, were just a few. Richard always referred to them as "dicks with guns", but generally they were just called runners. The profession had earned the nickname because they were almost always on the run from someone in the shadowy underworld of corporate espionage and crime for hire.

"Right this way sir," she simpered demurely, leading the otter and his rag tag group through the curtains that separated the lobby from the rest of the fine building. Roland heard Richard give a snickering whiney at the looks they got from the other patrons.

They followed the doe through the dimly lit hallways. Roland glanced into the various dining rooms as they walked past them. He recognized some of those people in the fancy clothes from before he became a runner. Some of them would have know him too, if they looked closely enough to see past his clothes and the subtle cosmetic surgery he'd had done. It had always fascinated Roland how people ended up in his line of work.

No sane person set out to become a runner, but society had many cracks a person could fall through. If you didn't have the right connections or didn't have the right identification, it was impossible to get by legally. Roland was once part of the right crowd, only leaving behind a lucrative job as a corporate security specialist after a rival corporation's hostile take over had became unusually hostile. The otter knew Brian from back then, and had even been his boss before the German Shepherd had lost his position in the same shake up that left Roland looking for work.

Boris was a gun for hire because it was one of the few jobs an ex-military specialist and illegal immigrant could do, the only way he could hope to make enough money to support the extended family he'd left behind him in the Russian consortium. Richard was just an adrenaline junkie who needed to keep in cash to upgrading himself. Gina, despite being involved with Roland, was still a mystery to him.

They were out of the normal restaurant area and in a hallway with several secluded private rooms for corporate functions. The doe led them to a heavy wooden door which she opened with a security card, and she kept her head bowed as she held the door open for them.

The five runners stepped inside the room and the door closed behind them, shutting out all sound. The room held one large table

151

set for six. Five places held plates of fresh sushi and warm sake, while at the head of the table sat a heavyset panda in a tailored blue suit, quietly eating a plate of bamboo shoots as his claws tapped on a commlink.

"Ah, Roland, sit down my boy," the panda said, wiping his mouth with a napkin as he set his chopsticks down. "Sorry to have started eating without you but I'm afraid I'm rather busy tonight. Tell me, do you have those family photos you mentioned last time we dined together?"

The team sat down on either side of the table as Roland nodded at their host. "Why, yes Mr. Johnson, I have them right here." The otter slid a tiny data chip across the table and sat down across the table from him, his crew fanned out along their side of the table. The otter picked up his chopsticks, snagged a piece of fish, and popped it into his mouth as the panda inserted the drive into his handheld commlink and inspected the files. It was all deliberate obfuscation; despite the Gilded Pearl's reputation for discretion and the white noise generator on the table, it was never wise to presume one had privacy. The panda's real name was Ryan Clark, and he was a middle manager for the mega-corporation Applied Dynamics. He specialized in handling situations that called for the talents of Roland and his friends, but they maintained the illusion that the team didn't know who their employer really was or what his motives were.

This verbal dance was an integral part of the business, almost as necessary as successful runs to maintain a reputation as dependable and a steady stream of work. The photos they had pulled out of the yakuza computer in the back of the Powerline that Clark was now viewing were of a priceless Chinese goblet, something from one of the old dynasties, back before magic returned to the world. Gina theorized that the panda was after it in case the goblet had become enchanted again with the return of magic, but they had no proof. The pictures clearly documented when and how the goblet had been quietly shipped to Seattle by the Orion

Corporation, a rival of Clark's employers. The most important piece of information, the part they had been paid a lot of money to get and had been willing to kill for, were the security codes for the case the goblet was being shipped in.

"These are very nice. You're a good photographer." The panda pulled the chip out and slid it back to the otter. "You have quite a cute pup there Roland. Perhaps you can bring him next time? I'd love to meet him." Roland grinned slightly as he plugged the chip into a wireless reader, transferring the files to his own internal commlink. There were new files on the disk now, and he glanced over them inside the privacy of his own head as they ate and chatted idly. The files contained detailed plans for an Orion Corporation warehouse and a simple set of instructions. 'Retrieve the goblet, kill anyone who sees you doing so, and return it to me here as soon as feasible. Payment is thirty thousand dollars each, with a ten thousand dollar bonus if the team leaves no witnesses behind.' Another job offer, and this time a lot more money was on the table.

Roland glanced at his team mates as he copied the instructions wirelessly to them. His silent question harvested silent approval, and he smiled at the fat panda bear.

"I think that can be arranged, Mr. Johnson." the otter said calmly.

Later that night, the team was riding in the large passenger van Brian owned. The Shepherd was in the very back seat though, stretched out across the seats, appearing for the entire world as if he were asleep. He was actually driving the van by remote link, his thoughts jumped into the big vehicle as it turned down twisting, narrow alleyways in the industrial complexes of Seattle's waterfront. The team was quiet as the van drove them closer and closer to their target.

"So Roland," Boris said casually as he buckled on a bullet proof vest. "What do you make of this target—San Diego or Rio?"

The otter winced a bit at the thought of the team's disastrous run down in Rio. "It had better be another San Diego." Richard said happily. "I've got bills to pay."

"You have a new arm design to buy you mean." Boris rumbled, and Richard just grinned at him.

"Think those two will ever stop complaining about money?" Gina whispered to Roland as the two men began their familiar argument about how to spend their cash.

"Not until Boris' family stops calling him for cash." Roland said as he calmly checked the slide of his pistol and holstered the gun under his jacket. "Or Richard runs out of parts to replace."

"I can't imagine there's much left now." Gina said with a smirk as she slipped her own bullet resistant jacket on. Roland smiled at her as Gina tied her hair back. Gina smiled back, and for a moment the ferret's paw touched Roland's.

'We're coming up on your stop, oh fearless leader.' The message from Brian flashed across the bottom of Roland's vision, and Roland slung his satchel over his shoulder as the van rumbled along the alleyway, crushing and knocking things out of its path.

Brian had paid a lot of money to reinforce the van; while it wasn't fully armored, a few trashcans weren't going to stop it. The otter checked his gear one last time, adjusted the thickly armored coat he wore, and as the van slowed at a T-junction, Gina gave him a kiss on the cheek before he leapt out of the side door.

A short jog down an alleyway brought him to the backside of a tall building. It was a factory, part of the Orion Industries complex, and it was largely automated. The five story building had no windows on this side, and with a grin, Roland took a pair of thick gloves from his bag. He pulled them on, and as he did, another message from Brian scrolled across the bottom of his vision. "Are you ever going to make Gina an honest woman Roland?" The Shepherd's grinning icon mocked the otter as he began to climb the rough brick surface like a gecko, the gloves sticking to the wall perfectly.

"Are you ever going to stop staring at Boris and tell him?" Roland sent back, and he smiled smugly at the way Brian abruptly closed the conversation window.

An hour and a half later, Roland was laid out on the edge of the factory roof, carefully calibrating the scope sight of his sniper rifle for the third time while keeping his body as still as he could as he settled onto the rooftop ledge. He could feel the dampness of the fog and light rain leeching into his clothes, but it didn't matter much right now. He had gotten up the wall and across the maze of factory rooftop sensors without incident, and the worm Brian had planted in the security system was showing no alarms had been raised by the otter's quiet climb or the rest of the team's approach towards the warehouse.

Roland pressed his eye to the scope of his rifle and used the scope's vision magnification to survey the grounds around their target. The warehouse was a large square building, with twenty feet of open weed covered ground between the building and the outer security wall. The outer wall was fifteen feet tall and made of solid brick with iron reinforcing, but there were several doors built into the wall at regular intervals around the building as fire escapes. From here, Roland could see along two sides of the building and through the long row of windows on the warehouse's third story. That offered him a comprehensive view of the warehouse floor.

The warehouse was fully automated, and even in the dead of night the machines inside were shifting heavy loads back and forth, loading delivery trucks that rumbled in and out of the front gate. Roland could see all the way down the long shelves, past the automated fork lifts, and right into the windows of the empty control booth. There were a dozen or so security guards patrolling the grounds in pairs, and Roland could see most of them easily from here. It was the perfect sniper's nest.

At the moment, the otter was tracking a pair of guards as they casually strolled down the length of the open space on the building's left hand side, checking the doors along the side of the building and the outer wall. Roland had seen this pair do the same routine twice already, and he was tracking their progress to make sure that they kept to the same schedule as before. If they did, then there would be a three minute gap between when these two guards rounded the far corner of the building and when the next two would move into position to see the west side of the building, and that was exactly the opening the team needed to get inside.

Roland whispered, "Alright folks. Our window is going to be coming up here in five. Everybody ready?" There was a crackle of static, as the radio in the otter's ears connected with the rest of the team.

"Check," rumbled the deep voice of Boris.

Gina sent the words "Check Baby," via her commlink, unable to speak because she was casting a spell at the moment.

"Check, one, two," Richard mumbled, his voice muffled this time by the lock pick he held in his mouth.

"Signal strength is strong, everyone is ready." Brian said calmly. "I'm accessing the warehouse security cameras now and bringing the tactical network feeds online." Brian said quietly, and Roland smiled. The German Shepherd was always the most professional of the crew. He was sitting in the van parked two blocks away from the warehouse, and yet still he had whispered those words.

Once again, the familiar video windows opened and began streaming the live feeds of everyone in his crew, but that's not all that happened this time. Along the bottom of each window was a vital sign readout for each of them. His commlink also began processing the new tactical and spatial info provided by the hundreds of security cameras all across the warehouse complex, and in a slightly dizzying way the otter was suddenly able to see the entire building from almost every direction, inside and out.

Roland looked out across the warehouse complex as walls and obstacles grew semi transparent as the visual feeds integrated into something not unlike x-ray vision. Using his cyber eyes this way, Roland could see every guard and checkpoint, every piece of moving machinery and storage bin. It was a sniper's dream come true. He could calculate firing arcs and trajectories on any target on the grounds without ever having to change his position. He focused for the moment on the individual feeds from his team.

Boris' feed showed Richard and Gina crouched alongside the outer wall of the factory compound in a shadowy alleyway, but in the bull's night vision the place was as bright as day. The bulky horse was on one knee in front of the door, his chrome arms gleaming as he rewired the security panel. Beside him, Gina's paws moved in a snake-like dance, shrouding the three of them from view to everyone outside their little bubble.

Roland could see the horse's metallic hands working the lock, deftly rewiring the electronics with a skill and finesse the otter knew Richard didn't possess. Brian was the one doing the actual work, guiding the horse's robotic fingers remotely via their commlinks. It was one of Brian's favorite tricks, since the dog hated to go in guns blazing.

The otter tensed slightly as Boris checked the magazine of his huge gun calmly. The click, clack of the bull checking and readying the weapon sounded loud in the otter's ears, and he could see the whole team's pulses spike. "Hey Boris, be careful with that thing." Richard said, his confident voice betrayed by his rising heartbeat. "I don't want this ending up like Lagos."

"What do you care?" the big bull snorted. "You're replacing those arms anyway."

"So," the horse said frowning. "It's still no fun having them torn off first." There was a soft click and buzz, as Brian finished using the horse's hands to rewire the door and the magnetic lock disengaged.

Boris went back to checking his gun. The bull refused to go anywhere without that gun, and the sleek, compact lines of the matte black Omega series assault rifle belied the power it held. A combination assault rifle and grenade launcher, it had an advanced targeting computer, the ability to detonate a grenade mid arc, and was so finely engineered that it could be fired on full auto with only the barest hint of recoil. It was the gold standard in big damn guns and dwarfed the weapons the rest of them had brought, even Roland's own sniper rifle. Roland should have complained that it was the wrong kind of weapon for an infiltration mission and made him leave it in the van, but the bull's superior firepower had come in handy one too many times when a run went bad for the otter to say anything about it. Roland just wished that the assault rifle was a quieter weapon.

Roland watched as Richard's heartbeat climbed as the big gun was readied, and the horse's bio-monitor indicated he was starting to sweat. The horse knew exactly what having the bull fire that thing would mean. One shot from that monster and the warehouse security alarms would be blaring, bringing the on site security teams running. Or if they were smart, they'd be running the other way, since Boris would probably mow the rent-a-cops down like weeds. After that, the team would have less than ten minutes to get out before the local Orion tactical response team came raining down on this place like a ton of bricks, and they would have a hell of a fight on their hands then. It would be another fifteen minutes after that before the state police arrived, and if that happened then no one would be able to get out of that building alive.

"Alright people, let's do this." Roland said quietly. "You will have one minute, two tops to cross the green space and enter the factory side door. Richard, you're on point. Once inside, head directly for the control room. I'll be watching the guard's patrols and warn you when to stop. If you stumble on someone I can't see, try to take them out quietly. We should be out of here in less than twenty minutes. Brian, you ready with the door?"

The radio crackled as everyone's adrenalin began to pump. "Yes sir, ready and waiting," Brian said, his fingers hovering over the button.

"We are go on my mark. I have the security team rounding the far corner in three, two, and one... mark." Roland watched as the picture in picture views of his three companions in crime shook and bounced. Through his expanded sight, he saw them sprint across the open field, their passage leaving a trail in the weeds only he could see. They reached the far side of the green space, and with a click one of the emergency exit doors disengaged as Brian cut the power to its circuit. Fire code demanded that such a door fail open, not closed; with little trouble Richard pulled the thing open, and they were inside.

Boris was through the door first, his huge gun leading the way into the dark warehouse. The bull shifted his stance, sweeping the gun across the row they were in, searching for anyone who might have spotted them entering the building. Gina and Richard scrambled through the door behind him, the horse pulling the fire door closed just in time as the second squad of security rounded the building. Richard pulled his handguns as the door resealed with a soft magnetic chunk as the door's power was restored.

Boris nodded at Richard and Gina, whispering, "We're clear. Let's get to the control room and do this." Boris walked down the row of boxes and containers, keeping one eye on the view with Brian's video feed. The bull could see the dog frantically checking the alarm systems and interior controls, but there were no flashing lights on the dog's monitors. "We're clean Roland," Brian said with a grin, and the team collectively breathed out. Boris sent the dog a silent message, "Good job," and then he accessed the layout map Mr. Johnson had given them.

Gina kept up the illusion around them, preventing anyone from noticing them visually as the three began to move cautiously down the row. Boris kept himself tensed and ready to spring as Roland did another visual sweep of the warehouse floor. The

159

otter guided them around one security team, and then told them to pause for a minute behind a storage rack as a heavy automated forklift moved past them.

They reached the control room without incident, and everything looked good. No guards were breaking from their routines. The only unexpected movement at all was a van passing the building on the street outside. Everything was going smoothly for once. Boris grinned as Richard accessed the controls, and initiated a retrieval request for the crate they wanted.

The machines spun to life and brought the team the storage container. Boris shouldered his big gun and pulled out a crow bar as the crate reached the loading platform. With a grunt he pried open the wooden crate, lifting the heavy lid off it. Inside, padded by a foot of foam, lay a black bullet proof carrying case. The bull grinned and lifted it out, setting it on a table nearby before replacing the crate's lid. Boris' video feed showed Roland and Brian what was happening as the bull punched in the unlock code, and with an electronic click the latch opened. Gina came round on the bull's left side as Boris opened the case. The stylized golden goblet glittered in front of him, just where they knew it would be. Boris stepped back as Gina examined the thing to make sure it was genuine, and she nodded with a grin. Mr. Clark was going to be very happy with this. Richard tapped a few keys to send the crate back where it was supposed to be.

Just as the wooden crate was lifted away, the door on the other side of the control room from where they had entered opened. Boris looked up, shifted his shoulder to swing his gun into position, but he could tell it was too late. Things had just gone very wrong.

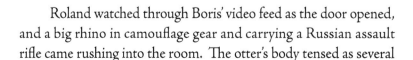

Roland watched through Boris' video feed as the door opened, and a big rhino in camouflage gear and carrying a Russian assault rifle came rushing into the room. The otter's body tensed as several other people, all heavily armed, came in quickly behind him. There was a whole separate runner team in the warehouse.

There was a breathless moment of stillness as the two groups of criminals stared at each other. Roland sighted on the rhino's face, and he could see the look of shock on the man's face when he spotted the goblet's open case. Then, the rhino's mouth twisted into a sneer, and he pulled the trigger bare seconds after Roland.

Gunfire echoed over the commlink and Roland heard Gina scream as the rhino's head jerked back. A huge pane of window glass on the south side of the building shattered as Roland's bullet went through it. The rhino's rifle rattled gunfire across the warehouse as he fell, and the other team stood there in shock as they were showered in blood.

Roland released the trigger and cocked the rifle as he counted out the other team into his commlink. "Four left! Two punk foxes, a zebra, and a panther! Cover is blown, open fire!" For a moment the range finder of Roland's scope was filled with muzzle flashes as the other team opened fire, and the glass windows of the control room exploded outward.

Everyone was screaming now, all pretense of stealth gone as Roland sought desperately for another shot to take. The voices of his team and the other runners were muffled screeches over the otter's commlink as the other team laid down a hail of gunfire. In seconds, the first security patrol was inside the building and rushing to the control area, and all hell broke loose as the rent-a-cops began shooting at everyone not wearing an Orion security uniform.

Roland checked the vital signs of his friends. Boris was hit, his blood pressure dropping fast but Richard was unhurt. Judging from his video feed the horse had ducked behind the console for cover. Gina... his heart skipped a beat.

Gina was flat lined, her feed showing nothing but the exposed steel ceiling of the warehouse. Roland shifted his scope frantically to find her, and he saw her lying in a pool of blood, her lifeless eyes open to the sky.

161

Cold rage filled the otter, and Roland sighted through his scope at the other team. They were all going to die for this. He chose one of the foxes, a female red fox with feathered green hair and a lip piercing. She was firing a pair of pistols at Boris, and she fell screaming when Roland pulled the trigger, a bloody stain covering her side. The zebra threw his hands up and magic leapt out at the security team that had rushed behind the other team's position, and the Orion men died screaming. Roland waited, watching the zebra's determined look as he charred the men, and when the sparks coming from his hands died the otter put a bullet in his skull.

That's when Boris began to fire. The bull walked out of the control room into the warehouse proper, his huge gun blazing as he cut down Orion security like wheat before a scythe. The bull was bleeding from a shoulder wound he was ignoring, and with a heavy boom he launched a grenade that forced the panther to dive for cover and took out a whole squad of Orion security as Roland sighted on and killed a guard trying to circle behind the bull.

Richard meanwhile squared his shoulders and faced down the fennec ganger who rushed at him and the goblet. The fennec was a hardcore punk in a leather jacket with fur tattoos all over him. The fennec was also seriously juiced or seriously cybered up, either way he was apparently new at being a runner. The biggest clue was the fact that he was swinging a sword at the horse instead of using a gun. The katana he held had become the favorite weapon of the young go-gangers who raced through the urban sprawl on crotch rockets and fancied themselves as modern samurai. Many of them tried to take up running to pay for their cyber or drug habit, and they were usually very bad at using the swords they carried.

That didn't mean they weren't dangerous as hell. Thanks to modern technology, even the most foolish looking sword could cut through two feet of steel like it was butter. Even Richard's augmented arms wouldn't stand up to more than a couple of blows from the thing, so it was bad luck for the fennec that he didn't know how to use it worth a damn. He swung high at Richard's head, going for a quick kill. Richard ducked under the blade, and tackled the punk like the horse was a linebacker making a sack. The horse's metal arms gleamed as he pounded the smaller fox into the ground mercilessly.

"Richard! Boris, you have to get out of there now!" Brian shouted over the comm, and Roland felt the pit of his stomach open up as he glanced at the dog's video feed. Every security system on the dog's screens had begun to blink an angry red as the whole site started to go into lock down. "Go out the front gate! Everything else is locking down!" The dog said frantically as he gunned the van to life, driving it quickly into the main road. "I'm bringing the van to open the gate… Shit!"

Roland jerked his head away from his scope and watched the crash happen with just his cyber eyes, and he wanted to throw up at the violent way Brian's video feed shook. The other van had rammed Brian's hard, and it sent the Shepherd's van rolling down the street like a thrown toy. The second van screeched to a halt, crippled from the collision, and Roland could see the façade of the van had been torn away to reveal a heavily armored vehicle underneath. It had to be the other runners' transport.

Brian's vital signs were wavering wildly, and Roland cursed as he adjusting his angle to get a bead on the second van's driver before whoever it was could overpower Brian. Then suddenly the tactical feeds froze, and the tacnet went dead as the van's communications server gave out, taking their personal wireless network with it and cutting Roland off from the security system camera feeds. Roland cursed loudly as he put his eye back to his scope and searched for Brian the manual way.

On the street below, he spotted Brian as the dog came crawling out of the van. Roland could see the dog was hurt badly. He had a bone sticking out of his leg, and blood was running down his face. The German Shepherd looked up at someone Roland couldn't see, and the otter shifted his aim smoothly to follow Brian's gaze.

The otter saw a battered lion holding a pistol, pulled the trigger of his sniper rifle instinctively, shooting the man in the leg rather then the chest. The shot still saved Brian's life, as the lion staggered backward, but it took Roland three frantic shots to finish the man. "Thanks," was all Roland caught in the crackle and pop of the radio transmissions before he lost contact with the Shepherd completely, but at least Brian was alive. Unfortunately, it meant Roland only had two rounds left before he had to reload.

Roland shifted his aim back to the warehouse, and back to the firestorm taking place inside. Boris was still unleashing hell in the rows of storage containers, and the Orion security teams were powerless to stop the bull's superior firepower. Most of them were probably dead by now, because the bull seemed to be focusing his fire on the panther. Roland tried to get a bead on the panther as he ducked and dodged Boris' fire, hoping to take him down with the bull's help.

The panther was bleeding from a shoulder wound where one of Boris' bullets had gotten lucky, and he was heading towards the bull in a dead run. Roland fired, placing his shot in front of the panther to prevent the cat from reaching Boris, and then he cursed as the shot went wide. The lithe cat had changed directions and was charging Richard instead, leaping through the broken windows into the control room once more. The fool horse was scrambling to get the case with the goblet closed, when he should have been trying to get out alive. Roland's final shot barely missed the leaping panther as he bore down on Richard, but the horse got the case closed and locked before the panther got to it.

Roland frantically reloaded his rifle as he watched the two men fight. The horse loved hitting people, and thanks to his metal arms Richard had a punch that could go through a concrete wall. That only mattered if he could land a punch though, and this panther was fast. Too fast, and too smart for Richard, it turned out. They ducked and weaved around each other, blocking and punching at each other as Boris finished gunning down the last of the warehouse security team. Just before Roland could finish reloading his sniper rifle, he saw the panther use a blade of his own, and it was much more impressive then the fennec's had been.

Richard dodged a wild roundhouse punch by jerking his head back as the cat's arm came around in a wide sweep. There was a flash of light as a foot long blade sprang out of the cat's forearm, and the blade threw Richard's blood across the wall in a wide arc. It was a nasty trick. The panther had hidden a foot long razor sharp blade inside a cyber arm made to look like real flesh and fur, and Richard hadn't pulled back far enough to avoid the blade as well. Roland watched as the horse felt to the ground in silence, as the panther grabbed the case and leapt over Richard's body. Roland cursed and spat as he tried to sight on him, but the cat was too fast and the otter was too upset to aim properly anymore.

The panther dashed through the rows, passing behind Boris' position as the bull finished off the security teams. The cat buried his blade in the bull's side as a parting shot, and Roland felt sick as he watched the bull fall to his knees as the panther ran on past him. Roland fired again and again at the cat, tracking the panther across the warehouse, but it was almost pointless now. The cat knew he was there, and he ducked and wove as he ran, using cover and making it almost impossible for the otter to hit him. Roland managed a single good shot, putting a bullet through the man's shoulder, but it didn't stop the panther before he left Roland's field of vision for good and disappeared into the back end of the warehouse.

Roland screamed as he threw his rifle down, grabbed his escape line, and slid down it in a rush. The rope tore his gloves off and burned his paws, but there was no way in hell that cat was getting away, not after killing Richard and Boris. Not after Gina. The ground rushed up to meet the otter's paws and he grunted in pain as he landed on the pavement. Feet protesting, Roland raced towards the back of the warehouse as fast as his enhanced body could go. He rounded the corner just in time to see the panther come flying over the top of the back wall. Like an acrobat, the panther was tumbling smoothly through the air in a high arc, his body clearing the razor wire topped wall by several feet. Roland's paws flew to his sides as his tactical software began computing the panther's trajectory, telling him exactly the spot the graceful cat would land.

The otter drew both his pistols as the panther came down in a perfect gymnastic pose. Roland's eyes met the panthers as the cat finished his landing, yellow eyes widening as the cat registered his presence. The otter emptied the guns into him, walking forward as the gunshots knocked the panther over backwards; the shots followed him down to the ground until the augmented cat lay still.

A flash of light made the otter look up, and fear gripped Roland as a large armored van swung round the corner and into the alley. The van's headlights flooded the area with hard white light. The Orion tactical response team was here. The otter looked at the vital sign readouts of his friends arranged around the edges of his vision, and saw nothing but static and white noise. The warehouse was being jammed. He had no way of contacting them or finding them—if they were even alive. Roland dropped the guns on the cat's chest, grabbed the case, and ran.

Boris gasped, staggering as he hustled out the front door of the warehouse, his gun trailing along the ground as he tried to hold his guts in. He cursed the bastard black cat with what little breath he had and tried desperately to make it off Orion corporate property. If he could do that, then the security team should in theory leave him alone—but considering how many had died in the warehouse he doubted that would save him if they caught him in some dark alleyway.

He could hear the sound of helicopters as the Orion security forces began to arrive, and he stumbled as he reached the wall of the compound. He tried to open one of the emergency doors, and he grunted in pain as his side burned. The door creaked as he put all his weight on it, but it refused to open. "No, no, no, no!" the bull pounded on the door, and he felt his augmented muscles twinge as they failed to break the door down. The bull looked up at the high brick wall, and Boris knew he would never get over the wall, much less past the mono-filament razor wire on top.

"Brian?" The bull grunted, activating his commlink and trying to raise the dog. He was close enough, he should be able to get a signal to the dog, but there was no response. "Brian I need an out, buddy I can't open the door." The bull felt the world tilting, and he looked down at all the blood trailing behind him. "Please Brian, you got to get me out," the bull muttered, but all his commlink was receiving was static. He was being jammed; the whole complex was probably being jammed. Boris hung his head, and that's when he noticed the second blood trail. Boris looked up and across the field, and saw where a trail of blood led to another security door, which was half open.

The bull staggered to the door as fast as he could, and realized why it was still open when all the others had been sealed. The vixen with green hair was there, her body holding the door open as she lay bleeding, half in, half out of the alleyway beyond the door. Boris tried to step over her and fell against the door instead, tumbling over her and onto the pavement beyond. He panted, shaking as he leaned against the wall.

Boris' guts were on fire, and he looked up as a van screeched to a halt at the end of the alleyway and a search light swept over them both. The bull's heart sunk. The Orion tactical response teams were here. There was nothing he could do now, he was basically dead. There was the crunch of boots on gravel, the cock of a gun, and when the first lion came sprinting into view, Boris laughed a bright booming laugh. The man, dressed in bright red and white swat gear and armed to the teeth, wasn't an Orion security guard but a damned EMT.

167

The man rushed up to him, his gun focused on the bull's face for a moment. Boris grinned, looked into the light, and held as still as he could. Boris knew he was being scanned and his identity checked, and he knew damn well how bad an idea it would be to move too quickly as the lion did it. Cross Emergency Services were very particular about this sort of thing, and the lion would shoot him without any hesitation if he threatened the man. The lion shouted, "Uninsured! Leave him!" to the other two paramedics who came stomping down the alleyway.

"What about her sir?" One of them yelled over the sound of the real Orion tactical response team's helicopter landing on the roof of the warehouse. "She's got a contract!"

"She's still on Orion Property!" The lion yelled back. "We're not pulling her out with a damn tactical response team hovering overhead!"

Boris looked down at the vixen who whimpered as the EMT passed them by. He watched the vixen's face as she reached out to red and white clad figure as they passed her by, her paw groping feebly. She had to have been the one to call them, and they had left her behind because of three feet of damned extraterritoriality.

With a grunt of effort, Boris reached down and pulled the woman through the door. It shut with a magnetic click and sealed, and she screamed in pain at being dragged like that on her wounded side. She whispered something as she passed out, and Boris shifted, trying to put pressure on his wounded side by leaning against the wall.

The three paramedics disappeared around the far corner of the security wall, guns at the ready as they headed towards the crashed vans. Brian had a contract with them; they'd get the Shepherd out safely and pick the vixen up on their way back. Boris grinned slightly as fresh gunfire rattled out of the night. The Orion team must have taken umbrage to the paramedic's presence. Oh well, it was their funeral, the Cross High Threat response teams were not the kind of people you wanted to mess with. Pay enough in this day and age and even ambulance drivers will carry guns when they come to get you.

A few minutes of pain passed, filled with the sound of Boris' heart beating and gunfire echoing down the alleyway before the paramedics came back around the corner carrying Brian on a backboard. The Shepherd started to struggle when he saw Boris lying there, but his movements were hampered by the paramedics. "No!" Brian shouted at the Cross EMT, "You can't just leave him here; he's going to bleed out!"

"He doesn't have a contract!" The lion shouted back, "Stay still sir, we'll get you to the hospital soon!" The lion ignored the dog's shouts from the ambulance as he and the other paramedic ran back to get the vixen.

Boris lay against the wall, his breathing getting ragged as he watched the paramedics work. The bull had no illusions about begging for their help. That's not how it worked anymore; the men in the white flak jackets were not charity givers. If he'd had the money to pay them off, he would already have a contract with them. The lion was half way through strapping the vixen onto the board when he stopped, cursed something Boris couldn't hear, and then turned to the bull as his partner continued strapping in the woman.

The bull blinked in surprise as the lion pulled him away from the wall and slapped a heavy self adhesive bandage over the knife wound on Boris' side. Boris bellowed in pain from the fire in his side as the lion applied smaller patches to the bullet holes on his arms and chest. The lion pulled a syringe from his bag, jammed it into the bull's leg, and depressed the plunger. Boris howled in pain again, and he watched as the silvery liquid shot into his veins. The commlink displays in his head lit up as his bio-monitors detected the invasive liquid, but it showed as some kind of nanotech blood replacement and his cybernetics didn't react to the stuff. Boris could feel the icy cold flow up his leg as they mixed with his blood and began to stabilize his condition.

Then the lion grunted with effort and forced Boris to stand. The bull's vision swam as he was hustled down the alley to the running ambulance. The lion was cursing constantly and holding him upright as the ambulance came more clearly into view. Boris squinted, trying to see inside, but all he could make out was Brian secured near the front of the van.

The lion shoved him into the armored vehicle and strapped him into a seat. Boris looked over at Brian, and he grinned when he saw that the slim German Shepherd had his arm snaked behind the driver's seat. He was holding a gun to the driver's head.

"This isn't going to work kid!" The Dalmatian behind the wheel yelled over the sound of the helicopters outside and the gunfire. "He still doesn't have a contract! You'll never get him treated at the hospital and the guards will gun you both down the moment they get back if you still have that gun!"

Brian laughed at the man, blood flecking his lips. "Then look at this!" Boris could see the German Shepherd was fiddling with the air like he was typing. The dog was doing something with his commlink, and Boris connected to his network so he could see the information that Brian and the copilot were exchanging. The little screens wavered to life in Boris' fading vision, and he saw a picture of himself on one of the screens.

It was a Cross Emergency Services Insurance Contract for him, under his real name. Alongside it was a bank terminal window, and he could see Brian sending payments to the paramedics and Cross alike. Boris couldn't tell how much, but a lot of money had just changed hands. "He's got a contract now, dip shits! So shove it up your ass and do your jobs!" Brian laughed at the look of disgust on the lion's face and the angry snarl he gave as he climbed into a seat beside Boris as the other EMT reached the van carrying the vixen. Boris felt himself slipping, and the last thing he saw was the dog grunting in pain as he holstered his weapon while smiling brightly at him.

Roland padded through the stark white Cross Applied Sciences hospital, his paw pads making soft leathery sounds on the linoleum floor. He glanced at the digital readouts of names and room numbers as he walked, and eventually he stopped in front of a door with the name Emily Pritchard on it.

The otter opened the door, and inside a vixen looked up at him, her eyes narrowing as she realized Roland wasn't hospital staff. "Who are you?" she said sharply, her shoulder length green hair falling over her eyes as she struggled to sit up. "What are you doing in here?"

"My name's Roland, Seraph—" the otter said calmly as he stood at the end of the bed. The vixen paused at the use of her codename, finger hovering over the call nurse button. She looked at him, as if judging distances, but Roland had been careful to remain out of reach of the vixen. It only took a moment to scan the woman, and while she had several cyberware enhancements she wasn't hiding a weapon under the sheets that could reach him at this range. Using the professional alias told Seraph she was looking at another runner.

"—and I'm the one who shot you," the otter finished, to make sure she fully understood the situation she was in.

The vixen sat very still for a moment, but she knew she was trapped. Roland could see it in the way she looked at his long, concealing coat and the way he had one paw in the pocket of the coat. "What do you want?" she said shortly.

Roland took out a data chip drive from his pocket and tossed it to her as she flinched. "I'm here to show you this. We share certain business partners and I thought you might like to know why both our runs went so horribly wrong."

The vixen stared at the thing suspiciously, and then she plugged it into a little port hidden in the crook of her arm. It was a popular place for datajacks these days, better than the ones behind your ears. Her eyes went unfocused for a second as she watched something only she could see. Then she screamed in rage and threw the little chip at the otter; who didn't flinch as it hit his chest and landed on the floor. "No! No, I do not fucking believe it!" Seraph screamed at him.

"Sorry honey, but it's true." Roland said quietly as he picked up the drive. It had contained only one file, a video recording made by Roland's own cyber eyes during their meeting with Mr. Clark earlier that evening. Her reaction was pretty much the same one Roland had had when Brian had shown him what he had hacked out of the vixen's cyber eyes—the galling recording of the panda's fat, smiling face. The otter felt sorry for her as tears ran down her face. She had lost just as much as he had tonight. "Clark sent both our teams after the goblet."

The vixen wiped her eyes and composed herself, and now instead of sad she looked mad as hell. "Why the hell would he do something like that? He gave us orders to kill anyone who saw us! He was even paying extra for it!" Green hair covered her face as she cried.

"He's liquidating his assets." The otter said quietly. "We checked with a few of our sources, and it looks like Clark's trying to pull a fast one on Applied Dynamics and make off with a lot of cash. We probably couldn't sell him the damn goblet now, even if we wanted to. It was just a tail chaser to get us killed."

She stared at him for a while, the anger darkening her face. "Right," she growled, "so we're just loose ends to him. How did you know he was our Johnson? We could have been after anything in the warehouse, not just the goblet."

"Two of my team hitched a ride in your ambulance," Roland said evenly. "One of them hacked into your commlink on the ride here and compared notes. I have to thank you for calling Cross; those two wouldn't be alive if you hadn't." That earned him a hard glare from the vixen. After all, he was the one who had shot her and triggered the arrival of the paramedics.

Roland didn't feel bad about that. It was true what Richard used to call him, he was a dick with a gun, and he made his living by using it. The otter had no pity for the vixen and her friends. They had known the rules of running the shadows as well as he and his team had, and Brian and Boris really wouldn't have survived the night if the paramedics hadn't arrived so quickly. The bull was having a long talk with the German Shepherd about why Brian had been willing to spend so much money on a contract for him. The probability that the two would hook up finally didn't at all assuage his emptiness at the loss of Gina and Richard on a fool's errand.

"So what do we do now?" The vixen said quietly. Her face had a calculating look to it, and Roland knew he had misjudged her back in the warehouse when he'd put her down as just another punk. She was a professional runner, just like him.

"Depends," Roland said, his tail tapping the ground. "You really want to run with the crew that iced your friends?"

"If you let me cut that panda's lying tongue out and feed it to him before he dies," Seraph said with cold fury. "Then I'm all yours." Roland smiled at her, and they shook on it.

*Cheetah Jones is a terror on the baseball dia-
mond—If he can keep it together long enough to
make it there. He's got one last shot at pro ball, but
if he's going to make it, something is going to have to
change.*

CHEETAH'S WIN

Phil Geusz

(With Special Thanks to Jacob O'Hare)

FOREWARD

Beep-beep! Beep-beep!

W*hy won't that jackass shut up!* I thought to myself, rolling over and clamping the pillow even more firmly over my head. It was hot— damned hot!— and hard enough for a man with a pounding head to sleep without some idiot and his horn to make things even worse!

Beep-beep! Beep-beep!

Damnit! I rolled over a little more, and instantly regretted the move. Something hurt like hell behind my left shoulder, and now there was bright, painful sunlight on my face. "Crap!" I declared to the world in general, trying to worm my way back under my pillow. "The whole universe is a load of crap!"

"Senor?" a young voice asked from very nearby, and suddenly I was wide, wide awake. Had I really...

"Senor?" the voice repeated, more urgently. "Senor?"

Beep-beep! Beep-beep!Beeeeeeeeeeeeeeeeep!

Jesus Christ almighty! I really had! And when Julio stretched out his horn like that...

Then a big turbine engine started, and I knew that I was in very deep doo-doo indeed. My eyes flew open despite the awl-stabs of pain brought on by the bright Dominican sunshine, and I sat bolt upright. "Senor!" the too-young prostitute in bed next to me repeated, looking terribly worried.

"Si," I muttered, clambering to my feet and balancing as best I could on the heaving, rocking floor. My billfold was still on the nightstand; at least I'd engaged an honest prostitute. Even if she *was* a little young. Perhaps the two went together, I reasoned fuzzily. I knocked over two rum bottles, one of them not quite empty, before finally grasping my prize. The wallet still had a wad of bills inside of it; I snatched them out and threw them down on the nightstand, uncounted. "Muchos gracias, Seniorita." Then the big motor on the team bus roared out, and there was no time left at all. My pants were lying right there in front of me, but there was no time for them. Instead I raced for the door like a gazelle.

I'd always been a fast runner; fastest in my elementary school, fastest on my track team, even fastest in the Major Leagues, once upon a time. Despite being barefoot and extremely hung over, I was down the stairs and halfway out the door before Julio managed to grind the team bus's balky gearbox into first. "Hold up!" I tried to scream through parched lips and arid tongue. "Hold up!" But all that came out was a pathetic little hiss.

There was an old man sitting on the hotel's porch. I vaguely remembered not having liked him very much the night before for some reason or another, so I didn't feel too bad about snatching the big Mexican-style sombrero off of his head without even slowing down and then using it to cover my privates. The man gabbled something, but it didn't matter. After all, he'd never been the fastest man in the Bigs. So what could he do about it? Steal a base, steal a hat. It was all the same thing.

177

Julio was into second gear when I finally came sprinting up alongside the team bus, beating on its metal flank with my free hand and hissing through dry lips. Finally, after an eternity, someone noticed me. The big vehicle squealed to a stop, and Julio threw the door wide open.

It was cold in the bus after my recent dash through the hot streets. A veritable wall of chilled air coursed down the steps and enveloped me as I stood outside the bus door for just a moment, catching my breath. Everyone was roaring with laughter, the whole damned team. There'd be another Cheetah Jones story going around the baseball world soon enough, another tale that'd grow taller with each telling. Which was fair enough, I supposed. My legend *should* grow, considering that my actual playing career was busily shrinking away to nothing.

My gorge was rising as I stood and panted, regaining my wind, and it took everything I had to climb the three steps up to where my team-mates sat. "Chee-*tah*!" my fellow players chanted, aware that they were in the presence of genuine greatness, if of a rather bass-ackward kind. "Chee-*tah*! Chee-*tah*!" They high-handed me and grinned and laughed in delight as I lurched down the aisle, my face steadily turning green. Coach Melendez was sitting waiting for me in my usual seat, however. And he wasn't smiling at all.

It was just as well that I had the hat with me. Otherwise, I'd have barfed all over him.

1

It was just as damned hot in Louisiana as in the Dominican Republic, I decided as I disembarked at the bustling Baton Rouge Metropolitan Airport. Even though it was still early spring, a wall of heat greeted me as I clambered through the little suborbital's hatch. Almost immediately my back began itching again; it'd been doing so almost constantly for days now. The rocket I'd taken direct from Mexico City hadn't been important enough to rate a jetway; instead they'd rolled up a stairway-on-wheels and let us pick our luggage out of a pile as we passed by.

"Cheetah?" a familiar voice greeted me as I headed for the terminal, and for the first time since God knew when I smiled.

"Buster!" I declared, grinning like a kid at my former coach. Old Buster had been my mentor all the way from the single-A's on up. In fact, I'd kind of suspected that they'd moved him along with me just because we got along so well; once upon a time I'd been a top prospect and considered well-worth pampering. And he was with the Catfish now? They hadn't mentioned *that* in my call-up letter! "I thought you were still up in Ohio."

"Heck, no!" he declared, grinning. Then, ignoring my outstretched hand he threw his arms around me as if I were his long-lost son instead of a good prospect gone bad. I ignored the pain this caused the inflamed skin on my back; Buster was one of the few people in the world whom I'd allow to hug me. "The General Manager up there was a real tightass. He even wanted everyone to cut their hair the same way." Buster shook his head, emphasizing the long, dark hair he still sported despite his age. "I finally got sick of it, and decided to go someplace where they play real ball."

I snorted, pulling away from the embrace and beginning to walk towards the terminal. "Come on, Buster. This is just a two-bit farm team like any other. We'll make a few bucks, have some good times, and move on."

But Buster didn't move an inch. Suddenly, his face was very serious. "You got fired down in the Dominican, didn't you?" he asked. "For farting around?"

I shrugged. It hurt, but I didn't let it show. "Yeah. Well, I didn't do anything that everyone else wasn't."

"And before that, from the Mexican Leagues."

"They were pissants anyway."

"And before that, you only made it through half a season in Japan. Right?"

179

"My numbers were good there!" I objected. "The umps wanted to be treated like gods! Besides, I was leading the league in—"

"—geisha girls, rice wine, and clubhouse turmoil," Buster continued smoothly. "But that wasn't your fault either, right?"

"You're damn right it wasn't! Anyone with any balls at all would've—"

"Would've, shmoud've," he interrupted me again. "Look, Cheetah. I've got good connections. No one else but me knows that you managed to get yourself canned down in the Dominican, of all places, and if you do what I know you can do on the field, then by the time anyone finds out they won't care anymore." He scowled, hard. "Damn it, Cheetah! You've got more natural talent than God gave a whole team of Lou Brocks. I've never seen the like of you, when you quit making excuses and actually care about the game. Are you going to use your head this time around, or am I going to have to watch you flush away what is for absolute certain the last shot at glory you'll ever get?"

I looked down at the ground again, then smiled. "So, what's the deal?" I asked. "I mean, why did they call me up all of a sudden like this? And straight to triple-A, at that? I never figured to be back at all, much less up so high."

Buster sighed and looked away. "Your new owner is a certain Mr. James Sandrell," he explained. "Mr. Sandrell believes that the key to exciting, winning, stadium-filling baseball is speed. He hopes by next year or the year after to field a team full of base-stealers." Buster stared me in the eyes. "Someone dropped your name in his ear as one of the great unfulfilled prospects of the era. After all, you're still only twenty-seven. Though God knows in your case it's not the years, it's the miles. So, he's giving you one last chance to show your stuff."

2

Cajun Field, located not far outside the heart of the bustling greater Baton Rouge metroplex, wasn't a bad place as minor-league fields went. The stadium was fairly old, and located downwind from a big genetic engineering outfit that spliced rice DNA with everything but the kitchen sink, producing franken-plants that grew alcohol, tailored lubricants, you name it. Pheew, did the place stink! But as Buster and I strolled up we could see workmen busily slapping on fresh paint, refurbishing the vending areas, and even repaving the parking lot.

"Mr. Sandrell is of the opinion that you get what you pay for," Buster explained as a bored-looking guard waved us through the front gate. "He believes that if he invests in his farm teams, they'll reward him with high-caliber, dedicated players."

I nodded absently, rubbernecking left and right as we headed down towards the training areas. The place was nearly empty save for the workmen; I'd been called into camp early. Finally we walked past the entrance to the locker room to where the coach had his little office.

"...ain't gonna get no better than this!" he was shouting into a telephone when Buster swung the door open. My new boss was maybe sixty, though he looked half that age when he smiled. Save for a beer-belly, the barrel-chested old guy looked to be in pretty good shape. He smiled and waved at Buster, then spoke into the phone again. "You'll either deal or you won't. I don't care anymore. Capish?"

"But... But... But..." I heard a distant voice stammer.

"But nothing!" the coach replied. "It's your decision." Then he slammed the receiver down and stood up.

"Tony," Buster said, pressing me forward slightly. "This is Cheetah Jones. One of the most talented young men it's ever been my pleasure to coach." He turned to me. "Cheetah, meet Anthony Turnbull."

My eyes widened slightly as I reached forward to shake Turn-bull's hand. He'd coached more than one Major League team to a pennant; what he was doing down in the minors, I hadn't a clue. Tony's grip was firm, and his gaze steady.

"Cheetah," he greeted me with a nod. "Glad to have you, son. Glad to have you indeed. I've heard more remarkable things about you than you can imagine. Some of them are even about how you play the game." Then his face turned to stone. "What's this about you getting fired down in the Dominican?"

I felt myself scowl. "It wasn't my fault," I explained. "There wasn't any alarm—"

"To hell with that!" Tony exploded. "You're a screw-up, Cheetah! You've never been anything *but* a screw-up, the whole time you've played ball. People I know and respect say you've got the makings in you. The genuine stuff, even." He nodded at Buster. "But you've got to get your head straight first. Or else you can walk out of here right now and never bother me again. Got me?"

My scowl deepened. I'd known up front that I was going to have to put up with a lecture before they let me play again, but this was a lot worse than I'd expected.

"I'll take sullen silence for a 'yes,'" Tony continued after a moment had passed. His eyes narrowed. "Kid, do you have any idea of what kind of life you're throwing away? Of how many people there are in this country who'd gladly die for a chance at the Majors?" He shook his head, then met my eyes again. "I've seen your kind come and go a dozen times over. Sometimes I don't know why I even bother trying anymore. But, every once in a great while, I find a player in the garbage pile worth the effort. And then it all makes sense."

There was another long silence before Tony spoke again. "You on the bottle, son? Drugs? Tell me the truth now, and there'll be no consequences. We'll get you treatment, and so long as you work with us we'll work with you. I swear it! But if I find out later, I'll fire your butt in a heartbeat. I won't have a liar in my dugout. Not for all the stolen bases in the world."

"I drink," I replied evenly. "I drink hard, even. But not all that often— maybe once a month, when I'm having a bad day. Other than that, it's just a beer or two now and then."

"Not any more," Coach Turnbull replied. "As of right now, you're on the wagon for the season. I ever catch the faintest whiff of liquor on your breath, you can go file for unemployment in Santo Domingo for all I care."

"You can't—" I began.

"The hell you say!" Tony countered. "I can and will fire you for any reason I see fit, even if it's because the laundry screwed up my jockstrap and I feel a little itchy that day. Wait until you see your contract! It's loaded with more reasons for me to fire you than you can possibly imagine. There's even a moral turpitude clause!"

My lips tightened. "My agent—"

"—is grateful as hell to be getting *anything* out of a dead-loss client like you." Turnbull smiled. "Go ahead, Jones. Walk out." He crossed his arms. "I have other, better prospects that aren't pains in the butt. See if I care."

For a long moment we tried to stare each other down. Then I remembered who was holding all the aces and lowered my eyes. "All right," I agreed, phrasing things very carefully. "If you catch me drinking, I'm gone. Fair warning, and all that."

He nodded.

"But that moral turpitude thing..."

"Cripes!" Buster exploded. "Cheetah, the reason you went to Japan was because you got caught porking the owner's daughter on the shower floor! By the press, even! They got it on film! You've gotta be reasonable, here!"

I waved a patient hand. "It's not like that, Buster." I turned back to Tony. "You said I could unload about booze and drugs right now, and not have it be held against me, right?"

He nodded. "Yep."

I smiled uneasily and shrugged my shoulders. The skin on my back was beginning to itch again. Wouldn't the damned thing ever heal up? "Does that go for other things, too?"

He crossed his arms and looked interested. "Try me. I haven't heard a new one in ages, though you might be just the guy to do it. I'll give you that much."

My smile widened. Despite myself, I was beginning to feel like this was a man I might be able to get along with. "You see, I picked up this tattoo one night in the Dominican Republic. The night before I got fired, in fact. I don't even remember getting the thing, and... Man! You won't believe..."

"I don't believe it!" the team doctor declared. I'd been hearing that exact phrase all afternoon, first from coaches, then from trainers, and now from the doc. "I simply do not believe it!"

"It's really there all right," I reassured him. "Trust me to be the one who'd know for absolute certain."

Doctor Jorgenson shook his head. "I've heard of these things, but..."

I sighed. It was quite a tattoo, I had to admit, one that pushed the limits of the new electro-cellular tech. "It itches all the damn time," I complained.

"It probably always will," Doc Jorgensen replied, his voice sounding sad. "The idiot who applied the thing ran the power lines so close to a major nerve trunk that I'm surprised you're not in agony every time the ah, ah..."

"Every time the girl sorta lights up and rolls her eyes?" Buster asked intelligently.

"*Which* girl?" Doc Jorgensen countered, his lips wrinkled in distaste. Then he shook his head. "There isn't a thing I can do for you, Cheetah. That... That abomination is rooted way down inside you. To ablate it, I'd have to cut so deep that it'd be months, maybe even years, before you got your full range of motion back— if then. And your back would be half scar tissue when I was done."

"Jesus," Buster muttered. Then he turned to me. "For God's sake, kid? Why did you go and mess yourself up like that? Them things ain't even legal in the States!"

"And for good reason!" the doc agreed.

"It wasn't my fault," I explained. "I was drunk, see? I don't remember much about how it happened, except that the needle stung like the devil and that the artist's wife made one fine margarita."

"He can't hide it," Jorgensen pointed out needlessly. After all, Buster and Turnbull and I had figured it out long since. "Not in a locker room environment. The press'll be all over it in a week, maybe less." The doc frowned. "Frankly, I've never seen anything more ludicrously obscene in all my years. And I haven't exactly been a choir boy."

Buster frowned too, then crossed his arms in decision. "He can't play like that. It's simply not possible. What if the kids heard about it? Baseball is a family sport."

I nodded. So my trip up north was for nothing after all, it seemed. I'd finally gone and done it, screwed myself up so bad that no one in baseball would have me. I'd messed up in the Majors, Japan, Mexico, the Dominican Republic, and now here in Baton Rouge. And for what? A tattoo I couldn't even remember asking for?

"...refund your airfare," Buster was saying, his face much more deeply wrinkled than I ever remembered seeing it before. "And I can probably get you two weeks pay for showing up, seeing as how upper management still thinks you quit a good job to come."

"Right," I agreed. Two weeks pay? Well, I'd been fired before, hadn't I? Two weeks pay would buy me a nice bender, and a hotel room for three, maybe four days to enjoy it. And then I could...

...do what? There wasn't anyplace left to run. Or at least not anyplace where I could play baseball.

Suddenly I felt very cold and empty inside. "Look," I said, turning back to the doc. "I know you can't abrade this thing, or whatever the heck it was that you said. I understand that. But can't you do anything else? Like tattoo over it, say? Make it a great big black spot? Or else cover it up somehow?"

Doc Jorgenson pressed his lips together. "I'm sorry, Cheetah. You can't tattoo over one of these electro-cellular jobs. The thing will burn its way back through in days, if not hours. It's actually alive, you see. So long as it lives, it'll use every resource at its disposal to display the, ah, message it's programmed with. Since it's a form of parasite drawing on your body for energy, the more you mess with it the worse the drain on your body becomes. Trying to submerge it in black ink not only wouldn't work, but would also make you sick as can be along the way. If the tattoo ever dies, which is very unlikely indeed, you have to ablate it immediately. With the unfortunate results we discussed earlier."

Jesus Christ! "What about covering it up? Look, maybe I could wear a bandage or something all the time, even in the shower."

"The area involved is far too large," Jorgensen explained. "Especially for a professional athlete. Your movements would be restricted. Eventually, a corner would come off." He frowned. "And with *that* thing, even just a corner would be quite enough."

"How about if we grew new skin over it?" I demanded, clutching at straws. One more bender, then the whole gaping future ahead, empty, empty, empty! "Like, over a burn? Don't they use nanites or some junk like that?"

"Yes," the team doctor agreed. "But we're still talking about a long period when you'd be unable to play. Just about the same amount of time that it'd take for the tattoo to burn back through, most likely. About the only thing..." Suddenly, Jorgenson's voice trailed off, his eyes narrowed, and he raised his right hand to his mouth. "Maybe. Just maybe..."

"What?" I asked, suddenly desperate. My God, what was I going to do with myself? Become a truck driver? A hamburger flipper? Deal weed on the streets back home and have kids point at me and talk about who I used to be? How could I live, without baseball? "I'll try anything! Anything at all! Even if it might kill me!"

"This wouldn't kill you," the doctor replied. "Not exactly." Then he sighed. "All right, Cheetah. I've got an idea, but I have to do a little research before I can say anything more. And you're going to have to be very open minded for it to work." He turned to Buster. "So is the team, for that matter."

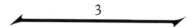

3

"I still can't believe I'm doing this," Coach Turnbull declared as our insanely aggressive autotaxi darted left and right through the heavy New York City traffic. I'd never ridden in an autotaxi before; we'd left my stomach behind several swerves back. Judging by his pallor, Tony had the same problem.

"*You* can't believe *you're* doing this?" I countered angrily. "I'm the one that's going to have to put up with all the catty remarks and teasing and stuff..." I sighed, then for about the tenth time made a conscious effort relax back into my seat. But it was impossible; every time I tried, my tattoo stung like a wasp.

"You think all of it's going to be on you?" Tony countered. "The other coaches are going to give me more lip than you—"

"Now approaching Freedom Center," the pleasant and incongruously female voice of the autotaxi interrupted as it swerved hard right, squealing its tires and setting off a veritable symphony of horn-blowing. "Please have your fare in hand, and be ready to depart the vehicle promptly. Thank you for choosing the Yellow Checkers Cab Company."

"Right," Tony muttered, digging out his credit card. Neither of us had any luggage, this being a mere day-trip. "I still don't believe it. Here I've got my whole lineup checking into training camp today, and where am I? Sitting in a cab in New York City alongside the biggest screw-up in baseball getting ready to beg permission to—"

The cab lurched hard left, once again setting off an orgy of hornblowing. "Five," the sweet, gentle voice intoned. "Four. Three. Two. One..."

...and then the automated vehicle came screeching to a halt right in the middle of a traffic lane! More horns blared as Tony clumsily ran his card through the reader; he had to do it twice because he got rattled and dropped it the first time. Then we went dashing for the curb, the little cab nearly clipping me on the ankle as it blasted away under full acceleration.

"Jesus!" Tony muttered once we were safely ensconced on the sidewalk. His head swiveled left, then right again; clearly, he was more than a little out of his depth. Finally, he nodded firmly towards a large entryway off to the left. "That way," he declared.

"Right," I agreed, leading off. Between suborbital flights, autocabs and waiting around at airports, I'd been in Tony's close company for almost six hours already, and had at least another six to go. It wasn't much fun, and if I could put him out of my sight by walking a little faster then he did, so much the better. I was maybe halfway to the big public entrance when I heard a squeaky voice cry out. "Cheetah!" it declared. "Cheetah Jones! Wait up!"

I practically froze in my tracks; who did I know in New York, anyway? Then Tony stopped close up behind me, and I amended the question. Who did I know in New York that was about to embarrass me to the quick in front of my new coach? A hooker? Someone I owed money to? A former drinking buddy, now begging on the street?

But it turned out that the voice belonged to none of the above; instead, it was the property of a pimply-faced boy of about fourteen. "Cheetah!" he declared again as he came rolling up in his power-chair, middle-aged mother bustling up behind him. "I knew it was you, just as soon as I saw you get out of that cab. I knew it!" He grinned from ear to ear.

I cocked my head to one side. "You know me?" I asked.

"Sure!" he declared. "You played with the Springfield Minutemen for what, five months?" He looked back at his mother. "I've got your card, in my collection. Too bad it's at home."

"He'd bring his cards everywhere, if I let him," the kid's mother explained. She looked down at his shriveled legs. There were darned few crippled people left in the world who couldn't be helped with modern tech, but this young man was clearly one of them. "They mean the world to him."

My head nodded slowly. I hated being around crippled people. They weirded me out. "I see."

"You were the fastest player in the Majors!" the kid exulted. "Still probably would be, if you hadn't gone for the money in Japan." His face fell a little. "Do you like it over there?"

Just then my companion cleared his throat, and I introduced him. "This is Tony Turnbull," I explained. "Coach of—"

"The world champion San Jose Toros!" the kid cried out in exultation, his eyes bugging in pleasure. "Oh, wow! What a great day this is! I'm so sorry I didn't recognize you, Mr. Turnbull! I've got your card too, of course. But once I saw Cheetah, there..."

Tony handled the situation with all the class I didn't have. "Sure thing, kid," he said with a smile, leaning over and extending a hand for his young fan to shake. "What's your name?"

"Raymond!" he exclaimed. "Raymond Belanger! I'm from New Hampshire; we're just here to see a specialist."

"Right," Tony continued, his smile never cracking for an instant. "Do you by any chance ever get down to Boston?"

"Sometimes," he answered, looking a little puzzled.

"Well," Tony continued. "I have a colleague there who can make special arrangements. And, it so happens, she owes me a favor." He pulled out a little piece of paper, and scrawled rapidly on it. "If you were to call my friend Angela at this number in a few days, after I've had time to make a call or two of my own," he explained, "you might just get to watch a major league game from the dugout."

189

Young Raymond's eyes widened until I thought they were about to pop out of his head. "Wow!"

Then he scribbled a little more. "And," he continued, "if you were to send Cheetah's and my baseball cards to this address here, there's a distinct possibility that they might come back autographed, too. With pictures, even." He paused thoughtfully and looked at me. "Though you might want to wait a few months on his," he added. "Or maybe not. Who knows? Maybe it'll be more valuable this way."

"I... Uh..." Raymond was totally at a loss for words, it seemed, but his mother wasn't.

"Thank you!" she gushed. "Oh, thank you *so* very much!"

"No problem," Tony replied, doffing his cap and smiling one last time. Then he made a great show of looking at his watch. "I'm sorry, folks. But..."

"Oh!" Mrs. Belanger gushed. "Don't let us hold you up! And thank you again, one last time. Thank you so much!"

"No problem," Turnbull assured her. "Our privilege." And then we were walking side-by-side towards the door.

"Jeez!" I said once we were out of earshot. "You pretty much shot the wad for that kid."

He shrugged. "It's what's expected."

I pressed my lips together. "Maybe it's what's expected of you," I answered evenly. "But you're not getting paid league minimum. Coach, I get twenty bucks for an autograph! And here you promised that Raymond kid one for free!"

Turnbull stopped dead in his tracks. Then, very slowly he turned around. "Cheetah," he said very quietly. "I've met some real world-class jerks in my life. But you, you miserable jackass, have just taken the cake."

"Why?" I demanded. "Lots of players charge for autographs!"

"Are you *blind?*" he demanded at the top of his lungs, totally ignoring the stares of the pedestrians detouring around us. "On top of every other screwed-up thing about you? Am I going to have to send a seeing-eye dog out into the field with you, to lead you to the balls?"

"So he was in a wheelchair!" I countered angrily, my own voice rising. Damnit, I was entitled to autograph money, when and if I could ever make any! "Big deal!"

Turnbull's eyes narrowed, and then he looked away. "Jesus," he whispered. "You really didn't see." Then he looked up again, and this time there was a tear running down his cheek. "The kid was wearing a Cancer Society medallion around his neck," he explained. "And his mom was carrying a bunch of pamphlets. Pamphlets about hospice programs for children. Do you know what a hospice program is, or are you stupid, too? Do you need me to connect the dots?"

My mouth fell open, then closed again. "He's going to die?" I asked.

"Yes, he is going to die," Tony replied, looking dead into my eyes. "And if you'd paid half as much attention to that poor kid as he so clearly did to you, if you'd cared half as much about what is probably the one single solitary fan you have left in this world as he did about you and your pitiful excuse for a career, you'd have figured that out all by your lonesome."

I blinked. "That kid is going to *die?*"

"Jesus!" Tony declared, rolling his eyes in frustration. Then he pulled out his wallet, removed a twenty, and slapped it into my hand. "Payment for the autograph," he explained. "In advance." Then he turned and stomped away.

And no matter how hard I tried, he wouldn't take the money back.

4

James Sandrell, my team's owner, was clearly a very busy and important man. His offices were up near the top of the Freedom Center. Once we got past the public areas, the place looked as if a mahogany-eating dragon had vomited all over the inside. I'd never even heard of such expensive furnishings.

Even Tony seemed a little overawed as we made our way back to the innermost sanctum of TransGenics Incorporated's office suite. He shuffled his feet a little, and spoke nervously, in short little sentences. "Be quiet unless spoken to, Cheetah! Don't screw this up. It's all in the bag, if you'll just keep your trap shut. And try not to damage anything!"

At least Mr. Sandrell didn't keep us waiting; the secretary ushered us right in. "He's on a conference call to Europe," he explained, smiling politely. "But Mr. Sandrell hates to be kept waiting in anterooms, and tries to avoid causing others the same discomfort."

Tony nodded and thanked the secretary, stuttering abominably. Then the heavy door swung open, and we were inside. "Hi!" Mr. Sandrell greeted us from behind what seemed to me to be quite an ordinary, unexceptional desk. His voice was deep and rich. "I'll be right with you guys!"

"Sure," my coach agreed, smiling. "Take your time."

Sandrell grinned back, then returned his attention to the transatlantic call. He was a much younger man than I'd expected, maybe forty, with a coffee-colored complexion and perfect white teeth that flashed attractively when he smiled. "I say it's a go on the new mutagenic sequence," he said into the telephone. "We've passed every test that the EU can possibly throw at us. Our product is safe and effective." There was a long pause as someone on the other end of the line said his or her piece, and then Sandrell spoke again. "Yes, of course. That's a given. But how much will it cost us not to move up production, assuming the process is approved? Which I firmly believe that it will be. There's risk in everything, Maria, and there are consequences both to acting and to not-acting. I've always preferred the former."

There was another short pause, then he smiled. "Fine, Maria, fine indeed! Then that is how we shall do it. Forgive me, but I have important business waiting in the office here." His face lit up. "Baseball business! My favorite kind! Thank you, and good-bye. Hasta la vista!" And with that, he returned the instrument to its cradle. "Forgive me, gentlemen," he explained. "I know that we had an appointment, but business can sometimes be pressing."

"Of course," Tony answered for us both. "Believe me, both of us regret having to take up any of your valuable time on minor-league stuff."

"Nonsense!" the executive countered, gesturing for us to sit down. "Baseball is my passion, even at the minor league level. Besides, today's minor-leaguer is tomorrow's star." He turned to me and extended a hand. "Cheetah, it's a true pleasure to meet you at long last. I saw you play in Springfield, several times."

I've never known what to say when someone tells me that, so I just nodded, shook the offered hand, and smiled. I couldn't help but be aware of Tony watching me like a hawk. Somehow, I knew that at the slightest misstep he stood ready to interrupt.

"Your style of play was incredibly aggressive," Sandrell continued. "Angry, even. In the course of the three games I was able to attend, you stole seven bases and were thrown out once. At home plate," he added quietly.

My mouth instantly jumped into gear. I'd only once tried to steal home in the majors, so I knew exactly the incident he was referring to. "It wasn't my fault!" I explained. "And I was safe, too." Then Tony's heel ground into the top of my foot, and I shut up again.

"I think that you were safe, as well," the team's owner replied, a twinkle in his eye. "And I had a better angle on the play than the ump did." He shrugged. "But that's all water under the bridge, is it not? Umps make bad decisions sometimes; after all, they're only human. Just as all of us are human. Putting bad decisions behind us, learning from them, and then moving on into the future is one of the key skills of life. Until it's mastered, little else is possible." He looked deep into my eyes but, mindful of Tony's heel I said nothing.

Then Sandrell sighed and leaned back into his chair. "Perhaps some explanations are in order, Cheetah. Many years ago, I was a prospect myself. I was even signed onto a single-A team. I played the game much as you play it, wide open and with everything hanging out. I sometimes even sharpened my spikes." He smiled wistfully. "And then, before I ever played my first pro game, I did something stupid. Some of my friends asked me to go for a ride with them. I didn't know that the car was stolen. Nor did I know that some of the others were carrying guns. By the time I was clear of the law, the season was well underway and the team had, quite understandably, lost interest in me."

Tony nodded. "I'm very sorry, sir." He glanced around the expensive office. "But things seem to have come out all right, in the end."

"Heh!" the billionaire snorted. "One might say so. And then again, one might not." He opened a desk drawer and pulled out a dusty old fielder's glove. "I still play ball, you know. In an executive's league. Center field. For the sheer love of the game."

"Good for you, sir," Tony said.

"Yes," Sandrell agreed. "Good. But not as good as it might've been." He gestured all around him. "I love this corporation. Even more, I love what it can do for people, and what this new technology means to the future of mankind." Then he turned to face me. "But never doubt for a second that I'd gladly trade it all for the chance to try and steal home plate with the game on the line against Sasquatch Howard pitching and Tom Bowan catching, blind umpire be damned."

He was staring right at me, but somehow I had nothing to say. Finally Tony stomped down on my foot, hard. "I see," I said slowly.

"Maybe," Sandrell replied. "Maybe you do see, and maybe you don't. But I propose to find out." His mouth formed a thin, hard line. "Cheetah, once upon a time you impressed me to no end.

And, perhaps I see a bit of myself in you. Just in case there is any doubt at all remaining in your mind, let me make it clear to you that you are where you're at today because I've pulled a thousand strings on your behalf. Is that understood?"

I gulped and nodded. So having Buster pick me up at the airport *hadn't* been a coincidence? "Yes, sir."

"Now don't go getting any ideas that this means I'll tolerate any nonsense from you." He turned to Tony. "As much as you mean to me, your coach means far more. I've instructed him to give you one, and only one, more chance. I'll interfere to no greater extent than that, and if he chooses to let you go then I'll not only back him to hilt, but I'll also apologize for having stepped on his toes in the first place. There's no one in baseball I respect more than him." Then he sighed. "But so much for the best-laid plans of mice and men." He shook his head. "What on earth ever possessed you to get that incredible tattoo?"

I looked down at my shoes. "I don't even remember. It may have been the stupidest thing I've ever done."

Sandrell nodded. "Good. You're being honest. *That* we can work with." He turned to Tony. "You say that you have a plan for dealing with this issue?"

Tony nodded. "Yes, sir. We plan to cover the tattoo, very effectively and thoroughly, so that no one will ever know. With fur." He smiled hopefully. "We even plan on using products from your company. So, you could maybe… Sorta sponsor it."

Sandrell appeared shocked for a moment, then grinned wide and leaned back in his chair. "It could be done, of course. The technology is totally proven. We do up actors for movies all the time. And then there are the exotic dancers..." He turned to me. "You'd be willing to go through with this?"

I nodded, once.

"It's against League rules to modify the human body in such a way as to improve athletic performance," the executive mulled. "If we were careful, we could leave your basic structure untouched.

In fact, if we played it smart, we'd make you just a tiny bit weaker, so that no one could complain on those grounds."

"Our team doctor has put together a package," Tony explained. "Cheetah here would miss about three weeks of the pre-season in hospital. By the time he got out, he'd have enough fur to cover the tattoo. Though, he won't completely finish changing until September or so."

"Right," Sandrell mused, his eyes distant. Then he grinned. "You know, this has real possibilities, far and away exceeding the mere covering up of a tattoo. The fans might just decide they love it. If we can get the League to go along with us, that is."

"And if Cheetah can play effectively as, well, a cheetah," Tony pointed out. "After all, even as a normal human..."

"Right," Sandrell agreed again. Then he came to a decision. "Begin the treatment," he directed. "Cosmetic body modifications have never been against League rules, and when you get right down to it this is purely cosmetic, even if a little on the extreme side. I'll do a little back-door politicking, and then we'll present the other owners with a fait accompli." He looked at me again. "Expect stormy weather, son. I think you're going to find that there's a lot more involved in making big changes in one's self than you yet realize."

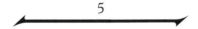

5

"There's a lot more involved in making big changes in one's self than you yet realize," the doctor explained to me as I lay waiting in bed. I smiled weakly, having heard that one before. "For one thing, you're simply going to have to get used to being looked at naked. That'll be happening more and more as we go on."

I blushed; Dr. Henway was a very pretty young lady, and they not only had me in a hospital gown, but one that was too short by several inches. Or at least I thought so. Plus, they'd already made a pincushion out of me. I'd never even imagined getting so many injections so fast! "I'm sorry," I answered, very slowly easing the sheet back. "You see, I was just in New York this morning, and—"

"—and they're pushing you just as hard as they're pushing me," she replied evenly. "Rush, rush, rush! After all, I woke up in Spokane with my husband. And, I can assure you, the last place I thought I'd finish out my day was in Baton Rouge, Louisiana." Then the doctor smiled. "Well, the recruiter told me that working for TransGenics would be interesting and exciting." Her face grew serious again. "Stand up, turn around, and open up your gown. I want to see this famous tattoo of yours."

I gritted my teeth, then stood up as ordered. It was freezing in my hospital suite, absolutely freezing. The soles of my feet stuck to the linoleum as I solemnly swiveled, and opened the flimsy garment.

"Oh... My... God!" my doctor whispered in awe. Suddenly she sounded about sixteen. "That is so incredible!"

"It itches all of the time," I pointed out. "Even aches. I don't suppose that you can—"

"Sure," she replied. "I'll add extra sheathing to the affected nerve. And the fur-job will cover it up just fine. Don't worry about that. I plan to make yours extra-thick, just to make sure." Then she paused for a long moment as I stood and shivered. "Your build and musculature are just about perfect for a cheetah," she went on after a time. "Long arms and legs, very thin torso, even your head won't have to be reshaped too much. Except for the muzzle, of course."

"Muzzle?" I countered. "Look, lady! I agreed to a coat of fur, yes. But—"

"And the tail ought to be fine as well. You don't have even a trace of scoliosis." I heard her scribbling on something. "If I didn't know better, I'd say that you were a professional athlete in the prime of life." There was a long pause, during which I said nothing. "That was a joke, Mr. Jones. Sorry. You can pull down your gown now, and get back into bed, if you like."

I took her up on it in a flash, noticing that Dr. Henway's eyes watched me intently the whole time. "Do you have any films of yourself running?" she asked. "I mean, out on the field?"

"There might be some in the archives," I replied. "Why?" Then my eyes narrowed. "What kind of doctor are you, anyway?"

"I'm your body sculptor," she replied, smiling prettily. "It'll be my job to design the new you. Detail work, like locating your spots and such. Mostly, I do exotic dancers. No one's ever done a pro athlete before. I can't believe that Mr. Sandrell asked for me personally on your case. It's such an honor!" She looked down at the floor for a moment. "You can call me Kris, if you'd like."

I nodded. "All right, Kris. But listen to me—No muzzle, no tail. I agreed to the fur, yes. But no more than that—got it?"

Dr. Henway's face fell. "But didn't you know?" Suddenly she seemed very disconcerted. "Mr. Jones... You've already received the basic injections. Mr. Sandrell gave the go-ahead, and I know for fact that you signed the papers. I verified them myself before we gave you the shot; professional ethics and all that."

I closed my eyes and sighed, remembering the endless stream of legal-looking documents that Coach Turnbull had passed across to me for signing on the flight home. I'd stopped to read one of them; it had relieved everyone in the entire universe, including yet-undiscovered alien intelligences, of legal liability for potential brain damage. "It's not like anyone would know the difference anyway!" Tony had snapped. "Sign the thing, or go try and find a new league to play in. It's up to you, Jones. Frankly, I don't care anymore. I've got better things to do."

So I'd resumed signing without reading until it was done.

"I'm a body *sculptor*, not a body designer," Kris explained. "All I do is tweak the details, to make the transition safe and artistically pleasing. It takes a whole team and lots of computer time to set up a whole new design. If we hadn't just happened to have to have the cheetah-form on file already, we wouldn't have been able to get any of this done. You see, there's this gay dance club in San Francisco where..." Her words trailed off, and she blinked twice. "Anyway, Mr. Jones, the basic new layout is already in your bloodstream, and it can't be reversed. Everyone here seems to think that this was done with your permission." She paused. "Don't tell me that in this insane rush, no one..."

I sighed and looked down. "I probably did sign the papers," I admitted. "I just didn't bother to read them first. So don't worry; you've done nothing wrong." Then I met her eyes. "Not that it probably would've made any difference if I'd memorized them. They've really got my ass in a crack. Or else I've got my own ass in a crack; the truth is, I'm not even sure which anymore."

I thought about young Raymond in his wheelchair for some odd reason, and then my vision blurred. Perhaps it was the drugs. In any case, once I wiped my eyes I could see all right again. "But whichever, it looks like I'm going to be changing a lot more than I ever planned for."

Dr. Henway nodded, trying to pretend like she understood what I meant. "There's a whole package of treatments associated with this procedure," she explained. "Physical therapy, mandatory counseling... The program is very supportive." She smiled again. "I think you'll be fine, Mr. Jones. You seem much more stable than several other transformees I've sculpted."

I nodded and smiled back at her despite my apprehensions. Mandatory counseling! Just what I friggin' needed right in the middle of attempting a comeback. What a waste of time! But it was that or the highway, it seemed. I'd already been warned that if I was in any way uncooperative with the medical people, there were a dozen other prospects salivating for my spot in the lineup.

"So," I continued, "I'm getting a muzzle and tail to go with the fur." The words felt very odd coming out of my mouth. But still, there were worse things in the universe, I supposed. Like going back to the Dominican and begging for my old job back. *Or being a suffering kid in a wheelchair that was never, ever going to grow up,* a little voice whispered in my ear.

"I can live with that, I guess. Anything a gay exotic dancer can take, I can take." I smiled reassuringly at Kris, who seemed a little relieved. "But please, tell me right now. How far is this going to go on the rest of me?" I suddenly felt very aware of my body as it shifted slightly against the clean soft sheets. Up until then, somehow, the whole change-thing hadn't felt real. But... The drugs were already in my veins, she'd told me. *Already in my veins...*

How exactly would lying in this same bed feel, I wondered, with a layer of soft fur between my skin and the sheets? Not bad at all, I was suddenly certain.

Maybe this whole cheetah-thing might have some interesting aspects, after all.

They promised me I'd only be in the hospital for three weeks. By noon on the second day I started to go itchy all over, not just on top of my tattoo, and by two in the afternoon I was out for the count, not to be brought back around for seventeen days. They kept me in a full life-support tank all of that time, while every cell in my body was reprogrammed and, in some cases, taught a whole new way of life.

Not that I noticed any of this; all I ever remembered of it was having the same dream over and over again. In it I stood in front of my fourth grade teacher with a Mexican-style sombrero in my hands, barfing my guts out while she glared at me with Buster's eyes and the rest of the class chanted "Chee-*tah!* Chee-*tah!* Chee-*tah!*" At least I got paid for those three weeks, full rate. And, for those same twenty-one days, Coach Turnbull found no fault with me. Somehow, I figured that would end up being the all-time record.

When they finally woke me up, my tattoo was covered with cheetah-patterned fur, just as thick and full as promised. So was my chest, for that matter. And my back, and my legs, and my face, and my arms...

"Hey!" I protested to Dr. Henway as she bustled by on my first afternoon of wakefulness. "Wait up a second."

"Sure, Mr. Jones," she replied smoothly, not sounding at all frustrated despite the fact that I'd stopped her in exactly the same way six other times in the past hour. "What can I do for you?"

"These hands!" I complained, holding up the offending body parts and wriggling them vigorously, just like I'd already done with several other bits of my anatomy. "There's fur all over the palm side! How in the world can I be expected grab a baseball and throw it like this? I can't even get a decent grip on my water glass, for Christ's sake!"

"You'll have to shave them every morning," Kris replied pertly. "Instead of your face. We'll show you how to do it before you leave our care. But that's only temporary, of course. You'll have the beginnings of your paw-pads growing in a couple weeks. They'll be a little sore and tender at times, but at least you can quit shaving your hands then. The pads won't grow fur."

"Paw... Paw... Paw..." I stuttered, but just like the other six times, Dr. Henway was gone before I could formulate the rest of my question. You'd have thought she considered me an unpleasant person to be around, or something!

But that wasn't the worst. I had to spend a whole afternoon with Dr. Forster before they'd let me leave. He was a shrink.

"So," he said with a smile, leaning easily up against his desk. "Your nickname has always been Cheetah, eh? It's not just a baseball thing?"

"Kind of," I agreed after a long moment of silence.

"Kind of?" the therapist countered. "How so?"

I pressed my lips together. Since whiskers were also hair cells, I'd already grown them along with the fur. The stupid things tingled and itched whenever I moved my mouth. It was even more annoying than the tattoo had been, though everyone told me I'd get used to it in no time flat. "Well..."

The silence stretched out again, until Dr. Forster spoke again. "Did they start calling you that because you've always been fast?"

"No." Another long pause. This time it dragged on and on and on, until I began to think that the damned doc was trying to bore me to death. "At first, they called me 'Cheater'" I finally explained. "Everyone did. But once I moved away from home, I managed to get people to change it to 'Cheetah'. You don't want people calling you 'Cheater' when you play ball for a living. It gives people the wrong idea."

"Ah," Dr. Forster said slowly, a big fake smile painted onto his kisser. "I can see where that might be a problem."

There was another long silence, and I stirred awkwardly in my seat. Geez! What a bore this guy was! And I was going to have to keep seeing him all season long, twice a week? Maybe being unemployed in the Dominican Republic hadn't been so bad, after all! "My brother started it," I finally explained, just to fill the empty silence. "When I broke one of his toys. It was a little car that his grandma gave him. Then I fixed things up so that Mom would think he did it, so that it wouldn't be my fault. All of the kids on our street found out, and soon everyone was calling me that."

"Did the other kids like you?" my therapist asked.

"No," I answered, half-smiling. "I was always the fastest and the strongest, see? I won all the races, even with kids a year or two older than me. And since I was so strong, they couldn't outrun or outfight me either one. So, mostly they were afraid of me."

"You must've been a very angry young man," Dr. Forster observed.

I shrugged and half-chuckled. "Maybe," I allowed. "Not that it did me any good. Mom was always shacking up with these losers, see? Pathetic no-goods, every one. Most of them druggies, none had jobs. With them it didn't matter how fast and strong I was..."

And so on and so forth. It was the biggest waste of time imaginable; if only the team paid me *half* as much an hour as it was paying my shrink! When Dr. Henway interrupted us because it was time to show me how to shave my hands, I was never so glad to see anyone in my life! At least all she wanted was to show me how to live with the cheetah-stuff I had to do, instead of asking me stupid questions about my true name and who I really was, deep down inside.

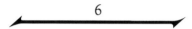

6

When the hospital finally released me, they sent a note to Coach Turnbull. He wasn't very happy when he opened it. "Light duty?" he asked, looking me directly in the eyes. Then he turned away again; my peepers were deep gold, now. They were the only part of the whole cheetah-thing I really liked so far. "What is this, Cheetah? You're already behind everyone else."

I shrugged. "It don't mean nothing to me, Coach," I replied. "I'll do whatever you want. The fact is, I didn't even open the envelope."

"Hrmm," Tony mumbled, pressing his lips together. Then he pushed a button on his desk. "Herman!" he demanded. "You busy?"

"Not at the moment," a youthful voice replied from the intercom box. "What can I do for you?"

"Cheetah's back from the hospital. He's got some kind of note from his doc. I need a trainer's opinion of what he can do and what he can't. We're in my office."

"Cool!" Herman exclaimed. "I can't wait to see him!"

I hadn't met Herman yet, but when he came bustling down the hall there was no doubt in my mind whatsoever as to who he was. Look up "nerd athlete wannabe" in the dictionary; the last time I checked his picture was still there. "Wow!" he declared once he stepped through the door, looking me up and down over and over again. "That came out *well!*"

"Thanks," I mumbled. Just about everyone seemed to think I looked good in spots, even though all I had so far was the fur.

My ears hadn't begun to migrate yet, nor did I have even the nub of a tail.

"Look!" Tony exclaimed, slamming the note down for Herman to read. "No running. No heavy exercise. No *emotional stress*, for God's sake! What am I supposed to do with this? I run a baseball team, not a girl's school!" He gestured at me. "Cheetah here seems cooperative enough," he added, just to be fair. "I don't think it's his fault. Maybe we can just ignore most of this crap?"

Herman smiled. My new trainer was much older than his voice and mannerisms would indicate, and the expression did nice things to the wrinkles in his face. "We'll work something out," he promised. Then he looked me over more carefully. I was wearing shorts and an armless shirt, all that was comfortable between the hot weather and the fur. In a few days, I was told, jillions of little nano-heat-exchangers would kick in to help keep my body temp where it belonged, and I would quit perspiring entirely. For the moment, though, I simply dressed for high summer even though it was still spring. "You've got excellent muscle definition, Cheetah," he proclaimed. "The fur seems to enhance it more than anything else."

I shrugged. "Whatever."

"Not much fat on you, either" he continued. "They do a pretty good job these days, maintaining conditioning while you're in a life support tank. And, you were playing pro ball just a few weeks back, weren't you? Fully in training?" he asked.

I nodded. "Yep."

"Good," Herman agreed. He turned to Tony. "We'll work something out," he promised again. "If I'm any judge, physically he's ready to play right now. Most likely it's just some little hitch with the transformation process. And the team's bought into that, right? So, I've just gotta call the doc first, and see what's going on. Plus, I really oughta sit down and have a heart-to-heart with Buster about where to take Cheetah's regimen. Give me until tomorrow to come up with a personal training plan. Okay?"

"Humph!" Tony snorted. Then he frowned and nodded. "All right," he agreed. "Cheetah goes to work tomorrow. But today he can hang around the field at least." Then the coach looked at me. "I've cut a deal with the press, on the side, like. They're gonna leave you alone for now, as a favor to me personally. So that's at least something you won't have to deal with right away. Though God knows they're gonna be all over that spot-job of yours sooner or later." Then Tony turned back to Herman. "He can get to know the rest of the team, and draw his uniform and gear. Can you walk him through that?"

"Sure!" the trainer agreed, smiling like a kid. He seemed to be the happiest guy in the world, Herman did, despite the fact that probably wasn't getting paid squat to be a trainer on a minor-league team. "Come on, Cheetah! I'll show you your locker and everything!

Two hours later, I was just finishing putting on my spanking-new jersey. The thing fit as if it'd been custom tailored, despite the fact that I'd never been measured. I wondered how it was they'd managed that, until Herman proudly explained that it had been his idea to call the hospital and have them measure me while I was still in the tank. He chattered my ears off, Herman did, nattering on endlessly about this and that like an old woman until eventually duty took him away. "You're going to love being with the Catfish," the young-old man predicted, slapping me on the back. "We're more a family than a ball team. Mr. Sandrell buys us the best of everything—you ought to see my training room! And Coach Turnbull is a real professional, much better than anyone we've had before. But I'll let you change clothes now. I'm sure you can find your own way around a clubhouse." And with that he was gone.

My locker was located just outside Coach Turnbull's window, where he could keep a close eye on me. Which was understandable enough, I supposed, even though it wasn't exactly what I would've chosen for myself. His and my eyes met several times while he stomped around hollering into his phone and I slowly changed clothes, making sure the fur was lying straight wherever the fabric was snug. I was just looking down at the ridiculous anthropomorphic catfish emblazoned across my chest for the very first time when someone knocked on Turnbull's door. He was a big guy, I noted, and despite the suit and tie his youth and overall healthy glow marked him as a fellow athlete. Probably a catcher, I judged from his build, or else maybe a first baseman. And a power-hitter, to boot.

"Yeah?" Tony replied, not even turning around. "Come in."

"Hello," the new guy said shyly, stepping inside and not quite closing the door after him. I could hear every word. "I'm Pudge Hiller."

"Hiller!" Tony replied, smiling wide and slamming the phone down, cutting off cold whoever was on the other end. He extended his right hand, and my new teammate shook it. "Hiller! I'm damned glad to see you, son! I traded half a team of good prospects for you, and don't regret it a bit."

The big man blushed slightly. "I just want to play," he replied. "That's the truth."

"And play you will!" Tony replied, wrapping his right arm around Hiller and sitting down next to him. They had old home week for a little while, as I put on my new cleats for the first time and adjusted them this way and that. I was a runner, after all. My cleats legitimately needed to be set up just right. I wasn't eavesdropping, oh no!

Why didn't Tony ever smile when he saw me?

"...only one problem," the coach was explaining as I finally finished with my left foot and switched over to lacing up the right. "We already have a 'Pudge' on this team, son. Pudge Jefferson. You may have heard of him. He's a catcher, too."

"I have," Hiller agreed. "He's a great man. I hope to learn a lot from him."

"That's why he's here," my coach explained. "His Major League career may be over, but Pudge caught in the Bigs for almost twenty-five seasons. He's more of a coach than a player these days, you see, especially for the pitching staff. The man has four Gold Gloves to his credit, and while he and I both think it's a long shot Pudge just might end up in Cooperstown." Then Tony sighed. "Hiller, I can't ask a man like that to change his nickname. I simply can't. Yet having two Pudge's on one team would be ridiculous, especially with both of them being catchers. Surely you can understand the position I'm in."

Hiller nodded. "I do."

Tony brightened. "Good! So, I checked your records, and everything says 'Pudge'. What's your real first name, anyway?"

Hiller blushed. "I was named after my mother's father. He was a great man, a doctor and philanthropist. There's a statue of him on our local town square. It was such an obvious thing at the time, me being named after him, that no one really thought—"

"I'm sure," Tony interrupted, still smiling. "What's your real name, son?"

"Adolph. My full legal name is Adolph Hiller."

You had to give Tony credit; his smile never wavered, even though he did blink. "*Adolph* Hiller? Your real, honest-to God legal name is Adolph Hiller?"

"Uh-huh," the young giant replied, looking as if he were about to cry.

"Well..." Tony answered, looking thoughtful. Then his face brightened once more. "Welcome aboard, Pudge!" he declared, standing up and escorting his new catcher to the door. "Glad to have you aboard! I'll call Herman, our trainer; he'll have you all sorted out in no time. Batting practice is at three. See ya there!"

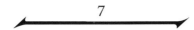

7

The inside of a dugout is relatively dark compared to a sunny ball field. This makes it difficult for anyone out practicing to notice someone inside, especially if the person in question sits in the back row and remains relatively immobile. I'd taken full advantage of this fact many times in my baseball career, starting back in high school when I'd sat and rolled joints when I should've been shagging flies.

So, the new fur aside, it felt quite natural indeed for me to slink along the dugout's back wall and then sit hunched-down on the end of the bench. Practically the whole team was working out; some were swinging bats under the watchful eyes of coaches, a little machine was pumping simulated fly balls into the outfield, and a remarkably young right-handed pitcher, eighteen years old if that, was standing out on the mound with his toe on the rubber, trying to hold a runner on first.

"Come on!" I heard the pitching coach cry out. "Smooth and sudden, just like I know you can."

"Easy, son," Buster's voice countered from the first-base coaching box. "You can take a bigger lead than that. Be confident, be bold."

Despite myself, I sat up and paid close attention. The runner at first was built just like me, I realized, lean and long of bone. But he wasn't leading off worth a damn. And then, when he finally decided to stretch things out, he leaned so obviously that a nine-year-old could've picked him off.

Which was precisely what the kid on the mound did, smooth and sudden just as he'd been coached. His form blurred into motion, the brand-new ball made a long white streak in the air, and there was a cloud of dust at first base. "Jeez!" Buster muttered; his runner had been thrown out by a foot or more.

The pitcher grinned, then turned to his beaming coach. "Good job, kid," the older man muttered.

Then they set up and did it again, and again, and again. And, mostly, the same thing happened. Each time, the runner became more hesitant, and his lead-off shrank to almost nothing. "Damnit!" Buster muttered to himself while the pitching coach called a time-out to work with his prospect on the finer points of things. Then he pursed his lips angrily.

I pursed my lips, too. Mr. Sandrell had wanted to put a team together based on speed, I knew. The kid looked fast enough, but...

Finally I stood up and strolled leisurely out into the sun. Almost immediately I began sweating heavily under the fur. But how could I let Buster suffer like that? "Heyas!" I called out, making sure that my head was held high and that I strode as arrogantly down the baseline as if I owned the entire stadium. The pitcher would be watching me every second, I knew, and it was vital that he get the proper message from the very start of things. Stealing bases was every bit as much a game of the mind as of the body, just like most of baseball. "How's tricks, Buster-Boy?"

"Cheetah!" he cried out in reply. For just a second his eyes widened in wonder at my new look, then he smiled just exactly the same way that he always did. It was impossible to dislike Buster, I suddenly realized, probably because he himself liked pretty much everyone else in the world. Which was just as well for me; the trait was probably the only reason he was the one coach in baseball who didn't actively hate me. "Good to see you again, son. *Good* to see you!" His smile widened, then he turned to the would-be base-stealer. "Cheetah Jones, meet Thump Morris."

Thump's eyes widened; I thought it was the spot-thing at first, but he never even mentioned it. "Jeez!" he exclaimed, taking my hand and shaking it enthusiastically. "I've seen so many of your game films! Buster shows them to me all the time."

I blushed a little, though of course no one but me could ever know it. "Really?"

"Uh-huh!" Thump continued, grinning like a kid. "You're awesome, man!"

"When he's not porking the owner's daughter in front of the press," Buster added sternly. "Or cussing out the fans. Or getting drunk on game days. Or..."

"Right, right, right," I countered. "There's no need to get into that. I'm sure he's heard the stories. Everyone else has." I held up my spotted arm. "And now there's this, too."

Thumps looked away. "They told us not to talk to you about that."

I blinked, then looked at Buster, who simply shrugged by way of an answer. "What's with this?" I asked. "I mean, we're a baseball team, for Christ's sake! We're going be living together for months!" I raised up my arm again. "How can we *not* talk about this?"

Buster grinned. "Your doc came and gave everyone a strict lecture. Coach Turnbull backed up every word. She said you're probably gonna have 'identity issues', whatever those are, and that everyone should give you a little space by not talking about it."

"She... I... Jeez!" I complained, turning away from Buster and looking around the field. Sure enough, everyone was staring at me. Though once they saw that I was looking back, everyone went right back to practicing as if nothing had happened. "I can't believe it. They went and messed up things even worse!"

"It's really all right," Thump explained. "No one's got a problem with it, I don't think. I mean, if a cheetah is who you really are, if that's your inner identity, well..." He smiled. "Who are we to complain? There's all sorts of strange people who play this game."

I turned to Buster. "Did he get that 'inner identity' baloney from Doctor Henway?"

He nodded silently.

"Jeez," I muttered again. After all, I couldn't tell anyone the *real* truth about why I was getting a morph-job. I'd known that going in. But the made-up story was even worse!

"Dancer Jenkins was especially supportive," Buster added, pointing out towards right field. I followed his finger to where a player stood with his very long legs crossed, waiting for the little machine to loft him another fly ball. He saw me looking, and gave me a furtive little grin and wave.

"Don't tell me..." I mumbled.

"Yep!" Buster replied. "You're absolutely right. Nothing wrong with your eyes at all, son! Like the kid said, all *sorts* of folks play this game." He grinned again. "And guess what! That little problem is all yours. And I can't wait to see how you handle it!"

"Right," I murmured, looking over at the mound. *Gay exotic dancers*, I reminded myself. *That's who mostly get the fur thing done to them. Gay exotic dancers...*

The coach was done now with whatever he'd been telling his pitcher, and they were clearly waiting for Buster and Thump. The right-hander was standing a little taller on the mound than he'd been before, I noticed, and smirking just a tiny bit after having made Thumps look so bad. "You know," I said slowly. "I'd like to take a crack at him."

"He's mighty fast!" Thumps warned me. "Reggie swivels like a big cat—"

"I've seen him," I interrupted.

Buster's eyes narrowed. "You ready to play yet?" he asked.

Clearly he hadn't gotten the word that I was supposed be taking things easy. Which meant that probably no one else out on the field had, either. "A little," I answered. "Until I get hot. My sweat glands are still all screwed up."

"Right," Buster answered, looking a little dubious. He eyed me up and down, then nodded. "If you want to run, run. I'm sure not going to be the one to stop you!"

Five minutes later, after doing some quick stretches, I was standing with my toe just barely touching first base, waiting for the pitcher to come to the set position. The first baseman, a big leftie who'd introduced himself simply as Steve, stood just behind me. But he wasn't important, not really. Not in this contest.

211

Instead, I locked my newly-yellow eyes onto the far more conventionally brown ones of young Reginald. It was already perfectly clear to both of us that we didn't like each other.

Not at all.

He toed the rubber, and I led off towards second. It was hot out in the sun, and I could feel sweat streaming down my back under the fur. For a long time we stood immobile, neither giving a centimeter. Then he pivoted and fired. I made it look easy, coming back in standing up. He'd not shown his best, in turn I'd not moved my fastest. It was the nature of the game. Then Steve tossed the ball back to his pitcher, Reggie set up again, and I took six inches more lead than I had the first time.

Now! a little voice inside me screamed as big Reginald pivoted once more. He was smooth, all right, but not smoother than me! I came back into first on my belly this time, raising a little cloud of dust but once again easily safe. "Time!" I called, and Buster watched as I patted the dust first out of my uniform, and then out of my fur.

"That's gonna be a pain," he sympathized.

"I'll live," I muttered. "We'll work something out." Just then I had bigger fish to fry than the fur-thing. It was an offense against the natural order of the universe that a pitcher should be allowed to remain poised and confident with a man on first. Not even pitchers on my own team could be exempted. Once I was as brushed-off as I could get, I returned to the base, smiled real big at Reginald, and kicked my feet theatrically. Then, very carefully, I scratched my nose.

With my middle finger.

The pitcher's mouth formed a hard thin line. *Message received,* I noted. All was going according to plan.

"Time in!" Buster cried. I grinned towards the mound again. Once Reginald was set I led off just a little further than the previous two times...

...and then flew like the wind for second as Reginald pivoted and threw to Steve. Something was wrong with the throw, I knew

212

from the way the kid had moved, though I couldn't have explained in a thousand years just *how* it was that I could tell. My heart pounded, my legs pumped, I filled my lungs once, twice, and then I was at second, with nary a shortstop nor second baseman in sight. The third-base coach was waving me on just as hard as he could, literally jumping and down in excitement, so I rounded the corner and pounded on with all I had. Then in a flash I was at third, sliding hard with my spikes riding up high and nasty...

...just as Steve emerged from the dugout with the ball that young, angry Reginald had so clearly just thrown there.

"T... T... Time!" I called again, and the beaming coach at third, whose name I still didn't even know yet, held up his arms and stopped play. Everyone on the field was staring at me now, I suddenly realized, everyone on the damn team; somewhere along the way they'd all stopped practice to watch the show. But they weren't staring at the spot-job anymore, or at least I didn't think so. Instead they were all grinning; Dancer was even jumping up and down and doing cheerleader kicks in a rather paisley sort of joy display. He must be a base-stealer too, I decided, to be so pleased with what I had just done; after all, with legs like those how could he *not* be?

Then the world started spinning around me, I sat down very hard on third base, and everything went black.

"...shouldn't be allowed back on the field!" the pitching coach was shouting at Tony, as I sat on the little bench beside my locker and allowed Herman to pour cold water over me. "If you'd'a seen it, Tony, I swear you'd feel the same way. It was a lousy *practice*, for crying out loud! Not guerilla warfare!"

Young Eric, I'd been told, hadn't been able to throw a single strike all afternoon once I'd finished with him. Apparently, I'd quite thoroughly rattled him. A pity, that.

"Now, Roger," Turnbull countered, a consoling note in his voice. "This is as close to the Bigs as you can get without actually being there. Your kid is young. Too young, I think. We've been rushing him along ever since high school."

"Yeah!" the pitching coach answered, not sounding the least bit placated. "Because he's the hottest pitching prospect in our entire farm system! Or at least he was until that two-bit street-fighter of yours started screwing with his head!"

Suddenly Tony didn't sound happy. "Cheetah is *your* two-bit streetfighter too, Roger. Every bit as much as he is mine. We're all on the same team here. And don't you make a habit of forgetting it." There was a long silence. "The kid's going down to double-A tomorrow, Rog. Physically, he's the hottest thing in the minors; I'll give you that. An arm like his doesn't come along once a decade. But he still has some growing up to do, which is right and natural at his age. This isn't the first time he's gone wild, not by a long shot." He sighed. "People are *going* to screw with his head, Roger. Can't you see that? Cheetah did his job out there today, and he did it well. If Reggie isn't grown up enough to play mind games and win, then he doesn't belong in triple-A ball. And that's that."

"Damn!" Roger declared, slamming his hat to the office floor. A long awkward moment passed, then the pitching coach bent over, picked up his headgear, and went storming down the hall towards the bullpen without so much as sparing me a glance.

"You feeling any better yet?" Herman asked after a few moments of silence had passed. He was smiling again, all happy wrinkles. The pitching staff had their own trainer, I knew, which explained much.

"Yeah," I answered, even though my brain still felt like it was about to explode. "Do I still have to go back to the hospital?"

"Nope," my trainer replied. "I managed to talk them out of it." Then the wrinkles hardened slightly. "But, you've got to stay out of the sun, Cheetah—for another week, at least."

I nodded, "Right." This time, I actually believed it.

"While you were out on the field," Herman continued, "I was doing some checking up. It seems that if we turn the air-conditioning down real low, and also keep a close eye on your core-temperature, there's at least some workouts we can do right now."

"Really?" I asked. "Like what?"

Herman frowned. "I've been talking to Buster," he explained. "You're fast, Cheetah. And your glove is just fine at either shortstop or second. But you don't hit well for average."

I sighed and looked away as the water continued to trickle down my back. Wet fur smelled really, really bad, I decided. Though, I was clearly going to have to get used to it. And it felt even worse, clammy and cold. "That's true," I admitted eventually. "It's not my fault. I've always been a weak hitter."

"Of course it's not your fault," Herman replied reassuringly as he continued to dribble cold water over me from his big yellow sponge. "But, I had an idea, see? And Buster likes it, too. How about if we bulk you up a little?" I started to object, but before I could get the words out Herman was speaking again. "Just in the right places, not enough to slow you down. For example, bigger wrist muscles would give you more control of the bat. And improving your upper body strength in general could help you at the plate. You hit lots of grounders up the middle. With a little more zing on them, how many more of them might dribble through and turn into singles? I think you could stand to carry a little more weight, so long as it's all muscle." He smiled again. "Besides, we can do extra speed-drills, to make up for anything you might lose in that department. I've got some ideas that just might help there, too."

I frowned. *More* speed drills? And weightlifting too? "Look," I began slowly "That's a lot of work, probably all for nothing. I don't know if..."

"Great!" Herman replied as if I'd agreed with him. "Good deal! I'm looking forward to spending a lot of time with you, then."

"He's bought into the new workout schedule?" a new voice boomed out; it was Tony, who'd apparently just then stepped out of his office to come and check up on me.

"Yeah!" Herman agreed, squeezing his sponge over the top of my head so that for a moment I couldn't speak without getting sweaty-fur flavored water in my mouth. "He seems real enthusiastic about the whole thing, Coach. Just like Buster told me he'd be."

"Hmm," Turnbull muttered, his tone dubious. He bent over and, squinting his eyes, examined me like a rancher looking over a prime beef. "Well. Whaddaya know?"

Then he was gone.

The next few weeks were absolute misery.

My body changes should've been the worst of it. Yes, the paw-pads did in fact begin to grow in, just as promised, on both my hands and my feet. But the damned things itched like the devil, all day long and into the night. Doctor Henway gave me some cream to rub into them. It stopped the itching, sure enough, but the stuff also stank; so badly that no one would willingly sit downwind of me. Even worse, I was told, I'd soon need to rub the same ointment into my lips and nose. How I'd ever manage to tolerate *that* was beyond me!

I'd asked Buster to find me a place to stay before going into the hospital. He came up a nice apartment, located in a clean little complex within a short drive of the field. I couldn't really complain, considering he'd also loaned me enough money to pay my first month's share of the rent. It would've been ungrateful to do so anyway, because it really *was* such a nice little place. Still, Thumps was not at all whom I'd have freely chosen as a roommate. It wasn't that there was anything to dislike about him; far from it. But jeez! He was so, like—wholesome.

"I've got to go, Mom," he was saying into his cellphone as he opened the door for me the very first time. "My new apartment mate is here." A pause, while he smiled apologetically at me.

Thumps wasn't more than four years younger than me, yet he seemed like such a little kid! "Yes, Mom, I know him pretty well. He's on the team with me, remember?" Then there was another pause, as Thumps rolled his eyes theatrically. "Mom and Dad are coming by next weekend," he explained, placing his hand over the mouthpiece. "And Mom wants to know if cannelloni is okay for dinner? With steamed broccoli?"

Inside my purported home, I felt like I was living in a dollhouse. Thumps was neat, almost compulsively so, and it was nerve-wracking in the extreme to have him constantly chasing around after me closing cabinet doors and picking things up. He never uttered a word of complaint about my slovenliness, which actually made things worse. Thumps was a good kid, maybe even a great kid, in his way. This was precisely why he made me so uncomfortable. I mean, he didn't even *drink*!

Practice wasn't any fun, either. I didn't mind batting practice, or fielding practice, or even a few wind sprints considering my specialty. But Herman, I'd decided, was trying to *kill* me! No sooner was I done with the weight machine then he wanted me to sprint like a maniac through his special course, where I had to place my feet in painted boxes and lift my knees high. Then I did squats and lifted dumbells until the cows came home, long after everyone else on the team had gone.

All except for Dancer and Thumps, of course. Impressed by my first-day showing, they'd decided to adopt my new training regimen, too. So, I was never left alone to suffer in peace. Instead of just me and my trainer, I was stuck with having two fellow players at my elbow all of the time. It wouldn't have been so bad, except that Dancer was easily stronger than I was. And, worst of all, Thumps was always a tick or two faster every time we raced.

I'd never, ever been on a team with someone faster than me before. It was much harder to take than I'd have expected. Every time he beat me in a race, I wanted to take the little jerk by the throat and throttle the life out of him. Then, I had to go home and eat his Mom's leftover cannelloni.

At least having Dancer stay over with us meant that Thumps and I got a ride to and from the field. I couldn't afford a car, and rather to my shock Thumps had never learned to drive. Dancer's life-partner Dasher (people always called him that, and he seemed to like it well enough) had an old beat-up sedan, so we always had wheels.

Did I mention that Dancer and Dasher lived directly upstairs over us? My teammate had earned his nickname fair and square, it seemed. Every morning, just after the break of dawn, he began his daily routine by performing classical ballet in his living room. "It's *great* for the balance!" he'd explained to me the first day. "And for agility and flexibility, too! You could work out with us anytime you liked!" He looked very hurt when I explained that things weren't necessarily as they might appear about me, despite the fact that I was as gentle as possible about it.

After all, I needed his wheels.

And, when I wasn't doing ten-thousand dumbbell lifts or sprinting like a fool around the basepads, I was back at the hospital having tests run. It was absolutely essential that the team be able to prove at a moment's notice that none of my modifications were performance-enhancing in any way, and that my athletic abilities were still limited by the same natural factors that they'd always been. So, I spent hours patiently enduring electrical stimulation of my nerves and muscles, bright flashes in my dilated eyes, and a thousand other torments from the innermost circles of hell. Sometimes Dr. Henway came to look me over, and made little cosmetic adjustments here and there to keep things under control. In truth, I had to give her credit. Even with my face still looking all funny from the long whiskers that didn't really belong without a muzzle, I couldn't help but find my new self considerably more attractive than the old. Instead of looking gaunt and haunted, I now came across as lean and determined.

The absolute worst, though, was the shrink. I didn't understand what was up with that from the very beginning; all we ever talked about was how things had been when I was growing up. One session we talked about how Mom's boyfriends had beaten me up so often, another time about when I'd come home from ball practice and found her overdosed on the couch. I'd had to call an ambulance, and she'd nearly died anyway. "Why did you work so hard at baseball?" Dr. Forster asked me one day. "When you had so much else going on in your life?"

I shrugged, then frowned at myself for having done so; the gesture had felt childish, somehow. "I dunno. It was just there."

My shrink nodded and smiled. An endless silence ensued, while I sat and thought. Jeez, how should I know why I did anything? "I was good at it," I answered finally.

Dr. Foster smiled, and once again said nothing. There was more silence.

"It was, like, the only thing that meant anything to me," I explained. "The only thing that felt good. Mom was a piece of garbage, her lovers even worse pieces of trash..." I frowned, a little surprised at how angry I was suddenly becoming. "No one ever gave a damn about anything I did—except the coaches."

"They spent a lot of time with you, I'd imagine."

"Heck, yeah! I was always, like, the whole team. Best hitter, best pitcher, best runner... I was their ticket to bigger and better things."

This time Dr. Forster frowned. "So, it was Cheetah Jones the player you felt they really cared about, then? Not Cheetah Jones the growing young man?"

"Heh!" I barked, leaning back and folding my arms. "Let me tell you something, Mr. Headshrinker! Back then, I was the genuine item! I carried our team to the State Championship not once but twice, and everyone knew it. No one cared if I sold a little weed for pocket change or cut a few classes, if you know what I mean. No one! Not even the friggin' principal!"

219

"I see," Dr. Forster replied mildly. "I think I really am indeed beginning to see."

All the sessions were like that, really. One time I asked the old man if we were ever even gonna talk about me growing fur. "Would you like to talk about that?" he'd asked in return, and I just about wept in frustration. What was I doing wasting time in therapy for, anyway? Didn't I have enough to deal with, what with the extra training and all that? All it ever did was stir me up; I always left all mad about stuff that had happened years ago. And why couldn't Buster have roomed me up with someone who at least kept a few cold beers in his fridge, like any normal human being? Why?

But, worst of all, if I had to listen to "Swan Lake" at five in the morning even one more time, my head was gonna explode!

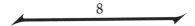

8

The best thing about spring training is that it eventually ends. The winners get to stay up with the team, the losers get shipped down a level, and finally everyone gets to play real baseball games instead of stupid simulations. Dancer, Thumps and I all easily made the cut. I hit leadoff and played short, Thumps moved over to second from his natural position of short to accommodate me and batted in the number-two spot, Dancer batted third and played left field, while Pudge Hiller hit cleanup and caught most days.

The idea was that if one or two of us fast-movers could get on base, then all sorts of good things could begin happening all at the same time. With a base-stealer on, for example, Pudge would be certain to come up to bat in his number four spot. The threat to steal might unbalance the pitcher enough, say, to hang a curve ball for Pudge. With his bat, one hung curve was all he needed to put a couple runs onto the scoreboard. Or, alternatively, the stress of facing Pudge might make the pitcher forget about the runners on base, allowing them to steal at will so that a mere single or sacrifice fly might bring them home. Plus, having all three speedsters in the top of the order put a huge stress on the opposing lineup's fielders; if they made the slightest mistake in ball-handling, we'd eat their lunch on the basepads. And even worse, they knew it and would fret about it, sometimes even for days before facing us on the field. So, working together, we hoped to induce a lot of fielding errors.

The rest of the lineup was mediocre at best, though we had an outstandingly good pitching staff for a minor league team. I'd once heard Coach Turnbull claim that he'd traded half a team of prospects for Pudge Hiller, and the evidence was clear to see in the rest of our teammates. We four top-of-the-order types would either score enough runs to carry the team, or we wouldn't. It was just that simple. On us, and on the pitchers, rested the fate of the entire club

The press seemed to know it, too. All four of us had been getting interview requests every day for weeks. The other three had been talking to the reporters for ages now, but so far I hadn't. Our opening game was at home, and after our last pre-season practice Tony called me into his office for a private talk. "I can't tell you anymore how you ought to handle the press," he explained. "So far, I've ordered you to stay away from them, and I'll give you full credit for obeying instructions. You're looking pretty fair out on the field, too. Working hard, even, and it shows." He folded his arms and leaned back in his sweat-stained swivel chair. "Eventually, though, you've gotta grow up. You want to talk to them, you've got the green light. You don't, I'll keep 'em off your back. Whaddaya want to do?"

I frowned for just an instant, then winced and flattened out my mouth again. It hurt to frown; perhaps my muzzle was beginning to come in? "My agent says that I ought to make friends with them," I said slowly. "Make my name just as big as I possibly can. That's the way to get sponsorships."

Tony nodded slowly, but remained silent.

"On the other hand," I continued, "what have reporters ever really done for me except get me into trouble? All they are is a pain in the butt." I sighed, then shook my head. "You know, I haven't done a thing but play baseball since I got here. Not a single thing!"

My coach nodded his head again.

"Play baseball, run sprints, work out until the cows come home..." I tried to frown again, being a slow learner. It hurt even worse the second time. "Plus turn into a friggin' cheetah. Jesus Christ!" Finally I shook my head and opened the office door. "Tell the reporters to stay away the hell away, Coach. Only pretty it up some, willya? I've got *enough* on my plate just now.

Opening Day was an impressive event, for a minor-league operation. A bunch of local business leaders turned out for the Monday afternoon game, and the franken-plant factory actually shut down their smelliest operations as a favor for us, so that we weren't half-choking for once. The stands were almost two-thirds full, an outstanding turnout for AAA ball. I broke a shoelace just before the Star-Spangled Banner began to play, and went jogging down to my locker to pick up a spare.

"Hey!" Tony cried out as soon as he saw me, banging on his office window. "Hey, Cheetah!"

"Coach!" I answered, smiling slightly. Everyone was wondering where Tony was. Most of us figured he was in the crapper; rumor was he'd eaten half a ton of jambalaya the night before at some kind of season-opening dinner.

He banged the window again. "Cheetah!" he demanded. "Get over here!"

I wasn't really supposed to be in the clubhouse so close to game-time, I knew, but I had a perfectly good reason; surely Tony would understand! "I've got a broken shoelace," I explained, holding up my foot so that he could see the dangling end. "I'm trying to get fixed up before the first pitch. See? It's not my fault."

"Damnit!" Tony roared. "I don't care about your shoelace! Get over here! My door is stuck! I think the lock is broken."

My jaw dropped for just an instant, then I jogged across and around. "Grab the other side," Tony directed. "See if you can help me force it. I've got our lineup card in here with me!"

We yanked and pulled and shook together, but got nowhere. "Damnit!" Tony roared. "Go get Herman! And tell Buster, too!"

Presently everyone and their brother was standing around Tony's office while he raved and cursed and threw things. "Opening day!" he roared out. "Opening damn day! I'm the laughingstock of the league!"

"It's okay, Tony," the opposing coach reassured him. They were old friends, having played together for a few years back in the day. "Look at the bright side. With a half-animal playing short and a flamer in left field, you'd have been the laughingstock anyhow."

"Probably," the chief umpire agreed, smirking. He was holding the game up until Tony could be freed.

"Let me try," Pudge Hiller suggested, holding up a bat. "Maybe I can knock the knob clean off." Everyone backed off a little, then Pudge raised his bat to the vertical and brought it down with all the hard, trained muscle of a professional power-hitter behind the blow.

Wham! the bat went as it slammed into the knob—which sheared off clean, ricocheted hard off of the cement floor, then flew back up and hit Pudge square in the face. "Damn!" the big man moaned, dropping his bat and bending over double.

"Damn!" Tony echoed from inside his little prison. He tried the door again; it was still just as stuck as before. "Damn, damn, damn!"

"Let me through!" Herman cried out, forcing his way to the front of the crowd. Pudge was sort of rocking back and forth now, moaning. Ominously, there was blood trickling down the back of his hands.

"Damn!" Tony repeated himself, seeing the blood himself. "What a stupid, idiotic way to..."

223

"It's *all right*," Herman interrupted, sidling up to Pudge's side and staring daggers at Tony. "Everything's going to be all right, Pudge. Here, let's get your hands down so we can take a good look at that face of yours..."

Just then, with perfect timing, the stadium loudspeakers came to life. "Attention, ladies and gentlemen! Your attention, please! Is there a locksmith in the house..."

It was just as well that we won the opening game; had we not, I fear that Tony might have done something foolish. Buster had been forced to rush Pudge to the hospital for x-rays and then a proton-scan, but despite a truly nasty bruise on his cheek and a gash that took seven stitches to repair, no serious damage was done. Still, no one at the ball park knew for sure that he was okay until the bottom of the fourth, and by then we had well and truly gone to town on our arch-rival Grenada Muskrats. I went three for four with two stolen bases, Dancer hit what by rights should've been a double but which his long legs stretched into a triple, and Thumps walked twice while I distracted the pitcher out on the basepads. Even gray-haired old Pudge Jefferson put on a show; he hit two homers for no less than five RBI's, looking fifteen years younger as he limped across home plate for the second time in one afternoon.

Still, the magic couldn't last forever. Soon Dancer was struggling at the plate, and the elder Pudge's gimpy knees were keeping him from running out singles. Even worse, Thumps never really got started; we were into the third week before he quit being zip for the season at the plate. He took more and more batting practice, but just couldn't seem to connect. I was feeling pretty sorry for him, just like everyone else. But, what can one player do for another when he's in a slump? I left him in Buster's capable hands, and tried not to make too big a mess back at the apartment.

Things might've sucked for the team as a whole, but personally I was living high and wide. At least I was hitting all right, even if no one else was. Plus, I was stealing bases. A few fans were beginning to show up wearing cheetah-spotted hats and sometimes even makeup jobs. If I got stranded all of the time, was that my fault? What could I do about other people's problems?

Once I got a few full paychecks in and had paid off a few collection agencies, I was finally able to buy myself a few nice things. Thumps had furnished the apartment, so there wasn't any need for anything along those lines. So, I went down to the mall and priced myself out a big, heavy gold chain just like the one I'd treated myself to when I'd first broken through into the majors, then had pawned in the Dominican Republic for airfare back home. When I tried it on in the store, though, my fur kept getting caught in all the little links. It hurt whenever I moved. Finally, I gave up on the whole thing as a bad idea.

My credit rating was nothing more than a fond memory, but I still had a nice roll of bills burning a hole in my pocket. So, I went down and bought myself an alcohol-powered scooter to run back and forth to the field with, and maybe to get around town when it wasn't raining. Dancer and Dasher were bickering all of the time about another man that Dasher might or might not be seeing, and riding with them had definitely ceased to be fun. A better ride would've been nicer, but given a choice between the kind of piece of junk car I could afford to pay cash for and a brand-new scooter that would actually start when I pressed the button, I felt like I made a pretty good deal.

Pretty soon I was zipping all around Baton Rouge. Buster looked worried when I first showed up on the thing, but Tony never complained; he had plenty of other stuff on his mind. Plus, I suspect, Thumps was probably glad to be rid of me from time to time. "How do you read the pitchers so well?" he was constantly asking me. "Do you keep a book? This guy Hastings who's pitching tomorrow; have you ever seen him play before?" It was all baseball, baseball, baseball with Thumps; between his continual nagging and the ongoing ballet recital upstairs, a man

225

couldn't get any rest! It was a good thing that our division was mostly concentrated in the delta country; at least our bus rides tended to be short and we weren't often on the road for more than a week or two at a time.

Things got even worse when Pudge Hiller came back off of the disabled list. Everyone expected that his bat would give the team a big lift, but it didn't work out that way at all. *Whoof!* *Whoof! Whoof!* his bat would go, and our finest hitter was down on strikes. Something seemed to be really bothering the man. "Heya, Cheetah" he mumbled glumly sometimes in passing; more often he said nothing at all. If he'd smiled once since spring training, no one had noticed. But, I had my own problems.

Most of them were with my shrink. "What do you feel when you look into the mirror these days?" he asked me one week, not too terribly long before mid-season. We were eight games under five-hundred, and nearly in last place. Even worse, I'd gone nothing for three at the plate that afternoon, and made an error in the field. And now here I was, having to talk about feelings. Talk about a miserable day!

"Like I'm a real dork," would've been an honest answer; things were getting to the point where it was hard to see the old Cheetah behind the new. Sometimes, it felt like I was wearing a mask that wouldn't come off, and somehow that really bothered me. I was having freaky dreams, too. My muzzle was beginning to grow in, and I missed three days while I had a bunch of old teeth pulled and new, more ferocious ones implanted. I kept biting the inside of my cheeks for a week after that, which was even worse than my itchy tattoo had been. On top of that, the base of my spine was continually burning where my tail was about to emerge. "I feel just the same way as I always did," I answered instead.

"And how is that?" Forster asked, grinning slightly.

Jesus! Would *nothing* satisfy the man? "Like I'm looking at me," I explained. "Like, I'm checking to see if there's a speck of dirt in my eye or something." My eyes narrowed; I was truly growing tired of this game. "How do *you* feel when you look in the mirror, doc?"

"Like I could stand to lose fifty pounds," he answered, grinning his most annoying grin. "Do your team mates seem to treat you any differently?"

I shrugged. "They hardly ever speak to me anymore."

The shrink's eyebrows rose. "Really?"

"Yeah," I agreed, shifting a little in my seat. Dr. Forster had been kind enough to find one for me that was easy on my tail area, but with all the swelling I still wasn't very comfortable. "That's how it always is, though. I don't think it's because of the fur."

"You're a loner, then?"

I nodded. "Pretty much. When you stay off to yourself, people don't keep asking you to do things for them, see? You leave them alone, they leave you alone. No one gets hurt."

"When you get close to people, they hurt you?"

"Usually," I answered, wriggling uncomfortably again.

"Do you have any friends at all?" Dr. Forster asked.

I shrugged. "I live with Thumps. He's all right, I guess. Though, he's a pest sometimes. It used to really piss me off."

"He bothers you?"

"Yeah," I answered, curling my lip slightly in disgust. It looked a lot better with the new teeth. "He's always acting like I know stuff he doesn't. Like, how far to lead off first. Or how to mind-game a pitcher." I frowned. "He irritated me all through spring training, and even after. But now, it's finally slacked off some."

"Uh-huh," Dr. Forster said, smiling encouragingly.

"He followed me around like a little kid," I continued, my frown intensifying. "I'm glad he's past that."

Dr. Forster frowned, then hesitated a minute, like he was thinking about something. "You mentioned to me once that you had a younger brother," he said slowly.

I felt my lip curl still further, into a definite snarl. "What about him?"

"Well..." Forster smiled. "People are generally pretty close to their brothers. Yet I don't recall your ever mentioning his name. Have you seen him lately? Are you close? How does he feel about the 'fur thing', as you call it?"

I sat still for a very long time, until the cramps from my suddenly-balled fists became painful. Then, very slowly, I climbed to my feet and stood towering over my shrink. "I don't want to talk to you about my brother," I said very slowly. "Not now or ever. Do you understand me?"

Forster visibly paled. "I... I mean.... Cheetah...."

I shook my head. "Doc, I'll talk to you about baseball all you want. I'll tell you everything you want to hear about my reflection in the mirror. I agreed to talk to you about that kind of thing, and I'll keep my word. But don't you *ever* bring up my younger brother again. He ain't got nothin' to do with anything. You hear me?"

Forster nodded, sweating visibly. "I... I..."

"Good," I answered, turning to leave even though the session wasn't half over. "I'll see you next Tuesday."

9

I nearly wrecked my scooter three times on the way home that afternoon; twice when I went into curves way too fast and once when I cut in front of a delivery truck with bad brakes. My hands were still shaking with rage when I pulled up in front of Thumps' and my little apartment; I lowered the sidestand with a savage kick, took off my helmet, and then headed up the sidewalk. Damn, but I needed a drink!

"Hey, Cheetah!" a voice called out from behind me. It was Buster, climbing out of his old Cadillac halfway across the lot. "Wait up!"

I closed my eyes and sighed. What else could possibly go wrong today? "Sure," I answered, letting a little of my anger make itself heard in my tone.

Buster came bustling up, then eyed me up and down nervously. "Are you all right?" he asked.

"Well enough," I answered. "What gives?"

He frowned, then looked away. "I've got a situation, Cheetah," he explained. "A bad one. I could use some help."

I felt my ears stir slightly. The sensation was... odd. "What kind of situation?"

"I'm not entirely sure yet," he explained, meeting my eyes once more. "Truth be told, I came to see if I could get Dancer to come with me. But when I got up close to the door, I could hear him and Dasher fighting again."

I nodded. "They've been at it for weeks."

"Yeah," he agreed, looking at the ground again. "I know."

"What about Thumps?" I asked, pointing at our window. "He could help you."

Buster shook his head. "No, I don't think so." Once again he met my eyes. "Cheetah, the fact is that things might get rough, see? And though I think the world of the kid most ways, Thumps isn't exactly who I'd want covering my back in a fight. Not that he wouldn't give his best, mind you. But..."

I nodded, intrigued despite myself. "Yeah. No street smarts." I paused and pressed my lips together, then nodded my head. "All right, Buster. I reckon I owe you one. Maybe even more than one. So let's go take care of this, whatever it is. But can you at least let me know what I'm getting myself into?"

"....been coming in every day with bruises," Buster explained as he drove us across town. "Not really bad ones, mind you. But enough to make Herman wonder."

I nodded. "Uh-huh."

"He's in a terrible slump," Buster continued. "Anyone can see there's something wrong with Pudge." He sighed. "When *you* don't talk to anyone, Cheetah, that's normal. But ever since his first couple of weeks, Pudge has clammed up too."

I shrugged. There were terrible bags under our star catcher's eyes of late. "Sometimes he really looks like he's at the end of his rope." Then I frowned. "But look, Buster. Pudge is a big, powerful man. If he's got bruises on him, I'd hate to see the other guy."

Buster nodded. "I know—which is part of why this is all so strange." He frowned. "I tried to call his house tonight, Cheetah. Someone answered, but then all I heard was yelling before I got cut off. It sounded pretty ugly. Expect anything."

"Gotcha." I curled my lip and looked out the window. We were in the older part of town now, where the lots were large and well-manicured. Our catcher made more money than any of the rest of us, and could well afford to live in such a nice area. He was married, though his wife never came out to the field to see him. None of us had met her at all, that I knew of.

Buster made two more lefts down quiet, residential streets, then a right into a long, magnolia-lined gravel driveway. The instant the car stopped, we could hear shouting.

"Damn you!" a female voice was shrieking. "Can't you do anything right? Move it back this way again."

"Honey," Pudge's voice answered, a little unsteady. "It's awfully heavy. Why can't we..."

Whap! Something hit something else, hard. "Ow!" Pudge objected. "Kathy, please! You don't—"

WhapWhapWhap! "Pick it up, you miserable bastard!"

I looked over at Buster, who was already looking at me. "Jeez," he muttered.

"Yeah," I agreed.

Buster went directly to the front door, and I sort of sidled off towards an open window. Sure enough, just across the room Pudge was bent over a heavy-looking dresser while his wife beat him about the head and shoulders with what looked like a curtain rod. "You... Stupid... Idiot!" she declared, punctuating each word with a blow. "You're fat! And useless! And stupid! And..."

"Honey!" Pudge answered, falling to his knees under the rain of blows. It was ridiculous, in a way; the young giant could easily have turned around and killed his wife with his bare hands. Yet at the same time, it was also touching. Clearly, he was trying his best to make things work. "I love you, honey! Ow! Please, put that down and let's... Ow! Honey, remember what the counselor..."

"To hell with the counselor!" she declared, redoubling the intensity of her attack. "And to hell with *you!*" I felt my lip curl back again; there was *something* about what I was looking at. I couldn't quite put my finger on it, but it bothered me. Way down inside, where it mattered.

Just then the doorbell rang, and Kathy threw down her weapon in disgust. "I'll be right back!" she declared. "And we'll see then if you can put something *exactly* where you're told to!"

Then she was gone, and Pudge was bent over the dresser, sobbing. "Psst!" I said. "Psst!" Over here!" I scratched at the window screen.

Pudge raised his head. "Who..."

"It's me!" I explained. "Cheetah! And that's Buster at the front door."

He turned, and I saw that his face was a mass of bruises. "Cheetah? What..."

"Come on!" I ordered. "Open the window!"

"Open the window?" he repeated, looking baffled.

Well, maybe he was stunned from the beating. "Come *on!*" I hissed. "We're getting you out of here. Now!"

"But... But..."

I snarled, then punched out the screen. "Come on!" I ordered, extending a spotted hand. "Buster and I will find a place to put you up. We've got to get you out of here."

Pudge frowned. "Cheetah," he said slowly, "I know you mean well. But Kathy's just a little hot-tempered. She really loves me, deep down, and—"

"Bullshit!" I declared. I'd heard enough of this same sort of crap from my mom, usually while I was holding an ice bag to either her battered face or my own. I tore the screen open wider. "Get out here, Pudge. We haven't got all night."

"Cheetah, I... Uh...."

"Damn it!" I declared, pounding the windowsill. "If you don't get your butt out here, I'll tell every reporter in the world that your real name is Adolph!"

Pudge's jaw worked slowly once, then twice. "Cheetah, you bastard…"

"I'll do it!" I shrieked. "I'm just the man for the job! And you know it!"

The catcher's jaw worked one last time, then he bared his teeth at me. "You are, aren't you? You miserable jackass!"

I took one step back and smiled wide, letting the pointy teeth show. "Try me."

All of this time Buster and Kathy had been shouting at each other through the front door; it now slammed. "Time's up, Adolph!" I declared.

"Damn!" he hissed through clenched teeth. "Damn, damn, damn!"

And then, to my intense relief, he climbed through the window and dropped heavily to the ground beside me. "Come on!" I urged, pointing. "Buster's car is right over there."

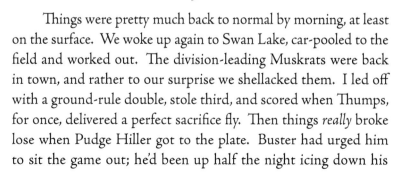

Things were pretty much back to normal by morning, at least on the surface. We woke up again to Swan Lake, car-pooled to the field and worked out. The division-leading Muskrats were back in town, and rather to our surprise we shellacked them. I led off with a ground-rule double, stole third, and scored when Thumps, for once, delivered a perfect sacrifice fly. Then things *really* broke lose when Pudge Hiller got to the plate. Buster had urged him to sit the game out; he'd been up half the night icing down his bruises and explaining to the police that no, he did *not* wish to press spousal-abuse charges against his wife.

The Muskrat pitcher made the mistake of confusing Pudge's obvious fatigue for weak resolve, and challenged him with a fastball right down Main Street. Our catcher drilled it up the middle, so hard that it was still rising when it left the stadium. After that, all we did all evening long was run up the score; I hit for the cycle, including my first honest-to-God over-the-wall home run as a professional. (I'd hit an inside-the-park one during my brief stint in the Majors, but somehow that didn't feel like it counted.) Everywhere I looked, cheetah-print hats were flying in the air. My bulging muscles were beginning to pay off. That night, Mr. Sandrell called me up and congratulated me; "Cheetah," he said, "I'm very pleased with your performance so far. It makes me believe in the magic of baseball more than ever." I couldn't believe that he'd actually *noticed*, much less taken the time to call.

But, even that wasn't the most memorable event of the day. After the phone call, Coach Turnbull stopped by my locker. "You and I have something we need to do when you're out of the shower," he said shortly. "Out in the business office." Then he was gone.

I wondered what it was about the whole time I washed up. I'd stayed clean, hadn't I? Not a single beer had passed my lips in weeks, though at times it'd been hard, hard, hard. My personal numbers were plenty good, even if the team was nine and a half back. That wasn't *my* fault! I hadn't given a single interview to anyone… So, what was his complaint? And why the business office?

It took me all of half a second to figure things out when I burst unannounced through Turnbull's office door. He was behind his desk—and sitting across from him was the wheelchair-kid we'd run into in New York… What was his name?

"You may remember Raymond," the Coach began, forestalling any difficulties. "And his mother, Mrs. Belanger."

I smiled and nodded, then awkwardly removed my hat. He still weirded me out, though I did my best not to let it show. Weirded me out, and something more. Though, I wasn't sure quite what. "Hi," was all I said.

"I just wanted to thank you for the picture," young Raymond said, his voice thin and weak. He didn't look nearly so good as he had in front of the Freedom Center, and that hadn't been all that great. "It was so cool!"

"We're down here visiting my in-laws," Mrs. Belanger explained with a smile. "Once we found out where you played, well..."

I smiled and nodded, then squatted down alongside the wheelchair. "It was a pleasure. Though, that pic is a wee bit... Outdated."

"Yeah!" Raymond agreed, eyes large. "It sure is!" Then he smiled again. "You hit for the cycle. It was so cool!"

I'd do it again, I heard a little voice say in the back of my head, *a thousand times over, if it could do a damn thing to help you.* "Not nearly so cool as seeing you again," I said instead. Then I turned to Coach Turnbull. "I presume you have the latest version handy?"

He smiled and passed it over. "To Raymond," I signed it, trying not to cry. Why was this kid getting to me so badly, all of a sudden? "Who believed in me."

"Gosh!" he said when I handed it over.

"Gosh," I repeated. Then I looked over at the coach again, eyes brimming with tears. "Is this the best we can do?"

Turnbull blinked, genuinely caught off guard. "No. Of course not." He got out his little pad and scribbled. "Mrs. Belanger," he explained, "If you'd simply have let us know that you were in town, you'd have watched the game from the dugout. Just like Boston."

"Wow!" Raymond gasped.

"In fact," he continued, still scribbling, "You two can watch any game you please from our dugout, from here onwards. We're officially adopting you. Or else they can fire me if they want; I don't give a sh... er, darn. And, if you'll let us know ahead of time that you're coming, every player on the team will sign a baseball for you, right in front of your eyes." He tore off the paper and handed it to Mrs. Belanger. "If you'd like, I can also try and arrange for a benefit game. For the Cancer Society, I mean."

"That... That..." she stuttered. A single tear ran down her cheek.

"Wow!" Raymond gushed. I was wearing shorts; he reached out with one arm and hugged my spotted leg. "I always *knew* you were all right! No matter what anyone else said."

"I'm not all right, really," I admitted, my voice thick with emotion. "I'm actually a pathetic jackass. But... But..." Then I shook me head, smiled, patted Raymond on the head...

...and got out of there quick before I broke down blubbering in front of them.

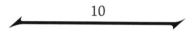

10

In some ways, it was tough being the only success story on the entire team. I didn't get along well with other people even under the best of circumstances. But now, with me developing my own personal fanbase and reporters coming from all over the world to watch and photograph me play in fur, even though they knew I wouldn't grant them an interview, well... I was more a loner than ever. About the only time anyone ever came to talk to me was the night that Pudge Hiller showed up at the apartment after a game and asked me to come outside so he could speak to me in private. Once we were alone together, he extended his hand. "I'm sorry I called you a jackass," he said.

"When did you do that?" I demanded.

He reddened. "Back at my house. The night that... that..."

"Oh!" I answered, smiling and accepting his hand without reservation. "Don't worry about it. You were..." My voice trailed off, for lack of words.

"Yeah," he agreed. "I was." Then he looked off into the distance. "I also want to thank you for how you've handled the whole situation. Not just for forcing me to make the break, though that's surely enough for me to owe you. But also for keeping your mouth shut ever since. I mean…"

I smiled back, then held up a furry arm. "I live in a glass house," I explained softly. "Thank you, and the rest of the team, for giving me so little grief over *this*."

"Heh!" He grinned. "Behind your back, I… We…" He colored again, then shook his head. "You're our star player," he said finally. "How much can we…"

"Right," I agreed into the sudden silence. Somehow I felt better, knowing that people were laughing at me. Though exactly why the knowledge made me feel better, I'd never figure out no matter how long I lived. "I understand."

"I've filed for divorce," he continued. "I plan to start all over again, or at least as near to it as I can manage. Once this is behind me, begin a whole new life. But, before I could even start, I had to make sure you knew how grateful I am, to you and Buster both." His hand reached out again, and I shook it a second time.

"Don't mention it," I repeated.

"If there's anything I can ever do…"

"Only one thing," I said softly into the moonlight.

"What's that?" he asked.

"Get mad, Pudge," I urged him. "You play your best ball when you're angry, just like I do. We're more alike than you think. Don't put up with anyone else's garbage ever again, on the field or off. I don't, and you shouldn't have to either."

The big young Kentuckian blinked in the darkness. "You know what?" he said softly. "I think you just may have something there."

We were scheduled to hit the road the next day for our longest scheduled trip of the year, to Jacksonville, Roswell, Raleigh, and Grenada. Because the bus was leaving at one, I had to see the shrink early in the morning. It didn't seem to matter much to him; he was still the same stubborn idiot he'd always been, turning everything back on me. This time, though, I surprised him. I opened up with a question. "Can this cheetah stuff change who I am inside?" I demanded.

The doctor tilted his head first to one side, then the other. "Not in any direct sense, no," he answered.

I shook my head angrily. "Don't weasel-word me," I countered. Then I pointed to my head. "I've been living inside here for as long as I can remember. And things are getting all *different* now."

"Different how?" he asked, looking interested.

I shook my head. "Like... There's this kid, see? He's sick. I should be charging him for autographs, but I'm not. Even though I'm perfectly entitled, and not exactly rolling in the dough. And there's Thumps... He's our second baseman. The kid I told you about who's always bothering me with questions."

The doctor nodded, but said nothing.

"I should've bit his head off a long time ago; he's *fast*, and like as not someday he'll be trying to take my position away from me. But, all the time we were in the dugout yesterday I was showing him how to read a pitcher better. That's *stupid* of me; I shouldn't be doing *that*! And then a little while back Buster and me helped another player run away from his wife; she was beating him, you see. Her beating *him*, and she maybe half his size! I shoulda doubled over laughing. Instead we got him out, and he came by my place last night to thank me for doing it. And upstairs, there's the biggest comedy opera in history playing itself out; two flamers who dress up in tights and dance *ballet* every morning, for God's sake! They're fighting now, and instead of busting a gut over it I'm laying awake at night worrying that they're gonna break up!"

The doctor stared at me for a long time, not the way he usually did when he was trying to bore me into talking, but rather like he was for-real thinking about something. Then he spoke aloud. "Your brother," he said at last. "You said he was younger than you. Was he a *lot* younger, maybe? And abused even worse than you were? Maybe even sexually?"

My mouth dropped open, revealing newly-fierce teeth. Then an icy, cold rage closed in over my heart. "You…" I began, feeling my still-new claws digging into my pawpads. "You…"

Then the doctor sighed and leaned back. "No," he said. "*I'm* sorry. You said you didn't want to discuss your brother, and that's certainly your right. I should never have brought the subject up. It clearly has nothing whatsoever to do with your cheetah-job, which is the only treatment you've signed up for." He smiled, icy-cold. "No, of *course* growing a fur coat can't change who you are inside. Your brain hasn't been altered at all, except in that the binge-drinking damage is responding well to treatment. If you feel different now about yourself and those around you, well… I'm afraid that you'll just have to look someplace else for the reason why."

I was still all pissed off about the shrink when I swung my scooter into the apartment lot. Because it was going to be such a long road trip, there weren't to be any workouts. All we had to do was get to the stadium by one. I was all packed and ready, not having much stuff to worry about in the first place. But on the way back to the apartment Dasher's wildly-driven car nearly ran me off the road, and when I got home there was Dancer, still in his morning ballet getup, weeping his eyes out on the parking lot. It didn't take a genius to put two and two together. I *could* have walked right past him. But, somehow, I didn't. "Come on," I urged the left-fielder, taking him by the shoulder and physically turning him around towards the building. "It's all over, now."

"I… I found someone's pants," he explained. "They… They weren't-"

"I know," I interrupted, not really wanting to hear the details. "Come on. Let's get inside, and then we can talk." I put my arm around his shoulders, and with an audible sob of

238

relief he sort of melted into my fur-job. *"What in the world are you doing?"* the little voice in my head screamed. *People are gonna see this, man!* But for some odd reason Buster's face flashed into my mind for a moment, and I refused to pull away. "We were supposed to be for *life!"* Dancer wailed. "I don't know... I mean..."

People were staring, it seemed. I felt as if there were a pair of eyes at every window. Fortunately, that included my own. Thumps was standing there, gaping like a fool. I waved for him to come out and help, but he stood frozen in place. Then I gave him the "steal-no-matter-what on the next pitch" signal, and that finally was enough to get him moving.

"Oh, God!" Dancer screamed, leaning back and staring up to the heavens. "I still love him so!" Then he squeezed me so hard I almost fell over. Probably would've in fact, if Thumps hadn't arrived just in time to catch me.

"Go call Buster," I ordered, once I was firmly upright again. Dancer was considerably larger than me, and every bit as much a professional athlete. I wasn't making progress towards the apartment with him anymore. "Go call him right now, and tell him I need him here like I've never needed him anywhere before."

"B-but..." Thumps stuttered. "B... B..."

"Do it!" I exploded, angry at last. "Get *something* right, why don't you?"

For just an instant, something died in Thump's eyes. "I..." I tried to explain as Dancer squeezed the life out of me and wailed. "I..." *I didn't really mean that,* I wanted to say. *I'm just too busy with another crisis to...*

It was too late, though. The damage was already done. "Right," Thumps agreed, his eternal smile gone. "I'll go call Buster. That much, I think I can handle."

The road trip would've been a total disaster, if Pudge hadn't finally found his bat. He went on an absolute tear at the plate, going four for five, two for three, three for four practically every game. He'd begun a beard; the deep-black stubble on his chin combined with the newly-wild look in his eyes made him look like he lived under a bridge and ate small children for breakfast. Soon, his biggest problem was that no one would pitch to him. Instead, he just walked, which quite often put him on base behind me.

So what'd I do about it? I encouraged him to steal. He'd never be fast, not with his physique. But the first time he made the attempt he got away with it on sheer shock value, and the second on my borrowed smarts. After that, the pitchers were almost as paranoid about him as they were about me; it was *humiliating* when a big lumbering dump-truck of a man managed to steal a base off of you. Word got around, when you let that happen. This was all to the good; the more paranoia there was in the world, the better for us base-stealers. One night, with Buster's permission, Pudge and I toasted our new partnership with half a mug of beer.

When Dancer caught back up with us— he was ordered to take three days off, and see a counselor—we went absolutely wild. No baseball team can succeed unless all of its parts are working. At the same time, however, there isn't a ballclub in existence that doesn't have deep, fundamental weaknesses built into it. So, it doesn't take much to alter the fundamental balance of things. Pudge's new success combined with Dancer's drive was enough to upset things sufficiently that we began to climb steadily in the standings. (It seemed that our ballet-master had grown a little angry, too. And determined never to be taken advantage of again.) We not only won four in a row, but romped our foes by at least a ten-run margin in every single game. The statisticians went nuts trying to keep up.

The only real weak spot remained Thumps. He was already hitting under his weight, but after the incident in the parking lot he slumped even worse. The coach finally pulled him out of the starting lineup, and there were rumors that he was on his way back to AA ball. Pretty soon the only time he was seeing action was when we needed a pinch-runner, or when we'd built up such a lead that the "also-ran" players, who knew that the odds were heavily stacked against their ever seeing the Bigs, were on the field. It was a major, humiliating step down for my room-mate, one that he bore in deep, frigid silence. And, he grew even colder and quieter after our team's owner, Mr. Sandrell, came to watch us play in Roswell and addressed the team.

"The parent club is taking a beating this year," he explained to us all. "We're going to finish dead last, likely as not. So we've decided that we're going to keep you people, our best prospects, right where you're at. That way, you'll have more time to work with the finest developmental coaching and support staff in the world. I know you all dream of the Bigs, and that it's hard to wait. Next year there'll be big changes upstairs, and many of you will be moving up."

Then he met with Pudge and Dancer and I, plus a couple of our best pitchers, and congratulated us on what great years we were having. "Everyone swore you'd screw up," Mr. Sandrell told me last of all. "But you haven't, Cheetah. Not once. In fact, I'm told you're emerging as a team leader. And your numbers are phenomenal." He laughed. "I *knew* you had it in you. Maybe I should talk more players into growing fur!" Conspicuously absent from this private reception was Thumps, who at the beginning of the year had been among the four big, hot prospects that were supposed to be the franchise's future. Now, apparently, we were only three.

I'd done many stupid things in my career. Many, many, *many* of them. But, never had anyone questioned my innate ability to play baseball at the Major League level. Indeed, my talent was

241

why I'd been allowed to screw up so profoundly, and for so long. Thumps, however, was apparently not so lucky. He was working as hard as humanly possible, living a clean life, paying strict attention to his coaches, and still getting nowhere. His level of natural ability, it seemed, *was* in question. There *was* doubt as to whether or not he'd make it all the way.

I could only imagine how bad that must hurt.

By the time we roared into Grenada, home of the league-leading and arch-rival Muskrats, we were hotter than firecrackers on the Fourth of July. The minor-league press, such as it was, converged on Upper Mississippi in droves to watch the expected pyrotechnics. There was thunder and lighting in the air.

I mean literally, there was thunder and lighting in the air. Hail and tornado warnings, too. Our Friday twi-night double-header was stormed out, then our Saturday game was cancelled because power hadn't yet been restored at the stadium. By Saturday night, therefore, most of us Catfish were feeling pretty restless and full of ourselves. In my own case, it was the first time since spring training that I'd found myself with too much time on my hands. Here it was, eight o'clock on a Saturday night. I was twenty-eight years old, and what was I doing? Lying in a lumpy hotel bed, watching a cartoon channel on the motel's small screen TV with a sullen, silent roommate. "Thumps," I said finally. "I can't stand it anymore. I'm heading out."

He sort of half-shrugged. "Whatever."

"We aren't subject to bed-checks until midnight," I pointed out, as if he'd argued with me. "It's not like I'm doing anything against the rules."

"Nope," he agreed. Then he half-rolled over onto his side, facing away from me.

"Right," I agreed. "I'll be back by midnight, then. Promise."

He nodded. "See ya."

Most of the time, we stayed in pretty cheap motels. They weren't nearly as bad as those in the Dominican Republic, mind you; I wasn't about to complain. But, they tended to be of low-enough class that they didn't have bars in the lobbies.

This one, however, did.

I'd promised myself back in my room that I wasn't going to have a drink. I reinforced this intention by swearing mighty oaths as I strode across the lobby. And by the time I eased my way into the little lounge, I'd pretty much convinced myself that all I was going to do was just take a quick look-see, and sort of check out the action.

In truth, I was a little nervous about going into the bar. Grenada Mississippi is a rural sort of place, and its inhabitants aren't exactly used to dealing with people who claim to be indulging their inner cheetah by growing fur and spots and the like. Sure, I'd run into people on the streets many times before this, mostly while going about my daily business back in Baton Rouge. For the most part they were nice, and even those who weren't tended at least to be tolerant. The worst anyone ever did was ask for an autograph. Somehow, though, bars are different. And, this was my first since the big change.

I stepped into the relative darkness, blushing dark red under the fur...

...and the damnedest thing happened. Nothing. Nothing at all. The juke-box played on, the waitresses walked briskly back and forth, and the murmur of conversation went on unchanged.

I smiled, keeping my lips over my fangs, suddenly feeling a lot better. Something in my life, at least, remained just like it had always been. Then, I strode in, and eased myself up against the bar. "A rum and coke!" I heard myself declare. "Have you got any rum from the Dominican Republic? The stuff'll take the enamel off your teeth, I swear!'

"Sure, hon!" the barmaid trilled, looking me up and down and clearly approving of every spotted inch. "I'll see what I can do."

I looked around the poorly-lit room, seeking team-mates. Pudge Jefferson and Pudge Hiller were sitting together not far away, probably rapt in a discussion about the finer points of catching. Nearer to me sat Dancer with some sort of fruit-filled drink; he was making eyes at a local man who might best be described as "pretty". But, other than them, so far as I could tell, the coast was clear. I'd just take my drink before anyone noticed, ease back into one of the darker corners...

"Why hello, Cheetah!" an acid voice suddenly exploded out of nowhere. "Out for a little drinkie, are we?"

I closed my eyes, sighed, then turned to face Coach Turnbull. "They serve just plain old soda pop here too," I countered. "It isn't my fault if you assumed that—"

"I found you some of that Dominican rum you were asking for, honey!" the barmaid interrupted, plopping down an oversized glass in front of me. "It's a triple, on the house." She smiled and looked me up and down again. "For helping to improve the scenery, like."

"Damn it!" Turnbull exploded, throwing his hat to the ground and stomping on it. "And *damn* you, Cheetah Jones! Just when I thought you might amaze the bejesus out of me and make good!" His face turned hard and cold. "If you hadn't lied, I might've given you another chance. But, my marching orders are clear. Go get your personal gear and meet me back here. We're going to get you a separate room, and then in the morning I'll fly you to wherever you want to go rot for the rest of your life." He shook his head sadly. "God, what a waste of space!"

My mouth fell open. "But... I mean... I was just... It wasn't..."

Suddenly there was a presence at my elbow. "Thanks, Cheetah!" Dancer declared, rubbing up against me in a manner somewhere in the vast unmapped region between very friendly and improper. "I've always wanted to try one of these Dominican rums you go on and on about. Thank you so much for buying this one for me! It was very kind of you."

I tried to engage my tongue, but it wouldn't go into gear. "Uh..."

"Damn!" Tony muttered, turning bright red. Then he bent over to pick up his hat. "I'm sorry, Cheetah," he said eventually. "It's just that you've done so well and all, and I naturally thought… I mean, I never imagined…" He looked at Dancer, then at me. Finally, he just shook his head and walked away. "Damn!"

"A plain coke for Cheetah, please," Dancer instructed the barmaid. "Charge it to my table." Then he smiled at me again, and winked.

"Thank you," I said finally, not referring to the coke.

"You're more than welcome," the left-fielder replied, understanding exactly what I meant. "I owed you one, after all." He smiled. "But even more, you deserved it."

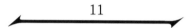

11

Our Sunday game with the Muskrats should've been full of high drama and tension, after all the media buildup and Mother Nature's free spectacle. And I suppose it fulfilled its promise, eventually. But, for the first two hours or so the most exciting thing to happen was the traditional tee-ball hitting game sponsored by a local bank during the seventh-inning stretch. A six-year-old girl hit the ball all the way to second base, a feat which won her a brand-new bicycle and free ice cream at a local establishment for her entire family.

Other than that, the game was boring as could be. I led off with a single, then stole second and was stranded there. My counterpart, the Muskrat's lead-off hitter, opened with a triple but also was in turn stranded. These remained the offensive highlights of the game right up until the ninth inning. Play was about as routine as routine could get; by the top of the ninth the Muskrat's pitcher had scattered six hits while our own hurler had allowed five, with neither side giving up any runs. So, we couldn't claim the pleasure of witnessing a classical pitcher's duel. There weren't even any exciting defensive plays to liven things up. About the only entertainment I found all day, in fact, was glancing over at the Muskrat's bullpen from time to time and grinning.

"Stop that, Cheetah!" Dancer objected at one point, catching me at my little game. "It's not fair to pick on children." Then he smiled at me, showing that he was kidding.

"Heh!" I chuckled back, kicking my feet up on the dugout's front-row bench and relaxing as best I was able in such intense heat and humidity. An old friend had joined the Muskrat's pitching staff during the storm days, it seemed. A nineteen-year-old prodigy of a short-reliever named Reginald Barnes, who was also rather a petulant child. I'd made a fool of him on my first day with the club—Reginald was the kid whose control I'd broken by getting him angry during base-stealing drills. His feelings had been hurt by the resulting demotion to AA ball, it seemed. Instead of rolling with the blow and accepting that the coaching staff knew what was good for him, he'd demanded to be traded. And now, finally, he'd gotten his wish. "On the count of three," I suggested. Dancer smiled and nodded. "One, two, *three!*" And on the last syllable, we turned and grinned together, the left-fielder making a silly face as well. It was great fun! By now young Reginald just *had* to be fuming...

It was the top of the ninth before the game finally showed signs of breaking free. I led off with a grounder up the middle, the kind of roller that, before I bulked up, would've been an easy out. But now, with just that little extra bit of snap behind it, the ball dribbled through the infield and I was safe at first by a hair. The crowd received my effort with an icy silence, as was to be expected, and while I was dusting myself off I took a moment to think about Herman, whose idea the new muscles had been. I owed him big time, and yet somehow I still hadn't found time to say so much as "thank you".

The Muskrat pitcher had been on the mound for eight complete innings; he'd been working very hard indeed in the hot summer sun. I figured that he was probably losing it, getting tired

and sloppy. But he held me on first just as tightly and profession-
ally as if he were fresh as a daisy; with the game on the line and
nobody out old Buster, coaching third, wouldn't give me the 'steal'
sign. I couldn't blame him, really. The pitcher and I played footsie
back and forth eight or ten times, then he finally served one up to
Dancer at the plate. And...

...*Pow!* My friend hit it long and high and deep, the perfect
sacrifice fly. I waited, waited, waited at the bag while the right-
fielder positioned himself just-so under the ball and caught it, then
tagged-up and ran for second. It wasn't even close: I beat the throw
standing up, as the crowd began to rumble unpleasantly.

Then it was Donnie Parker's at-bat. Parker was another
has-been, a player who'd spent most of a season up in the Bigs eight
years back. But he'd taken a line-drive to the head while there,
permanently doubling his vision just enough to drop his batting
average a good thirty points. He wasn't a pseudo-coach like old
Pudge Jefferson, on the team for the express purpose of sharing his
hard-earned wisdom after a distinguished career. Instead, Donnie
was a rather pathetic figure who'd once had a bright future but now
would never see the Bigs again. The only reason he was still playing
was that no one had the heart to fire him. Everyone always went out
of their way to be nice to Donnie, even our opponents. We understood all too clearly that there but the grace of God went ourselves.

Tragic figure or no, Donnie was a lousy clutch hitter. He
fanned, though he managed to run up a full count first. Somewhere
along the way the pitcher grew a little distracted, and I slid safe
into third.

Then it was Pudge Hiller's turn at the plate. Instantly, the
Muskrat's coach called time and jogged out to the mound, pointing
at his right arm on the way. There was going to be a pitching
change, about two outs overdue in my opinion, and a right-hander
was on his way out to the mound.

Since time was out, Buster gestured for me to come join him
for a private chat in the coach's box. "It's gonna be that spoiled

jackass Barnes," he observed, nodding towards the Muskrat bullpen. Then he smiled. "Could it be any more perfect?" I smiled back, showing my fangs, which was exactly what I knew Buster wanted me to do. He slapped me on the back wordlessly, and gently shoved me back towards third base.

There are certain times in baseball when everyone in the stadium is looking at you. Most of those times are when you're making plays; then, a player is far too busy trying not to screw up to think about all the eyes that are on him. But there are other times when you *do* think about it, when in fact you can't *not* think about it. Like when you step across the plate after hitting a home run, for example…

…or when you come walking out of the bullpen for the very first time as part of a new team, with the announcer making a big deal out of the fact so the home crowd will give you the traditional standing-ovation of a greeting. Most players try to look humble during those times; they keep their heads down and remind them- selves that they're as mortal as anyone else. Not Reginald Barnes, however; he *strutted* to the mound, head high, hat off, and eyes as bright as if he'd just won his tenth gold medal in the Olympic Games.

"Geez," Buster muttered, loud enough to be heard all the way from the coach's box. "I'm sure glad *that* one's gone."

"Wish you'da kept him," the Muskrat third baseman muttered under his breath. "What a jackass!"

Reginald's delivery was a thing of beauty. Warming up, he pumped fastball after fastball into the catcher's mitt, each of them clocking well over a hundred miles an hour. Then it was time for Pudge to step into the batter's box. He dug in, raised his club of a bat, squinted…

…and took the first pitch dead in the ribcage!

"Jeez!" the third-baseman muttered in sympathy.

An ugly mutter rumbled through the crowd as Herman came dashing out of the dugout, cold towel and icepack already in hand.

A hundred-mile-an-hour fastball is plenty enough to kill a man if it hits the wrong place; no one blamed Pudge for moaning and writhing on the ground under Herman's ministrations. Until, after a couple of minutes, in a complex feat of applied leverage the diminutive trainer hauled the power-hitter up onto his feet and supported him as he limped first towards the dugout, then the clubhouse, and after that directly to the x-ray machine beyond. Once again the crowd got on its feet, this time to applaud Pudge for leaving the field under his own power.

The Muskrat *fans*, at least, knew how to show a little class. For it was clear to every knowledgeable eye in the place that Pudge had been beaned, sure as could be. The only thing lacking was definitive proof.

Coach Turnbull sent Thumps out to run for Pudge at first base, then pinch-hit Pudge Jefferson in the number-five slot. The move was logical for several reasons; Jefferson was a lefty, and we needed a new catcher in the game anyway. But most of all, I suspected, Turnbull slid Jefferson into the lineup because of his vast experience and gray hair. *He*, of all people, wasn't going to let a pimply-faced teen rattle him. The umpire went out and had an earnest little chat with Mr. Barnes, who nodded soberly when it was over. Then the ump settled in behind the plate, called time in, and the next pitch was thrown. A strike, on the lower inside corner.

Pudge scowled, stepped out of the batter's box and knocked some dirt out of his spikes, then dug back in. The second pitch arrived. Ball one! Then another. Ball two! Once again Pudge called time and stepped out of the box, fiddling with something near his left knee. Probably a brace of some kind; he wore a ton of them. Meanwhile the Muskrat coach decided that he wanted a conference; the next thing I knew he was jogging out towards the mound again, and the whole Muskrat team was converging on him.

Suddenly Buster's lips were at my ear. "Squeeze," he whispered. "It's on."

I gulped. The squeeze, for my money, was the most exciting, difficult play in baseball. It derived its name from the fact that it was designed to "squeeze" the defenders, or force them to make difficult decisions much too quickly. Then, they'd have to *act* on these same instantaneous decisions as a unit, with total perfection, or else things would go wrong for them in a very large way. On the next pitch, Pudge Jefferson would do his best to get a hit; in any case he'd swing at the pitch, and do everything he could to be obstructive and make a nuisance of himself without quite breaking the rules. If he *did* get a hit, fine and dandy; I'd score easily. And if he didn't...

...then, in that case, I had to *steal* us a run! Meanwhile, Thumps would be tearing up the basepads as well. A single bad throw, a moment's misplaced hesitation, and we might just score *twice*.

It was clear from the moment play was resumed that the Muskrats suspected what was up. In fact, that was probably why the mound-conference had been called in the first place; to make sure everyone knew exactly who would cover what once the pressure was on. Barnes went well out of his way to hold me close at third, something that pitchers rarely bothered to do under these conditions. The Muskrats knew what was up, all right...

..but when I looked over at the first base coach, his hand tapped out the signal regardless. I bared my fangs—either Coach Turnbull didn't think there was much chance of anyone else on the team getting a hit off of Barnes, or else he had a lot more faith in me than I'd realized. I gulped and made the countersign indicating that I was ready.

Then, finally, after another flurry of pickoff attempts the long-awaited pitch was delivered to the plate. My heart thundering in my ears, I began driving for home. Old Pudge scowled ferociously, began to swing—then tried and failed to spin away as Barnes's fastball took him in the thigh.

It was deliberate again, and once more everyone knew it. But this time the Muskrat pitcher was unlucky. Because he was so old and his legs were so beat-up, Pudge Jefferson wore a virtual suit of armor under his uniform from the waist down. The ball struck and bounced off almost as if it had hit a cement wall—and, eyes narrowing in rage, Pudge, whose career was already over and who therefore had absolutely nothing left to lose, threw down his bat and charged the mound, unhurt.

There wasn't anything for it, really, but to join in the fun. After all, I was already sprinting towards the plate at high speed anyway. The Muskrat catcher was rising to his feet and trying to glom onto Pudge's shoulder, to protect his teammate from the hammering that he had to know was richly deserved, but which it was his job to prevent regardless. He'd forgotten all about me, apparently; I took his legs out from underneath him quite neatly indeed, shredding flesh all the way with my spikes. Then in an instant I was on my feet, ready for more…

…until something hard landed on the back of my head, just behind where my left ear was going to end up sometime soon. Then everything went black, and stayed that way.

I woke up little by little over a period of several hours. The first time I came around, it only lasted for a few seconds. There were faces above me, but they were only swimming blurs. I tried to speak, couldn't, then attempted to reach out and touch them. But, before the muscles even got the message, I was out again. And so it went on and on and on; each episode of consciousness lasting longer and growing clearer. Eventually I recognized Buster sitting at my bedside, with Dancer alongside him. "Unh!" I grunted intelligently. "Unh!"

As one they leapt to their feet and stood beside me. "Easy now, son!" Buster warned me, grabbing the hand I tried to raise. "You just lie there and take it easy. You're going to be all right, but you've got a subdural hematoma."

"That means you've got a pool of blood in your head, sort of," Dancer explained. He was really good at explaining stuff, Dancer was. In another life, he might've made a fine teacher. "It's not going to hurt you long-term, but for a little while you're going to have to do exactly what the doctors tell you."

I tried to nod, then realized what a terrible mistake that was. Dancer looked at Buster, who nodded. "You've got a hairline fracture in your skull, as well," he continued. "Nothing really serious; the doc had to magnify the x-ray to even see it. But, from now on, maybe you'd better play with a helmet."

I scowled; helmets were hot, sweaty things. They slowed me down. "Wha…" I asked, "Wha…"

Buster took over. "The squeeze was on—" he began.

"Fucker beaned Pudge," I interrupted, nodding so slightly that it didn't hardly hurt. "I 'member."

"Both Pudges, actually," Buster continued. "You were at third, coming home." He winced. "Don't get me wrong, Cheetah. I wouldn't have had you do it any other way. But you gave that catcher fifteen stitches and a sprained knee. You should know that. The League's going to be coming to see you about it."

I sort of half-shrugged. Surprisingly, it didn't hurt. "Man's gotta do," I muttered. "Protect my team."

"Right," Buster agreed, nodding. "Like I said, I wouldn't have it any other way. The fact is, I'm gonna be drawing a big suspension myself." He shrugged. Clearly, a man indeed had to do what a man had to do. "What happened to you was, the third baseman followed you home, to help back up the play at the plate. He was running full-out, and I heard from a reporter that he claims he didn't realize that Pudge had been hit by the pitch. When you stood up, he ran into you from behind. On accident, like. His nose is smeared all over his face."

"Just from hittin' my head?" I asked in wonder.

"No," Buster explained, looking both deeply proud of himself and twenty years younger. "From my fist. He hit you with his helmet. Accident my hairy old butt!"

There a long, long silence. "Jeez," I muttered eventually.

"It was *huge*," Dancer continued eventually. "Biggest blow-up in ten years. We'll be talking about it for the rest of our lives. Who was there, and who wasn't." Dancer had a shiner, I realized suddenly. A nasty one. "The whole bench cleared." He smiled. "And Old Pudge decked that jackass pitcher, too. He didn't get back up."

We talked about everything I'd missed for a long, long time, from how poor outnumbered Thumps had taken such a pummeling to how Pudge Hiller actually wasn't all that bad off. "That hillbilly has ribs like barrel-staves," Buster declared proudly. "He'll be playing again in a week."

I was feeling a lot better now, as much from the good company as the treatment. "Where's Tony?" I asked at last. "Coach Turnbull, I mean?"

Dancer and Buster looked at each other again, and I felt an icy stab in my chest. Was someone else hurt even worse than me? "He's just a couple rooms down," Buster finally explained. "In Intensive Care."

Pain or no pain, my head rose off my pillow. "What?" I demanded.

"Easy now," Dancer urged me, gesturing for me to lay back down. "Remember! This is serious! You're *hurt*, Cheetah!"

"Right," I agreed, lying back as ordered. "But..."

Buster sighed. "Both benches totally cleared. I mean, it was epic. And that included the coaches. Tony wanted a piece of that pitcher as bad as anyone. But, he never made it over the foul line." He shook his head. "You know, I've always wondered what he was doing down in the minors; a dozen organizations would pay top dollar for him, with his record. But, it seems he's got a bad ticker."

"Old nanites," Dancer explained. "From back in the day. He had heart trouble young, and took an experimental treatment. It worked, but because of it he can't take anything more modern to fix his new troubles. He's only got so long, and he knows it."

"So he went back to doing what he truly loved," Buster observed. "Coaching the minors. Who'd have thunk it?"

The docs held me for forty-eight hours of observation at first, then extended it to seventy-two when my brainwaves kept on doing funny stuff. "You expect *my* brain to be normal?" I demanded of my doc. But it didn't do any good; I was stuck. And, when the rest of the team headed back to Baton Rouge for the next game, I didn't have any more visitors, either.

You can only watch a cartoon channel just so long…

I wasn't actually hooked up to anything anymore except for some monitors on my head that would work just fine anywhere on the hospital grounds. So, in exchange for a solemn promise not to try and get up and walk around, they gave me a little power-chair and let me zip around to the conservatorium and the chapel and such. They seemed very proud of their conservatorium, and maybe they had a right to be. But I wouldn't know; I never made it there.

Tony was out of intensive care by the time I got my new wheels, and his room wasn't far. I spent pretty much all of my three days under observation with him, except for when the League came to hear me swear on my mightiest oath that, just like the third baseman who'd run into me, I'd not realized that Pudge had been hit by the pitch.

Apparently, I explained, both of us must've been at an especially bad angle to see that part. I blamed the spiking thing on the fact that the catcher wasn't blocking the plate in a defensive crouch, the way that he should've been and the way we always practiced. "It wasn't my fault," I summed up, picturing Buster laughing his butt off as I employed my favorite phrase from the bad old days. And Tony *did* laugh when I told him what I'd done, so hard that his beepers beeped and his flashers flashed and a nurse came running in.

"Get this, Cheetah," he chortled as the nurse reset the alarms. "You ain't gonna believe it. But I convinced the investigator that I was on my way out to *stop Pudge!*" Then we laughed again, and the alarms needed attention a second time. Luckily, the nurse didn't seem to mind.

Eventually, we ran out of things to laugh about, and silence set in. "I guess you heard about my heart?"

I nodded silently. "Coach, you don't hafta..."

He raised a hand in protest. "No, son. It's all right. Here, we're just two gimps together in the hospital." Then he sighed. "It's all true," he admitted. "There's about a hundred of us who took the early meds while they were still experimental—not that we had much of a choice! But it immunized us to the newer nanites, so we can't get anything more advanced done. There's not enough of us, you see, to justify the research it'd take to work something out. Not while there's about a bajillion others waiting for the same researchers to fix their problems." He scowled slightly. "They say this was just a preview, not the main show. I'll be out of here in a week, and then I'll pretty much be fine again right up until the Big Day. They say there's always hope, so long as you're sucking air. But..."

There was another long, long silence. I've heard that nobody else ever knows what to say to a dying man, either. So I suppose it was all right.

"Anyway," the Coach continued, scowling. "I'm glad it wasn't blackout time. Because, well..." He sighed. "I'm so sorry that I got you wrong about that drink-thing. I mean—you and Dancer, and..."

I couldn't help it. I began laughing again, so hard that I was afraid a nurse'd show up to reset *me*. "Don't sweat it," I finally sputtered. "In fact..."

Ton leaned forward, baffled.

You're out of your mind, a little voice whispered in my left ear. *You got away clean; you don't have to own up to this! No one will ever know.* "Look," I finally said. "I don't even know why I'm telling you this, but somehow I have to. I admit it; the drink was mine. Dancer covered me out of friendship and team loyalty. Dominican rum is about the last thing he'd ever drink."

Tony's face hardened for a second, then he let his head fall back onto his pillow. "I see," he said eventually.

I sighed and looked out the window. "So, I'm guilty. I got bored, and I messed up."

There was another long silence. "Well," he said at last. "Then it's a good thing that we're just two gimps here together in a hospital ward then. Because otherwise, I might have to fire your butt. And, Cheetah, if you don't realize it yet, that'd just about break whatever little heart I might have left."

12

They wouldn't let me play or even do much of a workout for another week, once I caught back up with the team. Buster, who was filling in for Tony, kept me extra-busy nonetheless; my guess was that word had come down to him from on high that I wasn't to be allowed to grow bored. Imagine that!

Anyway, he assigned me not one but two full-time jobs. "First," he said, "you're behind on your shrink-sessions. Not because you've done anything wrong, I know. But they still need to be made up. We've got a schedule all worked out for you."

I gritted my teeth and nodded.

"Second," he said, raising his eyes to meet mine, "I've got a special request."

My eyebrows rose. I looked really good doing that, I knew, as a cheetah. Whereas before, I'd just looked stupid.

"Thumps," he said. "Fix him."

My brows rose further. "Isn't that, like, *your* job?"

Buster's eyes fell to the floor. "It is," he acknowledged. "And I've failed at it. We're going to rehab him up here, since we can carry him on the DL. Then we're going to give him an at-bat or two to rebuild his confidence after what happened, to show that him getting beat up so bad in the big fight hasn't got anything to do with anything." He gulped. "Then we're going to demote him to AA level ball. I doubt he'll ever be back."

I nodded sadly. "He hasn't got the head for the Bigs."

"It's not his head!" Buster snarled. "It's his balls! At the plate he's afraid to swing, on-base he's afraid to steal…" He sighed. "Did you know that he's a track star? Never played ball at all in high school. The previous owners thought that anyone that fast could be trained to hit, field, and throw. And he *can* do all of those things, now. But what's he's not is *tough*! Apparently track stars don't have to make complex decisions under pressure, or know when it's time to charge the mound and face the music later." He sighed. "You… If anything you've got too much in the way of balls. You're not afraid of nothin'. It's like night and day." He shook his head. "I know you're no coach, Cheetah. And you're surely not being paid to be one. A few months back, I couldn't even imagine asking you to do this. But, do you think that maybe you can help this kid find his manhood?"

Buster's request weirded me out. So did my counseling session that afternoon. It was really strange; for once, I *wanted* to talk about something. "Are you *sure* that this fur coat can't change who I am inside?" was the first thing I asked Dr. Forster, once I was all settled in and he'd asked me about the knot on my head and all that polite stuff.

He blinked, twice. "That's the same thing you asked me last time we talked," he pointed out, crossing his legs. "Are you certain that something isn't bothering you?"

I frowned, then shook my head. "Well… It's strange, doc. Hard to explain, kind of." Then I sighed.

He smiled slightly. "You're doing better. Feeling better about yourself. Aren't you? You haven't messed up, like you invariably used to do. And you can't figure out why."

It was my turn to blink. "I haven't messed up yet, more like," I countered. "Though I tried once just last week, when I got bored. Even then though, it sort of…" I shrugged, at a loss for words. "It was halfhearted, like. I was being stupid on purpose, just *asking* to get caught. I mean, if I'd really wanted to get away with a quick drink, there were a million smarter ways…" I sighed. "I felt kinda bad about it even while it was going down." I wriggled in my chair. "Like I was about to hurt myself, but part of me didn't want that anymore."

Slowly, the doctor tilted his head to one side, considering. "So," he said eventually. "You used to need to hurt yourself, but now you're not who you used to be, and you don't need to cause yourself pain. Is that a fair summation?"

I wasn't quite certain what a 'summation' was, but it seemed to reflect the general idea. "Yeah. I guess."

Slowly, the doctor smiled. Then, still smiling, he removed his glasses and began to polish the lenses. "There's a lot of factors at work here, Cheetah," he explained slowly. "One is of course that you *are* going through a lot of big changes physically, in who and what you are, who you see in the mirror every morning, even in your grooming and personal habits. There are quite a few men and women in this business who believe that there just might be significant therapeutic value to major makeovers like the one you're having, because it forces a change in self-image at a very deep level. It gives those who need to change, in other words, a sort of excuse or maybe even self-permission to grow and develop in new directions. With physical change can come psychological change." He put his glasses back on. "I'm beginning to suspect that just maybe there's something to that theory."

I nodded.

"But," he continued, "in this case there's clearly a lot more at work than just that." He scowled. "At this point, I have to change the subject a little. While I currently specialize in dealing with physical transformation cases like your own, for years before that

I was a general therapist treating all sorts of patients. I'm a fully qualified psychiatrist, Cheetah. And while I was engaged specifically to do transformation counseling with you, as is invariably the case other issues have arisen." His scowl intensified.

"I've been torn, really, between trying to help you deal with your *real* problems and sticking strictly to the job I've been engaged to do. The job that you've given me *permission* to do." He sighed. "Of all the cases I've ever dealt with, in this one regard yours has been the most difficult. I've tried to help you a little around the edges, in ways that you probably haven't noticed. I took the Hippocratic Oath, after all. Yet, at the same time you unquestionably have the right to demand that we remain strictly on topic." He shrugged his shoulders. "So, before this discussion can proceed any further, I need to know something. Am I just your shrink regarding the cheetah fur, or am I your therapist overall? It's something that needs to be clarified."

I looked down at the floor. He had a point, I guessed, but...

"I'll also add," Doctor Forster continued, "that if I'm your therapist overall, I'm going to lead you down some painful paths. To places you don't want to go. Because I think that you very, very badly need to go there."

I continued to stare at the floor. "You think this is what's helping me then? The therapy?"

"Among other things," the doc replied. "You're also living in a highly supportive environment as well, which is of incalculable value. Almost an ideal one, even. But... a lot of that support is coming from the fact that you're making friends, and earning the respect and trust of others. You've never managed that trick before, have you?"

I gulped, then spoke the truth. "No."

"You're venting your anger here, instead of on the world in general. And, more importantly perhaps, on yourself." He shook his head. "God knows you've got plenty to be angry about! It's no crime for someone with your past to be enraged to the very core."

I gulped. "You mean… I'm not just being a wimp, being mad about my mom? And.. And…"

The doctor's face softened. "No, Cheetah, you're not. You've risen out of hell, son! Sheer hell! Is it any wonder that you still carry a few hot embers and personal demons with you?"

Suddenly everything went blurry. "You don't know… I mean, I haven't told you…"

Then the doc was by my side, hugging me and offering tissues. "I know you haven't," he said softly. "And that's okay. Whenever you're ready, and not until then." He smiled again. "We've got all the time in the world."

I wasn't supposed to even so much as work out for a week after leaving the hospital, so I had plenty of time to think about stuff. I'd grown up in hell, the doc had told me, and God knew he was right enough about that. But still carrying demons? Well… What was that little voice in my head that told me to get drunk and buy under-aged hookers and get awful tattoos, I asked myself, if not a sort of demon? So I went by the clinic and signed some papers making Doc Forster my overall, general-purpose shrink. The front office said nothing about it, for which I was grateful.

Even though I couldn't work out or anything, I still hung around the team as much as I could. They'd settled in for a long homestand, and despite the fact that half the lineup was either on the DL or suspended from the big fight we were still playing .500 ball. This wouldn't have been so great, but the Muskrats had gone into an awful tailspin. Not only had they suffered as many casualties as we had, but their own man was ultimately in the wrong and they knew it.

Baseball was a cold-blooded game in some respects; I didn't bear the Muskrat third-baseman a grudge for defending his catcher, any more than I figured their catcher hated me for defending Pudge. But, the chain has to eventually end somewhere, and once violence has broken out feelings can become quite intense indeed.

People don't *like* having to defend someone who's clearly in the wrong, even if they can't admit it right out. In fact, it upsets them at a very deep and profound level, so they take it out in other ways. I could easily imagine the fights and arguments that must be erupting all over the Muskrat clubhouse, as people took sides and assigned blame and pointed fingers. No one could play effective ball under such conditions. It was a miracle they ever won a game at all.

It was mid-August, and for the first time we were catching a whiff of the pennant.

Thumps was on the DL too; at his first step towards the mound during the big dustup, the much-larger Muskrat first baseman tackled him. Then he and the right-fielder and second-baseman had proceeded to spend the next several minutes pounding him. The bad news was that he'd lost a tooth and was seriously bruised almost all over. The good news was that nothing worse than that was wrong with him, and the League investigators had decided that a single step towards the mound, under the circumstances, wasn't enough justification to penalize a man. So, he was one of the few of us to walk away scot-free. If you didn't count the dental work, that was.

I walked away clean, too, as did the Muskrat who broke my head. The League accepted our story about how we thought the ball was still in play. The catcher was awarded a two-week suspension and a large fine, and both Pudge Jefferson and Reginald Barnes drew thirty days and a stiffer fine still. Pudge laughed when the official letter arrived. As an ex-big-league star, he could easily afford even the most punishing minor-league level financial penalty. "As for the suspension, I'll appeal and then appeal again," he explained. "That'll take at least until November. Long after the season's over, in other words—when I'll be retired anyway. Anyone else wanna try and bean my butt before the end of the year?"

261

Buster, as a coach who at least in theory was supposed to be nurturing the players instead of smearing their noses all over their faces, drew ninety days and enough of a fine to actually sting a little. He too laughed, then proudly framed the official reprimand and hung it on his office wall next to his ancient Golden Glove. He appealed too, but "Just so I have time to set up a base-stealing clinic off league property, so those three months aren't totally wasted." You had to love Buster. You just *had* to.

But Thumps and I walked away clean, or limped away, or staggered away, or whatever. We watched the games in street clothes from the dugout, sometimes sitting together and sometimes not, and then spent the rest of the day in our shared apartment, where Thump's mother had practically moved in to wet-nurse him back to health. "I'll get it!" she kept saying whenever her son rose to do anything, and I never ate so much cannelloni in my life. No matter how Thumps protested she was always at his elbow, adjusting, primping, fluffing. "My baby's been *hurt!*" she'd declare whenever he tried to do anything for himself. "You know, Mr. Simpson's still hiring down at the factory. People don't beat each other up when they can't get along there…"

I stayed in my bedroom, mostly, and thought. Thumps was on his way to a factory job, all right. Anyone could read the tea-leaves. And, after coming so close to the dream, such ordinariness would be even more soul-killing usual. It hadn't been at all fair of Buster to ask me to get involved in the kid's problems, to try and turn him around. Not only were turnarounds not exactly my specialty, but none of this was in any way my fault, now was it?

But, my fault or no, Buster expected results—and I couldn't let *him* down. So, one day when the team didn't play and I had all the time in the world to sit and eat cannelloni, I thought back over every minute of my relationship with Thumps. I also considered what Buster had said about him lacking the machismo for the game, and decided he was right. Next I pondered what he said about me maybe having a surplus of manhood, and about Thump's mother, and about *my* mother, and I grew very angry indeed for a time. Then, when I was done being angry, I worked out the kind of half-crazy gonzo plan that only someone gifted with a little too much testosterone and not nearly enough brain tissue could ever come up with.

A plan that, I reckoned, just might do the trick.

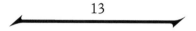

13

A couple days later, Thumps and I found ourselves zooming up I-55 on my scooter, running ten over the posted limit and living every mile to the hilt. Thumps had always been jealous of my scooter, I knew. He'd confided to me once that he really wanted a motorbike of his own, but his mother had made him promise he'd never buy one because it was too dangerous. So, it hadn't been any great trick to persuade him to come along and help me with a "little errand" up in Mississippi. "It's no big deal," I explained to him. "But I just had this head injury, see? And I don't want to be alone in case I get woozy and have to pull over…"

And so far, things were going well indeed. I whistled a happy little tune to myself as I swung out into the passing lane and overtook first an RV, then a line of heavy trucks. Thump probably felt like a very brave and bad boy indeed under his brand-new full-face helmet and reflective visor. He'd lied to his mother about where he was going, after all, and riding was always quite an adventure in and of itself.

It was well after dark when we arrived in Grenada. I was a little tight and stiff from the ride, and Thumps was probably suffering worse, not being used to a bike's hard seat. Still, he seemed pretty happy as I cruised up and down the peaceful residential streets.

"Whatcha lookin' for, Cheetah?" he finally asked, leaning forward and shouting so I could hear him. "Is something wrong?"

"No," I replied as, finally, I found what I sought. A scooter very much like my own, of a slightly different model but of the same exact color, was sitting a nice dark shadow where a large tree was shading it from the streetlight. I smiled, killed the motor, and coasted to a stop just behind it. "Everything's going just fine."

"Wow!" Thumps declared as he dismounted. "This is so much fun! I mean, I never…" Suddenly, he realized that I was pulling a large screwdriver out from under my seat. "Uh… Cheetah?"

"Yes, Thumps?" I replied patiently, as I began removing the parked scooter's license plate. "What is it?"

"I… Uh…" he protested, looking around nervously.

"It's all right," I assured him. "We're just borrowing it. I've done this before, lots of times." Though, I didn't tell him, in the past I hadn't slid two hundred-dollar bills into the glovebox to compensate my fellow rider for his troubles. Soon I had the "borrowed" plate mounted securely on my own bike. "Come on. Everything's going to be just fine."

"I… Uh…" Thumps stuttered. This was the crucial moment, the point at which my team-mate was most likely to back out on me. But, by my figuring it probably took even more in the way of balls to stand up to one's trusted friend and deliberately strand one's self on foot in a strange town in the middle of the night than it did to just smile and pretend that everything was still perfectly fine. Which was what Thumps, bless his innocent soul, finally did.

"A-a-all right," he finally said dubiously, climbing up onto the pillion behind me. "I g-g-guess—"

I never did find out what Thumps guessed, because instead of listening to him I fired up the bike, gunned it, and drowned out his voice in the wind and the roar of the motor. I knew exactly where I was, having studied up a little on Grenada geography ahead of time, and so was able to drive us directly to the Grenada Municipal Sports Complex and Stadium—Home of the Mighty Muskrats AAA Baseball Team!

"Uh," Thumps protested as I cruised by at low speed, checking out the setup. There were security cameras, I noticed, but placed in such a way that I didn't think they could cover anything right up against the building. "Uh…"

"Everything's *fine*," I reassured my nervous friend. "In fact, they couldn't be more perfect. Just keep your helmet on and your visor down, and I'll have to make sure that my tail stays in my pants leg as well. If we do that, what can possibly go wrong?"

The clubhouse was located behind the stadium; another slow circuit of the neighborhood confirmed my memory of the setup. There wasn't a soul around; the Muskrats had left two days before on a road trip to Arkansas. Even better, the whole area around the back of the place looked like an overgrown park; Mississippians loved their magnolia trees, and there were *huge* ones all around the building.

"Whew!" I heard Thumps sigh as I gave the scoot a little gas and effortlessly whirred us away. But, his relief didn't last long. Within seconds, I had us parked again, this time on a residential street just opposite the clubhouse.

"Cheetah," Thumps objected again. "I don't know what—"

"There's a little window in the visitor's locker room," I interrupted him. "It was always open, remember? To clear the stink." I grinned and showed my fangs, though Thumps couldn't possibly see them through the reflective visor. "It even stayed open during the big storms. I bet it's still up now."

For the first time, my friend began to see the possibilities. "I could get through that," he said after a time. "Or at least I think I could. And maybe you, too!"

"Both of us, for sure!" I countered.

"But…" Thumps stuttered again. "But…"

"Come on!" I declared, grabbing my carefully-prepared bag of goodies from under the seat. "Let's go!"

No alarms sounded as Thumps and I dashed through the big magnolia trees and crushed ourselves tight up against the building. This didn't surprise me any, as my boyhood experiences with breaking and entering had taught me much about the limitations of motion-detectors vis-à-vis large trees that tended to sway in the wind. The cameras probably got a shot of us, but in plain black riding gear and visored-helmets we might've been anyone.

The little window was open, just as predicted—even out here in the fresh air, it was easy to detect a trace of locker-room funk. "You first," I directed Thumps, cupping my hands so as to offer him a leg-up.

"I… Uh…" he stuttered again. "I mean, Cheetah…"

"Suit yourself," I answered, shrugging theatrically and looking around for inspiration. There was a medium-sized trash dumpster just a few feet away from where I needed it; without hesitating I strode over and put my shoulder to it. SCREE! the long-rusted wheels complained. SCREEE-EEE-EEE!

"Jesus Christ!" Thumps complained, bouncing up and down like he was terrified or something. "Stop that!"

The dumpster was still a long way from being in place. SCREEEEE!

"Damn it!" Thumps finally protested. Then, seemingly without effort, he leapt up, grabbed onto the windowsill and pulled himself up inside. "Here!" he declared, reaching down to offer me a hand. "Just stop that racket!"

I blinked. There was no way on earth that *I'd* ever have been able to leap so high from a standing start. And he was faster than me, on top of that! What exactly was I unleashing on the unsuspecting world of professional baseball, anyway? But, it was *far* too late to change my mind now. So instead of arguing I accepted the offered hand, and clambered in after him.

The locker room was dark and empty, which was all to the good. "I don't remember there being any motion-sensors in here," I explained into the silence. "Which makes sense, considering they use robo-janitors. But if the lights come on or if you notice *anything* weird, run for the bike. There's not a cop in the state who can catch either of us."

"Right," Thumps agreed, panting lightly. He sounded steadier, now that he was fully committed. "You've got lights, I presume?"

"Yeah," I agreed, pulling a pair of tiny penlights from the pouch and turning them on. "We have three things we need to do, as I see it."

"Three?" Thumps asked. "Then let's get them done and get out of here! Jeez, if Mom ever finds out..."

"She won't," I reassured him. "Just think about those bruises you're still wearing under that riding jacket."

Thumps scowled and nodded. "And your fractured skull. And Pudge's ribs. I get it, all right. And, well... Let's do this!"

"Good!" I answered, smiling again. "So, here's what we're after..."

By the time I was done explaining Thumps was laughing so hard that it took him twice as long to execute his mission as it should've. So I took a little extra time with my home-made template and brown spray can, painting primitive Baton Rouge Catfish logos on the Muskrat's lockers and then epoxy-ing all the doors shut. In fact, I ended up having so much time on my hands that I thought of a little something extra. I was still standing on the locker-room bench urinating into the air-vents of the locker belonging to one Reginald Barnes when Thumps finally arrived, carrying our main prize. "All right!' he declared, as excited as a ten-year-old on Christmas morning. "I've got it!"

"Good," I replied, finishing up my self-appointed task. "Care to take a squirt?"

Thumps's face screwed up in revulsion. "No. In fact, I think... No!"

I smiled again. "You come from a higher-class neighborhood than I do," I explained. "Lucky kid. Now come on! Let's get out of here!'

I'd done a good job of planning out our little raid, even if I did say so myself. But I *did* make one tiny slipup, which didn't become evident until Thumps and I were standing beside my scooter, eager to mount up and make miles.

"What do you mean, it won't fit?" Thumps demanded.

"Scooters don't have a lot of room in them," I explained, shrugging. "And, that damn muskrat suit is a *lot* bulkier than I expected." I frowned. "Maybe we oughta just go back and throw it in the dumpster..."

"Forget *that!*" Thumps replied, "Not after coming all this way!"

And so it came to pass that Thumps rode all the way back home to Baton Rouge on the back of my scooter dressed as The Mighty Muskrat. Even the head fit just fine over his helmet, without ripping it too badly. Being the discreet sort I took backroads most of the way home, and it being so late we didn't meet much traffic. But when we did, Thumps waved and capered and generally messed around so enthusiastically that he nearly wrecked us twice. We were pretty exhausted when we got back to the apartment. The suit fit just fine in the little storage area under our stairs, though Thumps seemed a little disappointed to take it off. We just had time for what amounted to a long nap before reporting back to the stadium. When we got there, my roomie was still sort of sparkling, full of laughter and life in precisely the way that'd been missing for so long. Buster noticed right away.

"Cheetah?" he asked me, looking across the locker room to where Thumps was engaging in his first towel-fight in heaven only knew how long. "What... I mean..."

"Get him to the plate just as soon as you possibly can," I said. "Don't wait a minute longer than you can help. The rest, you don't want to know about. Really, you don't."

So it was that Thumps suited up a few days earlier than he really should've, pinch-hit in the bottom of the eighth—and drove in the game-winning run.

Soon I was back in the lineup as well, and for the first time our team began to play the way it'd always been meant to. Thumps got two more solid hits off the bench, then he found himself back in the lineup. He was taking risks now, committing himself, being more assertive and self-confident both at the plate and on the basepads. I even cut back a little on the base-stealing, he was hitting so well…

…and at long, long last, our team was firing on all cylinders. Even better, no one was whispering about Thumps slipping down a league anymore. "You said I don't want to know," Buster said to me one day while we were watching Thumps do his wind-sprints. "And knowing you like I do, I don't doubt your word for a second. But, whatever it was that you did, you made me proud."

"Aw," I said, looking down at my shoes. "It wasn't no big thing. My great pleasure, in fact. And besides… Well, I owed him for the cannelloni, you see."

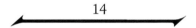

14

By Labor Day Weekend we were playing to sellout crowds. That almost never happens in the minors; usually, in fact, the clubs are forced to scrabble and struggle and offer a thousand promotional gimmicks just to fill the stands a quarter full. People simply aren't as interested in minor-league pennant races as they are the ones in the Bigs. Partly that's because even AAA baseball is by virtue of it own title admitting to the world that it's second-rate, and partly its because as soon as a player achieves something resembling stardom, he's immediately plucked from the fold and taken to join the parent organization. But our talent wasn't being plucked; Mr. Sandrell had made it clear that he wanted us to stay right where we were for the rest of the year, so that we could keep working with the coaches who were doing us so much good. Plus, the big fight with the Muskrats had fired up the fanbase to an unusual degree—why, there were even rumors floating around that rabid Catfish fans had desecrated the Muskrat clubhouse and stolen their mascot in revenge! And, well…

About half the fans these days showed up wearing cheetah-spots in one form or another.

"It makes me nervous sometimes," I explained to my shrink on Labor Day Friday. "I mean, all those people… if they knew the real me, they wouldn't wear that stuff. Instead, they'd demand I be locked up."

"Why do you think that?" he asked.

I sighed. "I'm… I mean, I've always been…." There was a long, long silence.

"But now you can't even say it anymore, can you? That you're a screwup, I mean?"

I tried to speak, tried my level best to prove him wrong. But, somehow, I couldn't.

He smiled. "You've climbed far and fast, Cheetah. In the really important ways, you've climbed higher than you ever have before in your life. It's natural that when you look down you should see a growing abyss, and be afraid of falling back into it." His smile faded. "But you're *not* going to fall, are you? Because now *you're* in control of what you do and who you are. Not some blind, enraged demon from your past."

I nodded slowly. "But I… I mean… I still haven't told you…"

The doctor smiled again. "I'm ready whenever you are. There's no rush at all."

We went on to sweep all five games that weekend, while sputtering Grenada went two and two. Now, we were only one game back, with five left to play.

The last one would be against the Muskrats, at home in Baton Rouge. Even in the big-league cities, knowledgeable sports fans took note and made plans to be near a television that night.

Anything might happen.

That last week was a busy one for us all. And it *was* of course the last week of the season; over the years the minor leagues have tried from time to time to generate enough fan enthusiasm to support playoffs and a Minor League World Series, but the fans never quite coughed up enough bucks to keep things going. So, the end of the regular season marked the end of the line for us Catfish, and the Division title was the highest laurel to which we could reasonably aspire.

And we wanted it. Bad!

This state of affairs was pretty unusual too. The sad fact is, minor-league players usually have as much trouble taking themselves seriously as their fans do. All most of us ever think about are the Bigs, Bigs, Bigs. If we're rounding third and see that the outfielder's about to make his throw, a minor-leaguer will tend to hold-up where a major-leaguer might dig in and give it his all, on the grounds that a pointless victory isn't worth risking a possible career-ending injury over. The longer a player is in the minors, the more risk-averse he becomes. The fans know it, the players know it, the coaches know it... The only people blissfully unaware of the true state of things are the promotional types, who spend their days in the front office trying to sell "future stars" and "traditional hard-nosed baseball" to the jaded public. Most minor-league seasons end more with a whimper than a roar.

But not this one! I'd only spent one full season in the majors, and we'd finished in fourth. The divisional race had been unusually close that year, however, and we weren't statistically eliminated until three days before the end of the season. So I'd very much been in a Big-League pennant race, had felt the pressures and been right in the center of it all. Yet, I hadn't detected half as much raw need, half the desire to win and dominate and be the Top Dog among my teammates that I picked up every single hour radiating from my fellow Catfish. It was like night and day, something I'd never seen before. In fact, I'd never even *imagined* such total focus.

Maybe if the locker room in my Big League team's clubhouse had felt more like this one, I might already have a World Series ring?

271

"All *right!*" Dancer declared, clenched fists raised above his head in the universal human gesture for victory. "All *right!*"

I reached over and high-fived my friend. I'd scored in the bottom of the ninth, and so had already been sitting in the dugout when Pudge Hiller hit it out of the park and drove both Dancer and Thumps home for a 6-4 win. "All right!" I agreed. Nothing more needed to be said; instead, we just looked at each other and smiled. The crowd was still going nuts outside.

"And Grenada's just lost!" Coach Turnbull declared, following Dancer down the little flight of stairs that we always swore someone was going to fall down someday. "It's official. We're tied!"

"Hooray!" everyone declared, breaking out in cheers. Naked and semi-naked men danced about and hugged each other in joy. I'd never seen anything like it. Then the pandemonium finally eased off a little.

"All right, guys," Tony continued, once he had everyone's attention again. "None of us here are stupid. It all comes down to tomorrow. So let's go home, get a good night's rest, and come back tomorrow fresh and rested, just like we always do..." He grinned, "...ready to kick some serious Muskrat butt!"

"Yay!" everyone cheered, and soon were dancing up and down the aisles again. I was a little surprised when Tony eased up next to me and tapped me on the shoulder—it was so loud that he had to press his mouth up against my ear to make himself heard. "...in my office," I finally made out. "Soon as you're cleaned up."

My eyebrows rose, and Tony nodded, letting me know that I'd heard right. "All right!" I confirmed at the top of my lungs. "I'll be there!"

He smiled, then leaned close to my ear again. "Take your time!" he shouted, gesturing at all the merriment. "You earned this, as much as any of them. Maybe even more than most!"

15

I was still thinking about my visit with Coach Turnbull in his office the next morning, while sitting in my shrink's chair. "So, this Raymond kid really means a lot to you?" Dr. Forster asked me from the other side of his big, heavy desk.

"Yeah," I agreed after the slightest pause. "He does, even though we've only met twice. I'm not really sure why." I sighed and shook my head. "It wasn't until last night that Tony told me he was coming to the game after all. Up until then, it looked like he'd be too sick."

"But you did already know that the season-closer was going to be a benefit game for the Cancer Society," he pointed out.

"Oh, yes!" I agreed. "Tony and I both signed the special letter inviting him to come sit in the dugout." I sighed again. "But... That was before this turned into such a big game. And now..."

"Ah," the doctor agreed, seeming to understand at last. "And you're nervous."

"I don't want to look bad in front of him," I explained. "I don't want him to have a bad day. I mean..." I shuffled my feet, then looked down at the tabletop. "It really bothers me, that he might not have fun."

"He doesn't have much time left, does he?"

"No," I answered, my voice very soft and low. "He doesn't. And what little he has, he wants to spend part of it with us. With me."

"He's young, he's helpless, he's innocent, he's suffering, he looks up to you, and he doesn't have much time left," the doctor observed. "That's enough to get to anyone, Cheetah."

There was a long, long silence, and I began to cry a little. Then I took a deep, ragged breath. "He reminds me of my kid brother," I said finally. "After."

My shrink's left eyebrow rose. "After?"

I nodded. "After." Then I shook my head and sighed. "Remember how I told you about how things were when I grew up? About how Mom always had her boyfriends over?"

"Yes. Of course."

"Well… They weren't exactly 'boyfriends', Doc. Though she called 'em that. Or at least most of 'em weren't boyfriends. She was a hooker; that's how she paid for her weed and pills. I never knew who my daddy was, and never will. And my little brother? He probably had another daddy still."

Doctor Forster's face remained impassive. "I see."

I sighed… "And sometimes…" My face screwed up, but I forced myself to go on. "Sometimes, Doc, when the money was short, she sold more than just herself. At first, when I was really little, it didn't mean nothin' to me where I put my mouth. But when I got older and figgered it out better, well… I told you that I was strong and fast. By the time I turned twelve, there wasn't too many men willing to try and take what I wasn't about to willingly give."

"I'm sorry," he said eventually.

"Heh!" I snorted, the sound wet and bubbly. "You think *you're* sorry! All the other kids knew what Mom was, and her johns talked." I looked down at the desk again. "Anyway, I didn't have any secrets. And, I found out that a hard fist shut down a laughing mouth pretty quick, like. So I didn't have any friends. Just kids I knew were laughing behind my back."

Forster's eyes blinked, slowly.

"Anyway," I said, after staring off into space for a long, long moment, "Like I said, I got to be pretty hard to sell. But Mom, she was a lucky whore. Because by then, Duncan was just about old enough. He was six years younger than me, Duncan was. And he worshipped me like a god. He wanted to go where I went, play when I played, eat what I ate." I sighed again. "I raised him, I suppose, in that he got raised at all." My fists balled. "Mom always made sure I had him back home by evening, in case she needed him."

"You didn't have anyone else?" my therapist asked. "Nowhere to go?"

"Heh!" I replied. "Half the kids I knew, their moms were whores too! I had grandma, sure enough, but she lived in Topeka and *never* came to visit. Her and Mom, they hated each other." I smiled sadly. "It's not like anyone really cared much about people like us."

Forster nodded, but said nothing.

"So... The more I watched this go on, the madder I got. Finally, I had a real brainwave. There was this little place up in the attic, where no adult could get to. Too small and tight, see? It was cold up there in the winter, and hotter than hell in the summer. But, it was a *safe* place. Or so I figured it. 'Go up there, every night after I bring you home!' I told my brother. 'Go up there, and them nasty men can't do you wrong no more.'"

"Actually," the therapist observed, "it sounds like a remarkably good plan, considering how young you were and what you were dealing with. All by yourself, mind you, and without support."

I scowled. "It was world-class stupid! The next john that wanted him paid Mom, then looked all over for him. She wouldn't give the money back, so he beat the crap out of her until she ran away." I looked down at the table again. "When he beat Mom, she screamed, and that got little Duncan all scared. So he started crying, and..." My voice trailed away to nothing.

"And?" the doc asked.

"Fucker went ape! The dude was drunk and high on I don't know how many kinds of crap. He tried to get Duncan to come out, but he wouldn't. So he set the attic on fire, to *drive* him out."

"Damn!" Forster whispered.

"Heh!" I snorted. "Just about then I got home, and what greets me in the hallway? A hopped-up monster with a lighter in his hand, lots of smoke, and the smell of my little brother *cooking* as he screamed." I raised my eyes and tried to meet those of Forster, but he had to look away. Then I lowered them again, so that a good and decent man wouldn't have to see what I knew was to be found there.

"He was all the way squeezed into the back like I'd told him to do, and his only way out was already burning. So I got a big stewpot, filled it with water, and poured on the fire. Three times was enough; after that there was enough space for me to wriggle back and drag Duncan out. But…" I scowled again. "Three times, I said! Keep in mind, that included running through the house, filling up the pot at the sink, climbing back up the steps with that big, heavy thing… He got burned all to hell."

"What about the sonuva… what about the man who set the fire?" Forster demanded. "Did he help you?"

I looked up again and smiled. It wasn't pretty, I was sure. "He tried to stop me. Said Duncan'd either come out and give him what was coming to him, or he could damn well burn."

"Oh," Forster replied, beginning to understand. "Oh." His face sort of melted. "Cheetah… I mean…"

"He burned up in the fire," I explained truthfully, if a bit incompletely. "I smelled him cook just like I smelled Duncan cook. And don't expect me *ever* to feel too damn bad about that!"

"You were thirteen," he whispered. "Jesus!"

"Almost thirteen," I replied, shrugging. "Anyway… The fire department was there by the time I carried Duncan out, and they took us both to the hospital. The cops asked me all kinds of questions, but because the newspapers snapped a picture of me carrying my brother out and ran it on the front page they didn't ask 'em very hard, if you know what I mean. Mom was all mad at me, told me it was *my* fault that her baby'd come so close to dying…" My eyes teared up again. "…and then, that was when the bad stuff *really* started happening."

Forster's jaw dropped. "I… I mean…"

I grinned again. "How can it get any worse? Use your imagination, Doc! Duncan was *all* messed up; when they finally let him out of the hospital he had clubs for feet and claws for hands and no lips… He was blind, too, so he couldn't take care of himself at all. And Mom… She was a druggy. Guess what happened to his pain pills?"

My therapist sat silent, mouth still agape, beyond shock. It was probably unprofessional, but who could blame him?

"Anyway... He didn't get his pills, so he'd scream and gurgle and drool all over the place. Then Mom'd get mad and hit him to make him shut up and take care of hisself better, and he'd just scream louder. We didn't have anything, not even enough to eat, because no one wanted to come and sleep with Mom while a burned child was screaming in the next room. At first I tried to take care of him, as best I could. But..." My face screwed up again. "But..."

Forster leaned forward. "Jesus, Cheetah!" he said, reaching out to touch my shoulder. "You were just a child yourself. And... What a nightmare!"

"It was a nightmare, all right," I agreed, no longer weeping. On this part, at least, I was long-since cried out. "The worst nightmare I hope I'll ever know." I looked down at my feet again. "They took Duncan away eventually, and me too. He died in a hospital room, alone, screaming to the very end. It was skin-graft infections that got him, something that didn't ever need to happen if I'd stuck around and taken care of him." I sighed.

"But no, I ran away from *that* part of the equation. A few days of him not getting his pills and screaming, and I broke down and ran off like a coward, sleeping on the streets. There's never been a kid in the universe got a worse deal than Duncan, and a lot of it's my fault. I didn't run away from the fire, and I didn't run away from the man who set it. But looking at Duncan, all messed up like that every day... *That* I ran away from, and because I did he suffered and died. They tried sending me to a foster home, but I tore the crap out of everything they gave me until they finally let me go back to Mom. Where I *deserved* to be. She finally OD'ed while I was in the single-A's; the last time I talked to her she called me a bastard for getting Duncan killed." I shook my head, then stared down at the desktop for what felt like forever.

"So," I said eventually, just to fill the silence like I'd done back when Forster and I had first started, "you can see that I've been square with you, man! I'm *garbage!*" I declared, punching the polished wood surface so hard I thought I'd split it for certain. "Just a pile of useless, worthless garbage that walks around on two legs and never gets nothin' right but messing things up and running away. Even my damn *name* comes from me taking advantage of that poor, innocent little…"

There was another long silence. Presently, I began to weep. Doctor Forster let me cry alone for a very long time, then he quietly got up and moved his chair alongside mine. He still didn't touch me, though, for which I was grateful. I didn't want to be touched just then, particularly by a man. "Cheetah?" he said eventually.

I didn't ignore him, exactly. But I was crying so hard that I couldn't do much to respond.

"Cheetah?" he asked again, a little later. "Can you hear me?"

This time, I nodded. "Yeah," I muttered. "I know. We're over time, and your associate needs the office, and…"

"No," Doctor Forster replied, his voice low and respectful. "He *doesn't* need this office, Cheetah. Or at least he doesn't need it half as bad as you do, right at the moment at least. You can stay and cry as long as you like; I'd stand off all the legions of hell for you, to give you time to cry. Much less Dr. Lang and his incurable eleven o'clock hypochondriac meal ticket." He sighed. "Cheetah… I'd do *anything* for you." He paused. "*Anything*. Do you know why that is?"

"No," I muttered, still sniffling. "Because you're supposed to do things like that for patients, I guess."

"Heh!" he snorted. "To an extent, yes. But…" His smile faded, and a strange expression spread across his face. It was almost, like, wonder. "In this case, it's something else."

"And what's that?" I demanded, not at all in the mood for games.

"It's because… They say the hottest fires produce the finest steel, Cheetah. And if you aren't the toughest, most remarkable

278

bastard of an honest-to-God hero that I've ever met in my life, well…" He sighed, then finally laid a hand on my shoulder. Somehow, by then it was all right.

"Where you fell short, in your own mind, at least, is merely a reflection of how high you aimed, what unreachable standards of perfection you demanded of yourself. You've no reason to feel any guilt, son. None at all! No one on God's green earth would hold you responsible for a minute for what happened to Duncan; in fact, just about everyone I know would praise you for dealing with things as well as you did. Compared to most kids, with far more advantages…" He shook his head and scowled. "Well, let's just say that it's been an honor to treat you, though I'd never have guessed that at first. And, it's even more of an honor to call you a friend."

"But…" I whispered. "Mom…"

"What was your mother?" he asked, his voice suddenly cold.

"A whore," I answered miserably.

"That's not what I meant," he answered, his voice cold and even. "I meant, what kind of person was she? Be honest, now."

My fangs bared, of their own accord.

"Precisely," Dr. Forster said, nodding and smiling again. "You just hold that thought for our next session. I think it'd be a mighty fine place to start, if you feel like it." Then his smile widened. "Now… You've taken a big step today, Cheetah. And it's been hard on you. But not so hard, I hope, that you'll be showing the Muskrats any mercy."

"Heh!" I laughed, this time smiling a little myself. Somehow, my heart felt a little lighter than it'd been when I arrived at the clinic that morning. Though why that should be the case beat the heck out of me. And, smiling was easier, too.

"You be on your best game, son!" he continued, standing up and reaching out to help me up from my chair. "I'll be three rows back, behind third base. Wearing a spotted hat!"

16

I always arrived at the ballpark a little late on therapy days, so I missed something really fun. Somehow or another, someone had arranged for Mighty Muskrat to be ready and waiting for our rivals. He was sitting in the visiting coach's office with his feet up on the desk, stuffed with straw and wearing a Catfish baseball cap. Not one but two Catfish pennants were taped to his paws. Mighty Muskrat was always grinning, but I thought that he seemed even happier and more carefree than usual in his new getup. The Muskrat coach protested that it was an unprofessional and childish prank, and Tony absolutely agreed with him between gales of hysterical laughter. So did most of the media, though you'd never know it from all the pictures they took. Somehow, they got in a little early, as well…

I missed most of our last real practice session because it was Cancer Society Day. Coach Turnbull had promised the Belangers that he'd try to get a benefit game scheduled, and he'd made good on his word. He and the front office and I worked out a schedule that, just barely, didn't require me to be in two places at any one point in time. First I showed Raymond and his mom around the stadium a little, which was more of a formality than anything since they'd been there before. Then I spent almost two hours signing autographs. Most minor-league players are required to sign autographs from time to time, because it's every bit as much a necessary professional skill that needs developing as throwing and running and fielding. Coach Turnbull had exempted me from the rotation early-on however, due both to the fur-thing and the fact that I'd been in the Bigs and therefore had some experience. So, this was the Catfish fans' first shot at me. And what a shot it turned out to be!

As a former big leaguer I was entitled to a minimum of twenty bucks a signature. Instead, I just put out a big bucket that read "Cancer Society Donations" and concentrated on having a good time. It went remarkably well, with none of the snarky fan-comments and innuendos I'd steeled myself to accept. Instead of making sure that everyone paid, I forgot the bucket was there and concentrated on smiling and trying to find something pleasant to say to everyone. The ugliest thing that happened was when one middle-aged man commented, "Geez! And the papers all claim you're a jackass! What do they know?" That, and a five-year-old girl became enamored with my tail and yanked on it ruthlessly. It was still pretty sensitive, having just achieved full growth. But I winced and went on like nothing ever happened.

The autograph line was so long that I couldn't possibly get to everyone. When the front-office people finally came to get me so that I could do my warm-ups, the queue was still nearly as long as it'd been when I started. But they came prepared; by this late in the season the merchandising types had developed a whole line of cheetah-spotted souvenirs, a good number of which I'd signed ahead of time with precisely this situation in mind. These proved to be acceptable substitutes. "Sorry, folks," my suited co-workers explained as I was escorted away, "but there's still a game to be played!" And, miracle of miracles, instead of complaining when I left, the crowd *cheered*! "Chee-tah!" they roared. "Chee-*tah*! Chee-tah! Chee-*tah*!"

Oh, and did I mention that they had to bring a new donation-bucket, too? Three of them, in fact.

While I didn't in the least regret doing the autograph-thing, it did have the effect of upsetting my game-day routine. Or, at least, that's what I blamed my poor performance in the early innings on. I was zip for two at the plate with a walk, and got thrown out attempting to steal. Even worse, I made a serious mistake in the field. What should've been an easy ground ball took a bad hop and dribbled through me for a two-base error, allowing a run to score.

No one said anything, but everyone knew I was having a bad day. Even young Raymond, whose wheelchair was locked in place right next to where I usually sat at the extreme right-rear corner of the dugout. It was about the safest place to put such a fragile, helpless kid, and though he didn't know it two of us were assigned at all times to make damn sure he didn't get hit by a foul ball or anything like that. "It's all right," he told me when I came in from the field, sweat pouring down his face despite the big electric fans we'd set up for his benefit. "Even Ozzie Smith made errors sometimes."

Raymond was always able to put a smiley-face on things; it was a special talent that he had. Somehow, though, I just couldn't. When the bottom of the ninth rolled around we were down 5-2, and suddenly Mighty Muskrat wearing a Catfish hat didn't seem quite so funny anymore. The 'rats were playing like machines; hard, pitiless, and impersonal. We were slowly being crushed in their gears. But there didn't seem to be much hope; the bottom of our order was up, and we'd never gotten a wet firecraker's worth of offense out of them all season long. Even the fans wearing spots were beginning to look tired and sun-wilted.

"It's all right," Raymond repeated, reaching out and laying his skeletal hand on my shoulder. He was a knowledgeable fan, Raymond was, for all his youth. Clearly, he knew what time it was. "You guys had a really, really good season. Especially you personally, Cheetah." He smiled.

I smiled back, but my heart wasn't in it. Donnie Parker of the double-vision injury, batting seventh, strode up to the plate. He swung at the first pitch, and—miracle of miracles, singled to left field!

"Well!" Raymond observed, sitting a little higher in his power-chair.

"Yeah," I agreed, as a little ripple of energy surged through the stadium. Now, I'd get another at-bat for sure. Not that it'd probably matter…

Our next hitter was Hank Greene, a third baseman who really should've been down playing *AA* ball, and would've been except that our organization was desperately short on talent at his position. I expected Tony to pull him for a pinch hitter, but he didn't. I couldn't help but wonder why, until with two strikes on him, Hank lofted a long fly ball to deep center. It *almost* left the park—but didn't. Donnie, however, was able to tag up and advance to second base.

"The pitcher's getting tired," Raymond observed.

"Yep," I agreed. Somehow Tony had seen it where no one else had, and held back his pinch-hitter. It'd almost worked, too; another few feet, and the ball would've been over the fence. We'd have been one run down with nobody out, and our best batsmen on their way to the plate.

It'd *almost* worked…

The Muskrat bullpen had been intermittently active all afternoon, but now suddenly both a right and left-hander began warming up. Even more significantly, the Muskrat coach came trotting out to the mound to hold a big conference, clearly just wasting time while his relievers loosened up their muscles. "Boo!" the fans began to shout, as the pointless gathering at the mound went on and on. "Boo!" Finally the umps decided enough was enough, applied a little pressure, and the coach pointed to his right arm, indicating he wanted the right-hander. His ace closer—Reginald Barnes.

The crowd began to boo immediately, and we in the dugout weren't particularly happy to see him either. But, as always, Tony was unflappable. "Pudge," he called out. "You're up."

It was old Pudge Jefferson he was referring to, of course, as Pudge Hiller was already in the game. "Right," the gray-haired old veteran agreed. He stood up and stretched his long-abused body, joints creaking and snapping. Then he smiled, something we almost never saw. "I guess this'll be my last at-bat. Ever."

"I reckon so," Tony agreed, nodding. Then he smiled, too.

Gradually, not all at once, the crowd figured it out as well. Pudge Jefferson had a long and distinguished career behind him, and in his day had been one of the more admired figures in the

283

game. An era was ending, and to mark it the fans slowly came to their feet. "Pudge! Pudge! Pudge!" they chanted, creating a sincere if pale echo of the elderly catcher's glorious past. "Pudge, Pudge, Pudge!" And, for the only time that I knew of in his entire career, Pudge tipped his hat to the crowd as he stepped up to the plate.

They went wild!

Our backup catcher was a real earthmover in the batter's box; it took him perhaps thirty seconds to shuffle around enough dirt to make him happy. Then he raised his bat and waited, the very picture of a calm, cool professional.

Out at the mound, Barnes shook off first one pitch, then another. There was a scar on his left cheek, still a little puffy. You'd never know to look at either of them that the batter he was facing was the man who'd put it there. Finally he wound up, kicked, and delivered a vicious, sizzling fastball way close inside! A brushback! Pudge leapt back from the plate and suddenly the chant of "Pudge! Pudge! Pudge!" turned into an angry mutter.

"Time!" the ump called. Then he jogged out to the mound to have a little discussion with Mr. Barnes.

"Jeez!" Raymond declared. "I mean… Wow! I've never seen *anything* like this!"

"That's why they call it hardball, kid" I muttered, grabbing my bat and heading for the on-deck circle. I really should've been out there already, but had waited in order to let Pudge have his last moment of glory to himself.

"I'll see you after you cross home plate!" Raymond declared, his voice as angry as mine.

Presently the ump returned to his position behind the catcher, Pudge stepped back into the batter's box and did his landscaping routine all over again, then the pitcher toed the rubber. This time, the pitch came hard, fast and straight right down the middle. An arrogant challenge, to which Pudge didn't rise. The count was now one ball and one strike.

I frowned slightly. Clearly, friend Reginald had his stuff today. This was not a Good Thing.

Then he delivered again. This time Pudge swung. There was a penetrating "crack" as lumber met horsehide and there was never a second of doubt. The ball was gone, gone, gone!

The crowd screamed, yelled, even danced in the aisles as Pudge Jefferson solemnly trotted the basepads, moving not much slower than what for him would've been a flat-out sprint with his gimpy used-up legs. Then he tipped his hat again, stepped on home plate, and ended a fine career with class and panache, despite Reginald's best attempt to spoil it all for him.

The score was now 5-4, with one out. There was nobody on, and it was my turn to face Mr. Barnes.

Baseball is a team sport. They drill that into your head over and over again, the coaches do, when it's time to share credit for a victory or to hone group-skills like double-play combinations. But it's also very much an individual game, as well. When a man stands at the plate, no one else stands there with him. I was a team player these days, more so than I'd ever been in my career. Yet I was also still very much who I'd always been, deep down, and if I were to claim that I didn't relish every nanosecond of these one-on-one encounters I'd be lying through my fangs.

Where Pudge was an earthmover, I normally took a pretty straightforward approach at the plate. A couple of kicks at the ground, one or two steadying swings, and I was ready. But, just this once... I aped every motion that Pudge had made, hoping that subconsciously it'd irritate poor young Reginald to death. Then, just as he seemed almost ready to deliver the first pitch I called time. "What's wrong?" the ump demanded.

"I've got something in my eye!" I complained.

They sent out Herman, who was intelligent enough to thoroughly work me over even though he must've known that I was faking it. Then he dabbed at me one last time and I returned to the batter's box and repeated Pudge's landscaping performance. At the last possible second I reached up and scratched my nose with my middle finger, just as I had the day Reggie and I had first met. But, this time, his face remained impassive. He shook off a pitch, then performed his beautiful windup and brushed me back from the plate, just as he had Pudge a few minutes before. The pitch was so far inside that I had to drop to the ground to avoid it.

"Time!" I called again, and the ump nodded. It was a reasonable enough request, after a brushback. I shook the dirt off my uniform as best I could, while the crowd muttered and complained. Then I patted down my fur, stepped back into the box, and scratched my nose with my middle finger again.

There are three ways to deal with being brushed back at the plate. One is to accept the rebuke and stand a little further away from the plate. Or, one could do as Pudge had just done— pretend the unpleasant event had never happened, and stand right in exactly the some spot.

But me being me, I crowded the plate even tighter.

Reginald scowled, then wound up and delivered. The pitch was low, almost in the dirt. "Ball two!" the ump declared.

I had a real advantage going for me now, with a 2-0 count. I stepped back out of the batter's box, took a couple steadying swings, then eased back in. Reginald shook off a pitch and something went 'click' in my mind. He'd thrown two brushbacks already, and both of them had flowed shake-offs. Well, I knew what to do about *that*. I gritted my teeth…

…then involuntarily flinched anyway as the bastard threw a hundred-mile-an-hour fastball directly at my legs. He was willing to let me have a base, it seemed—so long as I was too crippled to run once I got there! I skipped the rope, just like I'd done dozens of times before in my baseball career. But there was something different this time. I thought I was clear—then something yanked at my spine, and my tender, newly-grown tail was in absolute agony!

"Crap!" I cried, collapsing to the ground in pain. "You jackass! I think you *broke* it!" Herman came running out with his ice pack, and while he looked me over I realized dully that a crowd was forming around home plate.

"You aren't going to give him a base for *that*, are you?" demanded the Muskrat coach.

"I..." the umpire stuttered. "I..."

"If he hadn't gone and altered hisself," he continued, "he wouldn't even *have* a tail! Now would he?"

"It's an unfair advantage!" the Muskrat catcher, whom I'd once so viciously spiked, added sincerely.

"Uh..." the umpire declared.

"What kind of crap is *this?*" Tony countered, jogging up angrily. "My man here's been hit by a pitch. Everyone in the place saw it! And when he's able, I assume he'll be on his way to first base! It says right in the rule book that when a batter is hit by a pitch, he's to be awarded first base!"

"Uh..." the ump repeated, looking very lost.

"But," the Muskrat's leader countered, "when that rule book was written, batters didn't have tails, now did they? None of them! So, some of them didn't have an unfair advantage over others!"

"Aw, come off it!" Tony countered. "Pudge Hiller is twice Cheetah's size! If Cheetah gained a hundred pounds and got hit in the belly, he'd be awarded the base and you wouldn't have a single word to say about it. Or, say, if he'd stretched out his earlobes all long and dangly to wear jewelry, like some of the Carribbean players do these days? Getting hit *there* would have to count, wouldn't it? Or... what if his ankle was swollen, and he got barely brushed? Or, if he wore shoes a size too big?"

"Uh..." the ump stuttered.

"And I suppose that if I had my fielders grow hands the size of watermelons, you wouldn't object to that, either!" the Muskrat snapped back. "Baseball players are supposed to be *human!*"

287

"What is 'human', anyway?" Tony demanded, kicking up a cloud of dirt. "Can *you* define it?"

"You're kidding!" his Muskrat counterpart declared, tearing his hat off of his head and pointing at my now obviously-fractured tail. "Are you going to claim that anyone with one of those things growing out of his butt is still entirely human?"

"Immanuel Kant claimed that humanity is an end, not a means," opined the Muskrat catcher.

"You shut your trap!" his coach raged, pointing an angry finger at his player. "Right now!"

"The Objectivists think that a human is a being that can operate at the conceptual level," Herman declared as he began taping up my tail. It was amazing to watch; you might've imagined he'd done it a hundred times before. "Or at least that's how I understand their philosophy. But Plato defined man as a featherless biped." He shrugged. "Take your pick. I find them both pretty useless here and now."

The Muskrat catcher's eyes narrowed behind his mask. "I prefer the Turing test, myself."

"I told you to shut up!" the Muskrat coach exploded. Then he turned to Tony. "Never sign a catcher with brains! He'll be the biggest pain in the behind you've ever dealt with."

"Maybe," Tony growled, eyeing me. "And maybe not."

"Crap!" the umpire finally declared, removing his mask and wiping his brow. "How come I've never got a dictionary on me when I really need it?" Then he turned to the catcher. "I think it's pretty much impossible to assign a meaningful definition to the term 'human' in the absence of a godhead and/or divine revelation on the subject. We can't comprehend our own true natures, you see, any more than a kettle can contain itself." The man in blue blinked. "But, what's a Turing test, anyway? I've never heard of it."

The catcher smiled, and his eyes lit up. "It's where you take—"

"Jesus God almighty!" the Muskrat leader interrupted, raising his eyes to the heavens. "What did I ever do to deserve this?"

The ump finally did award me first, on the basis that it might be an affront to our Maker to define me as non-human and therefore a nonplayer. "Only God can define humanity," the umpire humbly explained to the two coaches. "Therefore only God can determine if an animal tail grafted onto one of His children becomes a human tail, and thus a legitimate part of a ballplayer. It's not my place as a mere mortal to define a tail directed by a human soul as *non*human, in other words. So, Cheetah gets first base. Play ball!"

"Damn!" the other manager cursed, removing his hat and stomping it into the earth. Then he kicked up an enormous cloud of dust.

"That's no way to pass a Turing test," Herman pointed out as he gathered up his gear and sent me trotting off to first.

"Go to hell, you little twerp!" the manager roared.

The ump promptly fined him fifty dollars for unsportsman-like behavior. "If you can't find it within yourself to operate at the objective level," he warned, "you can watch the rest of the game from the clubhouse! It don't matter to me!"

First base was a *much* calmer place than home plate, I decided once I got there. Or, at least to begin with, it was. My tail was throbbing, but I tried to shut the pain out. "A featherless biped?" the first baseman asked me when I arrived.

"Apparently so," I agreed," not much in the mood for conversation. "But only if it's a featherless biped that's an end, not a means."

"Heh!" the Muskrat chuckled. Then Barnes toed the rubber, and it was back to business again. I touched the bag ever-so-gently with my toe, and the eternal dance began. Reginald watched closely as I edged away from the base, then spun and threw to first as I danced back in standing up. It was just like spring training; neither of us had revealed anything like our best. Then we repeated the whole sequence over again; he swiveled and threw a second time, and I danced back in safe by an easy margin.

"At least I know he loves me," I pointed out to the first baseman, who seemed a nice enough guy. For a Muskrat, at least.

"Heh!" he laughed, throwing the ball back to the mound.

Reginald's next throw was to home plate. Thumps took the pitch. "Ball one!" shouted the ump, and I grinned a little.

"Kid's come a long way," the first-bagger observed as his catcher went out to the mound to talk things over. "You should be proud."

I blinked, then looked the Muskrat in the eye to see if he was kidding. "How... I mean..."

"Everyone knows you're mentoring him," he explained. "Kid's proud as can be of it."

"I... I mean..." I stuttered. But, before I could say anymore, the catcher trotted back home. My eyes narrowed. He was a brainy one, that catcher. Had a good head on his shoulders. And that little conference...

I stood up straight and tall at first base, and placed both hands firmly on my hips. It looked natural as could be, but was a signal. "I'm not stealing at this time," it meant. It just seemed like a bad idea, sort of. Buster could've over-ruled me, but he must have detected something fishy in the air as well. So he acknowledged instead. Then he repeated the signal to Thumps at the plate. That way, the kid could concentrate on nothing but his own at-bat.

Reginald, of course, had no way of knowing I wasn't going anywhere. So we danced again, he and I, and this time even though I had no intention of stealing I wandered just a tiny bit further from the base, so that he wouldn't forget me. Now I had to dive back in when he threw, making things *much* closer. Once I landed wrong on my broken tail, and it hurt like hell. "Owww!" I cried out, calling time and staggering around the bag. Herman started to trot out, but I waved him back. The umpires were prepared to cut a certain amount of slack to a player who'd just been hit by a fastball, but I'd be forced to leave the game if the trainer came out to see me many *too* many times. And how could I face Raymond then?

"That thing broken?" the first baseman asked sympathetically.

Once again, I smelled rotten fish. If I let him know where I was vulnerable... "Just bruised a little," I lied. "I jarred my head, is all. It's still tender from the fractured-skull thing."

"Oh," the Muskrat replied, smiling what I now understood was a very false smile. And, sure enough, when the next toss from the mound arrived, he tagged me right on the butt. Hard! It hurt even worse than my broken head had, and had to have been deliberate because it wasn't anything like the most convenient place for him. I got up and made a great show of patting the dust out of my fur, face impassive all the while. Then, just to drive the point home, I gritted my teeth and thoroughly patted it out of my tail too, no matter how bad it hurt. The Muskrat looked disappointed.

"Play ball!" the ump directed.

This time, I leaned a little further towards second, trying to make it look like I was going even though my lead was a little shorter than usual. And, Reginald took the bait! Instead of delivering a normal pitch, he threw a bullet a good three feet outside, which the catcher fielded standing up. A pitchout! But, it was wasted because I hadn't gone anywhere. A pity, that.

"Ball two!"

Now things were getting interesting indeed. Thumps had run up a count of two balls and no strikes, which put him well ahead of the pitcher. He could afford to take questionable pitches now, and try to draw a walk. Or, alternatively, he could reach out and swing at a bad pitch just to get in the way and obstruct things a little while I stole second. It was no surprise to me at all when the catcher went trotting back to the mound. *What are they going to do?* I asked myself. *What looks, to them, like the surest way to shut us down?* Then I frowned, looked down at my feet....

...and stood straight and tall once again, both hands on my hips. This time, Buster was already giving me the same sign, *telling* me not to try and steal. We'd obviously come to the same conclusion; they were convinced that I was going to steal, because that was just what I did, what my whole hyper-aggressive image as a ballplayer was based on. So, the pitchout was on again, and to heck with the ball and strike count. I wanted to grin at Buster and say something like "Great minds think alike, eh?" But, of course, there was no chance of *that* happening.

This time, they didn't try to hold me close at all. Or, at least not very close. *Come into my parlor, said the spider to the fly,* and once again I stood safe at first base while Barnes and his catcher executed a textbook-perfect pitchout. They'd have nailed me for certain, if I'd fallen for it.

"Ball three!" the ump intoned.

This time, the coach came out to the mound to hold one of his famous conferences. Buster came trotting over from his third-base coaching box with a big smile on his face. "You're doing great, kid!" he assured me.

"Well enough," I agreed. "For still being stuck at first." Then I scowled out at the big pow-wow on the mound. "They're going to walk Thumps intentionally," I predicted. "And hope for the double-play."

"It's what I'd do," Buster agreed. Then he grinned. "You could score on a fly ball from third. If you were on third, that is. I mean, you'd have to figure out a way to get there, first…"

I grinned back. "I would, wouldn't I?"

Then, wordlessly he clapped me on the shoulder and trotted away.

Dancer, in my opinion, was the most under-estimated man on the entire Catfish roster. Because he was very gay, because he wore a silly grin, because he crossed his legs while standing in the outfield, people tended to overlook his talents. But, even more, they overlooked the grit that lay close beneath the surface.

If someone were to ask the Muskrats who the toughest, meanest Catfish was, they might've named Pudge Hiller or Pudge Jefferson. Or, they might even have pointed at me. But Dancer routinely played with injuries far more severe than anyone else did, was batting just over .300, and had stolen enough bases to be leading most teams in the category.

He was a star in his own right, Dancer was, by AAA standards, at least. But while I filled up the stands with cheetah-spotted hats and Pudge Hiller's towering home runs often led the local news, no one ever seemed to notice when Dancer drove in the game-winning RBI, or scored from second where a lesser player would've been thrown out. Dancer, in short, didn't get any respect. Or, at least, he didn't get any outside our clubhouse; we appreciated the heck out of him, and he knew it. I asked him how he felt about it once, when the spotted-hat phenomenon was first taking off.

"Oh come *on*, Cheetah!" he countered, when I commented that his stats weren't any worse than mine, overall. "What are the fans supposed to do to support me? Show up in pink tights?"

He had a point, I was forced to admit. But it still never seemed quite fair that he didn't get the credit he deserved. And now, here he was at the plate, with the game-winning runs on base and the whole season at stake.

It's a lot harder for a pitcher to hold a runner at second than it is at first, for several reasons. One is simple geometry; turning a hundred and eighty degrees isn't as easy as pivoting a mere ninety. Also, the shortstop and second-basemen are the keystones of the infield's defensive structure; moving either one out of position to cover the bag upsets everything else. But, perhaps the *biggest* reason why pitchers have trouble covering second is that so few runners are willing to risk stealing third. A player at second is already in reasonable scoring position; most won't risk being thrown out just to improve their situation slightly.

I wasn't most players, however, and neither was Thumps behind me. We executed a perfect double-steal right under Barnes' nose, on the very first pitch. Now there were *two* runners in scoring position, and the heat was *really* on!

I didn't envy the Muskrat coach just then; he had some very difficult decisions to make. Barnes was his ace reliever, all right; in fact, he was his *only* quality short-man. So if he pulled him, who else could he go to? And, despite the fact that he was in so much trouble, Barnes was performing fairly well overall. The only hit he'd given up was that one home run to Pudge Jefferson. Other than that, no one else had even laid wood to the ball. Even Thumps' walk had been intentional. Plus, the Muskrat's leader had to consider the bigger picture, too. It wasn't his job to win this particular game so much as to develop stars for his parent organization. If Reginald Barnes went on to a major-league career, as even I was forced to acknowledge that he almost certainly would do, then he'd need all the confidence he could get. What kind of confidence-builder would it be for Barnes if his coach pulled him now, when he was arguably doing so well? I could almost hear the gears grinding over in the Muskrat dugout, but in the end Barnes stayed.

Dancer had swung at the first pitch to help us steal. The next pitch evened the count to a ball and a strike, then the third was a called strike. Dancer called time, stepped out of the batter's box, and proceeded to knock the dirt out of his spikes. He was well in the hole now, but seemed undaunted. Meanwhile, the crowd had gone silent.

Reginald coiled himself up, unwound, and delivered in his always-elegant motion. The ball sizzled to the plate. Dancer didn't bat an eye; he'd been taking all the way. "Ball two!" the ump intoned.

Barnes scowled, and before throwing the ball back the Muskrat catcher turned and looked wordlessly at the ump. The pitch had just missed the high outside corner. Or, perhaps, it hadn't missed at all and the ump had got it wrong. It was part of the game, something that one learned to live with. Or perhaps *didn't* learn to live with, in young Reginald's case. When the ball came back to him, he stepped off the rubber and then savagely slammed it into his glove, scowling mightily.

Meanwhile, Dancer was studying him very closely indeed. When the next pitch came, he took it again. "Ball three!" the ump declared, though once again it was a very questionable call.

"Aw come on!" the Muskrat catcher protested. "That caught the corner!" But the ump stood impassive, daring the player to push the argument any further. Wisely, he did not.

Once again Reginald slammed the ball over and over into his glove, his loss of composure clear for all to see. The right move would've been for the coach to come out and calm him down, but that wasn't possible because the rules stated that if he went out to visit the mound twice, the pitcher had to go. So instead the catcher trotted out, and he and Reginald had a long heart-to-heart. When it was over, the young man seemed a little calmer. On the outside, at least.

The next pitch was a foul ball, a line shot just wide of third that passed so close to me I could hear it hiss through the air. Had it the thing been hit two inches to the right, it would've been a game-winning triple.

The ump examined the ball when it came back in, and decided it was too badly scuffed to be used any further. So he pulled another from his pocket and handed it to the catcher. "Play ball!" he urged.

Barnes nodded and accepted the new ball. He was visibly upset now, having come so close to losing the biggest game of his career to date on the last pitch, and to a notorious faggot at that. Finally he toed the rubber, wound up, delivered, and threw the ball all the way to the backstop! Instinctively I ran two steps, then held up when I recalled that this was ball four. Dancer had walked, was all; it didn't count as a passed ball or wild pitch.

"Take your base," the ump declared.

And you damn well earned it! I didn't add, though I smiled and nodded when Dancer's eye caught my own. He was all excited and sparkly, like a big overgrown kid. He always got that way when he thought he'd screwed over someone real good, like.

Now the bases were loaded and Pudge Hiller was stepping up to the plate. *Folks,* I could almost hear the radio announcer saying, *It doesn't get any better than this!*

I expected to see a reliever when Pudge came to the plate, and probably so did most of the folks in the stands. Even Reginald himself expected to be relieved, I could tell from the way he kept glancing over towards his dugout. But no new hurler was forthcoming, and gradually it began to sink in on him that there was going to be no rescue, that he was going to be left to sink or swim on his own. Barnes gulped visibly, then turned to face the huge Pudge Hiller, who was already in the box and waiting.

Who he'd also beaned, the last time he'd faced him.

Pudge had been an amiable, happy sort of man right up until his marriage went sour. Things had changed considerably since then, however, and the changes had been accompanied by a surge in his stats. Where once he'd kept himself clean shaven, now a rough, unkempt beard grew in ugly patches all over his face. He was working out more, increasing his already impressive bulk. And even I couldn't meet his angry eyes for long.

Our catcher swung at the first pitch so hard that the sound was audible all over the stadium—*wooof!* It was a titanic swing, the stuff of pitcher's nightmares.

"Strike one!" the ump declared.

Reginald was sweating heavily now; in fact, it was pouring off of him. He shook off a pitch, and I wished there was a signal that'd let me warn Pudge that he was about to be brushed-back. The pitch was way inside when it arrived. Pudge didn't flinch a millimeter, however, even though it barely missed him. Instead he just dug in deeper, and grinned. It wasn't pretty.

"Ball one!"

The catcher returned the ball to the mound, and Reginald took a little break to finger his rosin bag. Then he paced around a little, still sweating furiously. Meanwhile, Pudge just stood and waited, patient as a mountain—or a tombstone.

Reginald glanced towards the dugout again, his eyes appealing. But, no one came forth. *This is what happens*, I noted to myself, *on the day when intimidation ceases to work. And, when a coach decides it's time for lessons to be learned.* Finally, Barnes climbed back onto the rubber, came to the set position, and delivered a white-hot fastball to the low outside corner.

"Ball two!" the ump ruled.

"Aw come on!" Reginald cried out from the mound. "Are you blind and stupid *both?*"

"Ball two!" the ump repeated, just a note of belligerence creeping into his voice.

Reginald scowled, and for just a moment I thought that he was going to resolve his difficulties by getting himself thrown out of the game. The way that I myself might've, once upon a time. But, just barely, he bit off the remark that he was about to make, and went to his rosin bag again.

I glanced over at the first base coach. He was fanning himself with his hat, looking for all the world like a sweaty middle-aged man with too much belly seeking a little relief from the heat. But I knew better, as did everyone else out on the basepads. First Dancer acknowledged the signal by kicking first base twice, then Thumps and I did the same at our own bags. Then, unable to help myself, I smiled. *Boy* was young Reginald in for a surprise! Especially since the count and other factors were, in theory, all wrong for what we were about to attempt. No sane coach would *ever* call such a play, in fact, unless he had three speedsters on base whose skills he trusted heart and soul.

None of us had been leading off much, because there wasn't anyplace for anyone to go. The only base available to be stolen was home plate itself, and to his credit once or twice Reginald had thrown to the third baseman to help hold me close, just in case I actually was insane enough to make the attempt with our finest batsman at the plate, the bases loaded, and only one out. Now all three of us edged a little further away from our bags—not enough so as to be conspicuous, but plenty to make a difference when play began. Reginald took a good long look at me, then scowled as he decided once again that I wasn't that nuts after all. He wound up, kicked, and fired a slider right down the middle. Pudge grinned like a savage, but then instead of swinging with all he had, he squared around to bunt!

I was already a quarter of the way home when the ball hit Pudge's bat and dribbled directly towards me, right down the baseline itself. For a brief but crucial instant not a single Muskrat moved; none of them could comprehend that such a dangerous, even notorious power-hitter might do such a thing. I'd taken three long steps before the catcher rose, pivoted and shifted his position to block home plate. He placed himself well, so well that for an instant I doubted that I was going to make it.

But, it was far too late to worry about *that!* What was going to happen, was going to happen. Carefully I danced over the slowly-rolling ball—if I'd touched it, I'd have been called out. This threw me off stride a bit, so I wasn't quite at full speed as I powered down the line, legs driving, heart pumping, face a ferocious fanged snarl. Meanwhile a sort of blur passed close behind me; Reginald on his way to field the bunt. I timed things carefully, leapt face forward as hard as I could, and watched with relief as first the catcher's eyes widened, then he leapt to his feet to shag Reginald's off-balance, thoroughly rattled and too-high throw!

I *could've* hurt the catcher and gotten away with it, just like the first basemen had deliberately tried to hurt me. Instead I slid into home like a gentleman, reaching between the catcher's legs to touch home plate a good hundredth of a second before he tagged my helmet.

"Safe!" the ump cried out. The tying run was home, but play was still underway. Hoping to salvage at least *something* out of the debacle, the catcher threw the ball towards first, where Pudge was still charging up the baseline just as quickly as he could. He'd have been thrown out, too—except that the first baseman, as stunned as everyone else, fumbled the ball! It went rolling out into right field!

"Come on!" I urged Thumps, springing to my feet and waving my arm in the big circle that's the universal signal for "keep going!" "Come on!"

Thumps had quite correctly slid into third; now he had to get back on his feet and pick up momentum from scratch. No one else in baseball, I sincerely believed, not even at the pro level, could've come sprinting down the baseline like he did after such a disadvantageous start. Apparently the Muskrat right-fielder had a cannon for a throwing arm; he threw right over the cutoff man's head and directly to home, where the catcher was now waiting for a *second* play at the plate. The ball came racing in, Thumps gave it all he had. Then there was a cloud of dust at the plate and a long, long silence. "Safe!" the ump finally declared. "The runner is safe!"

18

No one spends a lot of money on security at a minor-league ballpark. Sure, there's a few guards around to eject drunks and things like that. Normally, however, AAA ballparks are a sleepy, placid sort of place. No one really expects to see a lot of enthusiasm there, much less a riot. Not even on the day that the home team wins their division.

But a riot is exactly what erupted.

It still wasn't nearly as bad as you'd expect, compared to what sometimes happens after big-league victories. No one turned over police cars or looted the souvenir stands or assaulted us players or anything like that. In fact, I never for second felt like I was in any danger when the crowd mobbed the field. They were happy, was all. Not angry and drunk and vile and eager to make a name for themselves by hurting someone famous. In fact, the only pain or inconvenience they caused was when they lifted me and Thumps up on their shoulders and paraded us around the infield. That hurt my freshly-broken tail some, sure enough. But was I going to complain? Not hardly! Especially not after I looked down and saw that one of the fans carrying me and cheering his lungs out was my therapist, Doctor Forster.

Eventually we arrived in the dugout, where a second riot had also broken out. We might've been minor leaguers, but we sure as heck knew how to pop a champagne cork and spray each other down well enough! The stuff made my fur a sticky mess, and tickled something awful in my ears. It wasn't, however, anything that couldn't be fixed by being thrown time and again into an ice-cold shower while still fully dressed. The best part of all might've been watching Raymond sit in the corner in his power-chair, drinking it all in with hungry eyes. He might not have time to accumulate many memories, I figured. But at least we'd helped him accumulate some good ones.

Presently, as things finally began to wind down, I noticed a figure standing next to Raymond. He was long-boned and lean, just like I was, and had the same hungry look in his eyes. It was Mr. Sandrell, the team's owner, who none of us had even realized was in the ball park. I smiled in genuine pleasure, and strode across the wet, sticky floor to greet him. "It's just like you, sir" I said, removing my cap, "To come to the game and sit in an ordinary seat."

"Fourth row, center-field bleachers," he admitted with a grin. "Sometimes I *do* use my personal box, of course. But, the games have more flavor when enjoyed from the stands. And you meet the most *wonderful* people!"

I grinned, understanding exactly what he meant. "Well," I said. "Congratulations, sir. I know it's not much of a championship. But such as it is, it's yours."

Sandrell grinned, then extended a hand for me to shake. "It's *ours*, Cheetah. *Ours.*" Then the smile faded. "We came in fifth in the Bigs. Next year *will* be better." He cocked his head to one side. "Plan to start the season there. You and Pudge both. Probably Dancer, too."

I gulped. "What about Thumps?"

The team's owner frowned. "It could happen," he allowed. "Though I suspect another season down here would do him good. He still needs to grow up a little."

I nodded. "You're probably right. But know this. When he *does* grow up, he's going to be a superstar. One of the finest ever to play the game. Anything I can do, he'll do better."

Sandrell's eyes narrowed again, then he smiled. "You've grown up a lot yourself," he observed.

I felt myself blush under the spotted fur. "Maybe," I allowed.

"Heh!" the older man chuckled. "I've been keeping tabs on you, son. Better ones than you probably realize. I know what you've done this year, not just for yourself but for Thumps and Pudge and some others, as well." He smiled again. "You may be right, Cheetah, about Thumps outperforming you someday. But he'll never be more valuable or beloved in my clubhouse. Never! I promise you this, so long as you continue to walk the straight and narrow. Because you have *other* talents, young man, which you've barely begun to explore. You may not even realize you have them, or how rare they are." Sandrell's smile faded. "What are your plans for the off-season?"

I shrugged. "To tell you the truth, I haven't had much time to think about it."

He nodded. "I own two winter-league teams, Cheetah. They're bottom of the barrel so far as prestige goes; kids just out of high school, mostly. The rawest of the raw recruits. I'd never ask you to *play* at such a low level—it's not worth the risk of you being injured, among other things. But... Have you ever considered coaching?"

My mouth opened, but no words emerged.

"You don't have to decide tonight," he continued, ignoring my speechless state. "Your friend Buster's going to be managing one of them, and he suggested that you might make a fine assistant. The pay won't be much, but you'd be able to stay in shape, keep sharp…" His eyes narrowed. "And spend every single day doing what you love most." Then he turned away. "Forgive me. Sometimes, I grow jealous."

"Maybe you do, sometimes," I replied. "But you're *always* a gentleman, sir."

"Heh!" he laughed, smiling again. "Ask my ex-wife about that one. Or my other ex-wife!" Then, still smiling, he turned back to Raymond, who'd been taking it all in with wide eyes. "And you," he said. "Don't think that you're getting out of this scot-free, either."

"Huh?" the skinny little boy asked.

"I made a major donation to the Cancer Society today, of course. That was a given. But… You know that I own a team in the Bigs, right?"

"Uh-huh!" he replied, face a mask of awe.

"And a gengineering company, as well. A rather large one." He smiled again. "I can't make any promises, son, though God knows I'd like to. However, I have connections in the industry. Better ones, I'm sure, than your doctors can dream of. I've already talked to your mother, and tomorrow morning your medical files will be on my desk. They will remain there, the number-one priority of both myself and my staff, every single morning, until I find a promising experimental treatment program that will accept you. My sacred word of honor. Given to one of the few people I've ever met who loves the game as much as I do."

"Uh…" Raymond stuttered.

"In the meantime," he continued, "We owners sort of network together and exchange privileges. Starting next season, show up at any ballpark in the nation and you'll be treated as I would be. Again, my word of honor."

"Gosh!" Raymond gushed. And my heart sort of melted, because we all knew the odds were that he wouldn't live to take advantage of Mr. Sandrell's offer. But, a man had to what a man had to do.

Then suddenly Thumps was at my elbow. "Hey, Cheetah!" he greeted me after nodding his respect to Mr. Sandrell. "We're all meeting in the weight room. You're going to be late if you don't hurry."

"Right," the team-owner agreed, eyes twinkling. He nodded down towards Raymond. "I'll take charge here. You go to your meeting, Cheetah. Let me know when you decide about the winter ball thing."

"Sign me up," I declared. "I don't need a lot of time to decide to play ball. Thanks for asking."

Sandrells eyes twinkled again. "Excellent. Then… I suppose I'll be seeing you in the Bigs, Cheetah Jones."

It was a long walk back to the weight room, because it'd been added on long after the stadium itself had been built. We always held our team meetings there, since it was the biggest open space we had. "Cheetah," Thumps said as we strode along. "I want… I mean…"

I smiled, thinking of poor little Duncan, so long ago. And, for once, it didn't hurt. "Yes, Thumps?"

"I… Well…" he blushed. "I know what you did for me," he said eventually. "And, like… Thanks."

"Hah!" I laughed. "I had a blast too, Thumps. Someday when we're old we can sit down and laugh about it."

"I hope so," he said. "I mean… Even if we end up on different teams or something, I want you to know that I'll never forget you. And… Well, I'd like for us to end up on the *same* team."

I stopped dead in my tracks. "Do you really mean that?" I asked.

"Oh, yes!" he answered, nodding. "I do."

"Then," I replied slowly. "That's the nicest, kindest thing that anyone's ever said to me in my life."

We stood staring at each other for a long, long moment, then Thumps looked down at his feet. "There's something else I want to ask you too," he said finally.

"What's that?" I replied, still smiling.

He sighed, still staring at his feet. "That fur job. You've got the only one in baseball, and it's sorta like your trademark now." He blushed a deep, deep red. "It looks like *so* much fun! It seems to have done you some good, too. And the fans really love it. Would you mind if... I mean, I wouldn't do a cheetah..."

My jaw dropped, then I slapped my thigh and proceeded to laugh myself silly as Thumps grew ever redder. "No, I don't mind!" I finally managed to spit out. "In fact... It just might be good for you, too. Get you out of your own skin, help you loosen up a little."

He nodded, still blushing and staring down at the ground. "Thank you."

"Hah!" I laughed again. Then I grabbed Thumps by the shoulder and sort of steered him down the hall towards the weight room. We were the last ones to arrive, he and I. But it didn't matter. The room was full of happy players, happy coaches, happy trainers, happy front office staff. And up front, sitting happily in the middle of a happy folding table, was the divisional trophy.

"Cheetah! Thumps!" Coach Turnbull greeted us. "Late as usual!" But this time, there wasn't a trace of malice in his voice. He turned around, picked up the trophy, and raised it above his head. "This belongs to us all," he explained, and everyone cheered. "To each and every one of us," he continued once the noise died down. "Wherever we go from here, we'll always carry a piece of this trophy, of this victory, of this fellowship with us in our hearts. And it's right and proper that this is so." Then he set the big victory cup back on the card table. "But, deep down, I think all of us know that we've earned a greater prize as well. A year here together, sharing the joys and the pains and growing ever closer to one another; that's the true reward." He wiped a tear from his eye. "They call these the minor leagues," he declared, raising his voice like an orator. "But there's nothing minor about any of us, or what we've accomplished here together! About who we are, what we've learned, the experiences we've shared, our love for the game. Nothing minor at all!" He looked down at the ground. "Once upon a time, a man condemned to die far too young walked to the middle of Yankee Stadium and declared to a sellout crowd that he was luckiest man on Earth. Well, Lou Gehrig might've been the luckiest way back then; I won't argue with one of the greats about that. But today the honor is all mine."

There was a long, long silence after that, then the pandemonium broke out all over again. Half of us were cheering and half crying, and every few minutes we traded jobs. Then Buster called for attention. "And now," he announced, rolling in a training-table loaded down with smaller trophies, "The moment you've all been waiting for. Individual award time!"

Pudge Hiller won the home-run and RBI trophies, of course, while Dancer won the overall batting title. Pudge Jefferson took home a special appreciation award from all of us players. It was a pretty nice one; we'd taken up a collection to pay for it, to thank him for sharing his hard-earned wisdom. Thumps won the Biggest Individual Improvement award. And, last of all, I discovered that I'd been elected by my fellow players as the team's Most Valuable Cat.

Who'da ever dreamed it?

AFTERWORD

Thanks for reading. At this point, I'd like to share some background on the authors who's hard work has made ROAR 2 possible.

Shepherd J. Wolf, who just goes by ShepherdWolf online, debuts on the furry writing scene with "Trickster." Published elsewhere from major newspapers to corporate training manuals, Shep somehow manages to work, write, and still throw one hell of a dinner party. He lives in suburban Chicago with his favorite hyena and three fairly standard house cats, and firmly believes that authors should NOT be allowed to write their own biographies.

D.J Fahl lives in the Duke City of Albuquerque. He grew up there and credits the city for inspiring his writing. Mr. Fahl enjoys writing, hiking and playing with his puppy. Feel free to say hello and look for his upcoming novel, Save the Day.

H. A. Kirsch once got in trouble for pretending to be a werewolf and biting other students in fourth grade when he wasn't romping in the suburban woods. Now, he writes anthropomorphic erotica (and the occasional science-fiction piece such as this one) for anthro sites on the internet. He lives in southeastern Michigan with his partner and one too many cats.

Graveyard Greg is the writer/creator of webcomics such as Carpe Diem, Dungeons & Denizens, and

Gaming Guardians. This is his first publication for ROAR, but will certainly not be his last attempt. He also is a terrible devourer of sushi.

Teiran is the furry author behind the novel The Hero and the series High School Days. A wolf of no distinction, (Ed. note—Not true!) he lives in Texas with his mate Fuzzwolf. More of his work can be found at www.teiran.com and on Fur Affinity.

Phil Geusz is one of the better-known authors in the furry genre. A three-time nominee for the Ursa Major award, Mr. Geusz has been an ardent science fiction and fantasy fan since early boyhood. He particularly admires the work of golden-age authors such as Ray Bradbury, Arthur C. Clarke, and Robert Heinlein. Among his many other published works are the novel Transmutation Now! and, most recently, The First Book of Lapism. Phil is a Tennessee auto worker, originally from St. Louis, Missouri.

Finally, Buck C. Turner, your humble editor, is a rather solitary fellow. When not masochistically taking on work for publishers, he keeps himself busy with his art. A hanger on of the furry fandom for nigh on a decade, he mostly passes the time quietly in the Midwest. Not having enough yet, he looks forward to getting started on ROAR 3, eager to apply the lessons he learned in creating this volume to the next one.

Made in the USA
Charleston, SC
27 January 2010